THE DEVIL'S
ORCHARD

Acclaim for the Cain Casey Saga

The Devil Inside

"Vali's fluid writing style quickly puts the reader at ease, which makes the story and its characters equally easy to get to know and care about. When you find yourself talking out loud to the characters in a book, you know the work is polished and professional, as well as entertaining."—*Family and Friends*

"Not only is *The Devil Inside* a ripping mystery, it's also an intimate character study."—*L-Word Literature*

"*The Devil Inside* is the first of what promises to be a very exciting series…While telling an exciting story that grips the reader, Vali has also fully fleshed out her heroes and villains. *The Devil Inside* is that rarity: a fascinating crime novel which includes a tender love story and leaves the reader with a cliffhanger ending."—*MegaScene*

The Devil Unleashed

"Fast-paced action scenes, intriguing character revelations, and a refreshing approach to the romance thriller genre all make for an enjoyable reading experience in the Big Easy…*The Devil Unleashed* is an engrossing reading experience."—*Midwest Book Review*

Deal With the Devil

"Ali Vali has given her fans another thick, rich thriller…*Deal With the Devil* has wonderful love stories, great sex, and an ample supply of humor. It is an exciting, page turning read that leaves her readers eagerly awaiting the next book in the series."—*Just About Write*

The Devil Be Damned

"Ali Vali excels at creating strong, romantic characters along with her fast paced, sophisticated plots. Her setting, New Orleans, provides just the right blend of immigrants from Mexico, South America and Cuba, along with a city steeped in traditions."—*Just About Write*

Praise for Ali Vali

Carly's Sound

"Vali paints vivid pictures with her words…*Carly's Sound* is a great romance, with some wonderfully hot sex."—*Midwest Book Review*

"It's no surprise that passion is indeed possible a second time around"—*Q Syndicate*

Calling the Dead

"So many writers set stories in New Orleans, but Ali Vali's mystery novels have the authenticity that only a real Big Easy resident could bring…makes for a classic lesbian murder yarn."—*Curve*

Blue Skies

"Vali is skilled at building sexual tension and the sex in this novel flies as high as Berkley's jets. Look for this fast-paced read."—*Just About Write*

Balance of Forces: Toujours Ici

"A stunning addition to the vampire legend, *Balance of Forces: Toujours Ici,* is one that stands apart from the rest."—*Bibliophilic Book Blog*

Visit us at www.boldstrokesbooks.com

By the Author

Carly's Sound

Second Season

Calling the Dead

Blue Skies

Balance of Forces: Toujours Ici

Love Match

The Dragon Tree Legacy

The Cain Casey Saga

The Devil Inside

The Devil Unleashed

Deal with the Devil

The Devil Be Damned

The Devil's Orchard

THE DEVIL'S ORCHARD

by

Ali Vali

2013

THE DEVIL'S ORCHARD

ISBN 13: 978-1-60282-879-7

This Trade Paperback Original Is Published By
Bold Strokes Books, Inc.
P.O. Box 249
Valley Falls, NY 12185

First Edition: June 2013

CREDITS

EDITORS: SHELLEY THRASHER AND STACIA SEAMAN
PRODUCTION DESIGN: STACIA SEAMAN
COVER DESIGN BY SHERI (GRAPHICARTIST2020@HOTMAIL.COM)

Acknowledgments

This book was like visiting old friends. The Casey Clan and the battles they've waged started on vacation quite a few years ago, but I still remember the first conversation I had with Radclyffe about the eight-hundred-page book I'd just finished. Thank you, boss, for not only publishing the first book, but for always encouraging me to write more about these guys, and for offering advice whenever I ask.

I first met Shelley Thrasher in a bar, in New Orleans of all places, when the first book in the series was done. As an editor, she's taught me something with each book, and I'm looking forward to the lessons yet to come. Thank you, Shelley, for all the hard work you put into each piece and for your friendship—both are a treasure.

Writing might be a solitary craft, but it takes a team to produce the final product. Thank you to Stacia Seaman for the polish you put on each book and for your attention to detail. Thank you to Sheri for another great cover; you always seem to read my mind as to what the perfect image should be even when I don't have a clue. Thank you to Connie Ward and Kathi Isserman for the great comments and for always saying yes when I ask you to read something. And thanks to all my fellow authors at BSB for your words of encouragement and advice. I appreciate you all.

Thanks to you, the reader. When I started this series, you were the ones who wanted more, so thank you for embracing the characters and me along with them. I'm sure I'm on some FBI watch because of all the e-mails I get on ideas on how to kill people. Every word is always written with you in mind.

Life isn't always perfect, but it's a blessing when you have someone who travels the road with you no matter if the path is rocky or smooth. C, you are that blessing to me, and wow, have you made my life fun. You are my joy, my best friend, and I love you. *Verdad!*

For C
A lifetime is not enough

CHAPTER ONE

Y ou couldn't run forever."
Derby Cain Casey had waited months to say those four simple words, and Juan Luis's expression when she'd found him had been total disbelief. When she'd strapped him to a chair in the middle of her empty warehouse, any bravery he possessed disappeared as effectively as he had after she'd stopped him from attacking Emma.

Fat tears ran steadily down Juan's face, and she hadn't even touched him yet. "Did this day cross your mind when you tried to rape my wife?" He cried harder, proving what a coward he was. "You shot my friend and strapped Emma to a table. If that'd been all, I'd let Merrick shoot you in the head and be done with it. But you wanted my suffering to be complete, didn't you? That's why you picked that place. Your decision's going to cost you."

"I kill you if you no let me go," Juan screamed, and snot flew from his nose. "My mama come for me."

"That's true, she will come for you, and I'll hand you over a piece at a time." As Lou cut his clothes from his body, she tuned out his begging. Juan could get as loud as he wanted but no one would hear him, and she wanted him in the same state of mind Emma had been in when he'd tied her down.

"Did it excite you when Emma cried out?" She stood and took the safety glasses Lou held out. "Did her tears hit you here first?" she asked, and landed a punch in the gut. "Did it make you hard to have her tied down like an animal?"

Juan shook his head, but it was too late for denials. "Fire it up, Lou." He cranked the professional power washer and handed her the wand. The nozzle she'd picked could cut through wood, and the direction book warned not to aim at anyone since it could injure them. She was counting on it.

"No." Juan screamed when she aimed the water at him and started to get closer. The laser-like stream cut through his abdomen as easily as a filet knife through soft bread. His scream was so loud it—

"Damn," Cain said when she startled awake. Eventually the dream would be a reality, but so far Juan had proved elusive. The longer it took to find him, though, the more creative her imagination and dreamscape became. This dream had to have been caused by the painters they'd hired, since they were in the cleaning stage outside.

The bed was empty, so she got up, showered, and dressed to go find her partner. "Persistent," she said as she descended the stairs, buttoning the monogramed cuff of her new shirt. It was a recent gift from Emma, who'd gotten back into a shopping groove. She was grateful since she hated the exercise, so she simply said thank you when Emma handed her the box with five more just like it. That act, along with a thousand other mundane things, reassured her their lives were getting back to normal.

The FBI was outside keeping up their constant surveillance, her shipments of liquor and cigarettes minus the proper seals were still arriving without fail, and her family was happy and safe. She never took any of those things for granted, but a few pieces were still not fitting into the puzzle of her life. "Damn persistent," she said when she saw Special Agent Shelby Phillips sitting in her living room—again.

Shelby was on mandatory leave from her duties as the lead agent assigned to her family after both of her parents had been found murdered. The FBI couldn't take the chance of allowing Shelby back into the field, given her current mental state, so with all her free time she'd taken up a new routine. Shelby would arrive every morning and ask to see her, and she in turn would ignore her. This was the start of month two.

"What are you going to do about her, mobster?" Emma asked as she entered her office at the back of the house. She sat behind Cain's desk, borrowing the space for the project she was working on.

"When do you think she'll give up?"

"I lost the pool after a month, so I can't answer that question," Emma said, signing a check and attaching it to something that appeared to be a contract. "If you finally give in today, Lou gets the twelve hundred up for grabs."

"For a smart woman in law enforcement, surely she has a clue by now that I'm not giving in." Cain sat in a chair intended for visitors and crossed her legs. In an hour, she had to meet with the European vendors her cousins Muriel Casey and Katlin Patrick had been vetting for months. "It's not that I don't understand what's driving her. I do. But I'm not sympathetic enough to give her what she wants." She looked at Emma, and any anger over the situation evaporated when her gaze landed on Emma's swollen midsection. If she had the power to speed up time, she'd do it to see Emma holding their new baby.

"Considering you won't even tell her you won't meet with her, I thought she'd have given up by now, but she's—"

"Persistent." She laughed. "It's like being trapped in a sinking ship and not being able to swim. That's the best way I can describe Shelby's mind-set. You have to either drown or ask a shark for help."

"So either way she's screwed."

"That's right, lass. Lou will be out of luck today even if I was feeling generous. I've got that meeting at the office."

Up to now her business had centered on illegal hard liquors and cigarettes, a trade her great-great-grandmother had started as an Irish immigrant, but Cain saw potential in high-quality wines. A small portion of their operations dealt with them already, and considering its huge profit margin, it was time to expand. Wine would never make as much as the city's growing drug trade, but that wasn't a palatable future for her children.

"Then she'll be here tomorrow because you can give her what the FBI can't." Emma stood and lifted her hands over her head to stretch. "Either cave in or put the poor woman out of her misery."

"You think I should help her?" She didn't move when Emma walked toward the small leather couch with a gait that was slowly starting to change to accommodate the extra weight she carried.

"Look at all she's had to endure basically alone," Emma said with her hand out. "The thought of losing my parents like she did, or the kids having to live through that horror if something happened to us, makes me want to help her."

Cain joined Emma, took her hand, and kissed her. "You'd be willing to risk what could happen if I do?"

"Don't get crazy on me, baby. I didn't say help. I said I understood *why* she's here." They sat and Emma turned so her abdomen pressed into her side. Cain put her hands on their growing child, knowing Baby Casey was most active in the mornings. "What do you think today?"

"What I think every moment of every day," she said, and kissed Emma again. "This baby is another blessing to the miracle my life's become."

"We need to finish discussing this situation before you make any other romantic statements," Emma said as she unbuttoned her shirt, tugging it from Cain's pants when she couldn't go any further. "Unfortunately for Shelby, I don't trust her. Not with you, and certainly not with Muriel."

"Is there something you want, lass?" she asked as she sat with her shirt open, and Emma unbuckled her belt.

"Don't make fun of the big horny woman or I'll buy myself one of those rabid-rabbit things we saw on television late last night and evict you from the bedroom." Cain stood and her pants pooled around her ankles. Emma's fingers stilled at the sides of her underwear as if the urge to be bold had burned itself out.

The same thing had happened during Emma's pregnancy with their son Hayden, and if Emma hadn't run from this life she was sure it would've happened before Hannah was born. The extra weight and growing waistline made Emma's self-doubt about her attractiveness grow as well. Cain didn't enjoy Emma questioning how she felt about her, but she did like reassuring her.

The dress Emma wore was new, and Cain guessed it was part of the problem. Emma loved trips to the mall and her favorite boutiques, but not because she needed a larger size. She loved being pregnant, but her expanding middle was murder on her self-esteem.

"Mrs. Casey," she said as she dropped to her knees in between Emma's legs. They'd made love that morning, but her desire flared again when Emma lifted her head and looked at her. "I'm not making fun." She put her hands on Emma's belly and massaged it as she moved down toward the hem of her dress. The anticipation of touching Emma made the blood rush to her head, and she could hear her own heartbeat.

"I know you've got people waiting, so we don't have to," Emma said as her legs spread wider.

"The world can wait, this can't." She lowered Emma's panties, then stood to get out of her pants and shirt. Emma held her hand up again as a request for help off the couch, and Cain unzipped her dress as soon as she had her on her feet. She smiled when Emma groaned as their naked bodies pressed together.

"I need you to put your mouth on me," Emma said, and sounded desperate. "I'll do whatever you want, but I need you to do that right now."

The way Emma rubbed herself against Cain made it hard to think, but she lowered Emma back down and positioned her butt at the edge of the seat. Being able to lie back a bit would make it easier for Emma to breathe. She swept her eyes down the compact body, and her hips bucked forward into empty space at the sight. She needed relief from her pounding clit, but not until she'd given it to Emma.

"Don't torture me," Emma said as she squeezed her own breasts. They were fuller than normal, and her nipples were slightly darker. Cain thought about them at the strangest times during her day. She'd found Emma desirable from the first time she saw her, but seeing her with the next generation of their family made her insatiable. Emma didn't mind that her sex drive was over the top since she was at the point in the pregnancy where she craved sex.

She wanted to linger on the hard nipples, but Emma was dripping wet and tasted sweet when she put her mouth on her. Emma currently craved pineapple, so they had a number of containers of it in the refrigerator, and the amount she'd consumed had changed her taste. When Cain tasted Emma's sex, she assumed this must be what crack addicts experienced when they finally got their fix. It left a lifelong craving, but unlike any drug addict, she had no interest in rehab to beat the habit.

Emma took a deep breath and held it when Cain placed her tongue under her clit and ran it slowly upward, swirling it around the hardness as she reached the top. "Fuck," Emma said uncharacteristically, grabbing the sides of her head to pull hard on her hair. "Put your fingers in."

Despite what Emma probably wanted, she entered her gently, not wanting her desire to hurt Emma or the baby. To compensate, she sucked hard as her fingers went all the way in, and Emma smiled down at her when she stroked her fingers out and in. Before long, Emma put her feet on her back so she could pump her hips easier and position herself so her fingers and mouth were in the right place.

Emma came so hard she ended up crying, but Cain didn't have time to worry before Emma sat up and put her hand between her legs. "Come up here," Emma said as she placed kisses down her jaw.

It didn't matter that she would've gladly killed someone to have Emma's mouth on her, but her body got what it wanted. Emma's fingers slid across her hardness and she was helpless. She knelt there until Emma gave her the orgasm her body demanded.

"Do you think Muriel would be pissed if I don't show up today?" Cain asked when she fell forward until her forehead rested on Emma's chest. "We could go back to bed if you lie and tell me she wouldn't be."

"No lying to the boss today, my love, so come on." Emma kissed the top of her head before she pushed her off. "The sooner you leave, the sooner you'll get back here for the multiple orgasms I've got planned for later."

"Mine or yours?"

"Yes, so move."

❖

"Jerome Rhodes," Anthony Curtis said out loud as he stared at himself in the bathroom mirror. The name, his new identity, and the face he saw still unsettled him.

A year ago he'd been happy in the back of a van with his team of colleagues and friends, knowing where his life was headed. Only Special Agent Anthony Curtis didn't exist anymore. He'd died or, more accurately, been erased under the skillful hands of the plastic surgeon Gracelia Luis Ortega had found. Now he appeared more Hispanic—his lips fuller, his cheekbones more pronounced—but his eyes were the same. They were his only anchor to his past and the only physical trait he shared with his mother.

"What's wrong?" Gracelia asked as she dropped her robe and stood naked before him.

This was his savior; at least that's what she said constantly. Gracelia was a beautiful woman and the best lover he'd had, but all that didn't balance out her dark side. She was vicious, so much so that he realized everything her brother Rodolfo had done paled when compared to her actions. Rodolfo might've unwittingly been her teacher in that area, but she'd mastered her education so she could groom her son Juan to follow her. Her lessons had culminated with Juan strapping his uncle to a tree, coating him in honey, and unleashing ants on him. Juan had snapped before Rodolfo had suffered too much and shot him dead. They raised family dysfunction to new heights.

The elaborate death trap had been Gracelia's vengeance for Armando Ortega, the love of her life and Juan's father. When Rodolfo found out Armando had gotten Gracelia pregnant and then run, he'd handled the situation with a tree and ants. The thought of thousands of those little fuckers tearing off his dick made him cringe. Gracelia had never forgiven Rodolfo for the betrayal, so she'd taken everything from him, including his life and business.

"Nothing," Anthony said, not in the mood for a fight or a long discussion. In their time together he found Gracelia much smarter than her son, but just as psychotic, so he tried his best to keep her calm. "I'm still trying to get used to all this."

"Stop worrying and enjoy the time off before we have to return to the States to make sure everything is in order."

They'd fled New Orleans after killing Rodolfo and returned to Gracelia's home in Cabo San Lucas. From the reports of the men they'd left behind, things were starting to calm down and the police had moved Rodolfo's case off their priority list. The only problem Gracelia didn't want to acknowledge was Juan's disappearance. She'd had no communication from him in two months, and he hoped the stupid fucker hadn't gotten himself killed in a way that'd cause him a problem. A new identity wasn't ideal, but it was saving him from a life sentence in jail or running from Cain Casey.

"Nothing from Juan today?" he asked, risking Gracelia's temper.

"You've got to start using 'Gustavo,'" Gracelia said, as if speaking to a small child who refused to learn his lessons. "You are now Jerome and he is Gustavo." She jerked the knobs of the shower on, as if not wanting to look at him anymore. "You act as if you don't appreciate everything I have done to keep you safe."

He came up behind her and pressed against her. "I'm grateful, but you have to admit Gustavo has to be found before he gets into trouble," he said, using the name to appease her. "We've got a chance to build on what Rodolfo had, but we have to be smart about it."

"Juan is my problem. Yours is to deal with the business," she said, calmer. "He's upset with not getting what he wants. You should understand that."

"I know you don't like disappointing him." He turned her around to face him once they were in the shower. "But sometimes he can't have everything he wants. If you can't explain that in a way that'll make him understand, I'll be happy to do it for you."

"Is it so hard to give him this woman who's twisted his mind into a knot?" She cupped his testicles in her palm. Whenever she did, a tiny tendril of fear made him think she'd rip them off and show them to him as he writhed in pain.

"Do you want to go to war with three of the strongest families in New Orleans? Do you think we're in that position?" This was the last conversation he was having about this. If Gracelia refused to acknowledge the truth, he was leaving and starting over with the men who had begun answering to him since they'd returned to Mexico. Gracelia had quickly become bored with the day-to-day decisions, so he'd taken over, leaving her to pretend to make the big calls. The men still feared her, but they'd grown to respect his authority.

"If you want to give him everything even when it's not wise, you'll go down with him. Not me, or anyone, will be able to save you."

Gracelia grabbed him by the biceps, appearing panicky. "You can't leave me. I'll kill you if you try."

"Then kill me and put me out of this miserable limbo," he said, and shrugged her off. "If you want to cater to that idiot, do it. I'm out of here." Her smile was smug, as if she wasn't buying his bluff. But he wasn't bluffing, which was freeing. The worry and despair of living the same day over and over was gone. This was it. He wasn't interested in dying, but as he walked out of the bathroom he finally felt like he was getting somewhere.

"You're asking me to cut Juan out," Gracelia said as she stood on the bathroom tiles dripping wet. "I can't do that. He wouldn't survive."

"That's not what I want." He threw his towel on the bed and shoved his legs into his jeans. "Gustavo or Juan, whatever you call him, is fixated on Emma Casey. To get her you have to get through Cain Casey. If he's lucky enough to do that, the Jatibon and the Carlotti families will join with the Casey crew to hunt you down. I watched these people for years, so I know that for sure. Besides, Cain found Juan when he returned under the Ortega name with the help of Hector Delarosa. Do you have that much muscle at your disposal and haven't shared it with me?"

"Why would Hector help Casey?" Gracelia asked as she put her robe on, her skin covered in goose bumps.

"I didn't get to ask, but it might have something to do with what Cain brings to any of her business partnerships. Hector was smart to dole out the favors. He wants to establish himself, and getting Casey to back him is smart. Trying to get her wife for Juan to play with is fucking stupid, but knock yourself out since he needs you to prop him up."

"You want me to sacrifice him. It's not that easy."

"No," he yelled, tired of explaining himself. Gracelia had a talent for hearing only what she wanted. "You need to take a lesson from Rodolfo and keep him in line."

"My son hated Rodolfo."

"Obviously," he said as he put his shoes on. "Especially with you whispering in his ear about the god Armando."

"You are talking dangerous words now." Gracelia's voice had become low and threatening.

"Close your mind if you want, but while Rodolfo was alive he kept Juan on a short leash so he wouldn't do anything stupid. Rodolfo knew Juan's limitations and let him do only what he could handle." He picked up his wallet and passport and slipped them into his back pocket. "The only person who did learn from Rodolfo, and he's taking those lessons to heart, is Carlos Santiago, or Carlos Luis, since he took the name Rodolfo gave him. He's being smart about how he does things, and one of his priorities is hunting you and Juan. If you were thinking of rolling over the men loyal to your late brother, forget it. They belong to Carlos now."

"That won't last long."

"Good luck to you, then."

He made it outside with Gracelia a few feet behind him. "Wait," she said before he could walk out to the road. "I'll find him and tell him we have other, more important things to worry about."

"This is your last chance, you understand that, right?" He entered the house again but couldn't look at her.

"I do, but I must understand what you want." Gracelia gripped his biceps and forced him to face her. "Tell me honestly or you really can leave."

"I want the chance to build a new life where I'm not the asshole always taking orders. I thought that's what you wanted help with, but you're more interested in babying *Gustavo*." He spat the name out like a rotten piece of fruit.

"Stay, then, and we can start over together." She walked him back to the bedroom and began to take his clothes off after she'd dropped her robe.

He wanted to believe her because he didn't want to start over with another organization. A tremor went through him that made him think of the old saying, "someone walking over his grave," but the box of coke on the dresser dulled any anxiety and doubt. Staying was probably suicidal, but that magical white powder took the fear of that away as well.

"Sure. Why the hell not?"

Even if this ended badly, he was taking all these bastards down with him.

❖

Muriel Casey drummed her thumbs on her steering wheel as she waited for the gates to Cain's home to open. She noticed her ex-lover

Shelby had already arrived, as had a new paneled van across the street. When she'd left the previous afternoon she'd noticed a large delivery vehicle with a local bread company logo painted on the side.

"Because that's what you see parked on a street like this all the time," she said, and laughed.

From the beginning, Cain had advised her to laugh and blow it off when it came to all this. If you let the anger build, you either got sick or had a stroke, so she'd tried to listen. Her hands and stomach tightened as she stared at Shelby's small sedan. The government-issued SUV was either in the FBI garage or at Shelby's house waiting for her to return to her duties.

Their breakup had been easy. She'd sent Shelby back everything that belonged to her—every gift and any correspondence between them. After that she'd insulated herself from any further contact, and eventually Shelby had taken the hint. Only now, Muriel saw her every time she had to drop by Cain's.

They never exchanged words, and she still didn't understand why Cain hadn't given the order to stop her at the gate. Her cousin was smart enough to know this was another ploy for the FBI to worm their way in to where they didn't belong. At least she thought Cain was smarter than she'd been when for a brief moment she'd considered turning her back on her family for a chance with Shelby.

Her father, Jarvis, had died thinking that she was close to that decision, and she'd have to accept the disappointment of never getting the chance to make amends. That made her chest burn from shame and had made sleep for more than a few hours at a time impossible.

"Good morning, Muriel," said Ross Verde, Emma's father, when she got out of her car. His shirt was stained with sweat and the knees of his pants were dirty. Cain had gladly given him a large section of the yard for a garden, and Muriel often saw him out there with Hayden and Hannah pulling weeds and checking the multitude of fruits and vegetables they were growing.

"Be careful in this humidity, Ross. Pretty soon you'll figure out the only thing to miss about Wisconsin is the weather."

"Cain offered to air-condition the yard for me, but considering the mild winters here I don't mind the heat. Getting out here keeps me sane." He wiped his forehead after storing his tools in the small shed Cain had erected for him. "I'm not one to sit around all day doing nothing."

"You're part owner of a successful casino now, so maybe you should learn to gamble," she said with a laugh. "I'm glad you decided to stay." She put her hand on his shoulder for the walk to the house via the kitchen. "Emma is happier for it, and it's good to see Cain with in-laws."

"I don't know about gambling, but I'm enjoying my retirement for sure. I dreamed from Emma's childhood of what her future would be, and now that my prayers were answered, I'm having a great time being grandpa." He left the basket with peppers and tomatoes on the counter before joining her at the kitchen table. "How are you doing?"

"I'm fine," she said quickly, her now-standard answer to that question.

"Cain's my family now," Ross said, covering her hand with his. "That means I consider you the same. It's okay to admit that you miss your father. We didn't have much time together, but I think of him often. I'll be forever grateful to him for helping Emma make her way back here."

"I do miss him," she said, and had to swallow as a way to try to tamp down her emotions. "There was so much left unsaid between us, and that's how it'll stay."

"You don't have children yet, so let me explain a father's perspective." Ross seldom raised his voice, and she nodded, sensing her heart rate slow at the soothing tone with the slight Midwestern accent. "When you have a child, everyone says you pour your hopes and dreams into them from the moment you first hold them."

"You don't believe that?"

Ross nodded and closed his eyes momentarily. "I did as well, but along with all that sometimes you also give your child your fears, weaknesses, and insecurities. It's easy to do, especially when, like Jarvis and me, you have only one. For so long I let my wife beat Emma down as a way to try to get some sort of vengeance for what she felt deprived of. It was easier to not fight in an effort to keep some unrealistic peace." His eyes became glassy and his expression was one of regret.

"But you got to make it up to her," she said.

"And you think I'm lucky because I did and you're damned because you didn't?"

"Death isn't something you can undo."

"No, but Jarvis and I shared something very special. Even if I'd never had the opportunity of coming here to enjoy my family, I knew how wonderful my daughter grew up to be. Despite my failings she's happy and strong, and that's what your father thought about you."

"Thanks for saying so, Ross, but I knew my father. What I did was a betrayal not often forgiven in my family."

"Why are you here, then? Do you come every day to simply say hello to your cousin?"

She laughed at his persistence. "No. I still work for Cain and my family."

"No parent will ever fault you for following your heart, even if it doesn't work out. We bleed with you when it doesn't end how you hope, but it's no reason to shun your child. Not unless you're a fool, and Jarvis wasn't a fool." He released her hand so one of the staff could put the coffee mugs down. "If you're here with a full briefcase every morning, that means Cain trusts you, and your supposed betrayal wasn't as bad as what's rolling around in your head."

"How about in my heart?" She took a sip of her coffee, but this, like most things, didn't taste right. Her time with Shelby seemed to have dulled all the things she liked—even something as insignificant as a cup of her favorite brew.

"You have to either decide to believe my daughter and what she told you his last words were, or not. Emma wouldn't have lied about how much he loved you or how proud he was of you."

"Thanks, Ross, I'm trying my best, but it's hard on me knowing that was on his mind at the end."

"You could waste a lot of time worrying about that, which to me means your relationship with Jarvis boiled down to the very last days of his life. What came before was of no consequence at all," Ross said, then lifted his mug to his lips. "If that's the road you're on, you might miss out on a whole lot, like someone to love who'll love you and heal all those sore spots."

"You're not talking about Shelby, are you?"

"I'm sure he's not," Emma said when she walked in and headed for the refrigerator for some juice after kissing the top of both their heads. "You need to forgive yourself so your dad knows I did a good job of getting his message across. He's probably up there cursing me."

"You did great. It's just me questioning myself." She stood to pull Emma's chair for her. "She's waiting again?"

"Yes, and Cain's left her in there *again*."

"This is getting ridiculous." She thought of the hours of tape Cain had been able to get by bugging her house after she began to suspect Shelby's motives. All those nights Shelby had whispered how much she loved her, and how she'd held her hand during her father's funeral, had been part of an undercover operation. Now was the only time she regretted not having pulled the trigger to end someone's life. She'd come close, though, to begging Cain to order Shelby eliminated.

"You're angry, but try to think about what she's going through," Emma said.

"Have you forgotten what happened when that bitch's coworkers thought Cain was to blame?"

Emma swallowed so hard Muriel thought she'd spit the juice right back up. "The seizures are gone, but no one can promise they're gone for good, so no—I haven't forgotten," Emma said coldly.

When Shelby's parents had been brutally killed in California, Shelby had been the first to lay the blame at Cain's door. The agents she worked with weren't far behind. They'd cornered Cain on the way to work and used unnecessary force to take her down. The results had been a severe concussion, seizures that left her disoriented and sick, and a three-week hospital stay. Muriel's behavior had been so in question that Emma had kept her out of Cain's room for hours, but hell, she didn't blame her for the harsh treatment.

Had it been her lying in that hospital room she'd probably have cut Cain out of her life permanently, but Cain had welcomed her home. She'd been forgiven for her lapse in judgment and her neglect of her family. Cain had taken her word that she wanted back in and her promise to never put someone like Shelby above her blood.

"If you want, I can tell her to get the hell out of here," she offered Emma.

"I know you would, but she's here for Cain, so Cain will deal with it."

"Shelby's probably taking advantage of what happened as another way in. She's got no honor."

"Muriel," Emma said with a sad smile. "You have more reason than any of us to hate her, but I truly think her grief is real."

"Cain's not falling for this act, is she?"

"What act?" Cain asked, and surprised all three of them.

"Your lady-in-waiting with the crocodile tears," she said.

"It's like I always tell you, cousin, patience. There's a time for everything, and Shelby's turn is coming up."

CHAPTER TWO

Remi Jatibon stood off to the side of the camera crew as they set up their shots behind the St. Louis Cathedral in the French Quarter. Production of the sequel to the film *Lady Killers* had started the week before, and this was as close as she'd gotten to her partner, Dallas Montgomery, in all that time.

She missed Dallas in the morning, but seeing her focused on something other than the ordeal with her bastard father was a relief. In her position as the next in line to take over for her father, Ramon, Remi had always been the aggressor in any situation. No one could win everything, but weakness wasn't something she was truly familiar with.

For Dallas, though, it had been a constant companion from the moment Johnny Moores killed their mother. Remi hated referring to Johnny as the father of Dallas and her sister, Kristen, but that was the sad, unfair truth. Once he'd beaten Sarah Moores to death, Dallas's childhood had come to an end. That fateful night Johnny had committed murder, then crawled into his daughter's bed. It took time for Katie Lynn Moores to work up the courage to run, but she had, and morphed into Dallas Montgomery, successful actress.

"For an action movie, this is slower than paste," Kristen said when she arrived and looped her arm through Remi's.

The one happy casualty of Johnny's actions had been Dallas's place in the French Quarter when she and Kristen had moved in with Remi. The three of them were even discussing something more permanent than her condo, like a house. The condo was big enough, but Dallas always joked about the bachelor pad as just that, a shrine to Remi's unencumbered life. A new house would allow the sisters to put their mark on it and make it something they'd never had together—a safe and happy home. Until then she was getting to know Kristen and helping her finish her studies in finance.

"Welcome to the glamorous life of movie-making," she said, and kissed Kristen's temple. "Once you live through the process you'll think international banking is a hotbed of excitement when you compare both careers."

"Dallas has better perks, though," Kristen said, and waved to her sister when she emerged from her trailer with her costar.

"What, long hours with catering?"

"No, good-looking studio head and catering," Kristen said, and laughed. Since her arrival, Kristen hadn't dated or shown interest in anyone, but she had confided in Remi and Dallas one night at dinner. Kristen didn't consider herself a lesbian, but couldn't really imagine herself in a relationship with a man either. When she'd advised patience on that subject, Kristen's response had been firm in the negative. She'd told Remi it'd be hard to convince her otherwise after Johnny had locked them in a box for almost twenty-four hours as he drove them "home" to get "reacquainted."

"I don't know any of those, but we've dealt with some cute bankers through the years that I could introduce you to."

"Thanks, but I'm happy for now watching my sister enjoy being happy and in love. Being alone that way doesn't bother me."

"This is a nice surprise," Dallas said before Remi could respond. It was humorous to Remi that she was becoming one of those people who wanted what she had with Dallas to be contagious.

"I'm not surprising you. I'm here to oversee my investment," she said, and tried to sound gruff.

"All business, huh?" Dallas held her hand as if not daring to risk her makeup with a kiss.

"You having fun yet?" Remi kissed Dallas's palm.

"I'll probably have more fun tomorrow, since we're having the normal first-day catastrophes. We usually have problems, but today it seems like nothing's going right. Hopefully in a day or so everyone will be in the groove."

"It could be worse, sis." Kristen took Dallas's other hand. "You could be slinging hash somewhere wearing an attractive hairnet."

"Thanks for the pep talk, and we'll be at this until late, so you two should make plans for dinner that don't include me." The director started yelling, so their time was up. "Love you," she said to Remi, "and you too," to Kristen.

"Have fun, and if anyone gives you a hard time, tell them you know people."

Dallas laughed before taking her place next to the car they'd be using throughout filming. Remi and Kristen stayed for another half hour before Remi gave Kristen a ride to the Tulane campus.

"Can I treat you to dinner tonight?" Kristen asked when they pulled over.

"No, but I'll be happy to treat you if you don't mind that we'll have company. Name the place and time."

Kristen gave Remi the information and accepted a kiss on the cheek before she got out. Instinct told Remi to put someone with Kristen, but she wanted her to enjoy this time where a good time and fun were her only responsibilities.

"Is that going to be a problem?" Simon Jimenez asked as she rejoined the slow traffic on St. Charles Avenue. Simon was her personal guard as well as friend. She and her partner Juno had escaped Fidel Castro's regime with her parents years before.

"It's a crush that'll be crushed the moment she finds one of these college boys interesting." Remi read over the information her twin brother Mano had sent the night before. Their purchase of the casino in Mississippi and the studio in partnership with Cain was starting to increase their legitimate incomes significantly. Both businesses were perfect for laundering the money that was hard to explain to the IRS.

"The last few months have been hard enough, so what happens if this is more than that? Are you willing to gamble with what Dallas has brought into your life if something small turns into a huge misunderstanding?"

"We're nowhere close to that happening, but I'll talk to Dallas before we get there." She put the paperwork aside and looked out the window on the way to the office. "Anything else since this morning?"

"Muriel and Katlin confirmed for tonight, and Cain said she'll be at your father's in the morning for breakfast and conversation. That'll give you time to get through the list Juno made for you." Simon and Juno not only lived one floor down from the penthouse, but they both had worked for first Remi's father and now her.

"Is Papi or Mano going to the meeting today?"

"Both of them are going. Ramon trusts your brother the same as you, but this is all new to him, so he figured another set of ears couldn't hurt."

When Cain offered them a piece of her new venture as a sign of good faith to their fairly new alliance, Remi had agreed on the spot. While her father wasn't exactly upset with her decision, he'd gently reminded her where they'd made their money in the past. There was plenty of illegal liquor in their Pescador Clubs, but it was for customer relations, not money. Their money came from the gambling tables, not booze, and when you took huge risks with unknown things it could be disastrous.

"What's your opinion about all this?" she asked Simon.

Simon glanced at her momentarily in the rearview mirror. "When I was growing up in Cuba, this group terrorized my friends every day on the playground. They were cruel and didn't care who they hurt, and since they were always together, they had all the power." Simon had met her father when they were children.

"Papi put up with that? I've got a hard time seeing him as a bully."

"Ramon is a man much like his father, both in character and in choice of profession." Simon parked in their usual spot and turned in the seat so they faced each other. "He was no bully, and after suffering the humiliation of a fat lip and bloody nose, he learned a valuable lesson."

Remi was riveted, never having heard this story, which was strange considering her father's love of nostalgia. "Did he hire a hit team?" she joked.

"He formed an alliance with every kid who was tired of getting kicked in the teeth every day. Strength comes from our fists sometimes, but in most situations it comes from the people who stand with you and how many there are."

"So my faith in Cain is good?"

"Cain will always hold more power than you, Remi. Her operations are larger and better insulated from both vultures and the police, and because of the time her family's been in the city, she has more friends who are loyal to her."

Simon's expression was, as usual, controlled, not giving away anything in her head or heart. "So you disagree with me?"

"When you were shot I almost lost my sanity, and I believe Mano did as well. Had that killer succeeded, your parents would've never survived." The words put a crack in the façade, and Simon's voice trembled with emotion. Remi didn't really remember the impact, but her first meeting with her brother, her parents, and Dallas still made icy fingers spread from the spot on her chest where the vest stopped the bullet. Never had she seen her parents so broken by what she saw—fear.

"We've never really talked about that day."

"All I want to remember of that nightmare is the person responsible for keeping you and our family safe. Cain's planning and forethought kept you alive, and she proved herself to me as a true friend who'll not only stand with you, but who can be trusted." Simon took a deep breath as if trying to center herself again. "Your decision to join her on this is a good thing. I don't like going against your father, not that he opposes the plan, but it'll help you build your future. On the playground we navigate, it's good to be on the side you can not only count on but that has the biggest number."

"Thanks, Simon," she said as she squeezed her friend's shoulder. "What about Cain's enemies?"

"A true partnership is one where you accept not only the rewards, but the problems. I like Cain because her need for vengeance doesn't cloud her mind, so she doesn't become sloppy. I saw the same quality in a boy I met long ago, and that control worked well for him in all things. It's a trait he passed along to you and Mano."

Remi laughed at Simon's explanation and decided to let go of any concern she'd had about this venture. Cain would always be more powerful than her, but she did trust her not only in business but to stand with them in any circumstance. And after all the help she'd given to free Dallas from her past, she was forever in Cain's debt.

"Let's hope this goes as well as the rest of my life is." As soon as the words left her mouth she felt like she was tempting fate, but she was too happy to care. "Because that's as good as I could've imagined it being."

❖

Juan watched from the backseat of his rental as Remi Jatibon walked into her office building. He grimaced again, his jaw like a beehive where the doctor had placed the implants that'd completely changed his facial structure. It was like an itch he'd have to rip his skin off to get to.

"Gustavo, you want to wait until she comes out?" Enrique "Chico" Chavez asked as he tapped his palm against his knee, a nervous habit that was whipping Juan's anger into a froth. Chico and the three others who'd traveled with him were his mother's idea, and he hadn't been able to dissuade her.

"If you've got something better to do, get lost." Even though he knew it wouldn't do any good, he scratched hard from his ear to his chin, following his jawline. His true identity and the resemblance to his late father were two more things Cain Casey had stolen from him. "Tell me when she leaves," he said, and closed his eyes to wait for the small taste of coke to work away his discomfort.

Along with Cain he cursed Special Agent Anthony Curtis every day. The bastard was bedding his mother and gaining more leverage with her, but he'd been right. To get what he wanted he'd need to have a solid plan and practice patience. He'd do both, since his smash-and-grab approach hadn't gotten him anything but a lecture from both his mother and Anthony.

"Jerome," he mumbled, trying to get used to the new name. Even now when his men said "Gustavo" he at times didn't respond.

"I thought you wanted Cain Casey?" Chico asked, as if trying to make small talk.

"What the fuck do you care what I want? Your job is to do whatever I tell you." The temperature was starting to climb, and the sweat running down his back was making his clothes stylish straitjackets.

"Did I do something to piss you off?" Chico asked. They were the same age, but Chico was tall and handsome, with a personality that made him popular with his other men.

"I don't need a babysitter and a confessor."

"I volunteered to come and help you, we all did."

That was hard to believe. From the day he'd started working for his uncle Rodolfo until now, Juan was smart enough to know it was his name that garnered respect—not him. Had he been born to parents as poor as his father had been, he'd have been killed long ago, or left to die.

"You don't have to lie or talk in an effort to get close to me," he said as he opened his eyes. "Once I get what I want, you'll be free to run back to Gracelia for your reward."

"Don't you want to know why I volunteered?"

The heat, the itch, and this asshole were making him miserable. "If I ask, will you shut the fuck up?"

"Señora Luis is a smart woman, and I support her taking control of what Señor Rodolfo had, but the future always lies in the next generation. I volunteered to work with you because the power will fall to you next. This she's made clear." Chico seemed sincere, and had it been Rodolfo he was talking to, Juan knew he'd be dead. Pledging loyalty to anyone other than the boss was suicide. "How we got here isn't my concern."

"What do you mean by that?"

"How Rodolfo died and who killed him aren't important to me,"

Chico said as he pushed the lapel of his jacket back to expose the holstered pistol. "I served him, and now I want to serve you."

"Your pledge doesn't sound sincere if you don't give a shit about who killed your boss. If the same happens to me, will you try to cut a deal with whoever pulls the trigger?"

"Would you like me to avenge him?" Chico asked, almost as a taunt.

The pistol was still in his line of sight and he knew better than to try to bluff a man like this. He'd kill him and lay the blame on whoever suited him to gain favor with whoever would benefit from his death.

"We're here because the way to what I want starts here," he said, and pointed to the building. "Rodolfo taught me the way to knock something out of your way is to start with the foundation, not the roof. Gracelia tried that and failed, but she started too low to make an impact."

"This woman will do that? Make an impact, I mean."

He thought of Remi and Cain's partnership. "Yes, and even if I fail it'll break apart the strength of an alliance Casey depends on. Once I peel away the layers I'll finally not only take Casey out, but I'll get my reward."

"Her business?"

"No, her woman. With Casey out of my way, I'm going to fuck Emma Casey to death, and I'll enjoy every moment of it."

❖

The drab interior of the conference room in the FBI offices in downtown New Orleans was quiet as the people of acting team leader Special Agent Joe Simmons waited for Special Agent in Charge Annabel Hicks. Their surveillance of Casey and her businesses had been assigned to another team for the day because of this review.

"Let's get started," Annabel said as she sat with her assistant right behind her.

"Certainly, ma'am," Joe said, determined to keep his answers brief so Annabel would set the parameters of the meeting. His years in the field had taught him to never give any tactical ground if he didn't have to.

"Well?" Annabel snapped the word at him like a lash from a whip.

"What can we do for you, ma'am?" Claire Lansing asked.

"Let's start with where Shelby Philips is and continue from there."

"You put her undercover with Muriel Casey, and their relationship fooled even us," Joe said, not caring if his sarcasm got him written up. "You were her only contact, which is ludicrous considering who she was after. What was her out if things had gone south?"

"Watch yourself, Mr. Simmons," Annabel said icily. "Shelby is a capable agent, and her time with Muriel Casey did uncover some useful insights and leads on how Cain Casey does business."

"Ma'am, no disrespect, but we've been sitting on that warehouse for weeks and nothing," said Lionel Jones, the team's computer expert. "The closest we've come to any type of alcohol is the winos sleeping off their buzz in the parking lot surrounding the building. Could this be another Casey herring since she knows what Shelby was up to?"

"If you'd like me to find you all something more exciting to do, I'll be happy to oblige," Annabel said.

"Then to answer your question, ma'am," Joe said, in an effort to cool everyone down, "Shelby's somewhere inside Cain's house, just like she's been from the day you forced leave on her. Since we've been listening to 'It's a Small World' on a loop for most of that time, I have no report as to why she's there."

"Find out, then," Annabel screamed, uncharacteristically. "Can everyone wait outside, please?" she said after she pulled the front of her jacket down and took a deep breath.

"We've followed every lead from what you gave us, and we still don't have anything," Joe said. "Shelby has lost any inroads she made with the Caseys because of her initial reaction to her parents' deaths, and I'm sure she thinks we've turned our backs on her as well." He'd been a good agent for years because he followed the rules, but it frustrated the hell out of him when superiors at times turned that around on good people. Shelby had done everything Annabel had asked of her, and her reward now was banishment for as long as Annabel deemed appropriate.

"By next week this entire office will be under investigation for the actions of agents like Barney Kyle and Anthony Curtis." Annabel sounded flat, as if she was waiting for the firing squad to arrive.

"Who's Washington sending down?"

"Ronald Chapman."

Annabel said the name like a curse, since Chapman had complained all the way to the director when she'd been given the New Orleans office. Ronald had been raised in the lower Ninth Ward and had dreams of returning to his hometown riding the white horse of justice. Anyone who knew him, and Joe did, realized he had his sights on the governor's office eventually. He needed the exposure of cleaning up New Orleans to get himself elected.

"How would you like me to handle this?" he asked. Mentally he started drawing up an aggressive surveillance schedule that'd keep him out of the office as much as he could get away with. He had no desire to get stuck in the coming power struggle.

"I need you to get to Shelby," Annabel said, not making eye contact, "unofficially."

"For?" he asked warily as he pressed his fist into the table. Shelby was his friend, and as such he wasn't going to like where Annabel was taking this.

"I know you're loyal to her, enough so that you shut your eyes the day Cain Casey was brought in and left here on a stretcher. You, like everyone else, including me, thought Casey had slaughtered her family." She finally looked up with her mouth in a tight line, as if she were in pain. "It was my fault for letting it go so far, letting Brent take out his frustrations on her like that."

Special Agent Brent Cehan was still on desk duty and under protective order because of his actions toward Cain the day she'd been brought in for questioning. Joe had turned his head when Brent pounded Cain while she was cuffed and defenseless, and he'd gotten a perverse sense of satisfaction from her suffering. It was in that moment that he totally understood why Barney Kyle and Anthony had taken the easy low road. Even if Cain hadn't killed Shelby's parents, she was guilty of so many things, including murder, that he still couldn't muster up too much regret.

"In the end, though, ma'am, Brent might be the answer to taking Casey down permanently when she tries to get back at him for what he did."

"As much as I'd like to bring Casey down, Joe, this isn't frontier justice. Under my watch Brent beat a suspect and took her in under a false charge of resisting arrest, and another agent has gone rogue." Her list was probably much shorter than Ronald Chapman's, and he'd use every misstep as a way to strip away not only her place here, but her job as well. Annabel, after all, had been brought in to fix the fiasco her predecessor Barney had made by taking a job with the Bracato crime family. "If Shelby is able to convince Cain to help her get the revenge she wants, Chapman will bring us all down, and you know that's why she's at Cain's. Shelby's your friend, but are her motives worth losing your pension over?"

"I'll talk to her, but are you going to let her come back? She needs structure right now, not to be set adrift."

"She still has to pass the psych evaluation, but yes, I want her back." Annabel started to put her papers away but glanced up at him again. "My apologies for not cutting you in on what Shelby was doing. If it hadn't been for her parents, I believe we'd have the bones for a solid case against Cain by now. She was the one who insisted on the limited knowledge of what she was doing, and not because she didn't trust you."

"Why, then?"

"Muriel, like Cain, is smart. If you'd known the relationship was a scam, Muriel would've picked that up instantly and it would've ended the first day. Shelby needed all of you to display the wariness you did when she told you about her new assignment because of Muriel."

"The problem, though, is that relationship wasn't all a scam. It couldn't have been, because Shelby wouldn't have basically whored herself out as part of her duties." He had to believe that or lose all respect for his colleague. If she'd been with Muriel just for leads, it made her no better than Kyle and Anthony. "Why is Chapman really coming?"

"Muriel filed another protection order on behalf of her cousin, only this time in federal court. It was enough of a red flag for Ronald once it was granted." Annabel tapped the corner of her folder on the table when she was on her feet. "No matter what we do, we might've lost the war already."

"Do you trust me to go a little beyond talking to Shelby?"

"Will there be a record of what you have in mind for Ronald to add to his list of my sins?"

"No, and if I'm wrong I'll be happy to throw myself on Chapman's hand grenade to save you and everyone else."

CHAPTER THREE

L uce Fournier glanced around the inside of the warehouse as the driver Cain Casey had sent held the door open for her. "Looks are sometimes deceiving," she said in French.

"I hope you mean the building and not the group we're here to see," said Maximo Roux, the Chateau Michel Winery manager.

"Don't let the charm and smooth talk fool you." She followed the driver to a conference room to the left of what appeared to be a number of offices. "Our hostess is like this place—a contradiction with many layers."

"Are you sure that's not your own preconceptions bleeding into this?" Maximo's eyebrows came together as he asked. "This deal is good for us, and one the boss has been after for years."

"I'm not biased, old man." She dropped her bag next to the chair she'd chosen and took a minute to admire the grand antique table. It was as beautiful as the paintings on the walls. "We can take a lot of other avenues that are better than this. Either I'm trusted with the business or I'm not, but I'm going to do what I believe is best for the family until I'm told otherwise."

"Until you own the wine, and you don't, your job is to carry out orders."

Maximo picked the opportune time for his reprimand since the door opened again when he was done. "I'm Cain Casey," the woman leading the group said, with her hand out.

"Luce Fournier." She tried to match Cain's grip as she compared herself to the competition. And she did regard Cain as competition in so many ways.

They were, in her opinion, night and day. Cain's dark hair, tanned skin, and build were the polar opposite of Luce's slim physique and blond hair in its usual tight ponytail. Really, their only similarities were their blue eyes and height, though Cain's eyes were a much darker shade. Casey wasn't the ogre she'd hoped, not outwardly anyway, but she had time to dissect her to find the flaws and weaknesses.

"Is there a problem?" Cain asked.

"No, why do you ask?"

"You haven't let go of my hand, and I feel a bit dissected," Cain said with a smile that seemed cold and distant. It was eerie how she'd almost plucked her train of thought right out of her mind.

This wasn't someone who trusted easily, but then again, she wasn't here for a best friend. With a hard squeeze she released Cain and sat. After the endless hours she'd spent with Muriel, Katlin, and Mano Jatibon, she was anxious to book a flight home.

"I have no interest in you other than doing business, Ms. Casey, so if you'd like we can begin."

"The Jatibons should be here in ten minutes. Would you like something to drink while we wait? Or maybe you'd like to introduce your friend?" Cain sat across from them and smiled. Her poise and confidence radiated like a neon sign, and it only irritated Luce further.

"We are interested in doing business with you, so I'd like to finish. Once the Jatibons arrive, you can inform them of our final decisions, or whatever you'd like." A sudden heat made Luce's body flush, but her hands were clammy. That, along with the fireball in her stomach, was the familiar but unfortunate side effect of confrontation, but if they didn't gain the upper hand now, she'd never wrestle it from Casey. Her stomach acid doubled when Cain stood and her chair slid easily to the wall.

Cain rocked on her feet momentarily and stared at Luce before leaving without a word. "Lou," she said, once she'd cleared the door. "Escort them from the building."

"I'll get Frank to drive them back."

"Out of the building, Lou, but if it'll make you feel better, give them the number of a cab company."

"You do that and it'll kill the deal," Muriel said from a few paces behind her.

"Would I like this deal?" she asked as she dropped into her office chair. "Sure, but I don't usually go into business with hostile partners. You don't have to love me, but do you honestly think Luce Fournier has our best interest in mind? Especially if something goes wrong? We've got enough people trying to bring us down without inside help."

"I don't get it," Katlin said. "We've met with these people numerous times, and we had a solid deal in place with the understanding Remi and her family were part of the mix."

Cain heard the screaming in the hall, first in English, then French, between Luce and the older gentleman. It was the first time she'd seen who she knew was Maximo, but she'd heard plenty about him and his talent for creating excellent vintages. She had background on Luce as well but hadn't thought the woman stupid enough to allow her personal issues to get in the way of business.

"You'll get an apology in less than an hour and a request for another meeting," she said to both her cousins. "I don't care who answers that call. Tell them we're out."

"Do you have any idea what happened in there?" Muriel asked. "I agree with your decision, but if Katlin and I did something wrong I'd like to know what it was so we don't repeat it."

"You both did a good job on this, so obviously neither of you is the problem. Luce works for Michel Blanc but shares a special relationship with his daughter, Nicolette."

"The Nicolette Blanc you graduated with who was attacked before she went home?" Muriel asked.

Muriel had finished Tulane a year after her, but had to remember the French beauty who'd pursued Cain more determinedly than the FBI. "That's her, and she pushed her father to meet with Da from the first day of our freshman year. When that psycho caught her in that alley and carved a chunk out of her face, they went home without the deal Michel wanted."

"I thought Uncle Dalton met Michel before they left," Muriel said.

"He did, when he came to pick me up at their hotel. Nicolette didn't take no well to any question, but Lou, Merrick, and I got her out of that bind before the guy cut her heart out. Michel was grateful, so that's why I started with him for this."

Muriel nodded as if satisfied, so she turned her attention to Katlin. "Do you think it's a good idea to do business with an old flame?"

"Nicolette was a beautiful coed, but we were strictly acquaintances. Anyone who was that curious about Da, me, and the family back then was someone I kept at arm's length." She gazed at the family portrait on her desk and thought of Hayden's drive to please. Her son was going to be her successor, and she hoped her Da had been as comfortable with her at Hayden's age as she was with her son. "The day before I graduated Da gave me a promotion, so I wasn't too trusting with anything or anyone new. I didn't want to take the chance that I'd screw up."

"Should we start over or forget this expansion?" Muriel asked.

"I'm sure France has more than one vineyard, so start over with someone else. Only don't make this a priority. We've got enough to do, and things are starting to get back to normal on the streets."

"Our numbers are up both in shipments and income, so not having this won't hurt," Katlin said.

A knock stopped their conversation, and she stood to greet Ramon and Mano when they entered. "Good morning."

"I'm disappointed," Ramon said as they shook hands. "One small traffic accident and I missed all the fireworks."

"He means Luce Fournier is screaming in French outside," Mano said. "I'm sure she's cursed every ancestor we have as well as everyone in this room, and Papi set her off again when he waved on the way in."

"Ms. Fournier needs lessons in manners, so I apologize for the time you dedicated to this, Mano. The deal is off."

"Do you mind me asking what set her off?" Ramon asked.

"She started by disrespecting your family's part in all this, dismissing you like my flunkies."

"Puta," Mano said, spitting the word *whore* with venom. "Thank you for your backing. At least we know what we want from whoever we deal with."

"No need to thank me, Mano," she said as Katlin closed the door. "The most essential thing to the future we both want is peace. You have children, so you understand what a strong alliance with people you completely trust means."

Ramon nodded with a warm smile. "We're agreed, then, that we'll try again."

"I understood your hesitancy in the beginning." She spoke calmly, not wanting her words to carry any more meaning that'd insult either man. "We're both comfortable swimming in our own ponds, but combining our forces when it's appropriate will only strengthen our position against our enemies."

"As long as you know my questions had nothing to do with you. After meeting with Muriel, Katlin, and Mano a few times, all my worries disappeared."

Ramon's accent and mannerisms made her think of her father. Both of them always seemed so sure of themselves and left her with a sense of calm after only a short exchange. "I'd never speak ill of

Vincent or Vinny," she said of the Carlotti family, "but Vinny's business is going well. With success, though, comes power."

"Vincent would take him down himself if Vinny went against us," Mano said.

"You misunderstand me." Both she and Ramon smiled. "My partnership with you as far as trust is concerned is the same with Vincent, and I know your father feels the same. The Carlotti family and mine have a long history of friendship I've counted on, as they count on mine. The loyalty they've shown through the years is the reason both Remi and I backed Vinny in a business neither of us are really interested in."

"I agree with everything you said, but I still don't understand," Mano said.

"Power is like a popular toy on the playground. If someone has it, someone else wants it. Vinny's doing well and playing by the rules we set for him, and as he becomes more successful, the vultures will eventually start to circle to try to strip him clean."

"If Vinny's business is combined with someone's approximately the same size, it'll take all three families' resources to bring them down," Ramon said. "That's not a problem, but it's always better to avoid a fight if you can."

"Do either of you think that's going to happen?" Mano asked.

There was one fight she was willing to not only find, but win as well. Her problem, though, was that she hadn't found Juan Luis no matter how many people she'd thrown on the street. Many people, like Mano, she imagined, thought things came so easily for her. Her life had been blessed, but the ease came from meticulous planning. Knowing every angle that could blow up in her face and doing everything she could to avoid it had been like a religion to her, but nothing she'd done had made Juan surface.

"Am I worried about something specific?" she asked him as she held her hand up. "No, but it's something not to forget. We already know what happens when you leave something undone."

"We'll find these assholes, don't worry," Mano said.

"It's not your commitment I question, Mano. That's a nonissue. When you have someone like Juan lurking in the dark, I worry. I can't help it because for every one like him, a hundred more are waiting for their chance to take us down."

Ramon slapped his hands together as if in warning to his son that they'd eaten up enough of her time. "Until tomorrow night, Cain?"

"We're looking forward to it." She embraced both men and

followed them out to the expansive warehouse where their cars were parked. "I've already told Muriel and Katlin I won't be accepting any calls from Luce or anyone in Michel's circle. Their window to work with us is closed."

"Do you even want to pursue this? With everything else you've got going on, we can put it off if you want."

"It's a lucrative expansion for both of us, so I'm going to do what I should've in the first place. We'll deal with a broker that'll give us access to more than the few labels Michel presents. After today my debt to him for what happened to his daughter is paid."

"Dalton told me more than once that wasn't your fault," Ramon said as he placed his hand on her shoulder. "You owed him nothing to begin with."

"That's true. I didn't send the crazy nut in the alley, but what happened seemed to have deeply marred more than Nicolette's face. Hopefully with time she was able to put her fears in a cage." She thought back to that night and the satisfaction of taking Nicolette's attacker down. The man who'd professed to be a preacher found no salvation with her, or with Michel, if she had to guess. She hadn't pulled the trigger, but suffered no guilt when it came to sending him to a sure death at the hands of Michel's men.

"Thanks for everything, Ramon." She waited until their car had made it outside before returning to her office. "Is there anything else?" she asked her cousins.

"Just the day-to-day stuff," Katlin said. "We're moving out of New Orleans east into the warehouse we decided on in Metairie, so we're checking the surveillance before we transfer everything a little at a time."

She noticed Muriel's gaze drop to her lap. It'd take a few more talks before she released her self-imposed guilt. They were moving because of the information Shelby had been able to gather while dating Muriel. The FBI agent had exploited Muriel at the one time in her life she'd questioned her place and her future.

"Muriel, go ahead and start with the list we made up as plan B for this deal. It's not a priority, but I'd like to see who bites if we start looking."

"Do you want me to help with the move?" Muriel asked. "I'd deserve it if you made me carry every box."

"Don't fuck around like that," Katlin said as she slapped Muriel's back. "Everyone's entitled not to be perfect, and you've cashed that chip in."

Cain laughed at Katlin's razor-edge personality. If she wanted someone to cut to the bone without much buildup, Katlin was her first choice. "Listen to your family," she said as she pressed her hand to Katlin's cheek.

"You're never this forgiving, so I can't help but think it's charity. I don't want to be the pathetic and idiotic member of the clan you have no choice but to take care of."

"Do you think Hayden will make every choice and decision perfectly when he starts with us?" Muriel shook her head. "You're right, he'll make plenty of mistakes like his mother, and like Da, I'll forgive each one. It won't have anything to do with pity or charity, and I'll take everyone down who says otherwise. Don't expect me to treat you any differently."

"I'm not a child."

"Not gauging by your age, but if you keep talking like this I might change my mind." She laughed to not make the comment sound too stinging. "Face it, Muriel, I'll forgive you whatever sin you commit because I love you. We've shared a life and a friendship that outweighs any wrong you've built in your mind."

"What are you going to do about Shelby?"

"I'm going to give her what she wants."

Muriel came halfway off the chair and dropped back when Cain stopped her momentum with a hand on her shoulder. "You can't mean that."

"Well," she tapped Muriel's chin with her fingers, "I'm going to give her what she *thinks* she wants."

CHAPTER FOUR

Shelby's car was still outside the house. She and her need for revenge weren't going away, and Cain really couldn't fault her for that. If Shelby hadn't dedicated the whole of her career to convicting her of something no matter what the cost, she would've talked to her by now.

"Go around back, boss?" Lou asked.

"Yeah, I want to stop at the pool house before going in."

Her longtime guard and friend, Merrick Runyon lived with Katlin in the converted space next to the pool. She hadn't spared any expense to transform the structure into a handicap-accessible suite complete with a new bathroom and a heater for the pool. The physical therapist she'd hired was there six hours a day, and with the work they'd done in the water, Merrick was now able to get around with a walker. She'd retired the wheelchair completely.

Merrick had put it all on the line to save Emma, so no matter how long it took or how much it cost, Cain had vowed to get her back to full health. The bullet Juan Luis had put in Merrick's head was a favor she was impatient to return and something the first therapist said Merrick would never fully recover from. It'd taken willpower not to punch the guy in the face or give Katlin permission to shoot him, since the idiot had made his prediction in front of Merrick.

"Hey, Cain," said Diane Hazell, the physical therapist, as she slung her backpack on. "A few more weeks and we graduate to a cane."

"I'll owe you the world when you're done."

"A glowing recommendation will do." Diane laughed and held her brown, curly hair away from her face. "This is the easiest gig I've ever had."

"Good, I want you happy." She watched Diane walk away as she knocked on the door.

"Come in," Merrick said.

They'd spoken often after these sessions, and Merrick had commented on the sheer will it took to get through them. Cain couldn't truly appreciate what it was like, but could imagine the frustration that was now Merrick's constant companion. Gone from Merrick's life was the spontaneity most people took for granted. In the first months of her and Katlin's relationship, Cain had seen them having fun at her nightclub, Emma's. Their nights out now meant a trip up to the house for dinner a couple of times a week.

"You aren't beating on yourself with that big guilt stick you carry around, are you?" Merrick asked with her usual sarcasm and sense of humor.

"How'd it go today?" She sidestepped the question as she scanned the room, stopping at a small framed picture that was a duplicate of the one on her desk. That her family was so important to both Katlin and Merrick was a blessing.

"That girl, Diane, is cute, but she's a bitch." Merrick laughed and pointed to the chair closest to the sofa she was lying on. "There's something freeing, though, about that pool. The way I'm able to move around in there gives me hope for the future. Once I can walk without resembling Frankenstein I can start getting back into a shape that isn't quite so round."

"If Katlin was here, you'd get a spanking for that one." She held Merrick's hand and didn't feed into the self-deprecating humor. "My cousin's not perfect except for one thing." Merrick nodded and squeezed her fingers, as if her words had overwhelmed her emotions. "The way she loves you is the way I love Emma. It's perfect not because we don't make mistakes, but because we love without reservations. No matter what happens, trust that Katlin will always be here."

"Speaking of Emma," Merrick said as she dabbed at her eyes, "she's getting good at swimming laps while Diane tortures me. If I haven't said it before, that's one special lady, and I'm sorry for all the shit I said about her."

"Once she has you watching her back again, you might change your mind, so hold off on the praise," she said with a wink. "Emma's mood when she's really pregnant sneaks up on you at times."

"I was shot in the head, so I'm ready for anything," Merrick joked back.

"Until then, anything new?"

Merrick's body still wasn't where she wanted, but her mind was sharp, as it had been from the day of the attack. When Cain had given her an assignment, it'd helped with the rehab, probably because Merrick believed she hadn't lost faith in her.

"With Katlin's help we've talked to some of the smaller players," she said as she moved as if trying to find a more comfortable spot. "You know, the guys standing on the street corners."

"Sometimes the people holding the dime bags are the ones with the most useful information."

"Right, so since I'm stuck here for the moment, I've sent Katlin out a few nights a week with a list of questions I want answers to."

Cain crossed her legs and tapped her fingers on her knee. Maybe it was time to give Muriel more access to their daily operations, cutting Katlin loose to help Merrick. "She find anything?" If she had, Katlin hadn't shared it with her. A deep breath tamped down the sudden irrational anger that made her chest burn. These blinding episodes had been a side effect, not of her recent concussion, but in response to not being in control from the second she saw Merrick in that car and Emma not beside her.

Control was as much a part of her makeup as her blue eyes, and Juan Luis had plucked it away in one savage moment. Sometimes it was as if he'd ripped it from her body and held it up and gloated—a bleeding lump he'd ground under his heel that proved she'd never be able to let her guard down ever. That missing piece would forever be gone and cause her to lose all those special people in her life.

"Stop it," Merrick said with heat.

"What?"

"The gloomy thoughts that've been slicing through your soul like a hot knife through butter. What happened wasn't your fault." Merrick put her hands up when Cain opened her mouth. "Juan is an idiot who deserves whatever death you've planned for him, but that's not who I'm interested in."

"Anthony, you mean?"

"Without that motherfucker, Juan would've spent his life jacking off while he thought about Emma. No offense, but you know that's as close as he would've gotten."

"My problem, though, is that Anthony is now linked to the idiot and his mother because he has no other option. I don't exactly have an informant in the FBI, but there's no way Annabel takes him back."

Merrick stared at her for a long moment. "They were going to cut Barney Kyle loose. Have you forgotten that?"

Barney Kyle had turned Emma against her or, more accurately, had driven her away. Not only had he been the special agent in charge of the FBI office in New Orleans, but he'd been on a rival family head's payroll. Merrick had derailed his release from jail by putting a bullet in his head at Cain's order.

"Annabel can try cutting a deal with him, but to do that, she's got to find him. It's my goal in life to make sure that doesn't happen."

"It's what I really want for my birthday this year," Merrick said, in a way that made Cain laugh.

"So what answers do you have so far?"

"Hector is gaining strength from Florida to Texas, and only two speed bumps are in his way keeping him from total dominance."

"Carlos Luis has to be my first guess," she said of the late Rodolfo Luis's son, a son he'd claimed only hours before he died. Before that, Carlos had served him faithfully as the head of his security detail. Rodolfo had made it clear to everyone who worked for him that his business and money were to go to his son, not his traitorous sister and nephew.

"Carlos has been keeping what rightfully belongs to him in Mexico and is slowly branching north. Because the buyers find him fairer than Hector, he's got a steady stream of people willing to work with him."

"That gives me another guess." Merrick nodded when she held her index finger up. "Gracelia Luis is trying to make her way without her big brother."

"She's trying, but those truly loyal to Rodolfo are on Carlos's side, and because Rodolfo's house is like a fortified compound, Gracelia's homeless."

The pieces were starting to fall, but the major ones were still missing. "No word on Juan and Anthony?"

"So far, no." Merrick's face lost all expression. "Any mention of the Luis name mostly leads back to Carlos. Gracelia now goes by the name Ortega, and everyone fell in line when it came to compliance. I think that has more to do with insult than respect. No one, no matter what power they hold, agreed with the bitch's actions. In a way it amounted to Jarvis taking your father out to gain control. It just isn't done."

"Gracelia doesn't understand honor or code, but she'll catch on eventually. The Bracatos did, after all, and look what happened there. That name died out, and the world is a better place for it."

"Go home, and I'll keep digging."

"Thanks." She stood and placed a kiss on Merrick's forehead. "It's time to send the lost sheep on its way."

❖

Shelby glanced at her vibrating phone but didn't answer. Fiona O'Brannigan was calling again in an effort to tell her to drop this quest to see Cain, she guessed. They had the same conversation every day, so she wasn't expecting a change in topic now from the California detective who had led the investigation into her parents' murders. Her dad had been Fiona's mentor on the force, but even that close friendship couldn't make Fiona understand the enormity of what she'd lost.

The cops weren't ever going to find answers about the gunman, no matter how many man-hours they dedicated to this case. Shelby knew only that her parents were butchered as a diversion, nothing more. That's how little someone thought of them. Their deaths were meant to put the scent on Cain, and like an idiot, she'd fallen for it.

Her reaction had ensured the death of her relationship with Muriel and the once-strong tie to Cain. All she had left was Fiona and the team she'd worked with since arriving in the city, but none of them understood the ball of rage that was close to consuming her.

"Special Agent Phillips." Carmen, Cain's housekeeper, folded her hands in front of her.

"Did you tell her it was important?" Carmen welcomed her every morning and evicted her every afternoon. She was so polite and nice about it, Shelby left without argument whenever Carmen asked.

"I tell her every day," Carmen said in a tone that projected pity for her. "But I'm not here to tell you to leave. Ms. Casey said it's okay for you to go back."

Finally, she thought as she followed two steps behind Carmen. She saw Cain at her desk through the open door, and for the first time she was envious. Cain Casey wasn't simply attractive; she lived by no other code than her own. Every problem she'd ever encountered, she'd dealt with and buried the evidence so deep, no one would find it in this lifetime. How freeing that must be.

"Shelby," Cain said as she stood and moved around the desk to take her hand. "I never got the opportunity to offer my condolences on your recent loss. No matter our age we still need our parents, and their loss leaves a profound sadness that seems to cling to us like an oppressive blanket in summer."

"Thank you." When Cain touched her she had to swallow a few times in an effort not to cry. "Thank you for seeing me."

"It's no problem, since Cain understands better than most what you're going through," Emma said, and Shelby whipped around at the sound of her voice. She hadn't counted on Emma's presence, considering why she was here.

"Thank you, Emma, and you're right. Cain is the only one who understands my loss." She released Cain's hand and fully faced Emma. "Since we agree, do you mind if I meet with Cain privately?"

Cain watched Emma's reaction and almost laughed at the way Emma's eyes closed to slits. The only way she'd leave the room was if she ordered Lou to hogtie her and drag her out. "Shelby, have a seat." She pointed to the chair closest to the sofa before taking her place next to Emma. "Trust that whatever you have to say, you're free to do so in front of Emma."

"I'd rather not."

"Then this will be a short visit." The flash of anger that spread across Shelby's face marred her features and proved to Cain that Shelby still hadn't cooled off. Someone with this much rage wasn't in control.

Shelby stared at her with mouth set in a thin line and, after what appeared to be an internal struggle, finally relented. "I blamed you for my parents. I was so sure."

"You don't have to elaborate on that—we believe you," Emma said. "Cain has the bruises to prove it."

"I'm sorry for what happened to you," Shelby said sincerely. "The only family I truly have now is an aunt, and my team."

"Shelby." Cain wanted to interrupt Shelby's run down an emotional road that would get them nowhere. "Had you asked me, I would've been honest. But you should've considered how important you were to Muriel. I would've never hurt you or your family because of that fact alone."

"I *was* important to her."

"Muriel wanted more from that relationship than I think you were ready to give."

The skin around Shelby's neck turned bright red as she spoke, and her jugular veins were vivid. "I really don't need a lecture."

"I love Muriel, but I understand your motivations, so this is no lecture. When you examine your life truthfully, you'll see it's actually made up of priorities. We work and strive for the things we want most. I won't dispute that you care for Muriel, but you care greatly about your job. Muriel always came second to that."

"You know that's not true. Muriel is the main reason I do my job so well."

Cain put her hand up to make Shelby stop talking. It'd taken only one blatant lie for her body to tense. "You have interesting ideas about love, and I'm not in the mood to argue with you. Perhaps you saw yourself as a crusader who was saving my cousin from a life she's been forced to live."

"You honestly think she had a choice up to now?" Shelby asked, and the tentacles of anger spread quickly into Cain's skull, making pain flare above her right eye.

"Everyone has choices, Agent Phillips, but your self-imposed nobility has blinded you to that. You've also chosen to ignore the truth of who Muriel is and what she was willing to give up for you." She stopped to take a deep breath, realizing the volume of her voice was climbing. "Muriel is the daughter of Jarvis Casey, and she embraced him and the rest of her family proudly. Had Muriel chosen to stay with you, the rest of our family would've never turned our backs on her."

"But you would've locked her out, right?"

"You're the one with a lecture to give, it seems," Emma said hotly.

"Did you want something?" Cain asked, not in the mood for this bickering.

"I'm sorry, but I do love Muriel. It hurts that you'd think otherwise." Shelby sounded contrite as she rubbed her palms along her slacks. "I need your help, Cain," she said in a half whisper, as if she loathed the words and the request. "You're the only one I can ask."

"If I can, I will," she said, and almost laughed at Emma's hard pinch to her leg. "What do you want?" It wasn't difficult to guess, but she wanted Shelby to spell it out.

"I need the animals who killed my parents to pay." Shelby held up a finger as she spoke. "And I need to watch as the life of those who ordered the hit ends when I pull the trigger." She held up another finger at that. "You and I know we'll never make enough headway with the investigations to hold anyone accountable."

"We...as in the FBI?" she asked.

"Or the police, take your pick. The bastards who killed them are safe back in Mexico, and their bosses are having a good laugh about it."

"Shelby, let me share something with you before I give you my answer." Cain smiled to put Shelby at ease. "My father was a powerful man who, like yours, was taken from me by ignorant assholes. When he died I thought of nothing but revenge. The need for it consumed me."

"That's how I feel."

"My mother told me something before her life ended the same

way my Da's did. She said, 'To avoid the fruit of sin, stay out of the devil's orchard.'"

"What does that mean?" Shelby asked.

"Revenge is something you think will soothe the ache that loss leaves you with. Like apples growing in an orchard, it will tempt you, but it's an illusion. Once you pull the trigger, it won't bring your parents back or fill the hole in your heart. It might give you a brief sense of satisfaction, but it won't be the miracle cure that'll right your world. Take my advice and avoid the orchard, the sin," she said as she placed her hand against her chest, "and the devil you'll find there. This devil for sure will not lead you into that tempting place."

"You'll never admit it, but you willingly went into that place and gorged yourself. Don't lie and tell me otherwise." Shelby pressed her hands together as if in prayer. "Do you hate me so much that denying me this is a joke to you?"

"I don't hate you, Shelby. I don't trust you." She took Emma's hand as Shelby looked at her with an expression of disbelief. "There's a difference."

"You talk about sin and temptation, but you gave in. The Bracatos are dead just like anyone else who's ever crossed you, so don't preach or try to save my soul." Shelby clenched her fists and jaw as she spoke. "I don't need your advice, I need your help."

"Then what?" Cain asked in the same clipped pattern Shelby was using. "I'm supposed to deliver these guys, line them up, and watch you kill them all? After that, what, we shake hands and go back to opposite sides and pretend it never happened?" With so much talk about temptation, she tried not to go with the urge to fling Shelby out the front door. "To you I'm a devil who needs to be locked away, but because you're angry you're willing to look the other way. The Bracatos aren't my problem, so don't pretend to know what happened or how I fit in. You should be familiar with the Bureau's response when Big Tony killed my family. Did you close that case yet?"

"No, but there's no denying it is closed."

Emma squeezed Cain's fingers when she started to say something else. "You have a strange way of asking for a favor, Agent Phillips," Emma said in a way that telegraphed her bad mood. "I know you find it hard to believe Cain is simply a businesswoman, but there you have it. I'm truly sorry for your loss, but if you want a homicidal maniac's help, try your employer. Annabel seems to breed them. We can't help you."

Cain stood and opened the door, since Emma had wrapped up

nicely. She had nothing else to add. "Take care, Shelby, and give my best to Detective O'Brannigan. That's such a nice Irish name. I'm surprised she's still here in New Orleans."

"The case originated here, and she feels she owes it to my father to find these guys, so she's applying for transfer." Shelby hesitated, as if it would take Lou to carry her out. "At least she understands and is willing to help."

"I wish you both the best of luck, then."

"How do you know her name?"

"Fascinating people are a hobby of mine," she said as she waved her hand toward the front of the house. "If she's planning to settle here, we'll send a fruit basket."

The sarcasm made Shelby frown and got her moving. "I thought you'd be more sympathetic."

"I am," she said when Shelby stopped a foot beside her. "But your fight isn't mine to wage. Hypothetically, if I were in your place, the death of those most precious to me would be personal. It's not something I'd trust to anyone else, no matter how good at killing I think they are."

"What do you mean?"

"Grow your own orchard, Shelby, and decide how big a sin you're willing to commit. You'll have to carry your answer for eternity, so be honest with yourself." She smiled at Carmen and walked Shelby to the door herself.

"Hypothetically, how would you carry something like that?"

"Without guilt, but then my orchard is a place to…frolic. Yeah, that's a good word for it."

"So the devil has no remorse?"

"Even God feels remorse, and I'm not that perfect. What you asked for will stay between us, so be careful of talking to anyone else about it. From what I hear, the FBI and other authorities frown upon revenge killings."

❖

Fiona O'Brannigan stood in concourse B of the New Orleans airport staring down the slope and trying to spot her mother. Judice O'Brannigan had surprisingly decided to visit at the last minute, right after Fiona had told her about her transfer. She'd received a return call ten minutes after that conversation with the flight information.

The usually stoic and hardworking Judice didn't often indulge in whims like this.

Despite the last-minute warning, Fiona was happy her mom was here. Judice had been a single parent when society hadn't been very accepting of the concept, and the crap they'd endured together had made them extremely close. She planned to convince her mother to move to New Orleans too.

When her mother started toward her, she laughed at the number of men who stared. Even in her late sixties, Judice was an attractive woman who prided herself on her appearance. Why she did mystified her. She never sought companionship of any kind that Fiona knew of.

At first she thought her mother didn't feel comfortable sharing her sexuality, and when she'd told her mother it was okay if she was gay, Judice had laughed and assured her that if she were interested in women, she'd happily settle down with one. After that, with no further explanation, Fiona had no choice but to spin her own story to fill in those gaps.

In her version her father had died before they could marry and her mom hadn't gotten over him enough to allow someone else in. Perhaps she couldn't talk about him because of the pain she was still in. Whoever *he* was, her father and the rest of her mother's past were closed subjects.

"I'm hot already," Judice said as they hugged.

"Some of those guys you flew in with certainly thought so." Fiona took her mother's bags, freeing Judice to give her a light slap to her midsection. "You're beautiful, Mom, accept it."

"That's a small consolation. I'm losing my baby to this heat. You'll have a constant sunburn."

"I've lived in California all my life. I know how to use sunscreen." They descended on the escalator to baggage claim, and the teasing about her decision started taking on a different tone. Her mom wanted to change her mind but was trying to be subtle about it. "Did you have a nice flight?"

"Small talk, sweetling?" Judice asked with a smile that was the definition of melancholy. "You don't have to humor me that much."

"I'll have to until you admit you're either pissed with me or something else is going on." She hefted the hideous pink faux-snakeskin roller bag and led the way to her car. Her mother was right that it was easy to spot on the carrousel, but then she had to walk with the damn thing.

"I'm not upset," Judice said when they sat next to each other in the garage. "I just don't understand. You walked a beat for years waiting for that gold shield, and now that you have it, you run and hide down here." Fiona lowered her head when her mom held her hand. "Tell me why, and I'll accept it, but I haven't heard a good reason yet."

"You've kept books all your life, and you were good at it." Her mom had run her business from a home office, and she vividly remembered the parade of people dropping off and picking up documents and files. She'd never cared since her mom was always close by. "That's what I want for myself. I worked my ass off to make detective grade, and the brass kept me down for years. When I entered the academy I wasn't stupid or blind to the boys' club, but I'm past forty, Mom. I don't have a lot of time left to make my mark."

"The force here is that different?"

"It's good to be needed, and that's what I have now. They want me on their streets, and they trust my skills to close cases."

Judice nodded and smiled again, but she still wasn't happy. Fiona knew better than to push. Her mom would share whatever was on her mind only when she was ready. "Where are you staying? You never said."

"With a friend for now, but I thought you could help me decide on a place while you're here." Fiona glanced at her mom as she handed her credit card to the booth attendant. "Who knows, maybe you'll find a place close to mine and we can explore together when I'm not working."

"Maybe," Judice said with her head turned away from her. "Or you might get homesick."

"Hopefully I am home, Mom."

❖

"Pull," Cain said, then tracked the clay pigeon with her shotgun. At the height of its arc, her shot splintered it into pieces. "Pull," she repeated, so she could empty the other barrel.

"Good shot, Mom," Hayden said as he waited his turn. The range she'd found was an hour from the house, and after her meeting with Shelby she'd decided they had enough daylight left to go through a box or two of targets. "We need one of these in the yard in Wisconsin."

"You planning to curdle some milk when our place is finished?" She cracked the barrel and tossed the spent shells in the trash bag she'd brought along. "That place is crawling with cows."

"How long before we can go?" Hayden asked as he loaded his birthday present, the shotgun that was a replica of hers. "I think Granddad misses it."

"Jerry told me another month, so we'll go check it out when school ends." She watched as he took his turn, smiling when he shot at the same point she had with the same results. At moments like this she really missed her Da. Casey family traditions would be passed down for generations to come, if she had any say, but the lessons would've been richer with her Da looking on. "I'm ready for my milking lesson."

Lou and Mook stood close by watching for any potential threats. A gun range could be the perfect place for a hit, and she'd sighed loudly the fourth time Lou had said it. The second target fell to the ground intact, and she couldn't make out what Hayden was muttering. She guessed it was a litany of curse words he didn't think she knew he used at times. Cursing was something she indulged in only when necessary to get some idiot to understand a simple concept, like "don't fuck with me."

"It's a learning process, son," she said, waiting for him to clear his barrels before she put her hand on the side of his neck. "Eventually no clay bird will escape your clutches."

She tied up the trash bag of used shells and dropped it by her feet as she slid her gun back into the leather holder. Leaving the shells behind was an invitation for a rival or an unscrupulous cop to set her up, and she knew plenty of both.

"Can you make my game on Friday night?"

Hayden had spent the spring on second base for his junior-high baseball team, and she'd rescheduled whatever she had to so she wouldn't miss a game. "You know I'll be there, along with the rest of the Casey cheering squad."

They talked about their upcoming plans as they walked, and she barely noted the line of people on the pistol range shooting at paper targets. There were a few more men than women, but all of them were focused on their imaginary foes. Nothing about them stood out, but the guy closest to the exit made her stop so she could see his face. Nothing really seemed out of the ordinary about him, but an invisible hand to the chest and something in her mind whispered, "Look at me."

"What?" Lou asked.

The guy finished his clip and, as if sensing the attention, turned and stared back. His blond hair, pulled into a short ponytail, was much lighter than his eyebrows. He was short and slim, and he shrugged his shoulder in a *what?* motion. She'd never seen him before, but like stretching for something a hair out of your reach, she felt she should have. Something was familiar about him, but whatever it was eluded her. He pushed another clip into the big shiny gun, which struck her as a flashy piece for such a twerp, but he acted harmless.

"Nothing." She steered them toward the car and didn't look back.

"You sure, Mom?" Hayden asked as she walked away.

"Yeah," she said, but she wasn't being honest. At the car she gave in to the need to find the guy again, but he was gone. Probably into the restroom, she thought, since the entrance was close to where he was. "Maybe I'm hungry."

"That's Mom's line."

"Boy, you say that to her face, and you'd better hide that gun."

CHAPTER FIVE

"Mom," Hannah said from Cain's lap the next morning, "I need a pony."

"Has Mama been telling pony stories again?" She laughed when Emma stuck her tongue out at her. "Your mama's short, so what she had wasn't a pony. It was a puppy."

"I need a puppy, then," Hannah said quickly.

"Your birthday is the perfect time to ask your mama for that." Hayden laughed at her answer, probably remembering a dog that had slipped his five-year-old mind when he'd asked and been put off. "Are you ready for school?"

"I need my shoes." Hannah held up her bare feet.

"Come here, Miss Puppy," Emma said as she held her hand up. "You don't want to be late."

"It's okay, Mama," Hannah said. "I don't mind being late."

"I mind, so let's get your shoes on," Emma said, then shook her head when Hannah took off at a fast run. "Do you have your permission slip?" she asked Hayden.

"I packed it last night along with the money you gave me for lunch."

"Where are you headed?" Cain asked.

"The World War Two Museum. They got a local veteran to take us on the tour. Cool, huh?"

Trips away from school worried Cain. She always had to balance trying to keep them safe with letting them live as normal a childhood as they could. She didn't want either of their children to think of this time as a prison or a microscope, where they were constantly being watched.

"They needed some volunteers, so Mook offered his services," Emma said, as if reading her mind.

"Have fun." She hugged Hayden before he left to gather his things.

"You don't think they'd touch the kids, do you?" Emma asked as she came beside her and rested her arm around her shoulder.

"I don't ever like to worry you, lass, but to get what he wants, I believe Juan will do anything. To use children would be unacceptable to me, Ramon, and Vincent, but that's not who we're dealing with. If he got that lucky, I'd have no choice but to give him anything, aside from you, that he wants." The frustration of being so blind to what dangers lurked out there made her want to punch a hole in the table. All the time and money she'd spent on hunting Juan and to have nothing infuriated her.

"Because you're so self-sacrificing I called the school and suggested they needed more volunteers who were licensed to carry firearms," Emma said, and kissed the top of her head. Cain said another prayer of thanks to whatever higher power had sent her Emma as a partner. And she was certainly becoming that in every aspect.

"Thank you for that, my love. Maybe I should put you in charge of finding Juan and Anthony. We'd be done with all that by now."

"I appreciate the confidence, but I have a job." Emma dropped into her lap and kissed her on the lips. "Wife and mother is full-time enough, so you'll have to deal with the rest. I'm sure some women think I'm letting down females everywhere by sounding so domestic, but their last name isn't Casey. Those two roles carry a bit more meaning because my name is."

"Those are my most important jobs too, so don't worry about the rest." She laid her hand on their baby and felt Emma take a deep breath. "You need me to run any errands for you today?"

"I just have a few phone calls left, and I don't want you to change your mind," Emma said before she kissed her again.

"Change my mind?" She laughed as she stood with Emma cradled in her arms. "Juan has a better chance at stealing you away from me than me changing my mind."

"There's no chance in hell Juan's getting anything from me."

"Then I'll be waiting at the altar for you, Mrs. Casey. And once you arrive it'll be my honor to tell our friends and God how much I love you, as well as how I intend to spend my life with you."

"I'm looking forward to saying the same, and once I do the honeymoon begins." Emma bit her bottom lip with enough pressure to make her hard. She felt such a rush of emotion she had to sit again.

"You're going to make me late, and *I* have my shoes on," Cain said as she moved her hand up Emma's thigh.

"Just a little preview of things to come." Emma stood up and smoothed her linen slacks. "But that'll have to wait since I'm expected at Hannah's school this morning. I'm in charge of story time today."

"Be careful and call me when you're done."

"Should be right before lunch."

"Good, then you can't turn down my date offer." She held Emma's hand as they walked to the front door. "Will you be free for lunch?"

"For you, always." Emma kissed her again. "Good morning, Sabana," She wiped lipstick from Cain's lips. "Are you ready to go back to school?"

After Emma's cheery question, Cain smiled at Sabana Greco's expression. Sabana had asked to be assigned with her instead of Emma for so long she'd threatened to let her go altogether. Like their father, Sabana's brother Rick had worked for the family, but some of Juan's men had killed him. From her arrival, she had wanted the chance to avenge her loss and thought Cain was being unfair when she ordered her to keep an eye on Emma.

"I can't wait."

"One more bathroom break and I'll be ready," Emma said.

"I know you're still not happy with me, but you do realize I've entrusted Emma's life to you, right?" Cain didn't raise her voice, but she wanted to come across as stern. "If something happens to her while you're busy pouting, your mother will lose another child. Do we understand each other?"

"Perfectly, but I'd be more useful on the street looking for these assholes."

"My daughter, the word sponge, is running around here waiting for her mother, so watch your language," she said as she glanced up the stairs to see if Hannah was peeking back at her. "And when Juan comes back, who do you think might be at the top of his list of people to visit? Me, who wants to rip his balls off, or his crush, Emma?"

"Sorry, I never thought of it that way."

"Keep your eyes open and lose the attitude. If we have to repeat this talk, I'm going to hire you to pour drinks at the pub. That'll be your only option other than walking out the door."

"You got it," Sabana said, and smiled at Emma and Hannah when they appeared holding hands.

"Follow your own advice, mobster." Emma kissed Cain again. "Be careful, and I'll see you later," she said as Cain hugged Hannah.

Cain followed them out and got in the front seat with Lou. "How's Dino working out?" she asked of Lou's nephew, who was driving Sabana and her girls.

"He reminds me a lot of Rick. That's why I thought he'd be a good fit for Sabana, but she's too angry to see it. Dino's a good kid, and he knows how I feel about you and your family. My brother wants him at the restaurant with him, but Dino wants a future here. He knows what I expect of him, so he's not about to screw up."

"I don't mean to disrespect your brother, but has his cooking gotten any better?"

"He keeps warning me about the consequences of the life I live, but it's my cash keeping that place of his afloat. Idiot couldn't cook after I sent him to a culinary school, and it ain't gotten any better. He should've picked a different career after his retirement from the fire department." Lou laughed as he glanced in the rearview mirror. She'd already spotted their tail, so she didn't bother looking again. These guys never lost them unless they took evasive maneuvers. "I appreciate you giving the kid a shot."

"You're my family, Lou, and I trust you."

"If you add my brother to the mix, it gave you a reason not to trust Dino. Don't think I haven't realized that."

They entered the Ninth Ward, and Lou slowed and waved to a few of the guys sitting on the porches down the street. Jasper Luke's barricade was up and manned at the end of the street, and the other side was lined with cars. Jasper was a good six inches taller than her, bald, and muscled to the point of being scary. Like her, he'd taken over for his father eventually, but he'd been so young when he'd died that his uncle and Aunt Maude had tended to the business until he was ready.

Maude spent most of their working hours in the small café on the property, Maude's Kitchen, but like his father and uncle, Jasper depended on her unique brand of wisdom. Juan had come here with Anthony once to try to broker a deal, but like most, they weren't invited to lunch. That took Jasper's trust or Maude's friendship. Cain was fortunate to have both.

"Dino's lucky to have you," she said as they neared Jasper's roadblock. "Your brother isn't a bad guy, but it's got to be exhausting to live in fear of everything all the time."

"Yeah," Lou said as he waved again. "He loves to throw God in my face, but Dino gets the brunt of it and it's gotten old. It's good to see the kid happy, and he's taken Emma's safety seriously."

"Can't ask for better than that." They stopped at the barricades, and the guy who appeared the oldest rose from his chair and walked to her side of the vehicle. "How's it going? Looks like a party," she said as she pointed to the congested circle of houses. Every one of them, including the street, belonged to Jasper, so the city and the Feds couldn't do anything about the roadblock.

"Hey, Cain," the man said as he waved to one of the men to open the gate. "Jasper ain't too happy these days, so you know how that is. Even Miss Maude's a little put off. She'll be glad to see you."

"Thanks. We'll park here and walk, if you want."

"Jasper will skin me for that. Go on down and leave it in the middle."

A few people behind them climbed the front steps to the house on the end, but Cain led Lou to the left. The two window units on the back of the smaller place next door made a puddle under them, but Jasper would flood the city to keep his Aunt Maude happy. She'd spent more time raising him than his parents had, and Jasper was devoted to her because of it.

"Fall in love and forgot all about me, huh?" Maude said when they entered her large kitchen. "But I can't blame you. Jasper told me that girl is big and pregnant again."

"Number three, so cut me some slack, beautiful."

Maude hugged her, and the firm embrace never failed to remind Cain of her mother. The two women had plenty in common, starting with their devotion to family. But her mother had also loved running the one room that gave heart to a home, as she'd love to say. Sitting with her mother as she stirred a big pot, Cain had learned as much from her as she had from her Da.

"You here to take some of Jasper's worry away? If that man wasn't bald already, this past month would've sheared every hair from his head."

She sat with Maude at the small table in the corner. "He's got a lot of company, so let's us start in here first." Since Maude did have so much of Jasper's trust, and she knew him so well, Cain knew she had all the answers she needed.

"You don't dabble down in this neighborhood except with your shopkeepers and bar owners, so don't disappoint me because it ain't your business. Jasper's been kind to you and always answers your call."

"I may not visit as often as I should, but you have to know better than that. Da and Fats were friends long before I was a thought in his brain, and relationships like that don't die easy," she said, referring to

Maude's late husband. "You remember the first time he brought me here?"

"You were green still, but you were a charmer. I told Fats as y'all drove off that Dalton had himself a silver-tongued devil. Your father was a good friend to us, and he did a good job continuing his legacy, so don't take my request like an insult." She twisted the kitchen cloth in her hand as she spoke, and it was easy to read the anxiety across her forehead. "Someone is out to make a name, and Jasper's had to bury more men in the last few weeks than either of us can remember. It's never been this bad."

"Cain's got enough on her mind, Auntie." Jasper filled the door, and his voice carried even though he wasn't talking loud. He embraced Lou before joining them. He was alone, but the guy who'd obviously walked over with him stayed outside the door. "Thanks for coming," he said as he put his arms around Cain.

They all sat again and Cain reached for Maude's hand. She'd never ask her to leave, but she wanted her to understand the level of their friendship. "You're right about what business I do and don't do, but this is much more than that. Things here in New Orleans are changing, and it's my guess it's not going back to the way we know."

"That don't sound too encouraging," Maude said.

"You have to understand why. We're not as big as New York, LA, or Miami, but not as backwoods as some of the border towns. We're perfect because we have miles of under-patrolled waterways to get stuff in and more than enough choices to get the stuff out. Whoever controls the highways and distribution points will rule the city, and they won't give a shit about me, you, and everyone we call friends."

"That really don't sound encouraging." Maude's smile didn't form the wrinkles next to her eyes that appeared when she was truly happy or amused.

"We're dealing with cockroaches. We live in the South, so those suckers come in all shapes and sizes, and they like working in the dark. And like cockroaches, when you flip the lights on they run and hide. You might kill a few, but you know hundreds of them are there, waiting to get into things that belong to you. We're going to work together to exterminate as many as we can, but we'll never completely win that battle." She looked at Jasper when Maude seemed more reassured.

"Some asshole is taking out my people faster than I can put them on the street. I been hit, and Vinny isn't faring much better. Hell, even those thugs from the East ain't getting much done. When I called, I was hoping you had some clue as to what this shit is about."

"Do you think it's Hector?"

"Hector's so nice he's acting like he's running for mayor. If you listen to him for more than a few minutes you'd swear he was the reincarnation of that union boss that got capped." Jasper rested his elbows on the table. "He wants everyone to consolidate to make things go better, as he puts it."

"With him in charge, I'd guess," Cain said. She'd kept Hector in her sights, but not to the point that he'd mistake her observation for interest.

"You got that right, but really the person he wants in charge, here anyway, is that snake he claims is his daughter. That kid gives me the same case of the willies Juan did."

"Marisol is an interesting piece of work, but you're right. You can't trust her any more than you can trust her father." This was another dead end, she figured, but she didn't see any harm in trying to bounce some ideas off Jasper to see what would spark something new. "Hector would be my first guess, but if it was him he would've started with the small dealers."

"Why you think so?" Jasper asked.

"Taking out small dealers endears you to the two groups that you need to keep out of your business once you start in earnest. Taking out the trash is a favor to the police since it gives them less to deal with, and it makes friends with people like you, since it's like removing a splinter that's been bothering you. No one's going to die of a splinter, but it's a pain, so imagine someone coming along and erasing those guys trying to muscle in on your territory a street corner at a time."

Maude stood and stirred a few pots before joining them again. "Hector Delarosa is here to stay?" she asked.

"He's my new neighbor, which is making Emma as happy as the summer heat we both know is coming. Heat and pregnancy don't mix well." Her phone buzzed and she handed it to Lou when she saw it was Muriel. "Back to your problem and who might be causing it."

"Hector was first on my list, but he sat with me next door a few weeks ago and swore on his mother that he wasn't to blame," Jasper said.

"Did he know who was?"

"He wasn't that insightful. If he knows, he ain't talking," he said.

"My gut tells me we have something in common with what's happening in Mexico. There, the cartels gain or lose power with the numbers on the streets. If someone is getting too large, the killing begins until they balance power." Lou finished the call and shook his head when she looked at him. Whoever or whatever it was didn't merit an interruption. "The death squads there are becoming a problem no one wants to deal with."

"You think our friends down the street are going to let it go that far?" Jasper asked.

"If only they worked for us instead of trying to bury us all the time. I'm not sure they can do anything about it, even if they tried their best. The kind of people we're talking about aren't afraid of anything."

"A man with fear is a man with weaknesses, Fats used to say all the time," Maude said.

"It's true. Once Da was killed, my biggest fear was the safety of my family. 'Can I keep them alive' is a question that can consume you. Worrying about Emma and my children would paralyze me if I allowed it to."

"What do you need from me?" Jasper asked.

"We've been friends for a long time, so I think I can be honest without you getting pissed." She smiled and Jasper reciprocated.

"Compared to some in the city, what we got here ain't much," Maude said. "It's a cluster of old houses in a dying neighborhood, but this is our home. When Fats died it would've been easy for someone to take it away, along with the business. Your father didn't let that happen, so be as honest as you want. Jasper and me owe you that."

"Drugs aren't our business—never have been—and I'm raising Hayden to follow that philosophy. That is, though, the bulk of yours, and I know the power it takes to keep your share of the business. Power doesn't come simply from the force of your fists, but from knowing down to the bone who to trust."

Jasper nodded as she spoke, as did Maude. "You don't want to be my partner, but I trust you. That's not news or insulting, Cain, so what's your point?"

"That you do indeed need a partner."

"You offering?" Maude asked.

"I'm offering a suggestion that isn't me," she said, and both of them laughed. "Vinny's come a ways, hasn't he?"

"I like Vinny," Jasper said, and glanced at Maude before he went on. "You know that too, right?"

"I do."

"Vinny has come up good because he's bright, but I ain't ever going to be his partner. You know a lot of stuff, so you have to realize Vincent won't go for that, and I'm not going to start taking orders from nobody." His voice was low and steady, but she could hear the anger right at the surface. "I got enough to quit now, if that's what it takes to keep my pride."

"You won't consider it even if I make guarantees?"

He stared her down but she didn't look away. "You can speak for Vincent?"

"Not yet, but give me a few days." She stretched her hand across the table and was relieved he didn't hesitate to take it.

"Remember, Cain, who your friends are," Maude said.

"I will, and you do the same. I'm always a call away." She kissed Maude's cheek and hugged her again after she stood.

"Both y'all get out of here and let me stir in peace. Next time, bring Emma. It's about time I meet this girl of yours."

Jasper walked them to the car and opened her door for her. "Where to, boss?"

"To see a pregnant woman about lunch."

CHAPTER SIX

Y ou sure Señora Ortega okay with this?" Pablo Castillo asked. After Rodolfo's death and Carlos claiming his birthright, Gracelia had put Pablo in charge of the shipment and business end of things. He was the one person in the hierarchy of the operation that Jerome met with daily.

Jerome glanced up from his paperwork and stared at Pablo as he tried to calm his temper. He'd always been quick to anger, but the more time he spent with Gracelia and her cohorts, the more microscopic his fuse had gotten. If he'd had a gun in his hand he would've pulled the trigger with no problem. Gracelia had warned him that his mood swings were a result of the uptick in his coke use, but he knew it was from dealing with and being surrounded by idiots.

"Are you going to run to Gracelia like a scared little shit every time we talk?" He pressed his fingers together and tried his best to control his breathing.

"Ah…no?" Pablo said.

"Let's call her." He picked up the phone on the desk and started dialing. "You can ask her permission again to listen to me, and then I'm going to tell her I'll need a cleaning crew to come in here and wipe your brains off my walls." He hesitated on the last number so he could scream. "We've fucking been through this already."

"Señor, please," Pablo said as he motioned for him to put the receiver down. "My apologies, but in this job mistakes cost more than money. You understand me? You say we go to Mississippi, we go to Mississippi to talk to our workers there. I ask about Señora Ortega because she say we go through Louisiana for everything. She say Louisiana easier and no *peligro*." He shrugged on the last word, a sign he didn't know the correct one in English.

"Danger is everywhere, Pablo, so we'll try to minimize our exposure by going through the path of least resistance."

"What?" Pablo asked.

"No *peligro*," he said, his Spanish improving. It was getting tiresome to have everyone around him talk about him and not understand. "I want you to leave in the morning and start on the list in here." He handed over a cell phone. "Once you get three meetings, call me and I'll fly over."

"What do you want me to say if I never meet them before?"

"Start with the fact we're going to cut their costs by twenty-five percent. If they want the deal, this will be their only chance. Think you can handle that?"

Pablo wasn't a tall man, and unlike most of the guys Gracelia had working for her with their thick, straight black hair, his was short and curly. It made him appear younger and gentler than the others, but Jerome knew he'd kill on a whim. His loyalty to Gracelia was rooted in fear. Jerome wanted to start to chip away at that while building his own future. Perhaps with time he'd have to use fear to keep people like this in line, but right now he needed Pablo to think of him as someone apart from Gracelia.

"They might want to talk to Señora Ortega, no me."

"Either you're the man or you're an asshole who needs to be told when to take a shit, Pablo. Before you leave, let me know which one you want to be. If you can't handle it, I'll be happy to move you to help the women pack the bags." He sat again and started to go through his paperwork as a sign of dismissal. "Whoever I replace you with will get the bonus for every new buyer we get."

"Señora Ortega say that?" Pablo asked timidly.

"You see Gracelia Ortega here? Have you seen her lately?" His patience had snapped. "You're dealing with me, and I'm fucking tired of repeating myself while you sound like a cocksucker in need of a fix." He looked up and added, "Get out," with as much menace as he could put into the two words.

"I make calls for you, no problem," Pablo said as he held up the phone he'd given him.

"Do I need to tell you to get the fuck out in Spanish so you'll understand me?"

Pablo shook his head so vigorously he thought the guy would pull a muscle in his neck. "You have my word, señor, I no problem. You see, I do good work for you."

"You mention Gracelia to me again and it'll be the last thing out of your mouth. You understand that too?"

"You the boss, no problem." Pablo grabbed the phone and walked out backward as fast as he could manage.

"That's a crap shoot," Jerome said when he was alone again.

He had to start planning now if he was going to not only survive this, but end up in a position to be successful at something. Dealing drugs wasn't what he'd had in mind as a career choice, but it was time to take advantage of his position.

"Pablo's leaving?" asked Eduardo Fernandez, Gracelia's main guard and growing confidant. He'd entered the study he was using as an office without knocking. "I thought Gracelia wanted him here dealing with the buyers who've gone to other suppliers."

"I want to look at other opportunities." He glared at Eduardo for wasting his time. No way was he flipping this guy, so spending time with him was useless. "Where's Gracelia?"

"Señora is upstairs resting," Eduardo said with a tone that dripped so much contempt he suddenly desired a shower.

"Remember two things, then, Eduardo," he said as Eduardo stood and walked to the door. "Knock before you ever come in here, and don't tell me what my job is."

"I talk to Señora Ortega if you don't like my company." Eduardo laughed as he walked out.

Jerome would smooth Gracelia's paranoia later, but for now he wanted to get a few personnel matters out of the way. He stared at the phone number he'd written on a tattered piece of paper, irritated that his hand shook. When was the last time he was truly comfortable and not afraid his life would end because the lunatics in his life felt like putting a bullet through his brain?

Every one of them gave off a vibe that made him feel like the unwelcome outsider. He wasn't wanted, but that wasn't a new development. Even Gracelia treated him with caution, her secrets hidden in that psychotic head of hers. His main focus was to cull through the ranks and choose a group he could control. Pablo was his first recruit and Eduardo had proved his loyalty—only not to him.

He moved to the bookshelves, removed the thick leather-bound book of poetry, and grabbed for the phone he'd hidden behind it. The books in the room must've been left behind by the previous owner or been a decorator's idea, because no one but him here had spent time reading anything like the volume in his hand.

He turned the cell on and dialed the number he'd kept hidden in the folds of his wallet.

"Before you hang up, I have something you want, and for the right price it's yours," he said when his call was answered.

It was a cautious first step, but still, it was a start.

❖

Nicolette Blanc stared at her reflection, her eyes glued to the thin scar that ran from under her right ear to her chin. It was still visible, but not as bad as when it had first healed. Back then it was red, thick, and angry in appearance—an ugliness she'd never really learned to accept. After countless surgeries, this was her permanent souvenir that reminded her of a moment of childish irritation and stupidity.

Back then it'd been so easy to blame Cain Casey, despite the truth that Cain had actually saved her from further damage. It still stung that Cain had rebuffed her, even though she'd tried her utmost to get her into her bed. The anger over that rejection had distracted her enough for the pervert to easily catch her and drag her into an alley at knifepoint. Afterward she'd seen the relief in her father's eyes, but also his disappointment that she'd allowed this to happen. Cain had expressed nothing but deep pity, which had killed her dream of Cain's touch and a future together.

That was the last time she'd truly felt free, or at least had lived with the confidence that nothing could harm her. After all, she was Michel Blanc's daughter. Her father's name had always scared off anyone dumb enough to want to harm her because the consequences of doing so were unthinkable. During those college days she'd also stopped believing in love, or the kind of love that allowed her to show another person her true self without fear of rejection or humiliation.

Cain Casey hadn't wanted her, which had been acceptable for a while since Cain had gone through women like a swarm through fertile fields of ripe wheat. Obviously Cain wasn't capable of a relationship with anyone. That realization had made Nicolette immensely happy. She wanted Cain to drift unattached through life like she did. Eventually she would be able to convince Cain they were too much alike to not be together. When she received occasional reports that another woman had been replaced, she smiled, but that small joy had been crushed when the guy she'd hired to keep tabs on Cain sent her the name Emma Verde, along with her picture.

Her self-doubt had flared and the seed of hate for Cain had germinated. Why this simpleton from a farm in the middle of nowhere and not her? The question rattled around in her head, and she was ashamed it still did.

"Are you still pissed?" Luce asked, leaning against the door frame.

She hadn't said much since Luce and Maximo returned and reported what had happened. Luce loved her; that's why she'd tried to put Cain in her place. Their eyes met in the mirror, and she admired Luce's beauty again. She enjoyed this woman's touch, her friendship, but she'd never return her feelings. She defined love now as her relationship with her parents, no one else.

"I did warn you, did I not?" She cinched the tie of her robe tight before she turned and squeezed by Luce without much physical contact. "You could've possibly gotten away with that at home, but here, Cain rules just like her father did before his death. Also, we need her. Did your ego consider that before you decided to act like a spoiled child?"

"If only you'd defend me so vehemently," Luce said as she dropped into the wingback closest to the window. "I did what was necessary, and I'm only sorry you can't see and understand that. The Blancs bow to no one."

"Did my father adopt you and not tell me?" Nicolette opened the small box on the desk and took out a cigarette.

"You know damn well, Nic, that it's my job to make sure people respect the name, whether or not it's mine."

"Your *job* today was to close the deal my father and I wanted closed. We didn't need renegotiations, rudeness, and you beating your chest like a caveman. You failed on all three counts, and in record time, from what Maximo said."

Luce clenched both hands and opened her mouth to say something, then must've thought better of it. Her jaw clicked shut and she closed her eyes for as long as it took to count to ten. Luce's behavior was as predictable as the heat New Orleans experienced in summer; she hadn't figured out yet how easily manipulated she was. Nicolette didn't do it often, but when necessary it was easy to push Luce as much and as hard as she needed to get what she wanted. No way would Luce ever issue an ultimatum, even if she figured it out, since it would end both their personal and professional relationship. She enjoyed Luce's company, but it wasn't at all a necessity.

"If you want I'll meet with the bitch again and apologize," Luce said, sounding properly spanked.

"Cain Casey is done with you, but maybe she has some memory

of our friendship. You take Maximo with you and enjoy one of the good restaurants in the city."

"What about you?" Luce asked as she stood and reached to open her robe again.

"I'll be doing your job." She grabbed Luce by the wrists and stepped back. "Start at the bar. I need to talk to my father."

Luce hesitated like she was contemplating rebellion, but she turned and slammed her way out. It wouldn't be much longer before Nicolette offered Luce the privilege of keeping her job but expelled her from her bed. She didn't deal well with lovesick puppies who constantly begged for her attention and a pat on the head.

"Bonjour, Papa," she said when her father answered. "I'll keep it short since I have to go out soon. Did Maximo call you?"

"He told me the result, so I figured you're pleased. Your plan is working so far."

His voice echoed slightly off the marble in the bathroom, but she needed to finish getting ready. "Time hasn't tamed the tiger for sure, but that side of Cain is what I find most attractive. In a few days we should have everything we want."

"The contract isn't as important as your happiness, chérie. Forget the wine if you want and concentrate on getting back what's yours. You deserve this."

"Thanks, Papa. Your understanding and help mean everything to me."

"Keep in touch, and stay safe."

She hummed as she applied her foundation carefully, since too much caked around the scar made it stand out more. The dress she'd bought for this occasion would sear her beauty into Cain's brain, and that was what she wanted most. If she could focus Cain's attention on nothing but her from the start this time around, it wouldn't take long to remove Emma Verde from the picture.

"I'm not accepting the word 'no' this time, Cain, so I hope you're brighter than you were in your twenties. If you insist on refusing me, it'll be unfortunate, but getting rid of you might be the only way for me to move on."

CHAPTER SEVEN

W ould you zip me, please?" Emma asked as she held her hair out of the way. The dress was new, and Kevin, her personal shopper at Saks, had rushed her alterations so it would be perfect for tonight. It wasn't often that the families got together to talk a little business and have dinner together, so she wanted to look her best as Mrs. Casey, for Cain's sake. Not that she thought of herself as a cute arm decoration, but frumpy wouldn't do, even if she felt that way at the moment.

"Can I have this job in reverse when we get home?" Cain asked as she zipped her dress gently.

"I was hoping you'd volunteer." Emma gave Cain a fast kiss when she finished. "How did it go with Jasper today? Anything new?"

"Jasper is a man with problems, and I might have a solution for him if Vincent is in a frame of mind to listen tonight. If not, our friend down the street might make more of an impact than I'd like."

The last thing she had left to do was slip in the three-carat diamond earrings Cain had surprised her with shortly after they found out they were pregnant again. The square, princess-cut stones felt heavy, but she loved them because they showed how happy Cain was about this baby.

"If by friend you mean that snake Hector and his spawn, then I'll tie Vincent to a chair and beat him with breadsticks until he gives you what you want. It irritates me every time I think of them living a few blocks away."

Cain dropped her jacket onto the bed and put her arms around her. She lowered her head when Emma gazed up at her and very lightly pressed her lips to hers so as not to mess up her lipstick. "If I had enough manpower they'd be gone by now. You know that, right?" She nodded as she slipped her fingers into the hair at the base of Cain's neck. "Right now that'd be a waste on our part since I have other things to worry about, but I don't want to give Hector too wide a berth. He strikes me as the kind of guy who takes a thousand miles for every inch you give him."

"You're going to talk Vincent into letting Vinny partner with Jasper, aren't you?"

"They're friendly now, but there's still bad blood between Vincent and Fats, never mind that Fats has been dead for nine years. I sided with Vincent on that because Fats double-crossed him for a few bucks, so that he agreed for Vinny to work with Jasper was a minor miracle." Cain put her jacket on and held her hand as they walked down the stairs. "Asking for more than I got already might be suicidal, but I think it's the best solution. Having two people I know and have friendships with control that crap is better than the alternative."

"If anyone can charm them into cooperating, it's you, baby."

"Thanks, but I'll keep the breadstick threat in my back pocket in case what I have planned doesn't work out."

The noise level from the back room made them both stop and laugh. Both kids would be fine with their housekeeper Carmen and Ross, but Merrick and Katlin had volunteered to join in until they got back. Katlin usually went with Cain to meetings like this, but tonight Muriel was filling in since Cain had expanded her role.

"Let's hope there's no dog in whatever movie they're blaring back there," Cain said. "If there is, your rugs are toast."

"*My* rugs?" She pointed to her chest. "Any dog that comes into this house is going to live in the study."

Cain laughed as she followed her to the den. When they entered, the group was watching Hannah as she took her turn at the video game they were playing. Emma savored Cain's smile every time she saw it. They spoke often before going to sleep, and every time Cain thanked her for the happiness she'd brought to her life.

Their time apart and the guilt because of why it'd happened faded a bit more each time Cain told her the kinds of things that were meant for her heart only. Through everything they'd experienced together and during their separation, she'd never lost sight of what a blessing and a gift her life with Cain and their family was. That her father was here with them to share this with her only completed the sense of family she'd always wanted.

"Mama, look, I'm doing good," Hannah yelled as she swung her arm around with the game control in her fist.

Had Emma known Cain at this age, she probably wouldn't see much difference from their daughter. Hannah and Hayden both had a competitiveness that reminded her so much of Cain it made her optimistic for their future. Like their mother, both children would excel at whatever they did for the clan, and they'd assure the business for the generation that came after them. It was too early to daydream of grandchildren, but she did sometimes, wondering what Cain would be like surrounded by small Caseys again while their children ruled the clan.

"Have you eaten anything, Miss Doing Good?" Cain asked her when she picked her up and threw her in the air. Hannah squealed in delight since, like her brother, she loved to roughhouse with Cain whenever she was around her. With Cain there to catch her, Hannah was fearless.

"We ordered pizza," Merrick said. "And wine for later, in case they don't calm down from all this electronic stimulus."

"You're a funny woman," Emma said as she kissed Hannah's forehead when Cain held her out. Hayden had stood and put his arm around her waist and a hand on her growing belly. "Give him more time and he'll say hello."

"It's a boy?"

"It's a guess. Your mom and I are split on our choices. She says girl, and I say boy. Do you have a preference?" she asked, surprised she hadn't before now.

"Hannah and I are split too. She wants a brother, but I think another sister would be cool." He hugged her and kissed her cheek before he took Hannah from Cain. "Maybe one more so all of us will be happy if it's not what we wanted."

"Maybe," she said, "but let me survive the heat first."

"You guys have fun and try not to stay up too late," Cain said as she took Emma's hand again. "And tell your mama how beautiful she looks before we go."

Everyone, including Carmen, said something.

"Thank you, and be good," Emma said after she'd kissed Cain for her thoughtfulness. It was hard to not let her self-esteem deflate a little the bigger she got, but Cain derailed those thoughts before they could take hold. "I want you to know something," she said when they were alone in the backseat.

Cain had her arm around her and held her hand. "Last-minute advice?"

"No." She rested her head against Cain's shoulder. "It's really an apology."

"You haven't done anything you need to be sorry for."

"Let me finish, honey." She let Cain's hand go so she could spread her palm out on her lap. "I'm truly sorry for ever believing anything Barney Kyle ever told me. I remember that now, and I don't understand how I could've been so stupid. Running away from you, from us and Hayden cost us so much, and dwelling on it makes me insane."

"Lass, you really have to put that mess in its grave. That's where it belongs." Cain placed her fingers under Emma's chin so their eyes met. "We've both made our mistakes, and I mean *both* of us. What you have to know is my heart has no secrets from you. It knows you are what completes me, and in this lifetime and beyond there'll be no other who can take your place. Because of that truth, I don't want to waste my time on things that aren't important. All that happened, but it taught us what's important, didn't it?"

She gazed into Cain's eyes, trying to get the lump in her throat to dissolve. The tears were so close, and that wasn't what she wanted to do, considering where they were going. "This isn't me rehashing old hurts. Really, it's not," she said after a few deep breaths. "I'm apologizing because I want it to be the last time I do it. The stupidity I showed was colossal, but you're right. I want it to be a dead subject. Before we truly put it to rest, though, I want you to know that I'd die before hurting you like that again. What happened isn't something I take lightly, so don't think I do if I never talk about it."

"I'm glad we've come full circle, then." Cain kissed her before she went back to her original spot with her head on her shoulder. "As painful as living through that was, we're better together because of it. Had we gone along the way we did back then, maybe we wouldn't be here now."

"I love being your partner and helping you with the load you carry. I'm so grateful you and Hayden forgave me."

"We had no choice. You mean too much."

Lou drove slowly down the street Vincent's restaurant was on, so Cain kissed her again. "I didn't mean to be such a downer before dinner, but I had to get that out before it choked me."

"We've got a lot of good stuff to look forward to, so I'm glad you made that decision. If it makes you feel better about it, I accept your apology only if you accept mine for putting those doubts in your head to begin with."

"I never blamed you—well, not after I thought about it rationally. Unfortunately for me, by then it was too late, and the mistakes got easier after that. Besides, my mother's harping didn't help."

"Has Ross heard from her at all?"

Carol Verde had been vicious in her letters and phone calls when

Ross had first moved in with them. She'd threatened everything she could think of when Ross both ignored her and informed her divorce attorney she couldn't move back to the farm. The property had been in the Verde family for years, and her grandfather had done Ross's thinking for him before he married a woman he didn't approve of. Her dad had a prenup even when most of his friends didn't know what that was. The place would pass first to Emma, then her children once her father died, an eventuality she hoped was years away.

"She's been strangely quiet, which actually worries me more. The guy Muriel got to represent Daddy said she'd even stopped coming by his office to throw her weekly tantrum. Promise you'll spank me if I ever get like that?"

"You have my word, but don't worry, because you're nothing like your mother."

"Ready, boss?" Lou asked before he got out.

"That's a loaded question if I've ever heard one," she said, and Emma laughed. "I'm ready for something, but perhaps not this. Duty calls, though, so open the doors."

Their people exited the other vehicle that had followed them there and joined the crews of the other families. These meetings didn't take place often, but when the need arose it was good to have such good friends who shared views on so many levels.

"Cain." Patty, Mook's older brother and Vincent's head man, held his hand out. "Miss Emma." He took Emma's hand next. "It's good to see you both. I'll make sure Mama knows what a good Catholic you've become, Cain," he said with a large smile. "Though she'll give me a lecture to be more like my buddy Cain and not practice birth control. Congratulations." He kissed Emma's cheek.

"I'm sure there's a girl out there who'll help you find religion. We haven't given up on your little brother," Emma said.

They followed Patty to the private room in the back, and Cain recognized two FBI agents sitting at a table toward the side of main dining room. Both had an iced tea and appetizer in front of them, but she didn't believe this was a coincidence. Muriel shook her head from the door and waved her hand to get her walking again.

"They're just trawling, cousin. Let it go because there's nothing to fish here," Muriel whispered in her ear when they were close enough.

"Maybe, and maybe not," she said, but didn't explain as she led Emma to her seat.

The only ones missing were Remi and Dallas, and Cain was interested in how Dallas would react to all this. They all trusted her being there after her past had been verified and taken care of, but still—she wondered how the reality of who Remi was would compare to what Dallas's imagination had conjured up.

"Tell me again not to worry," Marianna Jatibon said when she approached them. They'd talked about this more than once, so Cain knew Remi's mother was happy she'd found love, but in their world that commitment and loyalty hadn't been tested—not really.

She kissed Emma's hand and pulled out the chair next to her for Marianna. "Do you need me to do it, or is this a job for Emma?"

"Go play. Your wife is who I need to talk to." Marianna laughed as she spoke. "Maybe it is time for us to retire and let our children deal with things. Ramon and I have become nervous cats lately."

"You're no different from Therese Casey when we met," Emma said. "Cain invited me to Sunday lunch, and Therese took pleasure in turning me inside out, even though I was the first girl this one had ever brought home," she said as she tugged on Cain's hand.

"My mother loved you and would've sainted you by now for the grandchildren who would've been the center of her existence." Cain kissed Emma. Their conversation in the car had to have been responsible for the pain that flashed across Emma's face, so she kissed her again. "I know Emma's backing is important, but would you mind if I say something?"

"I'd appreciate it if you would," Marianna said.

"It wasn't that long ago that my life was adrift in every aspect except for my business." Emma's eyes became glassy as Cain spoke, but she didn't interrupt. "I kept asking myself why someone who loved me would betray me and leave me alone. I never found an answer to make the pain go away until I finally figured it out. Emma came back, and in this woman I love lay the solution to everything I needed to be happy and complete."

"I'm happy you found your way back to each other," Marianna said.

"You're a good friend who prayed for that more than once," Emma said, emotion thick in her voice.

"I'm saying this because Dallas will never be perfect except for one thing. Her perfection in this life will be in how she loves your child. I can say that because I've found the same." Cain scratched the back of Emma's neck gently. "My mother would've told you the same had she been here," she said directly to Emma. "Believe that, and, Marianna, give Dallas the chance to prove it to you. Considering where she and her sister came from, she's going to cling to Remi closer than any of us will imagine. The freedom Remi's given her and Kristen to live in peace is the cement that'll bind her loyalty to your family."

"You had something to do with that, my friend," Ramon said from behind his wife.

"When we love, we feel the rest of the world should be so lucky. Right, Ramon?"

"We should form a lucky-bastard club," Ramon said jokingly. "That these beautiful women found something in us makes us so."

Remi came in, and with her first glance Cain could see how nervous Dallas was from the way she clutched Remi's hand. "Take a seat, Dallas, and keep my girl company while I steal Remi." She kissed Dallas on the cheek once she'd greeted Marianna and Emma the same way. "During dinner you can fill us in on how your new project is going."

Once Dallas sat, Cain took Emma's hand. The way she looked at Marianna made her think back to the day Emma had mentioned. They'd talked about it often and Emma had shared every bit of what she and her mother had talked about, but only after Therese Casey had passed and she'd asked. Only then did Emma feel she could share something she'd held so dear for so long.

Casey Home Fifteen Years Earlier

"Are you sure I look okay?" Emma asked Cain again as they followed Marie into the house. Cain's sister had waited by the front door for them, excited to meet her new girlfriend.

"You're beautiful, so relax," she said, and followed Emma's line of sight to the portrait of her father in the foyer and the vase of flowers under it. Her mother touched it as if to straighten it, even though it was perfect. "Mum, this is Emma Verde."

"It's a pleasure, ma'am," Emma had said in a voice so high she thought she'd pass out.

"I'm glad you're here," Therese Casey said with her hand out. When Emma took it she led her toward the kitchen. Cain had come as well after Emma gazed back at her with a panicked expression. "Tell me about your family."

Emma's story was stilted and hesitant, but her mother had nodded through it, already having heard Cain's take on the situation. The strain of telling it again had worn on Emma, so by the time the end came, she was leaning heavily against Cain. She straightened immediately when Cain finished, as if realizing then who her audience was.

"Go tend to your sister," Therese said, and the dismissal was only for her. "Emma, would you mind helping me finish?" she asked, in case her first directive wasn't clear enough.

"Sure." Emma sounded anything but sure of herself.

"Give us a minute, okay?" Cain took Emma's hand and led her out. "She deserves a tour before you put her to work."

The house was grander than any Emma had ever seen, but every room was comfortable and unpretentious except for the front parlor with its multitude of family photos, Irish lace, and a bar with the most beautiful crystal glasses and decanters she'd ever seen. She ran her finger along the etching on the one closest to her and wondered if she'd ever fit somewhere like this.

"Those have been in my family for generations," Cain said as she hugged her from behind. "They were purchased by my great-great-great-grandmother Rosin Casey after she established the family business in America."

"They're beautiful," she said, and dropped her hand to her side. "I'd be afraid to use them, considering how special they are to your family."

"Beautiful things are meant to be enjoyed, child," Therese said. When Emma turned, Marie was standing close to Cain's mother, smiling at her. "When Dalton was alive, we sat in here at least twice a week and shared a drink. Those are the moments I miss the most." Therese sighed and motioned her to a chair. "Cain, take Marie and yourself and wash your hands. Lunch is in thirty minutes or so."

Cain appeared to hesitate for the same reason she'd followed her to the kitchen. If Emma wanted to prove she was strong enough to defend what she wanted, she had to start now. If she folded and had to have Cain fight every battle for her, they'd never have a future together.

"Go on," she said to Cain. "We'll be right behind you."

"This is a first," Therese said as she sat across from her.

"What do you mean?" She sat and placed her hands on her thighs and tried not to move them. Rubbing them against the material of her dress would be a dead giveaway of the nerves threatening to run amok.

"My Derby bringing someone home." Therese smiled, and while she was an attractive woman, Emma found no resemblance to Cain in her face. "It's a development I really like."

"But you know nothing about this hick, right?" she asked, and Therese laughed. "I grew up with traditions too, Mrs. Casey, only we don't have any beautiful glasses to show for them. My father is a farmer, and he shared those things you need to run a successful dairy business with me."

"Only you don't want a future milking cows, do you?"

"Not until Cain becomes interested in cheese and butter."

"Even if your father's cows can spit whiskey out of their teats, I still can't picture Derby doing that," Therese said, and laughed again. "The Caseys are a rowdy bunch, but they love fiercely and are loyal to the end."

"It'll take time for you to understand and believe what a gift Cain is to me. I love her, and she'll be safe with me. You have my word on both those things."

Therese looked at the crystal, then her. "If that's true, then Rosin's glasses will be in good hands." Emma nodded at the small approval. "Remember your pretty words, Emma, because if they have no foundation, you'll have to pay a price that might be too steep for you, and one you might not recover from. Do we understand each other?"

"Yes, ma'am," she said, and hesitated. "It's crystal clear."

❖

"Are you okay?" Emma asked after Dallas tightened her grip on her fingers. Marianna had volunteered to get their drinks, so they were alone for a few moments.

"Just nervous, I guess. Every time we come to something like this, I expect someone to tell me I didn't get the part and I should leave. She really doesn't like me, does she?" Dallas asked about Marianna.

"I like you, so let me share something with you. The women we love both come from strong families that everyone thinks are headed by powerful men." She put her finger up when Dallas started to interrupt. "For us that used to be Dalton Casey, and for you, Ramon, but I figured out fast after I moved in with Cain that's only partially true."

"Of course, since Cain's in charge now."

"I never met Dalton, but I did meet Cain's mother, Therese. Marianna actually reminds me a lot of her. Cain learned to be strong not only from her father. Her mother was like a lioness at the gate when it came to her family and who she'd allow near them. Marianna is the same way with Remi and Mano, but be patient. She'll see what we all do when you look at Remi."

"Why did you believe me from the beginning? I could've been a cleverly hidden agent sent to take you all down."

Dallas Montgomery was a beautiful woman with a figure Emma was jealous of, if she was honest, for a moment every time they saw each other. Not that she was fixated on her looks, but Dallas was stunning. She was also successful and had Remi's love and devotion, but despite all that, Dallas had very little confidence. No one was able to fake that kind of all-consuming vulnerability and low self-esteem.

"I've told you before that I was glad you found Remi, since it was a chance for me to have a good friend who understood me and my life. This isn't the choice everyone would or can make."

"But how did you know you could trust me?"

"Because you don't strike me as a woman who prostitutes herself for a job, and sharing Remi's bed only to learn her secrets for the government would be that."

"But I have in the past, to make sure my sister had something to eat."

"I know, and I know you realize there's a difference in what we do for an employer and what we'd do for our families."

Marianna came back with a glass of juice and two wineglasses. Dallas accepted hers with a thank-you, but appeared disappointed they hadn't finished their talk. For Emma, it didn't matter how many lunches it took. She'd get Dallas to relax around Marianna and vice versa.

"How are Mano's children?" Emma asked, to get the conversation on firmer ground.

"Both of them are at our home with colds, and Mano and Sylvia are going crazy since he had to fly to Vegas for the week. I keep telling them I raised two children without a problem, so Ramon and I can handle a case of the sniffles."

"Can I come by and help tomorrow?" Dallas asked. "They're setting up shots out of town, so we'll only be on set for half a day."

"I'm sure they'd appreciate it," Marianna said without hesitation. Because she did, Emma thought she might be closer to accepting Dallas than she thought.

Both Remi and Cain came back and sat down after Marianna moved to be close to Ramon. The waiters had come in with the crab salads Vincent's was known for, but she'd have to pass. Her nausea had lessened, but it still hadn't disappeared, and the thought of vinaigrette dressing, no matter how wonderful, made her queasy.

"You ready to change diapers again, Cain?" Vincent asked.

"It's one of my favorite jobs, and I can't wait."

Emma smiled at Cain as she ripped the middle of the French bread Cain had passed her. Vincent actually had brought a date this time, and the much-younger woman had an elegance about her that made her seem above them all. It wasn't the kind of woman she'd have pictured him with, and from Vinny's expression he agreed with her.

The conversation stayed on safe topics, and Cain and the other family heads kidded in a way they could only do with each other. After the appetizers were cleared away, Vincent unlocked the door in the corner and followed the others inside. Vincent's date didn't say anything, but stood and headed into the main dining room after the others had left.

"Was it something we said?" she asked, and the others laughed, but Lou followed the woman out when Emma raised her eyebrows and cocked her head toward the door.

❖

"You're asking me to commit to a lot," Vincent said for the third time.

Cain could hear the anger starting to creep into his voice, but she wasn't backing down. Vincent wasn't much different from her father—they were both old-school. Her father, though, had learned the importance of building partnerships. Because he had expanded beyond Vincent and his family, she'd been able to keep what was rightfully hers when he'd been killed.

"Papa, listen to what she's saying," Vinny said. "Delarosa and these other fuckers are ready to come in here and cut our balls off. I've been working with Jasper, and he doesn't want to try for more than what we agreed to."

"You give up that much power to someone outside this room and you've already given up your balls," Vincent said, with a slam to the table in the center of the room.

"The world is changing again," she said in a low voice, to force them to calm down and listen. "These people—people like Hector— they don't believe in a handshake and our word. Money and power have replaced honor in their life, and they'll never have enough of both. If you don't understand that right now, you've already lost."

"The three families rule this city, Cain. That's what you don't understand," Vincent said, his temper still on hyperdrive.

"I plan to keep it that way, and if you listen to your son we might have a chance to guarantee it for generations to come."

Vincent slammed his hand down on the table again, in apparent frustration. He was a man used to getting his way and, more importantly, not being defied. "These drugs are in the hands of the thugs in the East and the housing projects right now. They don't bother me because I watch the news every night. All those murders they report are those animals knocking each other off when one of them gets too big. Nothing about that's changed in years."

Cain nodded and glanced around the room to gauge the reactions to Vincent's comments. "Right now Hector has three of the five largest crews working for him on the streets. That means the guys standing on the corners in each of our territories are his. Jasper Luke, with Vinny's help, still runs the largest crew, but when Hector feels ready, he's going to flex his muscle and crush whoever's in his way in less than a week." Remi and Ramon stared at her, but by their expressions they knew the reality of what she hadn't said yet. "Once he owns every section of the city, we and our businesses will become irrelevant. There'll be nothing left to pass to our children—we'll be the last."

Vincent laughed, but he was the only one. "You aren't serious?" He kept laughing. "No one is going to take me out, especially some slick fuck from south of the border."

"Then this meeting is over, and we enjoy the rest of dinner," Cain said as she stood and buttoned her jacket. "We'll talk again once we're retired in a way that'll not be on our terms. The one good thing about that will be finally shaking the FBI presence outside my door. They'll have much bigger problems than an Irish bitch with a taste for good whiskey."

"Wait, goddammit," Vincent said. "You're not shitting me, are you?"

"No, and my solution might not work, but it's better than rolling over and inviting Hector to fuck me over. Jasper is someone I know, and his father was someone my father knew. To me that's good enough."

"What makes you think he won't do the same once he gets big enough to crush us?" Vincent's tone had cooled and his question got a nod from Ramon.

"If he does it'll be with Vinny's blessing, and if that comes to pass, I'll leave the game and be content piddling behind the bars at my places."

"On my honor, I'd never do that to you, Cain," Vinny said.

"Then it's up to your father," she said as she walked up to Vincent and offered him her hand. "I graduated from that same old school, my friend, and my word is what means the most to me, aside from my family."

He shook her hand and stood to embrace her. "Thank you, and I do trust you. That hasn't changed, and if anyone can think their way out of this shit, it's you."

"I do love strategy, but sometimes you have to add a dose of something your opponent understands." She glanced at her watch and wondered if they'd get a visit from Annabel Hicks before dessert.

"Did you start without us?" Ramon asked.

"I'm not starting with Hector, but I did want to send him a wake-up call. I don't want him to feel like I'm not thinking of him. Tonight, though, is about dinner with friends and noodling."

"What is this noodling?" Ramon asked.

"It's a fishing technique," she said, as she spread her hands out and wiggled her fingers. "You walk along in the water and stick your hands in every hole until you wrap them around the neck of the fish you're looking for. That's my version of it, anyway."

"Isn't that dangerous?" Vinny asked.

"Perhaps, but think of how rewarding the gutting and fileting will be once I find the pathetic little bastard."

❖

Judice O'Brannigan watched her daughter study the menu, knowing she'd probably narrowed her options to three choices. Fiona had always been like that, no matter if it was Burger King or fine dining like this. "Do you want any help?"

"Do you think the veal or the steak is better?" Fiona never made eye contact, which meant she was leaning heavily toward her third choice.

"Veal makes you feel guilty from the minute they serve it, steak is probably a good choice, but it's an Italian restaurant—live a little."

"Lasagna it is." Fiona tapped her wineglass against hers after laying her menu down.

Vincent's was packed but, surprisingly, not that noisy, as if everyone there was engaged in soft, secretive conversations. "There's a lot of people not eating," Judice said, also keeping her voice low.

"Supposedly, according to Shelby, this is a mob hangout. If the guy's not eating, he's protecting his boss at the next table." The door across from them opened and a beautiful woman stepped out and walked to the bar. Before she had a chance to ask, the bartender poured her a shot of something. "This is a different planet compared to California."

"Is that why you really moved? You want to make a name for yourself as a king slayer? Because that's who these people answer to. Their king's word is law, not the one that badge of yours represents. If one of them gives the order to kill you—you're dead." Judice held up her glass and swirled the good Chianti so it briefly colored the sides. "They'll follow orders, then come here for a piece of veal, wine, and a cannoli to celebrate. They'll feel no guilt for your death, and certainly not for whatever they order."

"Are you studying to be a mob expert on your breaks?" Fiona laughed and stopped when her mother didn't join in. "What?"

"I've never asked you for anything," she said as she reached for Fiona's hand, "but I want you to come back with me. I love you for wanting to help your friend's daughter, but you know that's a crime with no solution. There's no reason to sacrifice yourself."

"You're more worried about these goons than the gangs in LA?"

"I worry about you all the time, but this," she discreetly pointed around the room, "you have to be a member to understand or get safely close to this. Your friend, Shelby, how long has she chased her tail on this?"

"She's assigned to Cain Casey, and she's honest about their lack of progress. I'm not FBI, but a fresh set of eyes never hurt."

"Have you met Casey?"

"Once, when I first got here," Fiona said, but the woman at the bar downing her second shot was a distraction she couldn't ignore because she was being watched by a guard much like the other patrons enjoying dinner. "Shelby was hot to see her, but Cain let us in just to taunt her. It was her son's birthday, so all Shelby got out of it was a slice of cake and a kick in the ass out the door. Who's that cruel to someone after her parents have been murdered?" The woman slid her glass toward the bartender and walked back to the room she'd come from, the large man opening the door for her. "I'd say her son, but from the files I've read, the children belong to the woman she lives with."

"You don't consider them Caseys?" Judice realized they hadn't had too many conversations about sex and sexuality except for the normal growing-up talks slanted toward education and safety.

"Genetically...probably," Fiona said as if she were picking her words carefully from a field of land mines. "They both look like Casey, so it makes the blonde an idiot for wanting to bring more of those killers into the world. Eventually they should let the bloodline die out—the world would be better for it."

"Children are a gift, sweetheart, no matter how or why they're born." The jump in her pulse and the ache in her gut was a warning to change the subject. Any more enlightenment on her daughter's views about this and she'd throw up. "No one is all good or all bad—no one."

"That's true, but some of us lean heavily in one direction or the other. The Caseys aren't nice people, and their files are so thick they're close to having their own room at the station. It's like they start their indoctrination program early and something in their genes soaks it up."

"All the reason to stay away from them." The place in her soul that housed the truths of her life knew Fiona wouldn't stay clear of the mobster. Her new bosses had dangled the carrot, and that's all it'd taken for her to bite down and not let go until she took them all down. At least she'd try, but sometimes even pit bulls got taken out with a bullet to the head when someone who didn't know any better thought them a threat.

"That's not going to be possible, Mama. I volunteered for the joint task force the NOPD and FBI put together for organized crime. I'm concentrating on Casey and her network."

"Why?" she asked. It didn't matter that she knew the answer. Fiona had always been noble and earnest to the bone, but that need to conquer sometimes blinded her to the patches of thin ice under her feet. So far she'd been lucky, but if she truly pursued this, Cain Casey would go out of her way to make sure Fiona not only fell through the ice, but drowned as well.

"Casey didn't kill Shelby's parents, but it ties into her. It's like they were killed not by her but because of her. They deserve the peace that'll only come by taking her down."

"Sometimes life isn't that simple, and you end up destroying yourself instead of the target you aim for."

Fiona stopped buttering her bread and stared at her as if she was trying to see the inside of her head to decipher her thoughts. "Do you think I'm incompetent?"

"No, but I don't want this to consume you to the point you waste years of your life. Is it really that important in the realm of all things?"

"Ah, you think I'll keep at it until either I win or die trying?" Fiona asked, using the same words Judice had spoken when she'd enrolled her in gymnastics and they were learning handstands. Five lamps and numerous knickknacks had been sacrificed until she'd perfected the skill.

"Yes. I don't think you realize what a real possibility that is."

❖

Dino Romero parked the piece-of-shit car his uncle Lou had given him the week before a block from the address he'd found in the glove compartment. This was the first assignment like this he'd been given, and he cursed that his hands wouldn't stop shaking. Sabana Greco didn't seem to have this problem.

"You look green," Sabana said in her blunt, annoying style.

She was young but, in his opinion, a vicious killer with no ability to feel guilt. "I just don't want to screw this up. Cain's counting on us."

"You feel bad for these fuckers, though, right?" Sabana looped her thumbs into the straps of her backpack and only gave him a glance before continuing to scope out the area around them. "If it makes you sleep better, think about my brother Rick. Your uncle Lou must have told you about him and what happened."

"He still hasn't gotten over that." He followed her to the backyard of a house close to where they were going. "If I never said it, I'm sorry for your loss. Uncle Lou said Rick was a solid guy."

"He was, and people like this killed him." Sabana pointed to the moderately large house with iron bars on all the windows and two guys guarding the back door. "They might do the same to me eventually, but I'm taking out as many of these fuckers as I can before they do. Odds are, I'll kill the bastards that murdered my brother for running an errand."

"I hope you're right about everything except them getting to you. When Uncle Lou partnered people up you might've wanted someone with more experience, but I got your back, so it sure as hell ain't going to be tonight."

Sabana momentarily relaxed, which transformed her face. She was a beautiful woman with real anger issues. "Thanks, and if you want, I'll do everything until you're more ready. I swear it'll be between us. Rick didn't kill anybody either before he died."

"I'd rather find out now if I can or not." He took his gun from his holster and checked the silencer before he aimed. When Sabana stepped closer to him the tremor in his hands calmed, and he took her advice and thought of Rick. They'd never met, but when the guy he shot went down, his sense of satisfaction covered any guilt he'd thought would overwhelm him. "You ready?"

"Yeah, and good job," Sabana said after she'd shot the other guy, so they had a short window before someone sounded any type of alarm.

He ran ahead of her and kicked in the back door. The noise started a series of screams, but he didn't hesitate to start firing once it swung open. Sabana threw the bag as hard as she could and yelled at him to get moving before it hit the ground. They didn't have much time to get clear.

They made it back to where they'd taken their shots before the explosion blew out most of the windows and shot a fireball out of each one. The screaming got louder, and they had to walk a block before they didn't hear it anymore. They'd done their part. At least he hadn't fucked up their end.

The money his uncle had paid out on the street had purchased three addresses, and after tonight, they'd all be burned to the ground. Fuck, he'd killed a guy and God knows how many others before the place was a pile of rubble. His father's warning rang in his ears: "There's no turning back." He couldn't undo or take back what he'd done, but he was too pumped to care. He did it, and he was okay with that.

"Let's go to my place and wait," Sabana said. They walked back to the other car they'd left ten blocks away, and again, she got in the passenger seat. "That's all we got for tonight, but you never know. Lou might need something else."

"Sure." He was so full of adrenaline he tried not to let his voice crack. He'd killed someone and lived to serve Cain like this whenever necessary. It hit him again and made him want to howl at the moon to get it out of his system. He was going to love this job.

CHAPTER EIGHT

Cain stood in front of the small television set in the kitchen and watched the reporter point to the still-smoldering pile behind him. The guy had the thickest eyebrows she'd ever seen on a human being, which almost distracted her to the point of missing what he was saying.

"The calls poured into nine-one-one late last night, but not even a quick response from the fire department could save this and two other houses in other locations. Fire inspectors suspect arson, but no word on how it was done. The neighbors we've spoken to are collectively relieved, since they suspected a large drug operation was working out of here," the reporter said. He was trying too hard, in her opinion, to appear serious, but his expression made his eyebrows come together in what looked like a freakish unibrow.

"At least he got the story right," she said softly to her coffee mug.

"We'll be updating this news throughout the day, but to recap, this and two other homes were destroyed last night, and authorities have confirmed that people were inside all three. No confirmation on how many dead, so back to you, Randi."

"Is an omelet okay, Ms. Cain?" Carmen asked.

"That's fine, thanks." She picked up the paper and sat at the table in the kitchen they used for breakfast.

The three places she'd ordered hit contained a large portion of Gracelia's inventory in the city, but she wasn't counting on it all being gone. Anyone with an operation supposedly as large as Gracelia's didn't stockpile that much product in only three spots. At least, Cain certainly didn't. Last night wasn't a deathblow to their business, but it'd be painful to recover from. However, she didn't know if any of Gracelia's top people were inside along with the local idiots she'd hired to move and guard her stash.

"Good morning, Mom," Hayden said, and Hannah repeated his greeting. "Don't forget my game tonight."

"We'll be there cheering. Right, Hannah?"

"I can't wait." Hannah clapped her hands.

Katlin entered and held the door for Merrick. After Merrick was seated next to Hannah, Katlin pointed to the headlines. The picture showed the place Lou had sent Sabana and Dino. She'd spoken to Lou the night before to make sure Dino's first job hadn't changed his mind about his future with them.

"Big news day," Merrick said, and pointed at the television where their action reporter had moved to another of the burnt shells. "You think it'll get any more exciting by the five o'clock cycle?"

"I predict the noon break will be unusually productive if you're an action reporter."

They finished their coffee and Cain took the kids to school on her way to the warehouse. It was important that she be visible today since her message to Gracelia wasn't complete. As they drove away, the van across the street surprisingly stayed put, and a smaller van took position a few cars behind them. She was sure it was Annabel's way of circling her wagons in hopes of an ambush. But the special agent in charge needed to realize that when you were so focused on trying to find the small crack to get in, it was easy to lose sight of your own defenses. That was the blind spot Cain was planning to exploit to the fullest when the time came.

"We might have company," Katlin said. She'd taken over for Lou behind the wheel for the day.

The Suburban she'd recently switched to sat so far up it gave her a good view of what was in front of them. About four guys with the same short haircut, gray suits, and boring ties were leaning against navy sedans that blocked her entrance.

"Take it slow, but if anyone tries to punch me in the head," she said as Katlin turned toward the gate, "shoot them."

"You want to move your cars?" Katlin said to the guy who'd taken a more alert stance by the first vehicle in line. The guy smiled but stayed put. "You deaf, asshole?"

"Is Cain Casey hiding back there?" The guy unbuttoned his jacket and put his hands on his hips, as if to show off his weapon.

"Why are you guys this tough only when you travel in packs?" Katlin taunted him. "Is that something they teach you at FBI school, or is that a New Orleans policy only?"

The man took a step toward them and Cain laughed. She opened the back door and repeated her order to shoot anyone who got within five feet of her with a clenched fist—only she said it loud enough for everyone to hear. "Is there a reason you're blocking the way into my office?"

Behind the now obviously pissed agent, the passenger side of the illegally parked car opened and Annabel Hicks got out. She stuck her hands in the pockets of her skirt and looked at her as if trying to decide the best way to start.

"Can I speak to you?"

"When you retire, Agent Hicks, you should consider a career in acting."

"Why?" Annabel asked. The dark circles under her eyes made her appear older and drained.

"You have a flair for the dramatic that'd come across well onscreen, I'd think. No matter what, you go out of your way to find the most extreme ways to get five minutes out of me." She tapped the spot over her eyebrow that held the scar Agent Brent Cehan had put there when he slammed her head into the trunk of her car. "Normal people, even those I don't like very much, either call or knock on the door. I'm not so inhospitable that I won't consider such an approach."

"I've never considered our relationship normal, and when I'm replaced you might actually come to miss my flair, as you put it."

"Going somewhere?"

"Not willingly, no." She motioned for the guy with her to move everything from the entrance. "Can I have five minutes of your time?"

Cain saw Cehan in one of the other cars and stared at him for a long moment before she answered. "If *you* want that, I'd be happy to accommodate you, but if you insist on guests I'll pass."

"Just me," Annabel said, and glared at the agent closest to her when he opened his mouth and complained.

"Let's walk from here, then. Katlin, drive in and we'll meet you." She waved Annabel ahead of her and turned to glance up at the apartment across the way where the team assigned to them usually spent their days when she was here. "What can I do for you, Special Agent Hicks?"

"Why so formal today? You usually take such pleasure in saying my name so I sound like a backwoods pig farmer."

"Annabel it is, then. Is there something in particular you'd like to talk about?"

"If that was you last night, it might've misfired. Explosions of any kind attract more federal agents, and it becomes sort of an acronym convention."

"If you're talking about what I saw on the news this morning, I hope you do bring in all the troops you can." She slowed her gait to make sure Annabel didn't twist an ankle by catching her low heels in the cracks spread across the front of their building. "Maybe if stuff like this keeps happening, you'll reassign some of these guys someplace they'd do more good. I'm not so dangerous that I need to be watched twenty-four hours a day. It's such a waste of taxpayer money."

"No, this," Annabel pointed to Cain, then herself, "is a waste of my time and taxpayer money, but do you have any idea what happened last night?" Annabel followed her inside and nodded when she pointed to the coffee service in the corner of the large open space.

They'd sit out there since Cain didn't want anyone with a badge in her offices. "I can repeat what I read in the paper and saw on the news, but I'd hope you have more information than that."

"So you couldn't tell me who owned those places?"

She brought back two full cups with a tray of sweetener and cream. Any more of this and she'd have to retire and become a Southern belle whose life revolved around genteel pursuits. "We'd get along so much better if you all would spit out what you want rather than trying to play these bullshit games. Let's try that approach. What do you want?" So much for her Southern belleness.

"The places hit last night, according to the DEA, allegedly belonged to the Luis family. From what the neighbors say, whoever owned them was moving inventory in and out in large quantities. Since no one ever reported anything out of fear, these locations weren't under surveillance."

Cain watched Annabel's mouth as she spoke and the way it set to a grimace when she finished. Annabel appeared to be a woman with a great weight, which, if she had to guess, was caused by the accumulation of failures she'd experienced since her predecessor Barney Kyle was relieved of his post. Desperate people were usually dangerous, but because of Annabel's position, she seemed almost gun-shy.

"Sounds like the beginning of a drug war," she said, when Annabel didn't add anything else.

"Or someone with a grudge against the owners."

"So I'm your first stop…again?" She smiled, finding the predictability of these people laughable, even though in this case Annabel was right.

"I'm not blaming, I'm asking if you've heard anything. For someone who owns a bar, you're surprisingly in the know about stuff like this."

The answer was another surprise because it rang true. "I can promise you that drugs and the people who sell them are subjects we agree don't have a place in this city. It's not realistic that you or any police organization will get rid of all of them, but whenever I can help you take someone like Juan Luis down, I will. I even spoke to the police department when Rodolfo Luis was found dead, and they asked for my help. All I discovered then was he was a major player who was partnering with Big Gino and his sons."

"We found Rodolfo," Annabel said, and finally smiled. "Gino and family are still MIA. Do you know Big Gino's wife still calls me about her grandson? She's accepted that her husband and sons won't be coming back, but that baby haunts her."

"Let's get back to what you need," Cain said so she wouldn't get sucked into this conversation.

"Hit a nerve?"

"You don't think much of me, but to hang the death of a child on me is a stretch even for the FBI. I have children and one on the way, so there are things I'll never be guilty of, no matter where your limited imagination skitters off to."

"Fair enough." Annabel spread her hands out and dropped them as if exhausted. "If you have contacts on the streets that tell you anything about this, I'd appreciate if you'd share that information with us. If your predictions of a drug war are true, the city's going to become a cluster of chaos. Nothing thrives in chaos, Cain."

"Give me a few days and I'll see what I can come up with."

Her assistant walked Annabel out, so Cain headed for her office. It was about the time Lou had set for the next part of her plan, and she only trusted the phone in there for his update. What Annabel failed to see was that war was at times chaotic, but also cleansing. The smaller dealers, who by nature were the most aggressive and vicious, didn't survive, and only the fittest of the larger operations were left standing. It was easier to see your enemies coming when you thinned the herd.

"So, Annabel, the war is on its way whether your people are ready or not."

❖

"Mr. Rhodes." The customs agent stared at the passport in his hand, then at Jerome. "Are you here on business or vacation?"

"Vacation," he said as he scratched his face, not used to the stubble of his new beard. He didn't panic because Gracelia's forger was too good for this idiot to figure he was holding a bogus document.

"How long will you be in the country?" the agent asked, his eyes back on the passport.

"Two weeks tops. My plans are flexible, though."

After another long hesitation, he stamped the document and waved him through. Had Gracelia been with him it might've taken longer, but he'd convinced her to give him a week before she came to meet him. He needed the time to bring her son in line and try to find a new partner. Staying where he was, surrounded by idiots, was suicidal, and he had no interest in that.

"Those two," he told one of the crew waiting for him in baggage claim. "Where's Gustavo?"

"He wait for you at the hotel."

"Let's go there first." He got in the car and shook Pablo's hand. He doubted Pablo had the opportunity to do what he'd asked, but he planned to keep hammering at him until he owned him. "Anything?"

"I speak with Miguel Gonzales and he promised a meeting with Señor Delarosa when you come. He sound *interesado*."

"Good, now tell me about Gustavo. What's he been up to?"

"He become a movie-star fan, so we ignore him. He no is a harm."

"What movie star?" He had to give Gustavo credit. His new face might've woken up some of his listless brain cells, and with time he could have maybe found out something about Cain by following someone close to Remi Jatibon. But Gustavo had run out of time. It was Jerome's goal to reel him in and ship him home to Gracelia. They could sit and spin revenge plots all they wanted together, with no hope of carrying any of them out.

"Dallas Montgomery," Pablo said, mutilating the last name but confirming he was right. "He go every day to see the film, the men say. They complain it too hot for that shit."

Jerome had broken down his theory of Casey's partnership with the Jatibon family for Gracelia and Gustavo, but something must've gotten lost in translation, because if Gustavo thought Cain would trade Emma for some piece of ass Remi Jatibon was bedding, he hadn't learned anything. The only reason to follow Dallas was a move toward

Cain. Gustavo had definitely inherited Gracelia's drive when it came to what they wanted, but he didn't have a fucking clue how to get it.

Gustavo had picked a place they'd never used, and the shabbiness of the lobby and the people in it made him think you could kill someone in the middle of it and no one would claim to have seen a thing. Jerome looked everyone who glanced his way in the eye, a trick from his FBI days. People with something to hide had a tendency to turn away from someone who did that.

"Where is my mother, *puta*?" Gustavo asked as soon as he opened the door, using his usual curse for him by calling him a bitch.

Gustavo appeared unkempt, had bloodshot eyes, and smacked his lips when he wasn't talking. The bindings keeping his sanity in place appeared strained and at a breaking point. Obsession complicated by heavy drug use was a recipe for disaster.

"Back home waiting for you." Jerome motioned for the men to wait for him outside. "She sent me to tell you that time's up. This shit you're doing is hurting business."

"You got here yesterday, and you think you can fucking tell me what Mama wants?" Gustavo laughed as he stripped his jacket and shirt off. He tucked his gun into the front of his waistband, and Jerome almost wished the stupid shit would pull the trigger and die from blowing his dick off. "You forget already who you listen to?"

"If you mean yourself, then you need to get your nose out of that nice box you love. Your mother and I came to an agreement, and you were the first thing she caved on. Either go home and pretend you're important to the business," he said as he chose the cleanest-appearing chair, sat, and crossed his legs, "or not."

"Or not?" Gustavo laughed hysterically as he slapped his chest. "What you mean?"

"Your mother needs to grow the business more than she's willing to give in to your craziness. Face facts, amigo. Some things are out of your reach. Emma Casey is number one on that list."

"Don't talk for my mama. You are not important to her like me." Gustavo slapped his chest again hard enough to leave the mark of his handprint.

"Call her if you don't believe me, but before you do, make sure you know everything that's happened."

Gustavo was almost panting as he stood closer to him, so he put both feet on the ground in case the guy got really stupid. "What you talking about?"

"Three of our places got blown up last night, and no one survived. Once the cops figure out that you locked up those women in only their panties like dogs, they will hunt you down." He'd deal with the others for not telling him. He'd actually heard about it on the news feed on the plane, and the demeanor of the newswoman on CNN was similar to a starving dog with a meaty bone being waved in front of it. The woman practically salivated as the investigators sifted through the rubble. This story wouldn't die a quick, quiet death.

Gustavo stared at him as if he'd suddenly switched to Korean. "You speak shit."

"Here." He handed over his phone. "Call them and tell one of your lap dogs to bring you a refill."

"That bitch," Gustavo yelled. "She did this to me."

"Shut the fuck up and start packing." The door opened and the order echoed out to the hallway. He screamed at Pablo when he entered without knocking. "What?"

"Someone killed many of our people."

"I know that, and you should've told me at the airport."

"No, señor, on the street. The men we have on the street, they die."

"Shit." Jerome stood and dialed another number. "Find out what the hell happened and get back to me," he said to the guy who answered. "Pack and get out of my sight. Everything in place went down in a day while you were busy waving your dick at a woman who hates you." Gustavo reached for his gun, but Pablo beat him to it and drew first. "Do you need a babysitter to see you get back to Mama?"

"Fuck off." Gustavo spat at him but kept his hand away from his gun.

"Who called you?" Jerome asked Pablo as he walked back to the car.

"He say he not shot, but everyone else dead. I call and no one answer, so I think they dead too."

"What's his name?"

"I don't know."

The call didn't come from one of their guys. In his gut he knew that was true, and it put him in a bad spot. He couldn't negotiate with Delarosa if he didn't know it was him, and he didn't know it wasn't him. No one gained an edge if he didn't have information.

"He spoke Spanish to you?"

"Perfect."

It couldn't be Cain, and he couldn't narrow down who it was with so little to go on. "Get out there and see what's going on."

"And Señor Delarosa?"

"I'll deal with that myself, but don't worry, I'm not cutting you out of that deal." He shut the door on Pablo and waited until he was calmer to make a call. "You know what to do, right?"

"Yeah, no worry."

"You should worry a little if you want to stay alive."

Nicolette Blanc linked her fingers together as if in prayer as she gazed out at the grand homes on St. Charles Avenue. When she'd attended Tulane University, she enjoyed walking this street and those around it because the area reminded her of home. New Orleans as a whole had a sense of history and old traditions not found in too many places in the States.

She'd left Luce behind, not in the mood for her out-of-control jealousy, especially after she'd tangled with Cain and been completely shut out. Luce was used to giving an order and everyone in their organization falling over themselves to be the one to get it done. It'd taken her a while to garner that type of respect, and Nicolette had often compared her to the one woman she'd never been able to bed no matter how hard she'd tried.

Cain had fascinated her from the moment she'd seen her walking across the front lawn of the campus with a beautiful girl hanging to her so tight it appeared like Cain would disappear if she let go. It hadn't taken much after that to find out who Cain was and what the Casey name meant. Luce had worked for the respect she had now, but Cain had been born with the type of charisma that people were drawn to and made them want to please her. Nicolette certainly had wanted to, even after years of rejection.

They pulled up to an ornate gate, which showed only a small glimpse of the house beyond it. The tall, solid wall reminded her of the defenses Cain had raised against her when she'd approached her about their families doing business together.

"Can I help you?" The man at her window had the thickest neck she'd ever seen on a human, but his white shirt and tie still appeared tasteful and sedate.

"Nic Blanc for Cain Casey. I don't have an appointment, but I don't mind waiting if she can give me a few minutes."

"Wait here, ma'am," he said, as if she had another choice. He had a short conversation with someone before he returned. "Go ahead in and park over there." He pointed to an empty spot. "If your driver's going in with you, make sure he's clean. Any guns you insist on will be taken and not returned, so don't make that mistake."

The garden to the side and the toys close to it didn't compute with what she remembered of Cain, but she put that out of her mind when the front door opened. It wasn't Cain, so the grand reunion she'd dreamed about for years with Cain coming to her and sweeping her off her feet wasn't going to happen.

"Welcome, Ms. Blanc, please come in," the woman said. "Mrs. Casey will be with you shortly."

"Mrs. Casey? Cain's married?"

"When I say Mrs. Casey, I mean Emma Casey, and she is Ms. Cain's wife, so she is married." The woman left her, but the guard close to where she sat kept his eye on her.

After a long fifteen minutes, a visibly pregnant petite woman stopped close to her and held her hand out. "Welcome to our home, Ms. Blanc, I'm Emma. I'll be happy to help you since Cain is out at the moment. What can I do for you?"

Nicolette didn't often dismiss someone after a glance, but this woman wasn't worth more than that. Everyone couldn't be perfect, and Cain had finally fallen from the heavens with this choice. Weakness in anything or anyone was the beginning of their ruination. This woman would be Cain's.

"You should've mentioned she wasn't at home," she said, and didn't care if her aggravation seeped into her tone. "I'll call next time." She walked out, not bothering to take Emma's hand. When she got outside, the mountain she'd figured they'd have to climb to get back into Cain's good graces was shaved to an ant pile.

Emma stared at her front door and laughed. It gave her a sense of pleasure to know Cain had never been with the French asshole who'd walked about with the same authority she guessed royalty was used to. From Hannah's squeals coming from the direction of the kitchen, the object of Nicolette's desires had arrived. "Is Blanc's car still out there?" she asked the guard close to the door.

"Yes. Would you like me to call her back in?"

"No, but thanks for asking," she said as she winked and walked to the back of the house.

She hung back when she saw Hannah on Cain's lap, recounting her entire day at school. Any worry she'd ever had that their daughter would have trouble bonding with Cain had died days after they were all under the same roof.

Cain, no matter what was going on, dedicated at least an hour every day to Hannah. All that time had erased the skittishness her mother had taught their daughter, and like Hayden, Hannah had embraced her role as a Casey heir with the gusto only Cain could infuse in her. Hannah had become confident in a way that no one experienced unless they were rock-solid sure of their safety net. It wasn't hard to fly high if you knew Cain was there to catch you.

"Mom, I told my teacher you and Mama would do it," Hannah said, her hand in Cain's.

"We'd do what?" she asked after she kissed Cain on the lips.

"We're hosting a pizza and cupcake party next week for Miss Hannah's class," Cain said with a smile. "It's close to the end of school, Mama, so we have to celebrate that."

"You missed someone who wanted to celebrate with you." She traced Cain's ear with her finger, which made her want to strip and beg Cain to touch her.

"You sure it's not you, lass?" Cain said, in a way that convinced her she could read her mind.

"You just missed Nicolette Blanc," she said, and described how the woman had treated her. "I haven't felt like a piece of fluff since our first date, but that woman managed it in a five-second conversation."

"I think someone convinced her as a child that she was a descendant of Marie Antoinette, but must've not told her how that story ended." Cain sat her on her other knee. "I'm sorry about that. I should've briefed the guys out front to make her go through the office."

"I'm not comfortable with the thought of her anywhere near you."

"Faith, lass." Cain's kiss soothed the vein of jealousy throbbing in her stomach. "We need to change so we don't miss the beginning of Hayden's game." Hannah ran out like they'd threatened to leave her behind.

"I shouldn't have said anything."

"Love, you can tell me anything. If you don't, then how would I know to tell you how unimportant it is to me to do business with the Blancs? If I was undecided before, I'm set to lock them out now. I should've made that clear when I met with that bitch Luce Fournier."

Cain locked the door to their bedroom, unzipped Emma's dress, and helped her step out of it.

"Thanks for the pep talk. Is that the only reason you're in such a good mood?" Her nipple tightened painfully when Cain laughed, wearing only her underwear.

"You know I love you, right?"

"Yes," she said as she pressed her hands to her chest in hopes that the warmth would relax the pucker.

"Then I hope it doesn't insult you when I say that sometimes I want to simply fuck you until you scream my name."

The words made Emma squeeze her breasts, which unleashed a flood in her panties. "Not nice, mobster. You don't make declarations like that when we have somewhere to be."

She didn't have time to react to Cain's laugh since Cain had picked her up and laid her on the bed. Her eyes closed when Cain's fingers slid in to the palm, gently at first, but then moved at a faster, delicious pace when she didn't object.

It was what Cain said, a fuck to relieve the need she'd obviously seen etched in her face. There was no buildup—it wasn't needed— but she didn't feel less loved as Cain touched her with the skill only a longtime lover would have. Her climax came as quickly, and she kissed the side of Cain's neck in gratitude.

"Thank you doesn't begin to cover it," she said lethargically.

"It's always a privilege, lass, that never loses its appeal. Tonight let's try for the long, scenic route. You know how much I love stopping at all the points of interest." She bit down on her nipple gently through her bra, making her hiss. "Right now, though, you need to get dressed to watch your son play ball. Eventually he'll learn the true meaning of second base, home plate, and everything in between, so we'll enjoy this while we can."

"Bite my tongue, mobster," Emma said teasingly as she adjusted the water for a fast shower. "And before you correct me, it's more fun if you bite mine than yours."

They finished and were dressed by the time Hannah knocked on their door. Emma enjoyed the sight of Cain in jeans wearing a shirt she'd gotten from Hayden's school with their logo on the breast pocket. As delightful as the afternoon had been so far, a small niggling of doubt started in the back of her mind like a cluster of dark, ominous clouds on the horizon.

"Come on, Mama," Hannah said. "Let's go have fun."

She tried to smother her fear so she could share Hannah's enthusiasm, but sometimes intuition wouldn't be ignored. Something or someone was coming, and it meant them harm.

"You got it, baby," she said brightly.

Fear, she'd discovered, had a way of getting stronger when you finally had almost everything you wanted. Once you'd arrived at that place, it was so easy for someone to take it away.

Not to tempt fate, but this time they'd have to take it from her by force. She'd never give it away as easily as she had to Barney Kyle.

CHAPTER NINE

Thirty-six," Special Agent Ronald Chapman said to the group he'd assembled for this meeting. "Thirty-six people dead in an hour's time, and you have nothing. Do you see this as a problem?"

Ronald had spent the last five years as a special liaison to the president, a job that had garnered him power, and it was time to use it. The next part of his plan was to knock Annabel and some of the other agents out of this office and replace them with people loyal to him. It was time to clean the streets of New Orleans all the way to the mayor's office, a position he wanted as a steppingstone to the U.S. Senate. The foundation to those steps he planned to climb would be built by toppling organized crime.

"We're working with the NOPD in an advisory position, Ron. We haven't been invited in, and they want to take point on the investigation," Annabel said.

"Leaders lead, Annabel. They do not ask permission, they simply do." He repeated the motto he religiously lived by. "Three bombings followed by this means the stitching has come off the seams holding this city together. Before that really happens, the citizens deserve for us to prevent an all-out war over drugs from breaking out."

"Great speech, but we still have rules and laws to abide by." Annabel, from her demeanor, was barely holding back her hostility. At least she was smart enough to know why he was here.

"You can go back to your duties...for now," he said, enjoying the knowledge that the asshole of everyone in the room had tightened from the unknown future they had here. "I'll be speaking with each of you individually, so reschedule whatever you have when I'm ready for you."

Brent Cehan got up and stood behind him with a clipboard. He needed an assistant for the investigation he was here to do, so he'd chosen the one agent who'd shown the kind of attitude he needed to see if he was going to succeed.

"Agent Cehan will be working with me, so expect to hear from him."

"Agent Cehan is restricted to light duty pending an investigation for a recent incident."

"He's been cleared of any wrongdoing as of this morning," he said, and Brent's cruel-appearing smile made Ronald feel a kinship with him. "There will be no further action and no mention of this in his file."

"Local and Casey family attorney Muriel Casey will have a problem with that, and she'll pressure U.S. Attorney George Talbot into something you aren't going to like," Joe said.

"Perhaps that's what the problem is," he said, glancing back at Brent, who'd given him a thorough rundown on office dynamics earlier. "You all seem to be under the impression you have to coddle these thugs. Not anymore. When you're at war, people, you must do whatever it takes to win. Whatever it takes—remember that."

"So our plan is frontier justice?" Joe asked.

"Our plan is to win."

"From my experience that's Muriel's plan as well, and she'll take great pleasure in reminding Mr. Talbot that the only reason Cain Casey didn't file charges against Brent for assault was because he agreed to be on desk duty for much longer than this," Joe said as he locked eyes with Brent. "I'm sure Brent must've forgotten to tell you that when he volunteered to work with you."

Annabel stared at Joe in hopes he'd keep his mouth shut and stop antagonizing Ronald, no matter how aggravating he was. She was upset with herself for not giving Brent his transfer to Houston like he'd wanted. The big bastard was now in position to screw her over, so it was time to strategize a counterattack. Brent had picked a side, but she was sure the others would back her.

"We do our jobs and we have results to show for it," she said as she stood, ready to leave. When you gave Ronald the opportunity, he could grandstand as long as you'd let him. Ronald was here to torpedo her career, but he didn't outrank her, so she'd had her fill for now. "*My* staff is here to help however they can, but I'd appreciate a heads-up if you're going to reassign anyone else."

Joe followed her to her office and forcibly closed the door. "I'm sorry for saying this, ma'am, but that guy's an asshole."

"Can I trust you, Joe?"

"What do you want to me to do?" he asked, dropping into one of her chairs.

"Be honest with Ronald, since I don't need to give him any more ammunition to screw us. I know he plans to split our teams apart and ship them out of the city." She stared out her window, and had Ronald not been there, she'd be tempted to go home and lie down. Being under constant attack was exhausting. "He wanted this job and never got over that fact that it went to an inexperienced bitch. I believe that's a direct quote."

"If he tries to replace you, ma'am, he can go ahead and transfer me. It's insulting to be accused of gross incompetence when it comes to dealing with people like Cain Casey. Special Agent Chapman," he said the name in a way that sounded like a curse, "is going to figure that out soon enough when Cain chews him up and scatters pieces of him all over the place. Especially once she gets a taste of his charming personality."

"Talk to Shelby again and let her know how important it is that she comes back. If she's not ready, I'll understand, and if she isn't, then tell her the daily visits to Casey aren't in her best interest right now."

"Anything else?"

"The rest…it's better if you leave to me."

Joe's silence made her focus on him, and his expression was hard to read, so she had no idea what was on his mind. "I don't mean any disrespect, but you need to cut this guy off at the knees, Annabel, before he has the opportunity to return the favor. We might not agree all the time, but we've got your back on this one."

"Thanks, Joe. If we're smart we'd take a page out of Casey's playbook."

"How so?"

"We've never been able to prove that Gino Bracato and his sons are dead, but we all know they are, and who killed them. Like Casey, we need to bury these guys deep enough that they won't be a problem, and then we can go back to doing our jobs in peace."

❖

Hayden's game was on the meticulously kept field at the private school the kids attended. This would be Hayden's last year on campus since he'd already been accepted at his grandfather and uncle's alma mater, Jesuit. The stands were starting to fill, and quite a few of the other parents came up to welcome the Caseys as they walked toward the bleachers.

Most of the faculty and parents had been wary at first, but the fund-raising committee had warmed to Cain once she'd opened her checkbook. Now that Emma and Hannah were back home, she was glad some of their money had gone to the comfortable stands that expanded out past first and third bases.

Hannah's teacher hugged the little girl and Emma when they were close to their seats in the first row near third base. Everyone had been good about saving the block of seats that made it easy for Merrick and Emma to attend. "I know Hannah volunteered you guys, but I wanted to make sure that was okay," the young woman said.

"I think we can handle pizza and cupcakes for everyone," Cain said, holding Emma's hand. "If you get some of the other parents to help serve, you can invite the other four classes."

"That'd be great. You two are any teacher's dream."

They sat and Cain glanced at Lou before finding Hayden on the field going through the warm-ups. The only blemish on the day was the constant fear that stayed with her, and would, until she'd planted Juan and his mother in the ground after a slow, excruciating death.

Keep having morbid thoughts like that, Casey, and you might prove the FBI right, she thought as she looked in the direction Lou was discreetly pointing. Cehan she recognized, but the man next to him was a new face in the game. Annabel's warning was perhaps coming true. She didn't glance away when Brent, unlike Lou, blatantly pointed at her. Whoever the new guy was, he obviously didn't have many manners. Only once before that had Annabel's goons dragged her away in front of her family, and Muriel had used that incident to add ammunition to her harassment claims. That'd been a bonus, but it hadn't helped her children forget.

"Stay put," Muriel said from the seat behind her.

"If that," she took a deep breath so as not to curse in front of Hannah, "*guy* pulls something, I'm going to pull something right off his body. Maybe I'll make earrings and send them to Annabel to wear with those drab suits she's so fond of."

"Let me go," Muriel said, and Katlin got up with her.

"What are they doing here?" Emma asked.

"Fishing," she said, but kept her eyes on Brent Cehan. She hadn't forgotten him or what he'd done, and the old Sicilian saying flashed through her mind every time she saw him. Her revenge was cooling, and long after he'd forgotten the misery he'd put her through she'd serve it cold and cruelly. The heat the authorities would bring down on them for killing him would be intense, but it'd be worth it.

"Haven't they learned their lesson by now?" Emma said.

"That you shouldn't trawl for sharks with the weakest rod in your arsenal? That lesson?"

"Different analogy than mine, but yes, something like that. Annabel and company must be getting desperate."

"The big guy with the belt buckle that clashes with his outfit is the guy who rearranged my face for me." Brent made eye contact with her, obviously not giving a damn or paying attention to what Muriel was saying. "Somehow I don't feel like this is an Annabel play because she testified he'd serve a long reprimand behind a desk for what he did if I agreed not to press charges. She also promised he wouldn't come anywhere near us."

"And you believed her?" Emma said, and let go of her hand when Brent shoved Muriel. "Let Katlin handle it, please."

"He's not here for Katlin." She bent and whispered in Emma's ear. "The kids deserve to play without distractions, so stay with Hannah and I'll be right back." She looked at Sabana and nodded when she took the seat Muriel had vacated. Lou had immediately taken hers when she'd stood up.

Brent was tall and thick, the type of guy you just knew played football because he took pleasure in hitting people. A habit he'd not outgrown, judging by his current behavior. He'd put his hand up again when Katlin stepped in front of Muriel but backed away when the guy he was with waved him off.

"Ms. Casey," the man said with a smile that reminded her of a used-car salesman. He probably thought it charming and disarming, but she saw it as oily and deceitful. "I'm Special Agent Ronald Chapman."

"Do you have a son on the opposing team?"

"No, I'm not a fan of baseball. It's too slow and lacking in action for me to really get into."

"Then go home and tune into some fake wrestling." She motioned her cousins behind her. They ignored her, probably because Brent hadn't moved back either. "I've already spoken to Agent Hicks today, only she was courteous enough to come to my office. If you need something else, this isn't the time or place."

"Only civilized people deserve to be treated civilly," Ronald said, and Brent laughed like a trained seal looking for his master to throw him a sardine. "We both know what type of person you are, so I'm going to enjoy showing up at stuff like this whenever the mood strikes me. People need to realize it's never a wise thing to keep a cobra as a pet. It might be fascinating and beautiful, but it's deadly even when put in a pretty tank. Your life might seem normal to these people here, but do they realize you killed about fifty people in a twenty-four-hour span?"

"Do you—" Muriel said, but stopped when she raised a finger.

"My cousin was about to ask where your proof is. Let's see the handcuffs and list of charges for that atrocity."

"Atrocity," Brent said, and laughed again, "is the wrong word for a bunch of drug dealers."

"Maybe you should do an internal review before you accuse other people of any crime that comes along." Brent's statement had knocked a bit of the cocky off the new guy. "Or did you just get here and decided to show the Irish mick who's in charge now?"

"Why do you say that?"

"Because you've arrived with the dumbest agent in Annabel's stable, like a guy trying to prove he's got a pair by picking a fight. Is that a good description of you, Chapman? A guy with a chip in his ass trying to boost his questionable manhood by flashing that pretty leather credentials wallet they gave you?"

It was like watching a thermometer in a pot of simmering water. Ronald's eyes closed to slits and his hands clenched to match Cain's. The angrier he got, the more amused she became and wondered why it was so easy to whip these guys into a froth. Annabel and Shelby were a little slower to irritate, but she'd managed it on a few occasions.

"If that's how you want to play it, I'll be happy to oblige," Ronald said in what she assumed was his best menacing voice. "You'll pray for the days of Agent Hicks and the team assigned to you now, because I'm going to make it my life's mission to bring you down by any means I can."

"Ronald," she said, and his anger clicked up a notch. "May I call you Ronald?" He didn't say anything, but he was shaking. "You should've learned the most important lesson in your years with the Bureau when throwing out threats."

"What, that pieces of shit like you always go down even if they think they're scary?" he said, loud enough to make heads turn.

"Not quite, Ronald," she said enjoying the sound of yet another name she could make sound the way *Annabel* rolled off her tongue. Annabel had accused her on numerous occasions of making her name sound hickish and simplistic. "You of all people should realize everyone has secrets. Some of us hide them better than others. How well have you buried yours?"

"Is that a threat, Derby?" Ronald said, trying the name game.

"It's more of a challenge. The thing about me is, if left alone, I don't bother anyone, but you all can't seem to leave me alone."

"So you *are* threatening me, a federal agent?"

"Digging up information isn't a crime, or that's my opinion since your agents have me under a microscope every second. Because you do, you're my best alibi." She smiled at both men and heard Hayden's team hit the field for the start of the game. "Privacy is something I crave but seldom get, so we'll see how you like a dissection of your life. I'm sure a guy like you is squeaky, but sometimes it takes something really freaky to keep that façade up."

"You don't know what you're talking about." Ronald's eyes opened wider and his fingers straightened.

"Sure I do," she said, louder than was necessary. "What is it, Ronald, a woman in tall leather spike heels with a whip to spank that bad little boy who loves to come out and play? Or perhaps a big bear of a man who does the same thing but with a butt plug the size of my fist? Come on, you don't have to be ashamed of that, and I'm certainly not going to judge."

"Shut up, you don't know what you're talking about," he repeated.

She'd taken her shot and hit a major nerve. "Now I do," she said softly as she turned and walked away, confident Katlin and Muriel would keep her safe from ambush. "All I have to do is find out what makes you sweat and show the world what kind of guy has a badge these days."

❖

"Stay alert out there and make sure you call for backup if you see anything out of the ordinary," Detective Sept Savoie said to the group she was working with. New Orleans was at times a dangerous place outside the heavily traveled tourist spots, but the last few hours were beyond the norm. That dark side that seemed to thrive like cockroaches in the dilapidated sections of the city where the junkies and the dealers lived had delivered the deadliest day any cop she'd worked with could remember.

"You think crime will go down after this?" one of the guys asked.

"I know you all aren't going to feel real warm and fuzzy about this, but it's too big to ignore. The houses that were blown were bad enough, but this latest development has even the governor's office involved. We need some leads, and the faster they come in, the better."

"We have nothing so far?" Fiona asked.

The new detective with the flaming red hair was still an enigma to Sept; even though Fiona was new to town, she had a crush on one of their infamous citizens. During their limited exchanges, she had managed to bring up Cain Casey every time. At first Sept had attributed the interest to the fact that Fiona was living with Agent Shelby Phillips, but now she wasn't so sure that's where the obsession was coming from—and she did see it as obsession.

"The first thing we have to nail down is whose real estate got smoked last night, and the only thing we have is a rumor that it was remnants of Rodolfo Luis's places. That I got from our friendly FBI office, since they're working with us on this." She'd received that tidbit from Joe Simmons, but he was leaving something out, in her opinion, so she was going to find whatever was missing on her own. "Right now I want you to treat that like a rumor. Don't tell me anything unless you can back it up with evidence."

"You want me to ride with you?" Fiona asked.

"Sure. My partner's out with the flu, so I can show you around some." *And I can find out what makes you tick*, she thought as they headed out to the car.

Her last stop was going to be the one place where she felt like she could trust the information she got. If Cain said it, she'd believe it. The only problem sometimes was getting her to start talking. They went to each location first and interviewed witnesses, but nothing shook loose.

"Where are we headed?" Fiona asked, her concentration like it had been so far, on the buildings outside, as if she was trying to memorize each route.

"Let's go by Cain's and see what she's got on this. Her opinion is usually golden if, and only if, she's in the mood to share it."

"Cain Casey talks to you?" Suddenly Fiona didn't seem too interested in the scenery.

"She and I graduated together, so she tolerates my visits better than most in our profession. Her father and mine were good friends."

"Were? Did your dad finally figure out they're nothing but killers?"

"Actually, Dalton Casey was gunned down by Big Gino Bracato, with the help of one of Cain's cousins who turned on the family. At least that was the word on the street when it happened. Dalton's case is still open and unresolved. My father was a pallbearer at his funeral and was proud to do it. Cain isn't exactly clean, but you're going to find out quickly there's way worse than her."

"I know my friend Shelby doesn't blame her for her parents, but I can't shake the feeling she had something to do with it. It's going to take a lot to make me believe she isn't anything but a thug that deserves to be caged."

"Cain tells me all the time that the devil has a lot of faces, some more evil than others, so I had to accept it or not. I could try to destroy them all or not, but there'd be a price I might not want to pay."

"You sound like my mother now. Why wouldn't you want to crush them all?"

"Because you have a tendency to end up destroying yourself before you come even close to accomplishing that." She stopped at the gate to Cain's house and waved to the guard, who waved back and let her in. "If you don't believe me, ask your friend Shelby about Barney Kyle and Anthony Curtis."

"Sounds like you really like her."

"Cain is my friend, but I'm not stupid to who and what Cain is. No one is all bad all the time. Keep that in mind."

Hayden and Hannah were outside playing with a man Sept now knew was Emma's father, Ross. She found it humorous that her mother had come over here on numerous occasions to share gardening tips with Ross, who'd been a farmer and dairyman by trade, but the Southern climate had thrown him a bit. For a guy who owned a very large share of a profitable casino, he liked to work with his hands. That tidbit she'd keep to herself, since Fiona was already prejudiced against the Caseys.

"Good afternoon, Sept," Ross said as the children jogged over to give her a hug. If they were recording this from the van across the street, her FBI file was probably as thick as Cain's.

"Hey, guys, how was baseball today?" she asked, since Hayden still had his dirty jersey on with a pair of shorts. "How'd you do?"

"Hayden won," Hannah said loudly, "and he hit the ball over the fence." Her sisterly pride was hard to miss.

"Congratulations, buddy," she said as she hugged him again. "Is your mom around? We need to talk to her."

"You people have harassed her enough today," Hayden said, uncharacteristically cold and disrespectful.

"Hayden, your mom can take care of herself, so apologize," Ross said.

"No worries." Sept waved him off. "Somebody came by already?"

"Two guys hassled her at my game," Hayden said, his face on Fiona, who was again in studying mode, looking around as if there'd be a test on the layout of the grounds when they left.

"Wasn't us. You know if I show up at a game, and I've made a few, I'm there to watch you play, not give your mom a hard time. Gray suits might not play by my rules."

"Sorry," he said, and pointed toward the yard. "Mom's out back. We were barbecuing and needed some stuff from Grandpa's garden."

Cain and Emma sat by the pool watching Merrick move around in the water with a woman Sept didn't recognize. Some of the kitchen staff stood around a large pit watching whatever was cooking. "Got enough for everyone?" she asked to announce their arrival.

"Sure. Since the city pays you peanuts, you need to bum a meal whenever the opportunity presents itself. Can I get you a beer, or do you take that on-duty thing seriously?" Cain asked.

"We're not some damn joke," Fiona said sharply.

"You're in the Big Easy now, Detective O'Brannigan. You need to learn to relax or the stress will eat you alive." Cain laughed in a way that warned her that she'd needle Fiona until she resembled a rabid dog. "I'm surprised you haven't explained a few things to her, Sept."

"I got a whole bunch of dead people that the mayor and governor want to know what happened to, so Fiona's education hasn't been a priority." She followed Cain to a more private table by the deep end of the pool after she'd kissed Emma's cheek in greeting. "I'm sure you've heard about that, right?"

"The Feds have already come sniffing around like I hold the key to the big chest full of secrets."

"You mean you don't?" she asked, and laughed.

"It sounds drug-related, and you know better than that."

"When it comes to you, sure, so I drove all this way for some great barbecue and that's all?"

"It's always about something, old friend, and I'm no cop, but has anyone considered Hector Delarosa? The guy lives like two blocks from here, and *Time* magazine named him an up-and-comer in the drug trade." Cain accepted a beer from Carmen, and Sept smiled and shook her head when Carmen pointed to the bottle, offering her one.

"No national publication has ever said I'm an up-and-comer in the bar business, but if you'd like, I'll ask around and see what pops up."

"You're not bullshitting me, are you? I find it hard to believe something like this happened and you don't know what, why, and who." From past experience, Cain was only this quiet when her fingers were sticky from involvement. This time it didn't make sense to her, only because it was drug-related.

"Give me a few days. There really isn't a good jungle-drum system working in New Orleans, and if there is, I don't have a subscription."

"We'll get out of here and let you eat in peace, then." Sept stood and sighed when Fiona stayed put. She understood Fiona's relationship with Shelby, but from what she'd heard outside of her talks with Fiona, Shelby didn't really blame Cain for her parents.

"Unless you're running down some more pressing leads, stay. Maybe if your friend here sees me eat and realizes that my kids aren't afraid they're on the menu, she'll figure out I'm not the monster she's built up in her mind."

"You're going to ruin Shelby's life, and you probably think it's a joke. I know your kind. You're no different than the scum that run the gangs in LA. Their whole life revolves around killing, crime, and totally disregarding human decency," Fiona said in one long breath. Sept watched Cain's face as Fiona threw the verbal daggers at her and came close to defending Cain, but figured she wouldn't appreciate it.

Throughout their friendship she'd always had a hard time reconciling herself to Cain's bad side. Judging by her father's stories of Dalton and his reign as the head of the Casey Clan, Cain had actually civilized the business. Long gone were the days of having to fight for territory and business opportunities by leaving a trail of dead bodies of those who'd gone against Dalton, yesterday being the exception.

Cain was forceful when she needed to be, but she reminded Sept of her uncle's old dog that mostly sat on his porch. The old boy was docile until her uncle said *seek*. Then whoever had stepped in his yard and didn't belong there would be missing a limb. It would be a sad day in her life when Cain no longer considered her a safe visitor because now, even though they were on different sides of the law, Cain would kill to keep her safe. There'd be no question or hesitation about it, of that she was as sure as her mother's love.

"If you're going to stay here, you've got to learn to decide who your real enemies are, Detective," Cain said calmly. She glanced at Sept and continued when Sept simply shrugged. "In a shark tank some know what their prey is and some will take a swipe at whatever swims by. If you don't know the difference, then don't swim in these waters. Because even the shark that knows its food source can be provoked into biting the head off an annoyance."

"Am I supposed to fall at your feet and beg you for mercy now? If you're waiting for that, you can fuck off."

"If you want to act and sound like an uneducated piece of trash, get out of my house, and don't make the mistake of coming back. No one comes in here and talks like that in front of my wife and children." Cain stood and leaned over so she trapped Fiona in her seat. "Good luck solving anything with this one," she said to Sept, and laughed.

"Mom, you hungry?" Hannah screamed from close by. The sight of Hannah's table manners always made Sept smile. She wasn't at all a picky eater and crammed food down her mouth with the same gusto she played and lived her life with.

"Set two more places. Aunt Sept and her friend are staying." Cain hadn't gotten too upset yet, but if Fiona rebuffed the hug Hannah was offering, she'd beat the idiot no matter the consequences.

"Thank you, Hannah," Fiona said, brushing Hannah's hair back gently.

Hannah was an affectionate child, even with people Cain felt didn't deserve it. "Go ahead and pick a seat, and try to control your language," Cain said to Fiona, but sat back down at the table with Sept. When left alone she looked at her old friend and raised one eyebrow. "What are you hearing about this?"

"The Feds told us it was the Luis family, so you popped up on their radar. Before you slug me, I'm not here to lay blame, but I do want your help." Sept ran her hand through her hair and appeared frustrated. "I know how you feel about the Luis family, but this isn't a good thing. What happened throws everything and everyone out of balance. You and I both know that's when innocent people get hurt."

"I know that, and that it makes your job harder, but I can't build up enough sympathy for those scumbags or the police. After what that animal did to Emma, no one but you gave a damn. Not Shelby, not her fellow agents, and not her boss Annabel. Not one of them came here and said anything about the fact that a member of their team helped Juan snatch Emma and shoot Merrick in the head." Cain's chest tightened and her stomach clenched like it had the first time she'd seen that car and realized Emma was gone. "That threw our lives out of balance, and no one gave a damn."

"So you aren't going to try too hard because of who's involved?"

"It's you who's asking, so I'll do my best," she said sincerely, but felt a twinge of guilt because she wasn't done with the Luis family. The police would have to accept that this tempest would rage and then die away just as fast. "You know I'll do anything to make you look good, even though you bring obnoxious people to my house."

"Kiss my ass," Sept said, and laughed harder when Emma put her arms around her neck from behind.

"You'll have to go through me for that." Emma kissed Sept's cheek. "What's with your friend?"

"She's rooming with Shelby, so I'm sure she's gotten a complete rundown on your partner. Give me some time and I'll set her straight."

"Good luck, but life's too short to deal with ignorant people." Emma glanced toward Fiona when Hannah took her hand because they were the only two people at the table.

"She's not leaving, so you might have to deal with her."

Fiona looked back at her, and the softness disappeared from her face as if she'd come with a predisposed hatred toward her. The coldness in her chest wasn't a warning she'd ignore this time. This woman meant her harm; she could sense it in every part of herself.

"We'll see."

CHAPTER TEN

S he needs you to come back, Shelby," Joe said as he twirled his beer bottle on Shelby's kitchen counter.

Usually she would've been embarrassed by the mess in her home, but she couldn't work herself up to that or any other sentiment. The more days that passed after her parents' death, the more numb she became. Her sounding boards and safety nets were gone, and she couldn't accept it. The sadness and despair were like wet, heavy sand piled on her. She couldn't concentrate on work with an outside investigator.

"I have a few more months of leave and I'm planning to take them," she said before she poured more Irish whiskey into her glass. The bite at the back of her throat helped her achieve total oblivion, something she'd done more than once since she'd come home. It was another type of numbness, one she desired more than bleakness.

"This isn't about guilting you into anything, but this guy Ronald wants to scatter us to the winds. Even if you don't, I need you to pretend to give a shit about that." Joe took a swig of beer then pointed the neck of the bottle at her. "You've got to realize your name keeps showing up in every report. All those visits to Cain's won't be forgiven forever."

"You think I give a shit about that? What I do give a shit about is getting the same satisfaction Cain did when her family was on the firing line. I want to put a bullet into the head of every piece of shit responsible for the death of my parents, and once I have, I'll think about worrying over some asshole who wants to knock us all down to make himself look good." She rushed through the words and watched him wince as if she'd physically hit him. Joe was such a by-the-book guy, or at least he'd been like that when he'd first come to town. In their time together he'd learned to bend the rules as far as it took to not actually break them. That was the only way to deal with Cain and get anywhere.

"Do me a favor and don't say that to anyone else. I know it's been hard, but do you think your father would want you to be locked up forever to avenge him? I met both of them, so don't think you can bullshit me about that."

"If I do something, whatever it is, I'm going to do it on my own. Cain won't help me, and I'm not about to involve you guys."

"Annabel really needs our help to survive this."

"Annabel is the most politically savvy person I know, so don't worry about her either. I've never met Chapman, but I've heard of him. If she puts up enough of a fight, he'll move on to easier hunting grounds."

Joe poured the rest of his drink out and threw the bottle away. She could tell he was disgusted with her, and months before, that too would've bothered her, but not now. "You still have to have a life, Shelby, so take the time you need, but try to find one that doesn't put you in a small cell for the rest of it. Call me if you need anything."

She watched him go and closed her eyes when the door shut behind him. She wanted to call him back and make things right, but she was exhausted, and that's what almost made her ignore the knock a few minutes later. Tears filled her eyes when she saw Muriel there with her hands in her pockets. Besides her parents, Muriel was the other person in her life she missed to the point of pain.

"I'm here for the rest of my stuff. It should only take a few minutes," Muriel said, so distant she might as well have sent a flunky to do it.

"Sure, but if you have time, I'd like to talk to you."

"There's nothing we need to discuss in this lifetime. You played me for an idiot once, but twice isn't going to happen. I'm all talked out."

"You can't honestly think I completely prostituted myself for my job, can you?" It shouldn't have mattered what Muriel's opinion of her was, but she didn't want to leave this hanging between them. "I'll admit I abused the situation, but I love you."

"Really?" Muriel said with a smile and opened her arms to her. Shelby blamed the alcohol for making her take a step forward. "God, you must really think I'm an idiot," Muriel said, putting her hands up to stop her.

"Muriel, I can't fake what I had with you."

"You know what, donate the clothes I left here. I don't even want them because I can't trust you didn't do something to them." Muriel turned to leave and glared at Shelby when she stepped in front of her and grabbed her by the biceps. This was no longer the woman who'd held her because she'd cared about her happiness or worried when she was hurting. "And *do not* come by the house or Cain's place again. If you're begging for me to truly humiliate you the way you did me, I'll give it to you in spades."

The door slamming shook something loose in her, and her thinking suddenly cleared. Tomorrow she'd do what she needed to get her life back, like Joe had mentioned, and she realized how to do it.

"Mom and Dad, I hope you know I'm ready to let go. You were the ones who told me sometimes it takes sacrifice to get what you want. I'm ready to make mine."

Gustavo sat in the bar close to his hotel and nursed his fifth tequila. He'd slammed the first four back to try to erase his meeting with *Jerome* and what he'd said about his mother. He thought the name a curse now and said it with contempt in his thoughts. That Jerome was comfortable enough to treat him so disrespectfully, and none of his men questioned it, meant Gracelia had tossed him aside to get ahead. And she'd tossed him aside for an ex-FBI agent.

He'd actually called her Gracelia per her request until he was about ten and she'd finally taken an interest in him. Before that, she'd left him with Rodolfo and Carlos's mother, who'd treated him no different than her own son. As a boy he'd enjoyed school and the way people treated him because of who his uncle was. There'd never been a day of teasing, bullying, or discomfort because Carlos had been there to protect him. That'd been Rodolfo's excuse for sending some kitchen help's son to private school.

At home Carlos had been free to play with him, but that'd changed when his real mother had come home that first time—for about six months instead of her usual weekend—that all ended in a screaming match with Rodolfo when he'd insisted she be a better mother to her son. His uncle had been the only person who'd confronted her about that, and the only one who'd cared what happened to Gustavo when he woke from regular nightmares as a boy.

At ten, Gracelia came home for good and pulled Gustavo away from Carlos and his mother in the afternoons. That's when she started sharing secrets with him about his real father, Armando Ortega, the great love of her life. His own life became a fractured pane of glass after that, and he'd never been able to put the pieces back together, especially since he'd killed Rodolfo.

To a young boy, a secret about the mythical hero his mother had described was too good not to share with his friends. The day after he'd told the boys he and Carlos played with at school, the ridicule began. Armando, they'd said, was an illiterate yardman who liked to drink and beat on women when he wasn't relegated to raking leaves because he wasn't bright enough to do anything else.

Gustavo raised his fists for the first time in his life when the other boys from wealthy families had joked that his mother was stupid enough, or desperate enough for dick, to fall for such a loser. She'd thrown herself at his feet every chance she got, no matter who was around to see it. In essence they'd said it made him a pathetic loser by default.

Carlos had saved him again from more than the bloody nose and split lip he'd gotten, but he never talked about his family after that. The only time he'd indulged in that pleasure was when he was alone with Gracelia and she told him about their future. That Shangri-La was a place where both of them would be together after they'd stolen everything from Rodolfo for killing Armando.

"You okay?" Chico asked after he'd shot this drink down his throat suddenly like the others and motioned for the bartender again.

"Go back to the room and leave me the hell alone." He wasn't done with his reminiscing. "Are you deaf? Get out of here and leave me. Didn't you hear the big boss? I'm being sent home."

"You're my boss, so I answer to no one else. If you want me to wait in the room, I'll wait, but I'd rather sit in the corner to make sure you're okay." Chico pushed his drink closer to him and sat back, as if to not get in his way. "You're an important man. If not, Señora Ortega would have sent you here alone."

"Señora Ortega can fuck herself, or she can get *Jerome* to do it," he said, laughing. Leave it to his mother to find a name she and everyone who worked for them couldn't pronounce. "Do whatever you want, but get out of my sight." He wasn't in the mood for all those eyes on him as he retraced the steps that'd gotten him here.

The more Gracelia had stayed with them, the more time she'd given him, and it'd made him feel special. He was her son and the anointed one because Armando's blood pumped through his heart. She'd told him to go out with Rodolfo and learn from him, but to never forget where his loyalties were. Rodolfo had killed his father in the most humiliating way he could think of, and eventually that would have to be avenged.

When he closed his eyes at night now, he thought back to Rodolfo's soft melodious voice and how often he'd called him *mi hijo*. His son, not by birth, but they had the same blood. Rodolfo seldom screamed about anything, and he'd been so patient with him as he learned the business. After all, it'd be his one day. His responsibility was to care for the people who worked for them and uphold the name he'd given him. Luis was, in Rodolfo's mind, a gift he'd spent a life building up to mean something. It was a name he'd given his son Carlos only hours before his death, and one he'd rejected to follow his mother.

The bitch who'd given birth to Gustavo, saddled him with the name of a bastard who loved the bottle more than both of them, and passed him over the first chance she got. She'd been smart enough to wait until he'd killed Rodolfo, because he knew Jerome had refused any part of it. He'd killed Rodolfo for her and it'd been for nothing. Gracelia was simply the weak woman who'd spread her legs for Armando and now Jerome, and neither of them were gods. Everyone in between was enough to make her nothing but a common whore.

He stumbled toward the bathroom and locked himself inside. It'd take the guys watching him a while to figure he'd made it out the window and to the room he'd gotten with no one else's knowledge. It took a block to find an empty cab and a few minutes to make it to the Piquant. It was the last place he'd stayed with Rodolfo, and the place where he'd start over.

"Hello."

Carlos's voice made two tears drop down his cheeks. If only he could find a way to go back and change what he'd done. He'd grown to hate Carlos because of his loyalty to Rodolfo, and he still did, only his hate was mixed with envy now. Even with both their fathers dead, Carlos had a sense of himself and knew who he was, while Gustavo had killed the only man who could've pointed him in that direction.

"Hello," Carlos repeated.

"Hello, cousin," he said, and only then realized that was actually true. They were family, the only family he had other than Gracelia.

"What do you want?" Carlos's voice took on a hard edge.

"I want you to know I pulled the trigger. I killed him and he cried like a woman, begging me not to." The intake of breath meant he'd hit Carlos where it counted. "You should've learned a long time ago that I'll always win, and I'll always get what I want. You were his son, yet he was grooming me to replace him. I'm the Luis heir. That's what Rodolfo wanted."

"Then come here and take it from me, because my name's on the deed to the house and the bank accounts, and the men work for me now. If you try, though, make sure you bring that bitch that bore you so you can die together for what you've done to my father. Before I kill you, I'll share with you what he left in writing about Gracelia and your father." Carlos laughed, which made Gustavo grip the telephone tight. "Armando with the big dick your mother couldn't keep out of her mouth, and she was so desperate for him she even spread her legs for him in front of the other yard staff. The woman had no shame then and she has none now."

"Rodolfo loved me, you son of a bitch. Your mother was no different when it came to my uncle."

"The true son of a bitch here is you, and don't think he left you out of the letters he wrote. You were his one true regret, though he had many of those, so you should be proud to have climbed to the top of that list. Of everything he wished he could've done differently, he knew killing you at birth would have done himself and the world a favor. With a father like Armando, it was a foregone conclusion that you'd grow up to be an idiot with delusions of importance. My father knew that when Gracelia spat you out, but he chose his heart over what needed to be done."

"Shut up," Gustavo said, his head spinning and his stomach rebelling from all the alcohol. It'd been a few days since his last real meal and bath, but he cared more about finishing with Cain and Emma than taking care of himself. "You didn't know how Rodolfo felt about me. He loved me."

"What, the brat who wanted for nothing but could never be satisfied? You mean the little boy who threw tantrums and acted like the world should fall at his tiny feet because he deserved it? To my father you were nothing but a spoiled boy who grew to be a spoiled little man who'd never amount to anything because you couldn't even get the pool boy to respect you, much less the men who worked for him."

"I'm more of a man than you."

"Then tell me the last time you had a woman you didn't have to buy or have someone help you tie up. You've chased Cain Casey and her woman so long with no luck that maybe you should take their example."

"What the hell are you talking about?" The call had been a mistake, but he couldn't hang up now without proving Carlos right about his immaturity.

"Find a big dick like your mother did to suck on and have it shoved up your ass. If you do that, then maybe, like the Caseys, you'll be happy after you admit you like your own sex, and you can stop pretending to be the stud you brag to everyone about."

Gustavo dropped the phone into the cradle and pinched the bridge of his nose. The sweat he'd just noticed was adding to the sour odor he couldn't get out of his nostrils. He needed a shower, a meal, and a long stretch of sleep.

His teak box was his greatest need, but it was still back in the shithole hotel room they'd been renting. Thank God he'd thought ahead and its twin sat on the desk.

"None of you will escape me," he said after he'd snorted a large amount into both nostrils. He whispered the threat again and gladly welcomed sleep.

❖

"What's the matter?" Judice asked. Fiona had been an hour late, and her mood had been horrible since she'd opened the door to her room.

"Nothing," Fiona said, but to Judice she resembled the pouty five-year-old who'd been denied a cookie.

"Nothing doesn't usually make you rude toward your mother." She finished putting on her lipstick and went to sit next to Fiona so she could take her hand. No matter how Fiona acted, she'd always brought her an abundance of joy. Having Fiona had filled the emptiness in her heart that no man had come close to accomplishing. "Let it out. It'll make you feel better."

"I rode out with Sept Savoie this afternoon, and it started out okay since someone like her can teach me the rules here. Her dad is the chief of detectives, so she has to be twice as good as everyone else. That's something I'm familiar with." Fiona seemed relaxed, and if she'd been talking to anyone but Judice they'd have missed the small signs, like the fast words that meant she was enraged about something.

"Did she say something you didn't like?"

"We ended our day at Cain Casey's home, and Sept insisted on staying to eat. Don't worry. I still want to go out with you because being there killed my appetite." Fiona rubbed the ring she'd given her years before with her thumb. "The way Sept treated that idiot was enough to make me sick."

"You think Sept is dirty?" Maybe this was a way in, and she could use it to get Fiona out of here.

"They went to school together and became friends even though Casey's an animal. They have this give-and-take relationship, and

Sept tries to get information out of her. I'm sure she's got to give up something, and I bet it's a lot more than she's getting out of that deal."

"If it's not Sept, then was Casey rude to you?"

"No, but I don't think it's a good idea to start hanging out with the type of people I've sworn to try to bring down."

Fiona sighed, and Judice figured whatever the problem was now simmered at the surface. "If you're this upset, either Sept is turning a blind eye to what Casey's doing because she knows what Casey's doing, or Casey wasn't happy she brought you there and treated you accordingly," Judice said.

"It's not that at all," Fiona said, the harshness gone. "She did seem so normal, and I didn't expect that. She has a partner and a family that loves her. I could see that in how they interacted with her. I've wanted that all my life, but I've never had time. Besides, no man has ever been interested after a first date when I tell them a little about myself. Who knew a badge could be so emasculating?"

"I'm sorry," Judice said, since Fiona's childhood had been missing so much she hadn't been able to provide. She'd actually been terrified to try.

"Is this the daddy lecture again?"

It hadn't been as hard as she'd thought to explain how it'd always be only the two of them. No man was in the wings waiting to swoop in and take her dead father's place. "It was a discussion, not a lecture, but I wasn't the best example when it came to relationships."

"Stop apologizing. You've been doing it since I turned eighteen, and it's not necessary. I know my sperm donor's dead, but eventually I'd like you to trust me enough and get comfortable enough to tell me something about him." Fiona stood and took her hand again, ready to leave. "Nothing you say is going to upset me. I'm too curious to get mad."

"Sometimes the truth about something is better than picking it to death. This isn't one of your cases, so let it lie."

"What choice do I have?"

"Would you rather skip this?" she asked, and Fiona squeezed her fingers. "I can appreciate you had a bad day, so don't feel like you have to entertain me."

"The day did suck, but I want to have dinner with you. I promise that we'll take a trip to the past, but only when you're ready. I won't ask about it again."

"Thank you." Judice had enough money to retire to a comfortable life, but she was on the brink of losing her greatest treasure—Fiona. "I love you."

She hoped it was enough.

❖

"We lose him," Chico said into his phone as he pulled the hair on the top of his head. The heat had a lot to do with the amount of sweat pouring off him, but he was sure it had more to do with the fear of what would happen to him for this screwup.

"Where?"

"He go to the bathroom and go to window. He gone before we know to look." The silence from the other end unnerved him, and a tingle started from the small of his back to his neck. "We look for him, and I call you back when we find him."

"Don't take too long. Do we understand each other?"

"*Sí*, I mean, yes, I understand." He hung up and pressed the phone to his forehead. He'd been allowed to come from Mexico with strict instructions to watch Gustavo and keep him from doing anything stupid.

That's a job he understood since this wasn't the first crew he'd worked for. Before this he'd kept the son of one of drug lord Caesar Kalina's enforcers in line. The kid had thought since his father killed people for Kalina, he could do anything he wanted. From what Chico had seen, the first and perhaps second generation of each family knew what it took to stay on top. Once they became successful, though, they indulged their children to the point of raising whiners who had a fit if they didn't get their way.

Gustavo was there for something, but sitting outside film shoots and sulking near the same locations were typical of an overindulged heir who'd get everyone killed the moment he took over. The problem was, he didn't know anyone named Katsura.

The American Gracelia had brought in was doing his best to pull the organization together, but the men hadn't been quick to warm to him. It'd been only after Jerome had made the tough calls on more than one occasion that they understood the danger of going against him. No crew was successful unless its men had a real fear of failure. If they didn't realize their actions had consequences, there'd be total chaos.

Chico tapped his phone against his head a few more times and thought of the chaos getting ready to rain down on him because he'd fucking lost some loser who was important to Gracelia Ortega and her enforcer.

"He's not back at the room," one of his men said.

"Put somebody at each of the places he loves going every day. This guy's crazy enough to go back because he can't help himself. If they see him, call me, and if we lose him again I don't think I have to tell you what'll happen to us."

"Who is this stupid shit?"

"I don't know," Chico said as he started to walk toward Bourbon Street. Maybe Gustavo had a sudden urge to see naked women. "But Jerome wants him found, so we're going to find him."

Hopefully somewhere along the line he'd figure out who this guy was, which would give him more leverage with Jerome. Or he could just kill the guy and maybe Jerome would assign him to something more important than babysitting duty.

❖

"Cain, you have a call in your office," Carmen said as Cain started up the stairs with Emma. "I tell them you were retiring, but he say it's important."

"Thanks, Carmen, I'll take it." She kissed Emma and placed the hand she was holding on the rail. "Keep the bed warm for me and I'll be right up."

"Don't take long," Emma said.

She nodded with a smile and wondered what else had happened that couldn't be put off until morning. It certainly didn't have anything to do with her, since she was waiting for the first part of her plan to flush Gracelia out to work. Once she had Juan's mother in her sights, Juan would be easier to find.

"Hello," she said into the phone as she stared out the window at the guard on the wall. The man was smoking a cigarette but still appeared vigilant.

"Señora Casey," a man said, and she zeroed in on the voice, trying to figure out who it was.

"Yes, who is this?"

"It's Carlos…Carlos Luis now. My father Rodolfo wanted me to take his name."

"I remember you," she said, really confused now. When she'd had to break the news about Rodolfo being found covered in ants and honey with a lot of bullets in his chest and head, she thought she'd seen the last of him. "Can I do something for you?"

"I have information for you," he said, his English much more practiced since the last time they'd spoken.

"Okay," she said, and stretched the word out.

"Juan Luis, he is in New Orleans."

The strength went out of her legs and she dropped into her chair. She'd looked forward to hearing that statement, yet feared it. She couldn't eliminate Juan if she couldn't find him, but having him in the same city as Emma and their family made her want to throw up.

"Señora, you hear me?"

"I heard you," she said, and took a deep breath to try to calm the nausea. "Please call me Cain." It took effort and concentration to stay seated, since she wanted to get up and run out and find Juan. She opened and closed her fingers to try to release the anxiety. "How do you know Juan's here?"

"He call me, and my men don't get all we need, but we know New Orleans is where he call from."

Juan had killed his father, a man who'd admitted who he was to Carlos right before his death, so it confused her as to why he'd share this information with her. She and Rodolfo weren't friends. "Can I ask why he called you? Rodolfo left everything to you, and Juan went with his mother, from what I hear, so he didn't have any reason to."

"He call to tell how he kill my father, and how he cry before he is killed. Juan say my father has no, how you say, honor," Carlos said with the Spanish pronunciation.

"Carlos, may I call you Carlos?"

"*Sí*, please."

"Your father and I weren't friends, only because he allowed Juan to disrespect my partner Emma and didn't do anything about it."

"He try to find Juan for you."

"He did, but only after he'd realized what kind of man Juan had turned into. But let me finish my thoughts before you think I'm only condemning Rodolfo. We weren't friends, but after he asked to do business with me and I refused, Rodolfo left me alone. He was not my friend, but he wasn't my enemy, and I believe he was a man of honor." It was as if she had a swarm of wasps under her skin, but she couldn't rush this. Carlos knew something and she didn't want to scare him away.

"Thank you, and I don't agree with my father when he do nothing the first time Juan see your Señora Casey and he talk to her like she a whore. He no do nothing and Juan go more brave to try again."

"We talked about what happened the last time he saw Emma and what almost happened. If I'd found him maybe your father would still be alive."

"I call you because if he come back, your family no is safe."

"Thank you, and I owe you a favor for telling me," she said, and decided not to worry about what Carlos might want in return.

"I want one thing from you," Carlos said softly. "Give me Gracelia."

He understood her need to kill Juan, to watch the life drain out of him, taking with it the threat to the safety of her wife. "Not Juan?"

"When I come to America we talk some more, but Gracelia must pay for what she done. Juan was *estúpido* as a boy and he never have to grow into a strong man. My father knew this. Gracelia took that weak in him and talk, talk, talk to Juan until he hate my father. Juan kill him, but I blame Gracelia, so he belong to you, but she must give me what I lose in blood."

"Is she here as well?"

"Only Juan call me, but I think you look and you wait for me if you find her."

"Call me when you arrive and I'll tell you anything I find out." She hung up and leaned forward to rest her head in her hands.

"Do you know the most scared I've ever been in my entire life?" she heard Emma ask before she felt her smaller hands on her back.

"No, but it's moments like this that should prove to you why, no matter what happened between us, I could never hate you. You left for something similar, and I never could punish you for it." She felt like a child afraid of monsters hidden in the closet. Control and ferocity had always been her strong traits, but Juan had gotten in and made her remember what had happened to her sister Marie. If she wasn't careful she'd look away for a second, and Emma and her children would be gone.

"The night I decided to fly back here after what I'd done to you in Wisconsin was the longest, most fearful of my life." Emma pushed her back and sat in her lap. "You were so angry when you'd left, and I thought you'd never see me, much less forgive me. That you'd cut me out was my biggest fear. I couldn't imagine a life without you."

"Maybe you should've," she said, to indulge her self-pity.

"Don't ever say that to me again." Emma framed Cain's face with her hands and roughly made her look at her. "You are mine, and you are what gives my life meaning. Do not *ever* disrespect that or me again."

"You're too forgiving," she said, and smiled even though it took effort. "That animal took you. He took you and strapped you to a table. If I hadn't gotten there—" She couldn't finish and she couldn't stop the tears that fell. No amount of time or cajoling on Emma's part would ever make her forgive herself for that mistake.

"You did get there, my love. That's why what happened wasn't the most horrific day of my life. You promised me in the beginning that there'd never be a moment you wouldn't be there for me, loving me, protecting me, and making my dreams come true." Emma kissed her and wiped her face with her fingertips. "Those promises gave me faith in the future we'd have together."

"I love you, but I failed to keep you whole. Twice I've let you down, and it kills me to admit it."

"Listen to me, okay? The world doesn't guarantee there'll be no bad days. What makes them tolerable for me is having you hold my hand, no matter how bad the storm." Emma kissed her again, only longer and with more passion. "The other thing that makes them easier is that you're going to find whatever threat is out there and eliminate it. I have no doubt that you'll kill this guy for touching what belongs only to you. I am yours as much as you are mine. Remember that you found him once, so find him again and end this."

Cain nodded and stayed silent until her emotions were back under wraps. "Sorry I freaked out on you like that."

"Do you know what an honor it is that you trust me enough to see you without your armor? To the rest of the world you're Cain Casey, but here when it's just us, I simply want you to be you. I want your strength, your tears, and your fears. I'll never judge you for showing me your vulnerable side because then I know you're sharing all of yourself with me. Believe me, I'll only love you more for it."

"Can you also promise me you'll be careful? He's here, lass, and if something happens to you my life would empty."

"Sabana may not like it, but we're going to be best friends."

"She won't be a problem, believe me," she said as the helplessness that had momentarily taken over subsided. "So he's here finally. I don't know how long or where, but finding him in New Orleans is going to be easier than chasing him through Mexico."

"Do you want to postpone our ceremony? Considering this, I won't mind waiting."

"No," she said forcefully. "Juan Luis has already taken up more of my time than he deserves, and I'm tired of making sacrifices for this fool."

"Good." Emma rested her head on Cain's shoulder. "What else did Carlos want?"

"He wants Gracelia, and if I find her first, I'm going to gift-wrap her and deliver her with a bow in her hair."

CHAPTER ELEVEN

W hat's going on?" Dallas asked as she got dressed to the sound of the phone ringing constantly.

Remi had taken every call, giving orders to each caller. "You got in late last night, so I didn't get to tell you that Cain called and said Juan Luis was back in town."

Dallas paused with her lips puckered, ready for the lipstick in her hand. "Is Emma okay? That guy has a lot in common with Johnny."

Dallas hardly mentioned her late father anymore, something that might've worried Remi had both Dallas and Kristen not gone through counseling about their ordeal. She'd wanted both sisters to talk to a professional so they wouldn't have any ghouls hiding in their thoughts waiting to ambush them in the future.

"Juan is going to meet the same fate as Johnny, so you don't have to worry about it. The excess calls I'm getting are Cain putting extra security in place, so don't be alarmed when you have more than Emile with you. I'm not taking any chances."

"What about Kristen?" Dallas stepped into her arms and gazed up at her.

"I took care of that this morning while you were in the shower. She left for school with a group of people dressed so they won't stick out, or as much as a heavily armed group of people can manage not to be noticed on Tulane's campus."

"I love how you take care of us," Dallas said before she kissed her. This was a rare day off for Dallas, and Remi was enjoying watching her get ready as she went through her morning routine in her underwear. Once the film had started production, Dallas usually threw on a pair of baggy pants and a T-shirt to make it easier for the makeup crew. "I guess this means I don't get you all to myself today."

"My first stop is Cain and Emma's, so you can tag along if you want. Cain and I have a little business, but then you and I have an appointment with the Realtor this afternoon, so you get me for the rest of the day. I think you might like the location this time."

"Am I being too picky?" Dallas ran her hand up Remi's thigh, pushing her breasts harder into her chest.

"You can be as picky as you want. We're not buying this for an investment. It's going to be our home." She reached behind Dallas and unhooked the navy-blue silk bra she had on. It wasn't until Dallas that she'd ever thought one woman would and could be enough to keep her interest and earn her trust, but she had that and more now. Dallas knew every aspect of her life and had never given her a reason to be wary that she was in danger of exposure. Since they'd moved in together, they'd both enjoyed the permanence that came from sharing their lives and waking up together.

"Do you have a few minutes?" Dallas took a step back so she could strip off her bra and panties.

Seeing Dallas like this, Remi understood the hundreds of proposals that came via her fan club. Her reps removed the scary ones, but every other person who posted to the page wanted a date with this beautiful woman. They saw the gorgeous façade, but to her, Dallas was so much more.

"I don't look stupid all of a sudden, do I?" she asked, a growing throb between her legs.

"I know we just got up, but I'd really like to go back to bed." Dallas started on the buttons of her shirt. "This shoot started this week, and I'm already looking forward to every hour I have off because I miss you."

Remi helped Dallas onto the bed and simply admired her as she took everything off. "The feeling is mutual." Usually she enjoyed the time they took with each other, but the world had been banging on her door all morning, so this would have to be fast. She kissed Dallas once before she spread her legs and put her mouth on her.

Dallas was sweet tasting, hard, and from the way her hips bucked forward, she was ready for her. Her cell rang, muted some by the fact it was in her pants pocket, and she ignored it to slide her fingers into Dallas's drenched sex.

"That feels so good," Dallas said as she gazed down at her through half-opened eyes. To Remi she appeared lush, sexy, and in need. The phone stopped but started again after a second pause. "Do you need to get that?"

"They can wait," she said, then put her mouth back. Dallas moved her hips faster and harder when Remi increased the pressure, and she smiled around the hard clit when Dallas shut her eyes as if she had to concentrate on the pleasure.

"Oh," Dallas said, sounding out of breath as she clutched the sheets. Her legs fell farther apart, and she dug her heels into the mattress so she could thrust her hips to meet Remi's fingers.

She sped up her strokes as Dallas's movements became more erratic and the walls of her sex squeezed her fingers. In their time together she'd tried to learn everything about what made Dallas feel good and turned her on, so she was sure her orgasm was close. "Don't stop, baby," Dallas said, and her hips froze. Remi stilled her fingers as well, and when Dallas groaned, she moved them out and slammed them back in until Dallas told her to stop.

The orgasm had made Dallas's skin slightly flushed, and she held the top of Remi's head so she'd keep her tongue flat against her clit. "I love you so much," Dallas said when the intensity had passed.

She moved up to hold her and cursed the damn phone. "I love you, and I wish these windows opened. If they did I'd toss that damned thing out," Remi said, and Dallas laughed.

"Answer it and tell the guys you have to turn it off for a little while." Dallas got off the bed and dug it out for her.

"Remi," she said, when she saw it was her personal guard Simon. It took effort to pay attention when Dallas got back on the bed, straddled her at the waist, and cupped her own breasts and held them up to her lips.

"I know you're not ready yet, but an agent's downstairs demanding to see you."

"One of the regular guys?" she asked as Dallas made room for her hand between her legs. If she didn't have to leave the bedroom soon, it would be one of those mornings when Dallas couldn't get enough.

"It's someone named Special Agent Ronald Chapman. He's with another agent, Brent Cehan."

Dallas put a lot of her weight on her knees so she could rub herself on Remi's fingers. The sight of that along with the way her head was thrown back was enough to make Remi come. "Did he say what he wanted, since he doesn't have an appointment?"

"He said it's urgent and whatever he had to say wasn't any of my business."

"Well, tell him he can either wait or come back when I'm dressed. And not to be rude, but I'm hanging up now." She threw the phone on the floor and put her other hand on Dallas's ass to pull her forward a bit so she could reach her nipple. When she sucked it in, it felt rock hard against her tongue. "For future reference, that's a really good way to get me off the phone in a hurry."

"All this time away from you makes me incredibly horny," Dallas said, grinding her hips slowly now and getting her entire hand wet. "How about you? Does time away from me make you crave me?"

"Crave is a good word for it," she said, then hissed when Dallas pinched her nipple. "You want to come again like this or do you want me to lick you dry?"

"Are you sure you can wait? I don't want to be selfish." Dallas moved a little faster when Remi sucked on the other nipple. She always looked forward to touching Dallas, but in the mornings when the room was lit with sunshine, it was even better because she could see every part of Dallas's body and every expression on her face. This position allowed her to really sit back and enjoy watching Dallas take what she wanted at her own speed.

"Take your time, *querida*." She squeezed Dallas's ass and added more pressure between her legs, the hard clit amazingly prominent under her fingers. She ran her tongue along Dallas's neck and opened her mouth when Dallas kissed her.

"Put your fingers back in and fuck me." She groaned at the command but did as Dallas asked. Dallas squeezed her shoulders as she came again and dropped her head against her when she was done. "You're such a giver, baby," she said, and laughed. "You deserve a reward."

Dallas moved back until she was kneeling between her legs and ran her finger from Remi's throat to the hairline of her groin. The slow, soft touch drove her desire to the point of excruciating.

Before she had to beg, Dallas moved her finger lower. "Lie down for me," Dallas said, brushing her hair behind her shoulders to get it out of the way. It was like her first time making love, and Remi felt uncontrolled and inexperienced when Dallas put her tongue under her clit since she knew she wouldn't last too long.

Dallas stopped and she came close to screaming. "What?" she said, and had to clear her throat because her voice was so raspy.

"I've got you all to myself," Dallas said, and kissed across her abdomen, "and you're ignoring the phone." She moved her lips to the inside of her thigh. "You're crazy if you're getting off that fast." Dallas licked the back of Remi's knee.

"I thought you wanted to reward me for my giving ways."

Dallas's smile made her take a deep breath and hope the torture wouldn't last too long. Her expression must've telegraphed her wish, because Dallas started again. As much as she'd learned about Dallas, she had returned the favor and sucked down hard enough to make Remi come. It was aggravating to have it so fast, but after a few more strokes she was done.

"When's your next day off?" She was so relaxed her muscles felt like oatmeal.

"For a couple of days and this weekend, all we have to do is run lines. If you want we can have everyone come here." Dallas kissed her navel as she moved back to the head of the bed.

"Call Vincent's place and have food sent over. Once the crew finishes work and dinner, we're going to bed." She carried Dallas into the bathroom and waited for her to adjust the water.

"It's a date."

They took a quick shower, and she had to pick another suit since the clothes she'd first put on were a wrinkled pile on the floor. As Dallas started on her makeup again, Remi called Simon back and found that Ronald Chapman was still waiting.

"Let me go see what this guy wants and we'll leave when I'm done."

Maria was in the kitchen making fresh coffee, a new luxury Remi was fast getting used to. For years she'd lived on her own and had eaten out often, so she'd been comfortable fending for herself except for the cleaning women her mother sent over twice a week. When Dallas and Kristen moved in they'd decided to hire someone full-time. Once they'd started asking around, Cain's longtime housekeeper and house manager recommended her cousin Maria. She was young but had learned and understood from Carmen that the most important part of her job was discretion.

"Good morning," Maria said as she poured her a cup. "Simon say she will be up in a few minutes with your guest."

"*Gracias,*" she said before moving to the dining table. She didn't want breakfast, but she didn't want to invite these guys too far into their home. The elevator opened and the two men followed Simon out but stopped a few feet in.

Her first impression was that both of them had an overabundance of arrogance, so she predicted a session of strong-arming. "Are you here to critique my decorating or to talk to me?"

The African American man in the front stared at her long enough and with an expression that made her guess he found her lacking.

Without a word he walked over and sat close to her and folded his hands in front of him on the table.

"Do you often keep federal agents waiting an hour?"

"It's not often the FBI shows up at my house without an appointment and demanding things of my staff. I don't treat anyone well who does that."

"I'm Special Agent Chapman, I don't need an appointment, and usually innocent people fall over themselves to not only see me, but to help and answer questions. It's called cooperation, which goes a long way in getting me to leave." Chapman spoke in a tone that encouraged her to react in a way that'd land her in handcuffs.

"What do you want, Agent Chapman? I actually make appointments to see people and I don't want to appear guilty, so I'm curious why you're here."

Ronald's laugh made him appear cruel. "You're as funny as your friend Cain. Both of you have had free rein in this town too long, and because you have, you're under the misguided belief that we don't know what's on the second floor of the Pescador Club." His delivery was smooth, and by the way he studied her, she knew he was waiting to see her reaction to his statements. "Or that we don't know what kind of liquor you pour there from Casey's supplies. I'm here to clear all that out of town."

"So the agents, like the guy you're with, have been incompetent up to now, and that's the only reason my business has thrived?" She laughed and didn't have to glance to the elevator to know Emile stood there.

The mountain of a man had spent years at her father's side but had enjoyed his new responsibilities protecting Dallas. At first he'd been there for Dallas's scumbag manager, then her father, but when given a choice even with no real threat against Dallas, he'd chosen to stay.

"I run a film studio, Agent, and I pay my taxes. My family does own a slew of businesses, and there's nothing irregular about them. If you'd like to try to prove otherwise, good luck. We've been under your microscope for years with nothing to show for it. Maybe you should all accept there's nothing to find."

"You've never been under my microscope, Ms. Jatibon, so we'll see, but that's not why I'm here," Ronald said, and almost as if he couldn't help himself, he turned around to find Emile closer than he appeared comfortable with. "We're investigating the large number of murders caused by three explosions, and numerous drive-by shootings. Would you have any information on that?"

"No, but even I read the paper, so you should try asking some of the gangs responsible for the city's drug trade. In the news that's who they reported the victims worked for."

"Did you and Casey rehearse your lines?"

"Only one person memorizes lines for a living in the house, and it isn't me," she said. The other guy leered in the direction of the bedroom, and she doubted he was admiring the artwork when she heard the click of Dallas's heels on the marble floor. "If that's all, I really need to get going."

"Ms. Montgomery, I'm a huge fan," Ronald said, his demeanor softening dramatically. "Are you and Ms. Jatibon friends? Such unsavory characters can't be a wise career move."

"Is that pertinent to the investigation?" Remi smiled at Dallas to reassure her.

"Like I said, I'm a fan." Ronald stood and smoothed down his jacket. "I'll be seeing you soon."

"Jackass," Emile said when the elevator doors closed. "We brought the car around if you're ready."

"Simon, did this Chapman guy visit my father or brother today?" Remi asked, still confused by the strange visit. Either Ronald was a real amateur at interrogation, or this had been about something else.

"No, he really was waiting for more than an hour downstairs, which made me believe he was some intern for the coming summer, but that's not what he said."

"Have the areas they were in swept, but tell me before you remove anything. Call my father and tell him to up the security at the club until I figure the guy out."

"You got it," Emile said.

"Not yet, but I'll catch on eventually," she said as a joke. The morning had been puzzling from the moment she'd left the bedroom.

"It's no fun when life gets complicated, huh?" Dallas asked.

"I can handle complicated better than bizarre. Him coming here and sitting around that long to toss out recycled threats is strange."

"Maybe it was like an audition," Dallas said as she put some items into her purse.

"How so?"

"He mentioned Cain and cleaning up the city, so if he visited her too, maybe he's searching for a partner to get all that done. Or you can forget that I love to ramble on about stuff I'm not sure of."

"In a strange way that makes sense," she said, and viewed Ronald more as a joke. "He's going to try to flip one of us. That's when he'll find he can't lift that kind of weight."

❖

Everyone was quiet around the breakfast table, as if taking their cues from Cain and Emma. No one had commented on the extra security that prowled the grounds and had already been assigned to every family member.

"Do you remember what Mama and I told you?" Cain asked Hannah as she held her on her lap after the little girl had finished her meal.

"Don't talk to strangers, and that means anybody I don't know."

"That's right, and you have to be careful about anyone who offers you an ice cream or maybe candy. It might look good, but we have the best candy and stuff here." She kept the conversation as light as she could and still get her point across to not scare Hannah. "Today we'll do something fun after I'm finished with work, so go play outside if you want."

"What's going on, Mom?" Hayden asked when Hannah left the room.

"Juan Luis is back, so I need you to not take any stupid chances. You stick to Mook and the other guys I've got with him."

"I'll be okay."

"I mean it, Hayden. If I'm worried about you ditching out with your friends, I can't concentrate on taking care of this problem."

"You don't have to worry, Mom. I'll be good, then you'll owe me one," Hayden said as he kissed first Emma, then Cain's cheek before he left.

"What's your game plan for today?" Emma asked.

"I need to see Jasper again. Depending on how that goes, we might have to have another dinner at Vincent's. This time we might need the other families to finish this."

"I thought you weren't fond of owing people favors."

"If Gracelia and Juan establish themselves here on the same scale Rodolfo had planned, it's in all our best interests to take out the trash. This business has too much of an allure not to thrive here, but having a major player with such a grudge against us isn't healthy."

Emma nodded and stretched forward to hold her hands. "Do you want me to do anything?"

"For now I need you to be pregnant and happy." She stood and leaned over so she could kiss Emma on the lips.

"I got that covered since I should get my own show at the aquarium soon."

Dallas and Remi arrived at the end of their conversation, and Dallas asked, "You don't think you're fat, do you? Get that notion out of your head, because you look fantastic."

Remi nodded, and after all their greetings were done, Cain and Remi headed for the office.

"What do you need us to do?" Remi asked when they were locked in the office with Simon, Lou, and Katlin.

"I might need a few people to cover some territory from here to Biloxi. We had enough for my plan for Gracelia, but I had no choice but to recall them after Carlos called me."

"Your first phase got some attention, but from the wrong people," Remi said, but laughed, which made Cain believe she wasn't upset. "Ronald Chapman and some other asshole he didn't introduce came to see me this morning."

"I got the same visit, but it was at Hayden's game. Ronald and his mentally challenged sidekick, Brent Cehan, I'm sure meant to embarrass me with the location."

"You know the other agent?"

"Brent's who put Cain in the hospital," Lou said in anger. "Asshole needs to be taken care of."

"He will be," she said, "but that's not my priority right now."

"So far no one from the list you gave me has come through any airport close to us. If Juan got here, he's got fresh papers with a name we don't know yet." Remi placed a thick file on the corner of her desk. "This is everyone through Houston, Dallas, and Miami in the last two weeks. If you get a clue, we have a starting point to verify from."

"Thanks." It was good to know Remi was as thorough as she was and hadn't minded the task she'd delegated her. "You up for a visit with Jasper?"

"Sure. We're looking at real estate this afternoon, but I can reschedule if need be."

"Snake Eyes is settling down?" She slapped Remi on the back. "Congratulations, my friend. Now I understand what all the wailing around town is all about. All those beautiful women are heartbroken they've missed their chance."

"Laugh it up, Casey. The same thing happened to you when Emma got here and wrapped you around her pinkie."

They told their partners they were going out, and she noticed the way Remi's eyes lingered on Emma. She wasn't concerned that it was inappropriate, but maybe Remi was ready for more than simply a new house.

"How's your mom with Dallas and Kristen?" she asked as they rolled through the front gate.

"After Emma talked to her, she's better, but it'll take her some more time to figure out that Dallas isn't on the FBI's payroll."

"Once you hand her that first grandbaby, she'll be fine."

"That might have to wait until Dallas's career is more set and she's ready for that kind of commitment."

"Buddy, Dallas might be waiting on you, so don't hesitate to ask all those questions she wants to hear."

Jasper's men pulled their barricades aside as soon as they drove up, and she wondered what the FBI and DEA were thinking about the large number of vehicles inside Jasper's little kingdom. She knew most of the old-timers, but Jasper had added plenty of new people, each looking scarier than the next.

Jasper ran his business at the main house at the center of the cul-de-sac, and that's where he stood and waited for them. "He might erect a statue of you out here since you've helped out so much in the last few days," Remi said.

"I'm not done." Katlin unbuttoned her jacket for easy access to the guns she had holstered under it. Then she opened the door and Cain got out. Katlin always reminded her of a walking armory, but it did give her a sense of safety.

"Jasper," Remi said as she embraced him. "You're looking healthy."

"Nothing but the good life will do that," he said as he put his arms around Cain. "And my life is good because I've got great friends."

Inside, Vincent and Vinny Carlotti sat at the long old cypress table Fats had supposedly won in a card game from a former chief of police. Maude sat in the corner, as if she didn't want to get in the way but still wanted to listen in. Cain walked over and kissed her cheek and pulled on the strap of her apron. Maude might've been better known for her cooking skills, but Cain had always thought her guidance had gotten Fats and Jasper through the tough times.

"Have you come to an agreement?" she asked when she sat at the head of the table across from Jasper.

"Right now it's a sixty-forty split only because we've had to take over where Jasper's missing people because of all the shit that's gone down. Once he's back up to full strength we'll readjust the numbers," Vinny said.

"You okay with that?" she asked, her eyes on Jasper.

"Still making more than before, so I got no beef."

"How about you?" she asked Vincent, out of respect.

"Kid's making it work and it's good business. I'm happy, but I don't think I'm here for you to ask me that. Am I right?"

"We're going to have to deal with the eight-hundred-pound gorilla in the room, and if left unchecked Hector Delarosa will take over every street corner from San Francisco to Miami, and all points north of there." They all looked at her with an expression that summed up her feelings. Life was extremely unfair at times, but you had no choice but to acknowledge it and move on. "I'm sure we all agree that none of us wants to answer to Hector in our city."

"That fucker's got a lot of muscle, though," Vincent said, and no one said anything even though he had no stake here.

"Alone, none of us has a chance, so it's important for both of you to establish everywhere that's suddenly become clear of competition."

She glanced at Maude and smiled when she blew her a kiss. She didn't have any reason to admit here, or anywhere, that she'd given the order to kill a large number of Gracelia's people, but Maude didn't need someone to spell it out for her.

"We're moving quick to do that, but not so fast we're not vetting people along the way. I want this to work, but not at the expense of letting a cop on my payroll," Vinny said. He was quieter than his father but just as savvy, so she trusted him as much as she did Remi.

"You got any clue as to what sections might be opening up soon?" Jasper asked. "You've always been good at predictions."

"Gracelia is about to run into some problems in Mississippi and Alabama. With the heat on Florida, she wisely located everything outside the state. They're shipping it in but ready for sale, no cutting or packaging there."

"Good to know," Vinny said, and glanced at Jasper.

"What kinda timeline we looking at?" Jasper asked.

"If you want in, have a group in place by tomorrow this time. I'd lay low so no one blames me for the Luis misfortune, but it'll keep someone from beating you to the territory." Her phone buzzed and it was Emma. "Excuse me a moment.

"Yes, lass, is something wrong?"

"Hector and Marisol Delarosa are here for coffee," Emma said flatly. "They're extremely disappointed you're not home, but they don't want to leave even though I told them you'd be a while."

"Could you put him on the phone if he's nearby?"

"Gladly," Emma said, and she heard her footsteps for a short walk.

"Hector," she said, but he immediately started talking.

"Cain, are you arriving soon? We have much to talk about."

"If you want to see me anytime soon, get the hell out of my house right now. You're upsetting my partner and our guest, and neither of them can help you, so there's no reason to sit and wait."

"No need for rudeness," Hector said, and he sounded suddenly angry.

"Rude is showing up and staying without calling first. My wife is expecting, and if you stress her, believe me I'll make you pay."

"Careful of such threatening words between friends." If she could've reached through the phone she would've strangled him. "Tomorrow, then, at my home."

"Tomorrow at a coffee shop of my choosing. There's no need for privacy since you've got my answer about us doing business together."

"Sometimes it doesn't pay to be nice, girl," Jasper said when she hung up. "I know he's a shit, but I get a craving to gut that oily bastard every time I see him. That is, if you were talking to Delarosa."

"Guy's like Juan. Neither of them know when to take no for an answer," she said, and cracked the bones in her neck to release the tension. "We'll get to Hector eventually, but one thing at a time."

"So back to the bad luck ready to fall like rain for the Luis organization," Jasper said.

"There's a possibility what happened here will happen in the locations I mentioned, and if it does, I'd consider it a favor if you'd take care of any problem that slips through the smoldering cracks."

"You need anything else?" Vinny asked.

"A little peace, and even if it means I have to kill every bastard who tries to keep it from me, so be it."

❖

"I'm sorry for the bad traveling conditions, señora, but anything too fancy stands out."

Gracelia and Eduardo were the coyote's only customers that late afternoon, but the guy's stench was making her carsick. The rut-filled road and dust coming through the open windows weren't helping, but they were at least getting close to the border, she hoped. She didn't think she could take much more of this.

"You're used to better than this, huh?" The guy persisted in making conversation, and that only accentuated the three teeth left in his entire mouth.

"You think this woman is interested in you?" Eduardo asked. He was the only one of her men she'd been comfortable bringing.

"This is my truck, and if I leave you out here the scorpions are going to eat for months on your hide."

"One more word and I'll put a bullet in your head and drive the rest of the way myself. At least the smell will be better."

Gracelia closed her eyes and rubbed her palms along her jeans. "Shut up, the both of you." When she slowly opened her eyes she noticed more trees along the side of the dirt road they were on. Vegetation only grew like that close to the river.

"Here," the man said, and got out and scrambled down the embankment. "The river's not too deep, and the car is waiting a mile down the road on the other side."

She handed him a wad of bills and took her boots off. This was humiliating, but it was important to get back into the States without any fanfare. Jerome had called her about the attack against them and the disappearance of her son. It galled her to admit Jerome had been right about Gustavo and his obsessions. The need to possess Emma Casey and kill Cain Casey had emptied her son's head. He'd put that over their business, and when she found him she'd have to tell him how disappointed she was.

"This way," Eduardo said as he helped her out of the water to the muddy bank on the other side. No sooner had he said it than a car pulled up with the headlights off.

Gracelia froze, a cold sensation coming over at the thought of dying beside the Rio Grande like so many who'd tried to sneak into the U.S. like this. The back door opened and she gasped, while Eduardo drew his weapon.

"Gracelia, come on," Jerome said as he stepped out.

"Thank God," she said as she stepped into his arms. "You scared me almost to death."

"I didn't want you walking along the road by yourself with all that's going on."

"Fuck you," Eduardo said, his gun at his side but still in his hand, obviously understanding Jerome's insult as to how safe she was with him.

"Eduardo, put it away," Pablo said in Spanish, his gun extended and pointed at her guard's head.

"We have no time for this. Save it for those who really want to hurt us, and, Eduardo, if you speak to Jerome like that again, you're out," Gracelia said. Eduardo glared at all of them but eventually gave a quick nod.

"You can ride in the next car, Eduardo," Jerome said as he held her, not caring she was getting him all wet. In the backseat Jerome kissed her and squeezed her breasts as if he couldn't wait to touch her.

Not that she cared about Pablo and the driver in the front, but neither man moved his eyes from the road, giving them as much privacy as possible. If they were quiet they could fuck, but she wanted to wait until she was clean and dry.

"We're driving the entire way?" she asked as she massaged his hardening cock through his jeans. The sensation of the material against her hand reminded her of the times she'd been with Armando. He'd loved for her to get him off in his pants while they were out in public. No man since had possessed her so completely, which was one of the reasons she still mourned him.

"We're an hour from the helicopter I hired to take us to Houston. From there we'll take a flight into New Orleans in the morning." Jerome returned the favor and rubbed the seam between her legs. It felt so good she forgot about her damp clothes. "We've got a lot to do to find the fuckers who did this. If we don't hit back and hit back hard, we're going to lose all respect on the streets."

"You really do want to help me, don't you?"

"It's no time to doubt me," he said as he unzipped his jeans and took his dick out. "I already told you, if you want I'll leave you, and guys like Eduardo can help you get what you want."

"Don't act like a hurt little boy," she said as she lowered her head. That Jerome had taken the time to come get her had made its impression.

He cared about her, which was another reminder of Armando. When she became too clingy he'd put her back in her place like a real man should, but when she'd distance herself he'd come chasing her. Rodolfo had tried to cheapen all those times he'd said he couldn't live without her with his snide commentary. Her brother always pointed out that Armando's professions of love always came when he was broke, and once she'd dumped cash on him he degraded her again.

"I'm not acting childish. I'm tired of having idiots like that think they can treat me like shit and get away with it."

She swirled her tongue around the tip of his penis and smiled when he thrust his hips toward her mouth. "Because you are with me, I'll make it up to you. Compared to you, Eduardo means nothing to me."

That was all the talking they did until the car stopped at a remote heliport full of equipment spray-painted with oilfield names. Their pilot barely looked at them as she, Jerome, and Pablo boarded. The thick envelope of money Jerome had given him was obviously too distracting.

"Tomorrow we start again right, sweetheart?" she asked Jerome as they lifted off.

"Something like that," Jerome said, and the same coldness she'd experienced when the car stopped near them came over her again. Perhaps there was something to fear in Jerome, but she did her best to put it aside. She needed him more than she was afraid of his betrayal.

CHAPTER TWELVE

A re you guys busy this afternoon?" Remi asked on the way back to Cain's.

"I promised the kids something fun, but if you and Dallas are up for it, we'll treat you to dinner. It might be noisier than you're used to, but it'll be good training for your future."

"Between me and you, I never factored in the possibility of children in my life." Remi put her hand on her knee and patted it a few times, as if glad to have her to talk to. "When you found Emma, I was jealous for so long, especially after Hayden was born. When Emma was duped into leaving, I saw your pain, but now I know you're happier than you've ever been because you had faith in her."

"My mother always said anything worth having is worth any pain or work you have to put into it." She took Remi's hand and turned it over so she could see her palm. "Everything I have, you've got right here if you'd stop being such a...Well, there's no good word for it that doesn't get me punched in the mouth." She laughed.

"What are you talking about?"

"Make the commitment Dallas is waiting for. Don't keep giving her the impression that what you feel isn't permanent. You do that and everything you've ever desired is in the palm of your hand."

"Did she tell Emma that?"

Cain laughed again. "You think Emma's going to share that with me? If Dallas said anything to her, she'd keep it in confidence even from me." She put her hand behind Remi's neck and squeezed. "I'm saying this because I've been there, and Emma was skittish until she walked into my house and found half the closet empty for her. When it became *our* home, that was the day she thought she wasn't another notch."

"That's what I was going to ask you. Do y'all want to go with us to the house I want to show Dallas? Emma's her best friend, so I figured she'd love sharing this process with her."

When they got home it didn't take much to convince the girls and Hayden to go along with Remi and Dallas. The drive didn't take long since the house Remi was interested in was four buildings down. It'd been years since Cain had stepped foot in the place she'd sold when her mother died, and she stopped and stared into the formal living room to see the changes the new owners had made. The family that had bought her parents' home was moving to Houston for a job change, according to what Remi said on the way over, and Remi held everyone back when they entered.

There was an open house for the weekend, so she ignored the people crowding into the place. So far everything was different, but as she touched the wood of the stair handrail, memories of her childhood seemed to be trapped in the grain of the wood. Her parents' voices echoed through her mind, and she ached from missing them.

"If it freaks you out I'll forget it," Remi said from behind her.

"I couldn't think of anyone my parents would approve of raising a family here more than you, so show it to her."

Hannah ran ahead of them, with Dino chasing her. They toured the first floors and moved as a group upstairs to see the bedrooms, and again Hannah moved ahead, but Cain didn't worry until she bumped into the legs of a man on the top step. He put his hand on Hannah's shoulder to keep her from falling back.

"Sorry, mister," Hannah said as Cain scooped her up and held her. Even though she was a step down she was still taller than the guy Hannah had collided with.

"It's okay," the man said in a low voice, too low in her opinion. It was like he was purposely trying to distort his voice. "She is beautiful." The guy had his hands behind his back and rocked on his heels.

Cain detected a slight accent in the four short words, but he kept his answers too short for her to get a real sense. The man sounded Hispanic, but he didn't really appear Hispanic, and she didn't recognize him. His face, though, struck her as familiar.

"Thank you." She settled Hannah in her arms and turned to put her body between them. It was a precaution, simply an overreaction since the man was wearing a pair of expensive-appearing linen pants and a golf shirt. He wasn't armed unless his piece was strapped to his leg, and he made no move to get closer.

"House shopping today?" she asked, her eyes locked with his.

"Yes," he said. His hand came up to comb back his longish dark-blond, highlighted hair. "You?"

"Hon, are we going up?" Emma asked, and the man briefly glanced at her.

"Sure, excuse us." The man moved aside and let them by. He descended after that and she watched him go, still suspicious. When he reached the bottom he looked at her, smiled, and left. She stood there until he was out of her sight and didn't move until Hayden asked which of the six bedrooms used to be hers.

"Let me show you," she said, but her feet were nailed to the floor. The man wasn't someone she knew, but her gut told her she should've. She closed her eyes and concentrated, trying to remember where she'd seen him, trying to put him in the right location for a clue, but frustratingly nothing came to her.

She walked through the rest of the house, but the carefreeness of the day strangely left her. It felt so important to jog her memory of where she'd known the guy. The only things that took her mind off the intruders on her day were Hannah running from room to room, with Dino now sticking to her, and Hayden asking her questions about everything. He'd always been curious about his grandparents, so she was happy he'd at least grow up with Ross. Her own grandparents had given her so much in a relationship so different than she'd had with her parents.

"What do you think?" Remi asked Dallas while they stood in the master bedroom.

"I love it." When Dallas answered, Remi smiled at the Realtor who'd been discreetly following them. After a short phone conversation, the others working the sale started clearing the other potential buyers out.

"Ms. Jatibon," the woman said, handing over an open folder and a pen. "Congratulations. I hope you have many happy years here." Once Remi had signed in all the appropriate places, the woman gave her a large ring of keys.

"Just like that?" Dallas asked.

"I can't wait for what comes next with you, so just like that."

Cain laughed and put her arm around Emma. She didn't really know the couple who'd bought the house from her well, but they'd had two small children. That's what had swayed her to sell the home where her parents had raised her and her siblings, once most of her family was dead. After all that death, not only did she and Emma deserve a fresh start, but these walls deserved the sound of children echoing through them. Now she wished the same for the new owners and the children she hoped they'd be blessed with.

"Let's go celebrate." She waved her family down to give Remi and Dallas a moment alone.

"Are you okay?" Emma asked as she ran her fingers along the spot on the wall where Dalton's picture had hung.

"I don't have bouts of intuition very often, but that guy on the stairs—well, it was strange."

"Strange how?"

"Have you ever met someone and wanted to punch them in the face before introducing yourself?" She decided to let it go for now. Sometimes that's what it took for something to come into focus.

"A few people, actually, but I leave the beatings to you since it's murder on my nails."

"You can help me redecorate, right?" Dallas asked Emma when she came down glued to Remi and cutting their talk short.

"Down to the pillowcases," Emma said, laughing. "Remi will have to work overtime to keep up with us."

"You're in trouble now," Cain said, having made up her mind to forget about everything until she had time to sit and really dwell on it.

❖

Gustavo sat in his car and beat on the steering wheel with his palms. It might've been his mother's idea to reconstruct his face, but it was his brilliance that had gotten him so close to Cain without her recognizing him. Everyone had made fun of him for following Remi, but through her, he'd gotten what he was after all along—a way in that would get him close to Cain.

"Fuck you, Jerome," he said. He laughed and stopped beating the wheel before he bruised himself. The next time he saw his mother's lover he was going to kill him, preferably in front of their men. That was the fastest way to show everyone who was really in charge and who had the brains to run the organization.

He kept laughing at the thought of Cain's expression. The gears in her head were almost visible as they spun, trying to place him, and even though it'd worried him for a moment, she'd failed. So much for that sharp mind everyone, including his uncle Rodolfo, was in awe of. No one wanted to believe him, but Cain was like every other woman he'd known—a stupid bitch with the audacity to tell men what to do.

He'd gotten close, but now he had to close the deal. He hadn't figured out how to get that done yet, but he wanted to take his time. If he failed again he'd have to give up his dream of having Emma before killing her, then Cain. But if he couldn't grab her, he'd settle for just killing them both.

The people in the house came out in a crowd, except the ones he was there to see. He slid down in the seat and decided to wait. As he stared at the door his thoughts drifted back to meeting with Jerome and the reaction of his men. Chico, Pablo, and the others were also dead for listening to the asshole he'd introduced to them. Jerome was one more thing Rodolfo had been right about, and he should've taken his uncle's advice and left Jerome to the dogs.

Only one guy had appeared uncomfortable with Jerome's display, and he had to fish a minute for the man's name. He searched the contacts in the phone his mother had given him. "Are you alone?" he asked when Andre Reyes answered.

"Who is this?"

"It's Gustavo, and if you warn anyone I'm calling you—you're a dead man. Are you alone?"

"I'm driving around looking for you, so yeah. Where are you, anyway?"

"Stop somewhere and I'll give you an address. Tell me when you're ready." It took Andre a while to say he'd pulled over. Now that Rodolfo wasn't in charge, it was hard to know who to trust, but he had no choice. He couldn't finish this by himself.

"What time do you want me there?" Andre asked once he'd repeated the information three times.

"Tonight at ten, and you'd better not bring anyone else. This place is crowded, so I'll know if you do."

"You sure you don't want some of the others?"

"Forget it, and don't ask for mercy one day soon."

"Wait," Andre said, loud enough so he heard him as he took the phone from his ear. "I'll come, and you have my word I'll come alone."

The door opened and Cain came out first. He disconnected and watched them through the gate. Emma, flanked by her children, made him ill, as did the sight of the swell of her stomach. It seemed almost satanic.

"I'll still fuck you so you can see how you wasted your life," he said as he looked at Emma. "And instead of killing Cain, maybe I'll let her live. That way the memory of the moment I hand her that baby after I cut it out of you will be burned into her brain. She'll never know another minute of peace."

❖

"Who is this whack job?" Special Agent Claire Lansing said as she took eyes off her targets to check out the man hiding in the car a hundred feet down the street.

"No one that pops to mind," Lionel Jones said. They were on their own today, since their team leader Joe Simmons had his meeting with Ronald Chapman set for the last half of the day. "I ran him through face recognition, and nothing."

"He's either really upset that Remi scooped him on the house or something else is going on." She took several pictures of the man but he was muttering into his phone, so even with their equipment at the highest level, they couldn't hear what he was saying. "You think we need to give Joe a call?"

He glanced at his watch and shook his head. "Give him three more hours, since he wanted to finish with Chapman today."

"So this is where Casey was raised?"

"I read through her file a few times and saw pictures of her as a baby being held by her father in that front yard. They didn't even have a gate and fence back then."

"Maybe they didn't need it."

Lionel pointed their microphones back toward Cain and her group, even if it was a waste of time, and recorded what was being said. "True, Dalton Casey wasn't the kind of man I would've messed with, but in those shots he was a father with his new baby. The way she talks about him makes me believe she idolized him. I never knew my father."

"Think about who he raised. Dalton wasn't all that wonderful, so your mother did a much better job."

Lionel's phone rang and he stared at it until it almost went to voice mail. He didn't understand why Chapman would be calling him if he was supposed to be meeting with Joe. "Yes, sir, can I help you?"

"Where are you?"

"We're with the Casey family, and we're covering Remi Jatibon for the team usually assigned to her. Remi is buying real estate, and it'd be too crowded out here for more than one surveillance crew. They're moving from one location to another, so can I do something for you?"

"I need you and Lansing to come in for your interviews."

"Sir, did you not understand me? Agent Lansing and I are the *only* two people out here. Joe and Shelby, when she comes back, are our investigators, but Claire and I are the surveillance experts." Claire stared at him with a disbelieving expression. "Are you sure you'd like us to desert our post?"

"This isn't the army, Jones. Get in here. I want to wrap this up as soon as possible so I can turn in our report. In my opinion you all could be holding hands with these people and they'd still be able to kill half the population of New Orleans without you figuring it out."

"Yes, sir." He hung up and got out of the van. It was bad enough for Cain to humiliate him. His employer didn't need to pile it on.

Claire followed him out and shut the panel door behind her. The move made him comfortable since he didn't trust that someone like Chapman wasn't spying on them. "He really wants us to pull out?"

"Wants to talk to us now. For some reason it can't wait until we can call in another team." He kicked at the ground in frustration. "For someone who bitches about how we do stuff, he's going out of his way to make it worse."

"I agree with you, but let's go. Remember what Joe said. We'll win this by cooperating."

He glanced across the street and noticed Cain looking back at them. It was as if she had a talent for seeing them at their lowest points and took notes of their weaknesses. No matter how covert their operation, Cain picked out the detail like she had a locator chip embedded in each of their asses. He slowly moved to the driver's side and got in, not caring that she watched him.

"What's Chapman's game, do you think?" Claire asked.

"He wants what we've worked hard for," he said as he turned toward downtown. "He wants the credit for toppling Cain."

"Cain might have something to say about that."

❖

The van's turn signal came on, and they actually turned and left an eerie silence. Cain wasn't used to it. She studied the street in both directions, surprised at their absence. When Lionel, who she'd talked to a few times, and his partner left, no one took their place.

"What the hell?" Instead of a relief, her sense of self-preservation for her family and herself kicked in. The last time the Feds had stopped watching, they'd beat her without fear of consequence.

"I think they left only one," Lou said, and moved between her and the street. "Car to the right, green sedan."

The only thing she could see of the person who sat crouched in the seat was their forehead and hair. She might not have recognized him in the house, but if he thought she'd forgotten him that quickly, he wasn't a great addition to Shelby's old team.

"Short guy with blond highlights?"

"That's him, but from the outfit, he's not carrying. Not the norm, for sure," Lou said.

"Have Sabana and Dion cut him off, then tell them to meet us at the restaurant. I want everyone visible tonight, from Carmen up to me."

Lou gave quick orders while she didn't move. "Same man from inside?" Remi asked.

When the two of them stood together, the man straightened as if he suddenly didn't care they were watching him. He started his car, backed up, and followed the same path as the van.

"With this new guy, something might shake loose, since they're confusing the hell out of me. Perhaps that's their new strategy—to get us to drop our guard and say something stupid," Remi said, but didn't appear to be worried. "I'll tell my people to stay sharp."

They headed to the restaurant, and Cain set her phone to buzz in her pocket at eight that night. Soon, Joe and Claire walked in and stood at the host stand. They were being overt so she'd see them. It'd be up to her, though, to move to talk to them, since they didn't come any farther.

"Do you two have a reservation?" she asked, after Emma urged her to go over. Emma wanted them out of the place so Dallas and Remi could enjoy the night without these people breathing down on their fun. "If you don't, and need my help getting one, let me know. My friend is celebrating her good fortune, so I'm feeling generous."

"You know damn well why we're here," Claire said. "And I'm not in the mood to listen to your bullshit."

"It only took you a few years to completely lose your cool, Agent," she said with a smile that might provoke Claire to slap her. "What's wrong?"

"We need a few minutes, Cain," Joe said, pointing to the foyer of the place she'd picked. "We've got four more explosions, one more here and now in Mississippi and Alabama. While the authorities were responding to them, we had another slew of shootings. When someone orders something this big, including sixty murders, it's not going to go unanswered."

"By you or the people this happened to?" she asked, curious as to his answer. Compared to the others in his team, Joe was the one, along with Claire, she had the least experience with. He seemed to stick to the background of her life and only came out for the big events that, like he'd said, couldn't be ignored.

"I've never had someone retaliate against me, so I'll go with the police and federal agencies who'll investigate this. I don't have a choice but to come and talk to you, since the DEA had more information on the places that were hit than the local agents did when it happened here." She followed him outside and motioned for Katlin and Lou to stay inside. "The places belonged to Rodolfo once upon a time, and now, I'm sure, to whoever took over for him. With this blow, whoever that is might be out of business, or they're pissed and getting ready to come out shooting blind at anything and everything that moves," Joe said.

"I'm not sure how I can help you. I didn't know Rodolfo well, and all I knew about his death was what was reported on the news."

"You were the one who told the cops who he was when they found him in the condition he was in."

"I knew that because of a story I'd heard about what he'd done to his nephew Juan's biological father. When you hear something like that you figure it's part of that family's folklore, because it's hard to fathom someone doing that to another human being."

"So you don't have a hand in this," Joe said, and sounded tired.

"You might need a nap if you think I'm answering that. Rodolfo approached me to do business, and I refused because I thought the guy was a bastard and his business is selling crap on the streets that'll eventually get into the hands of children. He didn't deserve what happened to him, but I haven't really thought about it since. I do believe his death has left a vacuum in the power structure and someone's trying to fill it."

"Someone like your buddies Jasper Luke and Vinny Carlotti? You've been pretty friendly with them lately."

"Don't mistake a visit to friends with knowing anything about me, Agent Simmons. Whatever you can prove about me, drugs and being involved in trying to advance that business won't be one of them."

"Would you come in and answer some questions?" Claire asked.

"No. Would you leave a family gathering for what is in essence bullshit, as you so eloquently put it? How about I show up at your parents' anniversary party, or your birthday celebration, and ask if you'd drive somewhere with me so I can act like I'm doing something about an issue I have nothing to do with?"

"I don't run a crime family in my spare time, so I can't answer that."

"Funny, Agent," she said. "If I decide to make that career change, I'll let you know. It actually sounds like a fun job."

"I might have to come back tomorrow, so don't leave town," Joe said.

"I'll be waiting," she said, but she meant she'd be waiting for Gracelia. She'd have no choice but to show up now, because with the night's activities she'd eliminated most of Gracelia's people. Depending on what she had going on in Mexico, Joe was actually right about one thing.

This might take Gracelia completely out of the game.

❖

Gracelia was in the shower when the call came in, and she rushed out when she heard Jerome scream at whoever was on the other end. She went back, rinsed the shampoo out of her hair, and stepped out sooner than she'd have liked, considering how she'd spent the day. Jerome stood at the desk and held the phone like it would slip from his hand if he let up the pressure.

"What?" she asked, and didn't care for the way he waved at her to shut up.

"When did that happen and how many people got hit?" Jerome asked the caller.

"Put the phone down a minute and tell me what is happening," she said in a way that would get Jerome's attention. No matter how much responsibility she'd given him and how much she cared for him, it was time for him to remember that the organization had only one head, and it wasn't him.

"You don't want me to find out why almost everyone we have working for us in three states is now dead? Gustavo missed the first attack against us, and while I was trying to figure out who did that one, they took out everything else."

"Everyone?" She sat down on the end of the bed and missed the worry-free life she'd had.

"Pretty much. Right now all I can find is the men I left looking for Gustavo when I came to pick you up, so hold on a minute."

He went back to the phone and finished his talk. Once he'd hung up he dropped into the leather desk chair and pulled on the hair at both sides of his head. Since she'd met him, this was the first time his FBI background didn't seem to make a difference, because he didn't act like he had a clue as to who had done this to them. The easy time they'd had after she'd killed Rodolfo felt like a thousand years ago.

"They have no idea? No one has moved in and tried to take over or sent in their own people?"

"It happened less than an hour ago, but whoever did this wanted to make sure almost everyone was neutralized. More than ninety percent of our people are dead. I think the best thing we can do is go back to Mexico and regroup. We need to concentrate on the export part of the business, and until we can grow that, it'll be suicide to try to continue with our plans."

"You expect me to run?" The shock of what happened faded and what she needed to do about it became clearer. "Call and order more of the men here by tomorrow. We'll meet them in New Orleans but won't move until I know for sure who did this. Once we do, we need to strike back twice as hard, to send a message."

"I think you need to get the message. You can't fight back from a crippled position, so be smart about this."

"You don't know the streets and how to navigate them." She walked back to the bathroom and turned the shower on again. "Harvard, or wherever you went to school, isn't going to help you now. Smart has nothing to do with what needs to be done now. These people understand power, money, and strength. If I run back to Mexico and hide, we can forget any future because it'll be like throwing gallons of blood in a shark tank. The others in the cartel will go into a feeding frenzy until we won't even be able to sell small bags to tourists on the beach." She finished her shower and stepped around him, tired of his indecisiveness.

"You bring the men we have left and the same thing happens, you'll be lucky to stay alive, much less worry about business. This isn't about strategy, Gracelia, and how we can outwit whoever this is. It's about survival."

"Go, if you're so afraid. When you choose this life, you must go all in. My brother was a bastard, but at least he understood that. He wasn't some coward who ran and hid every time something like this happened. I figured you had more *cojones* than this, but it's better I find out now."

"Listen to me." He knelt in front of her and grabbed her hands.

"This isn't about having balls or being the most macho on the block. When this has happened in New Orleans before, if the attacker was bigger and stronger than the people they went after, the little guy was completely wiped out. It made my life as an agent much simpler, but those poor bastards were still dead on the street. You want that? Because I know someone who would love nothing better than to put both of us out of our misery."

"If you mention Cain Casey's name to me, get out. You and my son have that in common. No matter what happens, you blame that bitch, and only her." She wrenched her hands free and started to formulate a plan. "This time it's not her, so start thinking of something else."

"Why do you automatically think it's not her? Your son tried to rape the woman she considers her wife and then ran. If I was trying to find him, this would be a good way to flush him out." Jerome stood and looked at her with an expression of exasperation. That too was getting old. "But you're right. This could also be someone like Hector Delarosa, and if it is, we can't win."

"Hector would never do this, and because you were on the other side of the law for so long, you wouldn't understand that either. I've never moved against Hector, and he wouldn't risk starting a war when we're all trying to start up our businesses here." She put on the hotel robe and started to comb back her wet hair. "No matter that you believe I'm as stupid as my son, I know enough. We're growing, but not fast enough to worry someone like Hector. Rodolfo, I know, made a deal with someone named Gino Bracato, but that didn't work."

"It didn't work because Cain is the main suspect in the deaths of him and his four sons. I'm not leaving, but I'm also not following you into the grave in some scheme to prove how tough I am."

"What do you think we can do besides go home and hide under the bed?"

"If you want, we can go back to New Orleans and start asking questions. The most important thing to do first is to find Juan," he said, and she cursed softly under her breath. "Don't get twisted out of shape. We need to find Gustavo and pin him down about what he's done to get close to Cain, her family or business partners. The only way to prove Casey had nothing to do with this is to know what she's been up to lately. Gustavo prides himself on knowing everything he can find out about this woman."

"Leave Gustavo to me, and to prove how much I trust and care for you, I want to do something for you. I planned to wait until we arrived back in New Orleans so everyone could watch, but their stories will be good enough. Know this, though, if you accept my gift, you're tied to me for the rest of your life. How long that will be is up to you."

"What gift can possibly be that important?"

Gracelia picked up the phone and talked to someone for a brief moment in Spanish. After she hung up, a knock sounded at their door and she opened it herself. Pablo looked at him as two of the other men dragged in Eduardo, who, because of the beating he'd obviously gotten, was having trouble walking on his own.

"What's this?" Jerome asked.

"You wanted respect, and I'm going to give it to you," she said, and motioned for the men to bend Eduardo's knees so he was at her mercy. Lorenzo Mendoza was the man who'd watched out for her from the moment she'd decided to break out on her own, and he'd been in love with her.

She'd never let Lorenzo in her bed, but she'd used his affection for her to turn him against Rodolfo, and she still missed him. He was dead, something else her son and Jerome blamed on Cain Casey, but it didn't matter to her. Once she'd figured out Lorenzo wasn't coming back, she'd replaced him with Eduardo. He was a man who loved getting ahead more than he cared for her and wasn't bright enough to hide that from her.

Now she was about to prove to Jerome how far she was willing to go to replace Lorenzo and her lover Armando for good. "This man spoke to you the way you have a tendency to speak to me." She nodded, and one of the men placed a plastic bag over Eduardo's head as she screwed a silencer onto the gun Pablo handed her.

"What are you doing?" Jerome asked, taking a step toward her with his hands up. He appeared almost afraid she was going to shoot him as well.

"If I must prove myself to you, I will every time you ask me to, so sit down." She poked a hole in the top of the bag, even though Eduardo was struggling from what she assumed was a lack of air and from the reality of what was about to happen to him. She put the muzzle of the gun on the top of Eduardo's head and pulled the trigger. A couple of drops of blood escaped the bag, but not enough that it'd be difficult to explain to the cleaning crew. Eduardo was dead and twitched a few more times before he went limp and still. The bag tied tightly around his neck was filling with blood.

"We're leaving in the morning, and Jerome is in charge. If any of you talk to him the way this piece of shit did, we'll do this again as many times as it takes for you all to understand my wishes."

She handed the gun back to Pablo and kissed Jerome in front of her men to further prove her point. "Get rid of him."

CHAPTER THIRTEEN

Y ou're going to behave and listen to everything Katlin and Lou tell you, right?" Emma asked as she helped Cain put on her jacket and straightened her collar. "I don't need to mention for you to stay away from Marisol Delarosa, but I will. That girl looks at you the way I do, and I'm not ashamed to admit I don't care for it."

Cain turned and wrapped her arms around Emma. The short, thin nightgown she wore made her smile, since these days Emma preferred comfort over style. During her pregnancy, at some point Emma's usual nightwear changed to her granny fashions, as she described them. Cain found them adorable since they displayed their growing baby well.

"I asked him to leave her at home, but I don't have any control over that. He probably won't listen since that crazy bitch is his heir apparent. He, like I will eventually with Hayden, will use this as a learning opportunity." She kissed the top of Emma's head and felt the swell of their baby against her.

They were into the second trimester, and so far everything was good with both mom and baby. The doctor had explained that since this was Emma's third pregnancy and she'd been so slim going in, this time around she was showing a lot more at sixteen weeks than with their first. Cain was thrilled about the development because she loved the proof of their growing family every time she saw Emma.

"Don't waste time thinking about that idiot." She'd called Hector back and asked him to join her for a drink at Emma's, their upscale nightclub in the warehouse district.

"She might be an idiot, but she's a beautiful one."

"You're beautiful, lass, and you're the woman I love. Even when we get Hannah her puppy, I'll still be your best friend, and I'll be twice as loyal."

"Can I pet you later?" Emma asked, and sounded in a better mood.

She had to stay home because while the place shared her name, the loud music and cigarette smoke weren't ideal for the baby.

"I'd even consider a leash, if you get me a leather collar with spikes." She ran her hand along Emma's back and kissed her. "I love you, lass, with my whole heart. There'll be no other for me."

Her honesty made Emma blink away tears and smile. "I love you the same, and I thank God for giving me such a miracle."

"Get some rest and I'll be back as soon as I can."

"Are you sure you don't need us to come with you?" Sabana asked when she got downstairs. "You might need us." Dino stood next to her, but from his expression he wanted no part of Sabana's request.

"Girl, Cain's lived her whole life without you, so sit and do the job I asked," Lou said bluntly, his normal tone when aggravated. "In case you missed it, Juan is back and wants nothing more than to take Emma somewhere you're going to have a hard time finding. If you allow that to happen, I'm going to rip you into pieces so small your mother won't be able to recognize you." He looked back at her. "Sorry, boss."

"Truth doesn't need an apology," she said, and pointed at Sabana. "Let's talk before I go."

Sabana followed her to the office and wisely stood behind one of the visitor chairs, not assuming she was there for a casual talk. "I only want to help."

"No. You want to get your way, and I'm getting tired of your whining when you don't. I thought what I asked you the other night would've tamped that lust to kill down some, but it hasn't." She was also damn tired of repeating herself with this girl, and the obligation she'd felt for Rick and his sister's future was starting to fade. "By now I thought you would've learned that everyone plays a role."

"I did a good job the other night, and I've been patient waiting for what I want. My brother's dead, and so far no one's paid for that." Sabana puffed herself up as she spoke and never lost eye contact, as if to prove nothing intimidated her.

"What do you think destroying that house was about? Has your anger made you stupid? Gracelia and Juan Luis are responsible for Rick's death. The house you hit and the people you killed work for them. Now that I know Juan is here, I trusted you to watch over the one person in my life he covets most, because Merrick can't."

"Trusted?" Sabana asked, and sounded like she'd stuck a pin in her and deflated her ego.

"Someone who knows more than me, Lou, and Merrick combined

has outgrown us. If you're constantly dissatisfied with what's asked of you, it's time to move on."

"You're firing me?"

"When I add someone to my crews, to my family, I don't do it lightly. When I do, it takes years before I allow them into my home and around my family. Rick understood that, and I thought you did as well. What your brother understood as well is how you get to leave."

"You'd have me killed?" Sabana didn't sound completely afraid, but her words had made cracks in her bravado.

"I didn't say that," she said, and spread her hands out. "But you seem ambitious. Sometimes to get what we want takes hard work or having something to trade up. Anyone out there not a part of this clan would love to know the inner workings of our family. You give them that, and they'll give you anything or any job you want."

"I'd never do that to you."

"I know," she said, and slammed her hand down. "The last person who did got my father, mother, brother, and sister killed. Betrayal cost me the whole of my family because some bastard wanted more responsibility and freedom. He wanted the life of the wise guys he'd seen in the movies, and when I refused, when my father refused, he ran to the first person who would give it to him. Only it wasn't free. He gave up everyone I loved."

Cain stood up and moved around the desk as she screamed. Sabana didn't move but gripped the chair so hard the leather creaked. "Do you honestly think I'd take that chance again?" Sabana shook her head and wouldn't look at her. "You must think me brain-dead if you do."

"I don't."

"Remember that," Cain said, her face inches from Sabana's. "Because if you can't, I'm not wasting my breath on you again, and I'm not going to have you killed."

"Thank you," Sabana said, obviously relieved.

"I'll kill you myself." She let that threat hang for a moment and saw Sabana swallow. "The next time you ask for something other than what Lou assigns, you're done. I've trusted you with Emma's life, something I'm seriously reconsidering, so spend tonight thinking about this conversation and we'll meet again tomorrow. Run tonight and I'll find you by morning, and you won't even have time for a prayer when I do."

She opened the door and called for Lou. He'd had a soft spot for Sabana since her arrival, but he didn't even glance at her. "Put her on the wall tonight with a warning about pouting while watching my family. I understand what motivates her, but I'm tired of being questioned and second-guessed."

"So am I. I'll handle it. Don't worry." Lou didn't take long, and Katlin and Dino didn't comment when Sabana headed outside without complaint.

"Nelson called," Katlin said about the manager of Emma's. "Hector and Marisol are there, and he personally escorted them to your private table. From what he was able to pick out, at least four DEA agents are posted around the club."

"Just what I want," she said as she got into the back of the car with Katlin, "more voyeurs in my life. What's your guess as to what Hector wants?"

"Same thing Hector always wants. The DEA is coming down hard on his business ventures here, and they're teaming up with the Federales south of the border. When you gun for that top spot in the cartel it puts you in the spotlight. If that's not slowing him down enough, ICE is doubling patrols, making it more likely they'll spot anyone coming in illegally. It's an extra added bonus when they're carrying lots of Hector's drugs."

"Did you lie and tell him I'm an agent with powers to make his problems disappear behind my back?"

"No, and the guy might have problems, but he is observant. You don't have near the sticky messes he does, so he needs your secret."

The drive wasn't that long, and Cain wasn't in a rush to sit with Hector, so she took time to shake hands with their security personnel outside. "It's not a secret, cousin. What Hector needs is a personality as charming as mine," she said, and Katlin laughed.

"Then I foresee plenty of messes in his future, because he doesn't come close."

It was early, so the dance floor was still quiet, but the bar and tables were full. At this time of night a conversation with friends was possible, since the music was mellow and soft. Nelson's estimate of four turned out to be about six, but she didn't feel like searching for and counting the others who were probably there. They weren't her problem.

"Hector, thanks for coming over," she said as she took his outstretched hand. He was like a boy with a crush who thought his persistence would eventually win her over.

"After our last talk I'm surprised you called. When you speak to me that way, I think you don't want to be my friend."

She accepted a whiskey neat from Nelson and took a sip before she answered. "Can I be honest?" she asked, not caring what his answer was.

"I've known you to always be truthful, Cain, but that translates into crassness at times. It's not in line with your education."

"I don't want to be your friend." His eyebrows came together and his smile disappeared instantly. "Before you order me killed, I don't really want to be your enemy either."

"The edge of a fence is at times too thin to walk," Hector said, but Cain kept her eyes on Marisol. The young woman had stayed silent, to her amazement. Marisol was beautiful but seemed to jump into situations and then consider her options. That was a flaw if she wanted to one day take over for her father, one Cain constantly preached to Hayden to avoid. Perhaps Hector was making headway. "I've never met anyone who has been able to do it for long. Eventually you lose your balance and fall one way or the other."

"And no one has ever threatened me so subtly, or tried to push me in the direction they want. You refuse to see I have nothing to offer you except my neutrality. I can't help but wonder what a friendship between us would bring into my life." She turned away from them, pointed out each agent, and described them. "You come with baggage I have no interest in carrying for you, Señor Delarosa."

"You say such things, but you *are* involved in my business."

"How so?" It must've chapped his ass to find Vinny and Jasper already in the big hole she'd blown in Gracelia's business. "You're sitting in my business, and unless someone kept you from dancing or drinking, I've done nothing to you."

"You don't play the fool well, so skip the performance. If we cannot be friends and will not be enemies, then we will agree to stay out of each other's way." Hector's smile was back and he again offered her his hand. "Be careful on your fence, and if you fall, depending on where you fall, I'll be there to catch you."

"Or to watch my head splatter like melon on the sidewalk, right?"

"I like you, Cain. I would rest easier if I did not, but you remind much of myself when I was younger. You will not consider any offer I present, so I will leave you be." When she took his hand he pulled her toward him and whispered in her ear, "You trusted my information once. Will you do so again?"

"It depends on what you want," she whispered back. "When the price is as steep as yours, I'd rather fumble around in the dark until I find my own way out of it."

"You won't accept even if the gift is free?"

"Last time you said it was free, yet it wasn't. You can't accept that I don't want or need what you're offering."

"The world will pass you by unless you decide to try new things."

"You'll do fine without me."

"Someone called me and said he had the information I wanted," Hector said, and his breath in her ear was annoying. "Gracelia Luis isn't someone I want, but that's who this guy offered me."

"I'm not really interested in Gracelia either."

"You are a bad liar. If you find her, you will find her son probably still suckling at her breast. Juan, I know, interests you."

"Thank you, but we're done."

"Are you sure?" he asked as he took a step back and out of her personal space.

"I'm sure, but I appreciate your generous offer."

He and Marisol left after that, and the agents followed him out. Cain didn't want Hector in her life, but she'd found his visit enlightening, so she was glad she'd come. Rodolfo was gone, and his men obviously weren't happy with the new management. It was the only way someone from this Luis camp would be brave enough to make Hector the offer.

It was the lesson she'd tried to explain to Sabana. The betrayals that cut you off at the knees came from within. Whoever called Hector proved that, for all Gracelia's posturing, someone with the keys to the kingdom she was trying to build was shopping for a new boss. With a little work she'd find out who that was and how much they wanted.

Once I do, almost everyone will get what they want, she thought. Carlos would get Gracelia, Jasper and Vinny would get a larger slice of the business, and she would get Juan.

"Anything important?" Katlin asked.

"Let's go upstairs and talk about it." In Muriel's conference room she told Lou to put more money on the street for information on Hector's mystery caller.

"We'll start tonight," Lou said.

"Good, and I want to personally talk to any takers. If they have a map to Gracelia, Juan, or Anthony, the reward will be huge." She glanced at her watch and figured Emma was still up. "It's not all I want for Christmas this year, but it's up there on my list."

"Boss, the holidays are months away," Lou said.

"It never hurts to shop early for the things you really want."

❖

"Did he tell you not to talk about what your answers were?" Claire asked Joe and Lionel. They'd both accepted her invitation for a drink in her apartment.

"Yeah, but since I figure our answers all match, I say fuck it," Lionel said, the language uncharacteristic for him.

Joe looked at both of them and missed Shelby all the more. These guys were great, but Shelby had a knack for seeing every angle. "He asked me about Barney Kyle and how we gathered the intel we turned over to George," he said as he twirled his beer bottle on his lap.

"Then he didn't ask us the same things," Lionel said. "All my questions were about Anthony and how Agent Hicks handled the situation. He asked a lot about Anthony's father too, but I had nothing for him on that." Joe found it humorous that Lionel stuck to Coke.

"What's that asshole's father got to do with anything?" Claire asked.

"We'll get to that." He sat forward and rested his elbows on Claire's kitchen table. "What did he want from you?"

"Shelby, and I mean everything about her. I feel like I'm betraying her, but we had no choice but to mention her visits to Casey in our reports. It's not like we can erase her from the video."

"Shelby knows what she's doing, or at least she thinks she does. Both my parents are alive and well, enjoying their retirement in Florida, so I'm not going to judge her for whatever she thinks she's going to get out of Cain. I've already gone to her and talked about coming back, but she's not ready."

"She's angry, Joe, and I can't blame her. I saw the crime-scene photos. What happened was brutal, and because she notices everything, that damn bottle got her attention. She thought it was Casey taunting her after she'd killed them for who their daughter was and what she did for a living," Claire said. "Her instincts failed her this time, and we're the ones paying for it, but I don't mean any disrespect by that. The assumptions she made took the leash off Brent, and Muriel Casey had a field day after he attacked her cousin. I wasn't too torn up about it when it was happening, but the hangover's been hell."

"Hicks hasn't shared with me what Ronald grilled her about, but if I'm right, it was all those things. I believe he's using our mistakes and missteps to boot Annabel as well as some of us out of here because she's right. Ronald wants her job for some reason, and he wants it badly enough that he's willing to smear all of us to get it."

"So that's it? We're out and there's nothing we can do about it," Lionel said, his shoulders slumped.

"Claire, you weren't with us when Shelby decided to meet Cain and accept the box of goodies she dangled out there. For the head of an organized-crime syndicate, Casey put together a solid case against our former boss." He counted off on his fingers that list of good fortune. "She had video of Barney meeting with Gino Bracato, pictures of him taking payments, and wiretaps of them planning Casey's death and covering it up as an FBI operation."

"George didn't care where the stuff came from, did he?" Claire asked.

"He didn't at first, and before it became an issue in court, Washington came down and started to negotiate a deal with Barney. If he cooperated and told them how he'd cracked the nut of getting someone like Big Gino to trust him, he'd walk and get to keep all that cash Gino lavished on him."

"Barney didn't get to spend a dime when someone spattered his brains all over the back of that van," she said.

"True, but the fact they were even contemplating letting someone go that trampled all over everything I stand for, and have worked hard for, ate at me. A small part of me applauded Casey for doing it, if she's responsible."

"You're not alone in that," Lionel said. "That guy was forever screaming at us for what he saw as our screwups, when all along he was screwing us over."

"I understand where you're both coming from, but what's that got to do with all this?" Claire asked.

Joe stared at both of them, sensing he could trust them, but how well did you ever know anyone? The FBI put good people like this in the field, but it was also a highly political organization. To get ahead you needed to not only know the game, but play it well. If he confided his plan and they turned on him, he'd be lucky to only lose his job. Someone like Ronald would use it to prosecute him.

"Barney went down because Shelby decided to take a chance and trust someone we all agree shouldn't be trustworthy. It wasn't our great investigative talent pool that brought a bad agent down. It was Cain Casey." He glanced between them again and tried to gauge if he should stop.

"Are you saying we recruit Cain to take Ronald down?" Lionel asked, and Claire laughed. "That might be the only way to save our jobs, so don't dismiss it right off," Joe said to Claire.

"You're serious?" Claire asked, and he and Lionel didn't say anything. "Come on. I just worked up the nerve to curse her out, and you want me to turn around and start asking her for favors."

"I'm not recruiting Cain, so don't freak out on me," Joe said, and Lionel appeared disappointed. "I *am* suggesting that we use something similar to what Cain did to make sure we don't get burned. Cain wasn't afraid of us, and still isn't, I guess, but Barney wasn't working as an agent of the law. I think an agent with impunity to kill did scare Cain, so she decided to turn things around and use the system against Barney, and it worked beautifully."

"Do you think Ronald's dirty?" Claire asked.

"I've met motivated people in this job, but never anyone who takes such joy in trying to remove good people from a post. Don't you think it's strange that of all the agents in our office that could've helped him, he picks Brent?" Claire finally nodded, and he felt as if he was getting through. "Brent jumped at the chance and got rewarded with a clean report. If you think he's not going to use that against everyone he feels screwed him over on this, you're crazy."

"You think Muriel knows?" Lionel asked.

"You read the report compiled by us and the crew that relieves us. Both Chapman and Brent went to Hayden Casey's game and called Cain out. The only way Brent could be anywhere near her is if someone forgave him. Ronald, with his obnoxious attitude, painted a large bull's-eye on his own forehead for that. Cain decided at the last minute to drop any charges against Brent if they gave her that one concession."

"What's our first move?" Claire asked.

"We need to talk to Annabel, because with only three of us, we don't have enough people to pull this off. Ronald might be clean, but if he's got any nasty habits we need to find them. The trick here is to have a better hand when he plays his cards."

"And if somewhere along the line Cain hands us another box, then what?" Lionel asked.

"We use it if she gets it the same way she got the first," Claire said.

"We're agreed?" he asked. This might be the lure that got Shelby to come back.

"Agreed," Lionel and Claire said together.

"Good." He held his bottle up for a toast. "Here's to standing up to assholes like Ronald and not going to the mat from a sucker punch."

CHAPTER FOURTEEN

A week went by and no one responded to the promise of big money on the street, Hector had kept his promise to stay away, and nothing out of the ordinary had happened. The end of the school year had finally arrived, and Cain had cleared her schedule for all the activities the kids had planned.

She watched their son come down the stairs in his school uniform, straightening his tie and mumbling. The white shirt with the school crest on the pocket, the tie with his school colors, and his slicked-back hair made him appear much more mature than his years. The timeline they'd agreed on would come faster than she thought when she saw him like this, but it didn't worry her.

Hayden, like she and Emma had been, was the top academic student in his class. He still had plenty of schooling ahead of him, but she suspected he'd do as well until his final day in college. The future of their family was secure for the next generation.

"You ready to move on?" she asked as she finished the tie job for him.

"I'll miss some of my teachers, but most of my friends got accepted to Jesuit, so that's good. It'll be a plus to know some people." He followed her to the kitchen and sat next to her at the table. They were the only ones ready, so they'd have time to talk before Hannah came down and told them about her pizza party for the thousandth time.

"Your mama and I are so proud of you. I remember the day you were born and I held you for the first time. It was like holding a mirror up to the past. You looked so much like my father and Billy, I felt ten feet tall. Those big blue eyes and that head of black hair screamed Casey, and you were going to be the center of my world. I knew that right off."

"What do you think this new baby will be like?" he asked as he put his hand over hers.

As much as she loved Hannah and Emma being back home, she missed this one-on-one with him. Summer wasn't goose season, but maybe they'd go up to the cabin she'd built next to Emma's lake in Wisconsin and set up a skeet machine. Like at their shooting range, it was something they could do together.

"If I get my wish, maybe this one will be a little girl with blond hair and green eyes that looks like her mama. Actually, that's been my wish for all of you, but my side of the family's not too bad-looking." She winked.

His exams were over and the only thing left was the graduation ceremony the school held for its students moving on to high school. Hayden had practiced his speech in front of them a few times, and Emma had cried every time. He wasn't only the kid with the best grades; he was also the class president, so the honor of speaking for his fellow students went to him.

"Today, though, belongs to you, son. Hayden Dalton Casey, you're mine, and I'm so proud of the man you're becoming. Remember to always do what's expected, but only if it makes you happy."

"You and me, we want the same things," he said, and stood. "I know I'm expected to claim my birthright as the next clan leader, but that's what I want. I'm a Casey and I'm yours, and I want to be just like you."

"You won't be." She hugged him and kissed the top of his head. She didn't have to bend as much anymore, and it was amusing that Hayden had to lower his head when Emma tried the same thing. "You'll be better than me because I trust you to make your own way when it's your turn."

"I love you."

"I love you, and I can't wait to see you grow. You've given me nothing but happiness, and I'm glad you're my kid."

When they broke apart Emma walked in with a gift-wrapped box in her hand. "You look so grown-up." Emma smiled when Hayden hugged her so hard he lifted her off the ground. "Thank God you didn't inherit my short genes."

"We made him tall so he can carry you around when you're a granny," Cain said, and Hayden laughed.

"One more crack like that and you'll be on the sofa, smarty pants." Emma fussed but laughed too as she held her hand out. "There's another reason we're glad you grew so big." Emma handed Cain the box and leaned against her as she thought about what was inside.

"Your grandfather treasured one thing his father gave him. Our business started in Ireland, and a few of the siblings came to the States to expand and make their mark." She sat them down for the abbreviated telling of this story, and even though Hayden had heard it all his life, he seemed riveted. "You know their plan didn't turn out how they'd envisioned, but they managed to survive the worst and started what we have today."

"You need to start telling this story to Hannah, Mom. She'll love it as much as I have."

"She tells your sister a little part every night at bedtime, and you're right. She loves it more than any book she owns," Emma said.

"Your grandfather received a gift that has been in our family for generations, and it was one of the saddest days of his life when it was stolen from him as a young man. He missed it so much that he had a replica made, and he wore it with the same affection as the one he was given. It's not the original, but Billy accepted it with pride as well the day I gave it to him." She slid the box in front of him and went back to holding Emma's hand. "Congratulations, son, from your Mama and me."

The ring inside had been Dalton's and he'd worn it every day until he died. In his will he'd left it to the new Casey Clan leader, but her brother Billy had fallen in love with it as a small boy and she couldn't deny him. It had gone into the house vault when Billy died, and she'd decided it'd wait there until Hayden's hand grew into it.

The gold band had *Mine But For A Moment* engraved around the outside and *Casey* on the inside. Her grandmother, generations before, had first said it to a baby born in the United States. The ring had been given to her by her grandmother in the old country and was part of their family's history.

"He'd have popped a few buttons seeing that on your finger," she said when Hayden slipped it on.

Hayden stared at it as if in disbelief. "Thanks, and I promise to take good care of it."

"You're welcome. Now get something to eat so they can hear you in the cheap seats," she said, grateful Katlin had hung back until they were finished. Her mother often said there were moments in life that should be locked away in your heart because they were so special. This was one of those.

Katlin came when she nodded and stopped to put her arms around Hayden, then Hannah, who'd run in dressed for school. "You have time for coffee in the office?" Katlin asked.

"Anything yet?" Cain asked when the door to the office closed.

"We got a call from one of Carlos Luis's guys. They're arriving in the morning and he wants a meeting."

"Did he find anything new? I would've thought one of those tweakers would've taken me up on the money we're offering, if only to keep their habit going for years."

Katlin straightened one of the frames on her desk, which made Cain glance at Emma smiling back at her. Why in the hell couldn't anything be easy? She'd lit a powder keg by going after Gracelia, but when Carlos arrived it might go off before she was ready.

"Set it up but not here." She stood, wanting to give business a pass today unless someone dropped Juan on her doorstep. Katlin, though, kept her seat. "What else?"

"Nicolette Blanc and her girl Luce went by Emma's last night. They had way too many drinks and made a scene. Nelson called me down, so I took care of it."

"What kind of scene?"

"Nicolette was screaming that either you showed up or you'd be sorry for blowing her off. She followed that by saying, 'FBI, sorry.' Nelson had the guys stuff her and her girlfriend in the office, and the guys with them went a little apeshit."

"Nic obviously hasn't learned that full-charged persistence doesn't work with me unless your name is Emma Verde Casey. Then I'm lucky to last the day."

"True, but this isn't Emma, so what do you want me to do about it?"

Cain drummed her fingers on the desk in her habitual uneven pattern and thought about the quickest, least complicated solution. After a brief conversation with Luce she knew that'd be impossible. Luce Fournier wanted to beat her chest and prove she was queen of the jungle to impress Nic. The obnoxious woman hadn't figured out yet that if someone had the title, while people were busy shouting *look at me*, it was easy to slit their throats.

"Nothing for now, except call her and tell her she'll have to wait a few days. Warn her that I won't tolerate another outburst like that. You can leave that up to her imagination or not—your call."

"I'll take care of it." Katlin glanced at her watch. "Who do you want with you this morning?"

"Lou and Mook should cover it. I told them to wait outside so the other people there won't be uncomfortable."

"Comfort isn't a priority for me right now, cousin, so I'm going to buck you on this one. Lou and Mook can cover the front, but I'm sending Dino and a couple others to cover the back." Katlin placed her hands on her hips, appearing defiant, as if she expected an argument.

Like her father, who'd had her uncle Jarvis watching his back all his life then did the same for her, Cain appreciated her family watching out for her and those closest to her. Muriel and Katlin would never betray her like her cousin Danny Baxter.

"Today I'm Derby, wife and mother, and all I'm interested in doing is listening to my brilliant kid give a speech and watching my other brilliant kid fill up on pizza. You can do whatever you think is best."

Katlin laughed and dropped her hands. "Come on, then, because if I'm in charge for the day I want to get going and take advantage of the opportunity."

Outside the school both sides of the street were lined with cars, so the van that'd followed them moved on after Claire got out. Cain shook her head in amazement, wondering who the FBI thought she was going to cut a deal with or kill inside.

They entered the auditorium with Ross and Hannah, who, along with the other younger kids with siblings in the morning's events, got to attend. After the awards were given out, the school's president introduced Hayden. He thanked his teachers, fellow students, and every parent for their commitment to their academic success.

Emma squeezed Cain's forearm as he spoke and had a smile that rivaled Cain's. Hayden was articulate, smooth, charming, and had pretty much everyone in the audience nodding as if they approved of everything he was saying.

"I'd like to thank my parents and my Grandpa Ross for teaching my sister, Hannah, and me that anything is possible if you work for it. It's the best feeling in the world to know I have people who love me and believe in my dreams. I love you, guys, and thanks for having my back."

They posed for pictures when Hayden's part was done, and then he walked Hannah to her classroom. The other children knew him and ran to him to beg him to read them a book. Every last-year student had to do volunteer work, and Hayden had given up his free period to spend it reading to Hannah and her friends.

"You'll meet us later? Don't forget we're taking Daddy and the kids to dinner to start the summer right," Emma said as they walked out together. It was early enough for Cain to get some business out of the way.

"I'll be home in a few hours, but I'd like to take care of something Katlin told me about before we left."

Emma tugged her to a stop and waited for her to say something, but they were outside under Claire's watchful eyes. "I know—not now, but you're not going to be out in the open, are you?"

"No. I have to figure out where Nicolette and Luce are staying so I can send them packing." She kissed Emma's forehead, then her lips. "Nicolette got stupid at Emma's last night and I'd like to avoid it happening again."

"I'm all for convincing that French twerp to leave, so good luck."

"Where is she?" Cain asked Katlin when she got in the car. The vehicle in front of them held her family, and another carload of guys was waiting to follow them home.

"They have a couple of suites at the Piquant and haven't been out of their room yet."

"How do you know that?"

"I've got someone in the lobby by the elevators and a guy up by the pool, and so far nothing. They have to be in their room."

"Interesting. Luce doesn't seem like the kind to lie around all day, but she might need the rest for her small bouts of sarcasm." They stopped at the valet stand, but Katlin had one of the guys turn the car around and wait. A few twenties for the man set to take it allowed him to wait inside.

"They're up on seven, and I hope they're still sleeping the liquor off," Katlin said as they rode the elevator to the lobby. "Bastards made me get out of bed to deal with that shit."

The Piquant's marble lobby was, as always, beautifully decorated and full of people, but it didn't seem crowded. Cain often forgot about the stained-glass restaurant and bar where the owner often played a few sets. After their life calmed a little she'd have to bring Emma back on a date.

"You've come a long way from the womanizing and partying of your early twenties. Merrick's been good for you."

"Same as Emma's been for you. Sometimes I miss it, but when Merrick's better we'll hit the town. I want to believe Diane when she says that's only a few months from now. Having a therapist come to us every day has sped her recovery a lot."

They got into the next set of elevators and she pressed her shoulder to Katlin's. "I wish what happened hadn't, and if I could've changed it—"

"I don't blame you. You're my family and I know that's how you think of Merrick." Katlin put her arm around her and kissed her cheek. "It's a privilege to live the way we do. We are true to our families, our tradition, and our rules. All those make us richer than most, but what happened to my girl is at times the price that comes of it. You want Juan for your reasons and I want him for mine, but that's who I blame."

"In a couple of months we'll celebrate together, because it's a blessing Merrick's still got that sharp mind."

"Your assignments have gone a long way in motivating her, and it makes her believe you haven't given up on her."

The hallway was empty, and they glanced at the sign showing which way to go. "Don't be offended, but she's always been the best on my payroll."

"I believe you, since she's kicked my ass from day one."

Cain stopped Katlin short of the door and smiled. "Let's hope you remember how."

"How hard do you want to go?"

"Let's remind them that stupidity is often frowned upon. If they're having trouble breathing out of their nose, they might be motivated to choose their words more carefully next time." Katlin took one of her guns out and held it by the barrel as she knocked. She heard only a muffled noise and someone saying something in an agitated way, and she looked directly at the peephole.

Luce Fournier opened the door in a robe, with tousled hair and bloodshot eyes. If she was armed she hid it well, so Cain let Katlin go in first. Before Luce could lift her hands in defense Katlin smashed the butt of her gun into the center of her face. The sound was like a pumpkin hitting a sidewalk from five stories up, and Luce ran to the bedroom and dropped to her knees, her hands pressed to her nose.

"Hello, Nicolette," Cain said as Nicolette sat on the bed and clutched the sheet under her chin. "You asked to see me?"

"What the hell are you doing?" It obviously didn't matter that she was naked, because Nicolette got up and went to Luce. The blood now leaked through her fingers. "You could've killed her."

"I still might," Cain said, taking another robe from the closet and throwing it to her. "And she might not be the only one leaving via the laundry chute, so listen carefully."

"Give it a rest," Nicolette said, her French accent still thick. "This is excessive even for you." The robe stayed where it'd dropped as Nicolette went into the bathroom for a towel, wisely leaving the door open since Katlin now held her gun correctly.

"Put the goddamn robe on and sit down. You stretched your limits last night, and that was enough to get my attention."

Nicolette took her time with the robe and didn't lose eye contact with her as she tied it. "If only you'd been this enthusiastic about seeing me when we were both free."

"Let's be clear about a few things so you can take this idiot you brought to do business in your name to the hospital. Once you get that opportunity, do I need to say what a bad idea it'd be to go with any other story except that she slipped in the shower?"

"Since you just mentioned it," Nicolette said sarcastically, "I guess so."

"You've left me no choice but to repeat myself. We cut a deal after months, and she," she pointed to Luce and was amazed how fast her eyes had bruised, "changed it. I say no deal, and you're throwing threats around in my club. When someone shows such a lack of intelligence I have to do something to get through their thick skulls. That's when everyone always figures out their hard heads are in reality incredibly fragile."

"Last night was all in jest, Cain. Have you lost your humor now that you are older?" Nicolette sat with half her body turned away from Cain, but she figured it was to hide the scar on the side of her face.

"I love a good joke and a good time, but I never find my name and FBI in the same sentence funny. If you can't understand that, it's time for you to go home."

"Have dinner with me so I can talk to you about what happened. We worked too long on this to give up so easily. We were such great friends once, and you risked your life for mine, so let us explore how good we can be together."

"Your brain must be wine-soaked." Cain glanced at Katlin and nodded. With her permission silently given to do anything, Katlin kicked Luce in the stomach. The blow made Luce let go of her face, and when she fell forward, a small pool of blood dripped onto the carpet. "I thought all these years would've taught you something, considering you have a father like Michel."

"So I'm an imbecile because the great Dalton Casey didn't raise me?" Nicolette said, and it appeared she held back from spitting on her. "You're an animal like your father, except for one thing."

Luce looked between them and put a hand back on her nose.

"You might want to reconsider this woman's commitment to you because this next question might hurt." Cain smiled and turned to Nicolette. "I'm dying to know. How am I different from my father?"

"The woman you picked. I would've predicted someone with more backbone, but you went for the blond American you could control. Are you so weak that you bypassed a spirited partner who could've been your equal? What happened to the woman who saved me from more than this?" Nicolette turned and ran her finger down the now slightly white line down her face.

That night, right before their graduation ceremony, Cain had almost given in to this woman. Nicolette had played her right, but she hadn't given in fast enough and Nicolette had run out into the French Quarter in a fit of temper. Bad luck had trailed her out of the bar when she ran right into the arms of a freak who'd given her the permanent souvenir.

"Let that go." She traced the same path Nicolette had on her own face. "You're better than to let something like that scar define you." She stood and motioned Katlin to the door. "Leave, Nicolette, while Lucy here takes all your lessons for you this time. Though," she bent and slapped Luce's cheek softly, "next time, Lucy, politeness will get you much further than this bullshit you think is tough."

"You're not going to defend the little woman?" Nicolette asked tauntingly.

"Emma is my equal partner, the mother of my children, and she asked me one thing when it came to you."

"What? Please come home to her and not cheat? Was she afraid I'd steal you away?"

"She asked me not to kill you in honor of our new baby. Leave today and I'll give in to her *weakness*." She walked to the door and stopped. "You've got a day, Nicolette. If you want to test me—stay. Lucy might not be too happy if you're in a defiant mood."

"Her name is Luce."

"If I learned anything at all through the years, it's that when you're the bitch on your knees bleeding profusely, I can call you whatever I want."

❖

"Why now?" Annabel asked Shelby after Shelby had told her she was ready to come back. "You have time left, and the more I think about it, the more I think you should take it."

"Unless you want to order me not to go back into the field with my team, I'm starting tomorrow. I've already talked to Joe so he can give me a review to get me up to speed." She tried to keep a mild expression so Annabel would relax, because getting back to work was the only way to get close enough to what she wanted. She needed to avoid a psychological exam that'd keep her out indefinitely.

"I'm only thinking of you. Losing your parents is traumatic for anyone when it happens from natural causes, but this way tripled the grief."

Judging from the way Annabel studied her, she was looking for that one weakness that'd make Shelby a danger if she put her back to work. That's where she needed to be, though, since Cain had been a dead end, but her wariness hadn't surprised her. Their relationship had always been adversarial, and what she'd asked took ultimate trust. Cain would never trust a federal agent that much. Not unless given a good reason to.

"Ma'am, I can't sit at home and think about it anymore," she said, going with a little of the truth. "I need to be useful and play a part in finding the animals that did this."

"Does that mean you want to transfer to California?"

"I know and believe that Cain Casey had nothing to do with this, but I do believe it's all related."

Annabel nodded as Shelby spoke and stopped when she'd given her the theory she knew to be fact. "How do you know that? I've asked the group investigating this for updates, and they haven't reported anything close to that."

"Because the only part of this they knew is what happened to my parents. But think about it. My dad was a police officer, but he'd been retired for quite a few years. Any chance these were retaliation killings is a stretch." The only way to convince Annabel was with more truth. "I've gone over all the information and the witness statements, and it feels like whoever did this wanted us to concentrate on Cain."

"I'll agree to your coming back, but you'll have to rethink your theory. We don't have any proof Cain's tied into this except for a liquor bottle you found on scene." Annabel spoke in a gentle, controlled way, which Shelby found insulting. It was like Annabel was trying to soothe an agitated mental patient. "Even that was explained away by your new roommate. That is, if Fiona O'Brannigan is still living with you."

"No one gets ahead in this job without listening to their gut every so often. I don't know how they're connected yet, but they are. Cain's not guilty of this, but someone used my parents because of her. Fiona agrees with me about that."

"Am I going to have a problem with Fiona being on the task force Ronald took over for us? Believe me, this guy doesn't need any more ammunition to cut us all down."

"Fiona's dedicated, but she won't bend the rules for anyone." That might not be true if they found the hit team sent after her family, but then she wouldn't judge her for vigilante justice. "If that's what Ronald wants, he'll be disappointed."

"Tread carefully, Shelby, and I'll be glad to have you back."

"I couldn't leave you to the vultures." The door opened behind her and Annabel's eyes closed to slits. No one came into the office of the special agent in charge anywhere in the Bureau without knocking first.

"Is the building under attack?" Annabel asked through clenched teeth.

"I saw Agent Phillips, so I thought we'd get her interview out of the way."

They'd met on a few occasions, but Ronald had a distinct, high-pitched, nasally voice that didn't go with his sturdy build. Even when he didn't seem to mean it, he sounded condescending. But usually he *did* mean it, since Ronald always thought himself to be the smartest guy in any room.

"Agent Phillips isn't available until tomorrow," Annabel said. "This is her last day of leave, and I'm sure she doesn't want to spend it with you."

"It's okay, ma'am. Today might be better since I'll probably be slammed tomorrow." Shelby turned and noticed he hadn't changed or aged much through the years. "What can I do for you?"

"I'm sure Agent Hickman has things to do, so come with me." He led her to one of their interrogation rooms, where Brent waited. Ronald clicked on a recorder and placed it between them. She stared at Brent as Ronald stated his name and the date for the record. "I'm glad to see you back at work."

"Why?" She put her hands on her lap. This wasn't a friendly chat, so she wanted to show no reaction that could help feed Ronald's inquisition. "I don't mean any disrespect, but you're here to implode the office and rebuild it into something that works better."

"So you admit that's necessary?"

"No one in their right mind admits to incompetence, Agent Chapman. I'm grieving the loss of my family, not mentally touched." Brent's snicker made her press her nails into her palm. He had to be the worst, most unprofessional agent she'd ever worked with. "We've done our jobs—most of us anyway," she said as she eyed Brent.

"There's no need for hostility, Agent. All I need from you is your opinion. Can we do anything differently in the Casey investigation?"

"Believe me, if there was a magic potion to end it successfully I'd use it, but it's a process. Only through surveillance, good investigative work, and persistence will we finally get the break we need. No one's perfect, and that includes Cain."

"Very true, and thank you for your time," he said, and turned the recorder off. "I'm sure everyone will be glad to have you back."

"That's it?" Such a soft approach worried her more than if he'd gone after her and threatened her with whatever came to mind if she didn't cooperate.

"Unless you have something to add, that's all I have."

"I have nothing else either," she said, and took her time leaving. Ronald was a complication she didn't need right now.

❖

"We got something," Lionel said while they waited outside the Piquant. Somewhere in the larger van they'd taken something pinged, and Claire and Joe glanced away from their monitors. They'd stayed inside since Cain couldn't be visiting anyone inside that made them worry.

"From inside?" Claire asked.

"Nope." Lionel typed quickly on his laptop. The speed of his fingers had always amazed Joe. "Remember the warrant we got for Matt and Brianna Curtis's phone?"

"Don't tell me their idiot son Anthony called and identified himself?" Joe asked.

"I set the parameters to warn me right away if it came from either Anthony's phone or it took less than the time people think we need to trace it."

"So which one was it?" Claire asked.

"It was a real short conversation, so the latter." He typed some more and smiled when he stopped to read. "It's the same number that called once before, and that conversation was as short. I gave them the benefit of doubt the first time since it could've been a wrong number."

"If that's the case, can we get any information that helps us?" Joe read the text that'd popped on his phone. Shelby must've sweet-talked Annabel for a deal—anyone else would've been in therapy for months. "Shelby's coming back in the morning with no restrictions."

Lionel glanced at him, as did Claire, but they remained silent.

They both seemed to be afraid that if they spoke it'd change what he'd said. Having Shelby on the team again was something they'd all been waiting for but weren't expecting this fast.

"She's coming back to work with us, right?" Claire asked.

"That's what it says here." He held his phone up. "Finish up, and maybe we'll have a starting point in the morning."

"Back to the phone call, then," Lionel said, his voice higher, as if he was excited. "I needed another one to verify the beginning of a pattern, and while they're too short for me to pinpoint the exact location, the first one came from the Cabo San Lucas area." He typed something else and turned the laptop so they could see the map he'd put up. "Anthony's parents live in Orange Beach, Alabama." Lionel traced the line from Cabo to the mock pushpin in Alabama. "The second call came from somewhere in here from the same number." He pointed to a circle that included the City Park area in New Orleans into Metairie.

"That's too much of a coincidence," he said, and the hairs on his neck stood like they did when he was chilled. When Anthony had slipped through the net they'd set up for him, it'd angered him more than anything Cain had ever done.

"I've got a better chance with some time and our towers here in the U.S. to come pretty close, if he gives me another shot."

Joe dropped both his feet to the ground and leaned closer to Lionel. "So do it."

"I would, but whoever this is disabled the phone, as in took the card out and probably destroyed it. We can guess it's Anthony, but whoever made the call knew what they were doing. The call was short and they didn't take chances once they were in the U.S. What we have to do now is keep tabs on the Curtis's home phone as well as their cells."

"I'll call the office in Mobile and have them put someone on the house. If this is Anthony trying to contact his parents, we might finally bring him in." Joe went through his phone, trying to think if anyone he could trust in that office would start the surveillance immediately. He made the call, and the agent who'd graduated from the academy with him said he'd be part of the team that'd move out as soon as they got the file.

"I want to see that asshole's smug expression when we cuff him and bring him in. It's still hard to fathom he helped Juan Luis kidnap Emma Casey with the intent to rape her," Lionel said.

"Maybe he learned a little of what it takes to be a dirty agent from his father. Agent Hicks gave me his file when I said I wanted to follow up on something, and the only reason Matt Curtis didn't end up like Barney is because he resigned when they put the heat on him. It was the deal he cut for the Bureau to stop looking into his business." Claire contributed her facts but stared at the monitors as if not to miss anything with Cain.

"From what I heard, they couldn't prove anything he did but pushed him out anyway. It was better than having someone in the office who was allegedly on Vincent Carlotti's payroll," he said, and tried to stretch out his back. By the end of their shift he was impatient with the cramped small space. "Who knows, maybe by hanging around Matt, Barney learned a few things."

"Heads up." Claire pointed to the center monitor where Cain's car drove out.

"Run the guest list to see what this visit was about. And to finish with Anthony, if he's got Juan with him at any sign of either of them, especially around Emma Casey, bring them in," he said as he watched their relief start after the car.

"I did already, but it'll take me some time to run the names. No one popped, but I don't think the bad-seed cousins decided to come downtown just for a drink," Claire said as they started to move. From this spot Lionel would have them back at the office in ten minutes.

"Yeah. Cain always does have a rhyme to her reason." Joe skimmed down the list of names and didn't recognize anyone either. "The shame of it is, we never know exactly what it is until we have to deal with the aftermath."

❖

"She was fucking Casey's cousin and attorney, Muriel Casey, and you're letting her walk?" Brent screamed. "I thought you wanted to take that shit out."

"If you're going to work with me, please refrain from that language. Obviously you're a college graduate, so try to sound like it." Ronald made a few notes in the small journal he kept in his breast pocket. "Find Fiona O'Brannigan and get her in here."

Brent didn't say anything else, thankfully, so he reviewed all his observations since his arrival. Everyone he'd talked to so far was correct about what they'd said about their jobs. The investigation into Casey's business had been by the book, with very few glitches, and so far the only prosecution they'd come close to was that of Barney Kyle. One of their own wasn't what the taxpayer had in mind, he thought, as he reread everything he'd written about Shelby.

If anyone could deliver what he wanted it was Shelby, but he doubted she'd do so willingly. After all, like Brent had said, Shelby had fucked Muriel Casey, only she'd done so voluntarily. Whatever she'd given Annabel from her time in that house was totally useless. Not one lead had turned up anything and or advanced them one inch.

To him it meant either Shelby had been made, or she was one of many peace officers on Casey's payroll. Either of those scenarios helped him. Shelby Phillips was the key, and he was going to exploit it until he closed this case.

An hour had elapsed by the time Brent knocked and entered with Fiona in tow. "I hope I'm not taking you from anything, Detective," he said, and pointed to the chair across from him. "Agent, wait outside." The long hesitation from Brent forced him to glare at him to get his feet to move.

"I was having dinner with my mother, but she understands the job's important," Fiona said after Brent slammed the door. "What can I do for you?"

"First, I need to be able to trust you. Can I do that?"

"I'm completely serious about my oath, sir."

"Thanks for saying so, but realize the penalty for lying will be steep. There's too much at stake for anyone to cut a friend any slack."

"No friendship is worth that."

"How about if I'm talking about Shelby Phillips?" He flipped to the right page in one of the files he'd stacked on the table so she'd realize he knew everything about her. "I believe her father was your pope on the police force and the reason you made detective grade so quickly."

"That's true," Fiona said, but didn't seem as enthusiastic as before. "What's Shelby got to do with this?"

"Don't you feel that your friend is uncommonly close to the people she's supposedly paid to watch?" He lowered his voice and leaned forward. "I don't know who I can trust here, but I need someone to watch the watchers. For me, it's better to go outside for a job this important, and you're a perfect candidate."

"You want me to spy on Shelby?"

"Not every aspect of her life, but I want to know about any contact she has with Casey or anyone associated with Casey." He pushed a phone toward her. "Use that if you need to call me."

"Are you expecting to catch Shelby in something illegal?" Fiona asked, but picked up the phone. "She's not like that."

"What was the purpose of all those visits to Casey's house?"

"She didn't say, but I figured she was there to try to talk to Casey about what she knew about her parents."

"You don't lie well, Detective," he said, as if he already had all the answers. "If you can't or won't do what I'm asking, then at least swear you won't mention this to Agent Phillips."

"If you need this, I'll do it." Fiona dropped the phone in her blazer pocket and glanced down at the file he'd referred to. "What exactly do you want me to do?"

"I won't forget this." He came close to bouncing in his seat over how easy it'd been to snare her. "And remember, this is about Casey more than anything else."

"When we're done I hope you tell her I had a part in destroying her life and family, like she's done to so many people throughout her miserable existence."

"I'll be happy to."

CHAPTER FIFTEEN

The next week, Hayden's baseball team finished their season on the road, winning their division championship in Baton Rouge. The kids had been thrilled, not only with their trophy and achievement, but with the fact they'd taken the title at LSU's Alex Box Stadium. With that accomplishment both children were now free for the summer, and despite everything, Cain decided to take a week for a trip north.

Remi offered the use of their plane and to work with Muriel while they were away. Cain had decided to take more guards than were probably necessary, but they were at the endgame. To finish this was something she could almost taste.

"Mook, be sure to pack all the shotguns and the sweepers. Jerry's been overseeing construction for me, but it doesn't hurt to play it safe," she said, mentioning Jerry Rath, the husband of Emma's lifelong friend Maddie.

They'd left the son of Giovanni Bracato Junior with Jerry and Maddie during their last visit, transforming Giovanni III to Jeremiah Cain Rath. From Emma's telephone conversations with Maddie, JC, as they called him, was a happy and healthy ten-month-old who loved riding the fields with his daddy. No one involved would ever reveal that secret to the world, but her heart did go out to Big Gino's wife. Hopefully one day she'd find peace, but she'd been her husband's biggest fan and supporter, so she should have known that one day she would have to answer for a life lived so poorly.

"Lou's already gone through both places twice, but you know how anal he is. By the time we arrive he'll have swept for every kind of bug, including the kind that crawls."

"A habit you thankfully share." Cain laughed. Hayden's guard had been assigned to him for years, and she was confident they'd be together for years to come. Mook was young, but he loved Hayden like a little brother. Anyone with an idea to hurt her son would figure out the handsome face and beautiful blond hair didn't mean Mook didn't have a hair-trigger finger and very little forgiveness in his soul. Mook would kill without hesitation.

"You bet," Mook said, and casually saluted her. "Anything else you want me to take?"

"Emma made a list, so check with her."

She walked to the pool house to see Merrick, who was now walking well with a cane. That morning she'd asked Merrick for a favor and loved the appreciation and relief that transformed her expression. Someone like Merrick would die without something to do, so it was time to start easing her back into a few responsibilities. When Merrick was almost back, she'd resume her duties at Emma's side, with the addition of someone like Dino.

"You ready to go?"

Merrick had her guns strapped on and wore a light jacket. Her cane had been a gift from Cain, and Merrick had gotten a kick from the handle that was a small replica of the gun she preferred. To see her getting stronger every day answered every prayer Cain had said from the day she'd been shot. She didn't pray often but had done so gladly for Merrick.

"Are you sure you don't want to take anyone else? You're not insulting me if you do. My aim might be off."

"I doubt that, so let's move. If I don't drive every so often, I'm going to forget how."

They took off and stopped at the Columns Hotel on St. Charles Avenue. Their lounge usually spilled out to the large front porch of the historically registered establishment, and Sept waited for them at a table farthest away from the street. They'd been friends long enough to know how dangerous it would be for her to chance a seat out in the open and close to such a busy street.

"Vacation, huh?" Sept asked when they joined her.

Two glasses already sat on the table and Sept didn't appear that thirsty. Fiona came through the front door, probably from the bathrooms. The new detective's attitude got under Cain's skin, and she couldn't believe Sept was able to work with this overly opinionated hothead.

"If you keep up this company, I might take a permanent vacation from you."

"For now I'm stuck training her, so don't take my job out on me." Sept motioned to Fiona to hold up. "Can I talk to you alone for a second?"

They entered and sat in the Victorian Lounge close enough to each other to have a quiet, private conversation. Merrick was in her line of sight, and Cain laughed when Fiona sat close to her so she could watch them as well.

"What's wrong with your partner besides Shelby's parents and their tragic demise? A little more attitude and I might have a harassment complaint."

"She got picked for the joint task force we formed with the FBI. That's what I wanted to talk to you about." Sept spoke in a whisper, only breaking away when the waitress brought them a menu and a refill for Sept. "You know I'll never break the law for you, but this time I want to warn you about this group. This talk would've gone smoother, but Fiona's not letting me out of her sight, especially if she thinks I'm coming to see you."

"We've known each other long enough to both realize someone with a badge is always after me. This bitch will have to go some to get anything on me."

"I know you've met Ronald Chapman, and that's who's hijacked the task force. Fiona's thrilled because they've been given the green light to skirt some of the rules as long as it brings results. This guy wants you bad, and he's stacked the group with cops and agents who want that too. If Fiona gets her way, I'll go down with you because of our friendship."

"Stop talking," she said, putting her hand on Sept's knee. "I don't want you to sacrifice anything that'll hurt your career."

"I'm not, but you've got to know that the game isn't fair this time around. Be careful doing business because they're gunning for you and Ronald's an asshole. I haven't really met him, but if Fiona's waxing this poetic about him and what he wants to do, I can guarantee he's got something against you."

"Thanks. I won't forget this, and I'll owe you a few in the future."

"Anything on what's happening on the street?"

"My contacts say the locations hit did belong to Gracelia Luis. Rumor is she killed her brother Rodolfo and took his business. Her problem is Rodolfo's crew fractured after his murder and went in three directions. Some stayed with her, some stayed with Carlos Luis, and the last small group went to Hector."

Sept appeared amazed. "How in the hell did you figure all that out?"

"I use cash instead of the shiny gold badge and intimidation. Well, police intimidation, anyway," she joked. "I don't know who, but Hector's the one with the biggest plans for expansion. He came by again and tried to strike a deal with me. The word no might've finally gotten through his head."

"So you think it's Delarosa?"

"I haven't gotten that far yet. If it was Hector, no one on the street is going to talk."

"How about Carlos Luis?"

"I don't think so, but I still have feelers out, so I'll let you know if something comes up. Thanks for the warning on the other end of this." Cain paid for Sept's drink and walked her out. "Take care of yourself and keep your head down. Your mother would miss you if something happened to you." She slapped Sept on the back.

"You too, since for whatever reason my mother loves you too." Sept shook her hand and stopped at the table where Fiona and Merrick waited.

Fiona had her hand over her glass, and her ring caught Cain's attention. The gold band resembled the one she'd given Hayden recently. "Can I see that?" She pointed to her hand.

"Some other time." Fiona closed her hand into a fist. "If we're done, Sept, I'll see you later." She headed across the street with her hand in her pocket, as if to not give her a glimpse into any part of her life.

"Forget about all this for a while and enjoy the time away with your family," Sept said, her eye on the retreating Fiona. "Don't let it slip your mind to call if anything new happens. Let me help you by doing my job. Too many people are watching you for you to try to go after someone."

"I'll make it easy on you and be good."

"That you're good is never in question, Derby. It's why everyone in the FBI has perpetual heartburn."

"You follow your own advice and take some time off. Instead of constantly trying to find me doing something illegal, spend some time looking for a woman to keep you warm at night." She helped Merrick down the stairs and saw the guy from Remi and Dallas's recent home tour. He sat in his car a half a block away and tried not to seem like he was there in a surveillance capacity.

"Who are we leaving behind that can do some research for us? Someone we can trust implicitly."

"If you want, Katlin and I can stay behind." Merrick stared at the man she pointed out. "What do you want?"

"So many things, it's hard to list them all."

❖

Jerome sat staring at Pablo as the man gave Gracelia an update on the search for Gustavo. For a complete idiot, Gustavo had managed to disappear and no one had spotted him. What surprised him most was that Gustavo hadn't called for help. Like his mother, Gustavo wanted so many things, but it was always up to someone else to get it done.

"When more men get here, we look more," Pablo said, his eyes on him. Pablo shifted in his seat as if he were nervous. "One man missing."

"We have a lot of people missing, and until they sift through the fires we might still not know exactly who's dead. Not that we should stroll into the police station and ask if everyone working in our lab has been identified." He swirled the wine in his glass and concentrated on not spilling any. It was how he thought of his life now. It'd become a whirlwind he had no control over and was on the brink of spilling over in a mess he'd never be able to clean up.

"Be quiet for once and listen," Gracelia said, exasperated. "Who is missing?"

"Andre Reyes, Señora." Pablo stood up and seemed ready to leave.

If he wasn't so pissed he would've found this humorous. Pablo acted as if he was stuck in the middle of two angry parents. He couldn't please both so he had to choose. "Do you think he's with Gustavo?" he asked.

"He leave the night Gustavo leave, so *sí*."

"Like the señora said, we have some men arriving in the next few days. When they get here we'll start looking again. For now we'll lay low and try not to be a good target for whoever wants all of us dead. Tell Chico to get up here and watch the door." How Casey made this look so easy was a mystery he wondered about every day. "Go," he said, when Pablo stood there like a dead tree stump.

He waited until Pablo left before he faced Gracelia, and her disgusted expression was the excuse he needed to follow him out. Pablo had wisely waited and followed him to the elevator. The hotel he'd picked was in Metairie instead of New Orleans, in an effort to keep from anyone accidentally spotting Gracelia or anyone with them. The place was on the lake and presented another challenge since a large number of Hispanics in the middle of a conservative, Republican, white-bread town was memorable. Hotel staff with good memories was the last thing he wanted.

"Call Delarosa and tell him as soon as possible," he said to Pablo when the doors closed. "We might not get the deal we want, but we need to cut out before things get worse."

"You think Señor Delarosa do all this? One man kill at house here is my cousin. His mama and papi raise me when my papi kill working for Señor Rodolfo. Mi mami run away, so I alone."

"I'm sorry," Jerome said because the story made him think of his parents. The worry, the stress of not knowing had to be a toll. "I really don't think Hector did this."

"Who you think?"

"Gracelia thinks I'm crazy, and she doesn't want to hear it, but I think it was Cain Casey. All this was payback." They walked out and headed to the top of the levee that surrounded Lake Pontchartrain. It was hot and humid, but it was freeing to be out of the room and away from Gracelia's crazy ranting.

"Señora Gracelia's son and Señor Rodolfo do bad things to Casey. I not know but the men say this. Juan and Señor Rodolfo gone now, so why Casey care?"

"She's got what's called a long memory. What Juan did was something Casey isn't going to forget or forgive. You're right, though. Juan's gone and we need to get that message across to Casey." He took out his pack of cigarettes from his shirt pocket, a new habit he'd taken up to help with his coke cravings. Smoking relaxed him, but when he'd been confined to small spaces in his previous job, it'd been impossible to enjoy a cigarette. "Go ahead and call me once you make contact."

"Gracias, señor, for trusting me. I do a good job for you."

He glanced back as Pablo left, and his mood improved. If only he could find a few more like this guy, he could get more done about fixing what was wrong with everything about Gracelia and her family business. The fix was near for him anyway, and in that second he decided to take Pablo with him.

"You want to see me?" Chico said, and his sudden appearance startled Jerome.

"I wanted you to watch Gracelia, but now that you're here, let's go over the last talk you had with Gustavo. Before he ran, what exactly did he say?"

"You think I did something to him? Who the shit is this guy, and why you care?" Chico asked, instantly combative. "You say watch him, and we do. No matter that all he wants to do is stupid shit."

"Just tell me what he said. I could give a crap about him, but Gracelia, your boss, is worried he's out doing shit that isn't going to be good for any of us." Every step was as much effort as climbing Everest.

Chico repeated the story hesitantly, but it sounded more like a translation delay than concern or covering something up. So it'd been his disrespect in front of the others that had made Gustavo run— interesting. He'd figured it was because he and Gracelia were going to keep him from his plans.

"I told Pablo we're going to continue the search once the men arrive."

"What we do now?"

"Stick with Gracelia, but keep in mind what happened to Eduardo. Let me know if she wants anything strange." Jerome crushed his smoke, picked up the butt, and stuck it in his pocket. Getting caught was always a possibility, but it wasn't going to be because of his carelessness. "You think you can handle that?"

"Yes, but I want better job when you can."

"Sure. Go sit outside Gracelia's room and call me if anything happens."

He took the throw-away phone out when he was alone at the water's edge. "Are you alone?" When the answer was yes, he paused and lit another cigarette. He kept his voice low to disguise it. "I've told you I have the information you need, but you have to be patient awhile longer. When it's possible you'll have what you've been waiting for." He hung up after that and took the SIM card out of the phone and snapped it in half.

CHAPTER SIXTEEN

The Casey family's flight left early the next morning, and Lou was waiting with the four new Yukons Cain had purchased from the local GMC dealer. Every chance she got, they bought from the locals so no one would think the new neighbors weren't a great addition to town.

Jerry Rath was driving the vehicle behind Lou, and Cain hadn't gotten such a strong embrace from a man since her brother was alive. She stepped back and let him greet Emma and the children the same way, which gave her a chance to notice the two large SUVs parked close to the building where the control tower was located. Every so often she had the fantasy of asking one of her people for their weapon and just opening fire. Her defense would be she'd had enough of the constant invasion of her privacy.

"Maddie and JC are waiting at the new place with lunch," Jerry said as the men unloaded the plane. "She's been in there cooking since yesterday. I hope you don't mind her christening your kitchen, Emma."

"I'd rather milk a hundred cows than cook, so don't get jealous when I kiss her on the lips for thinking about us."

They hadn't been to Emma's hometown since Cain had driven Big Gino to the hole she'd buried him in, and she loaded her family into one of the trucks and carried them to their new vacation home. She'd designed it large enough for Ross to stay with them if he wanted to, but he'd told her on the way there that he'd given up his room to Maddie and Jerry. Ross figured Emma would appreciate the time to catch up with her oldest friend and enjoy the Raths' new baby.

Even though the cabin was closer to the Raths, Cain had built the drive to it from Ross's farm. The patch of land was now hers and Emma's, but she wanted their place to connect to Ross and his family's heritage. She'd had the drive lined with the pines Ross told the kids his family had on their original farm in France generations before.

Eventually it'd be a beautiful addition, and they'd provide no cover for the teams the FBI insisted on sending with them.

"It's beautiful," Emma said when the cabin came into view.

The place was big, yet small when compared to the house in New Orleans. It was deep into the acres Ross and Jerry owned, so unless their friends had a warrant, they'd have to trespass to get anywhere near them. The hedges that surrounded the buildings also left them only one view, and that was from the front porch, so she'd told everyone that no business would ever take place there.

"I'm glad you approve so far, because I think it's perfect for us. We're going to finally enjoy ourselves without anyone looking on."

"Then I love it already." Emma reached across the center console for Cain's hand.

They parked on the side and entered through the back deck, where she'd installed a heated pool so it wouldn't freeze over and crack in the winter. Maddie was outside holding JC with a smile so wide Cain thought her face had to hurt, and even though Maddie was Emma's friend, she hugged Cain first. The baby was squeezed between them, so Cain took him from Maddie and held him up so she could get her free arm around her.

"God bless you," Maddie said softly, but she heard her words over JC's baby talk.

She was able to look at JC when Maddie let go. The little boy had gotten bigger, and his chubby cheeks were cherub-like. His hair had grown out and was curly at the ends, which made him resemble Maddie. Cain thought back to the waif of a girl who was his birth mother; her hair had been a bit wavy too.

"His hair's lightened up." Emma ran her hand over his head. "All that time outside with his daddy is doing him good."

"He's perfect even when he's cranky," Jerry said. "And that only happens when Maddie brings peas anywhere near him."

"I don't mean to mess up your routine, but while we're here let's play it safe and keep JC indoors. You all know how popular I am, so let's assume the trees have eyes and ears." Cain handed the baby to Emma, who immediately got a series of laughs out of him.

They took the tour of the inside, the kids running to their rooms, and Emma grasped her hand and asked for a look at their bedroom. When she'd had the architect lay it out she'd asked for him to pay tribute to a certain tree close to the shore. He'd actually built the master suite over the water, and the bed faced the lake and that one tree.

"I remember the first time you brought me to this place you love so much," Cain said as she stepped behind Emma and put her hands over their baby. "You said this was your wishing place, and I wanted you to know that I'd do anything to make every dream and wish you have come true."

"It's silly, but I think of this baby being conceived right over there," Emma pointed to the shore. "And you are my wish, my love. I feel selfish wanting anything more when I have everything already."

"I love you, and tonight when everything quiets down, I'll be honored to show you how much."

Emma turned and reached up for her. She kissed her, and when Emma's tongue entered her mouth she was ready to strip. "You're a bad influence, Mrs. Casey," she whispered in Emma's ear as Hannah came in and jumped on their bed.

"I've learned from the best, but I have years of lessons left to take," Emma said as she squeezed her butt. "Besides, you have yet to make an honest woman out of me, but you'll have your chance soon enough. For now let's go be sociable."

They spent the rest of the night laughing and catching up with the Raths. Cain didn't understand the cow conversation aside from the number that Jerry was now responsible for. With the number she'd purchased and Ross's, Jerry was now the largest operator in the area. He'd taken advantage of the huge land acquisition his silent partner had made from some of the neighboring farms that were happy to sell for the price she'd offered.

"The new star of the farmers' market is the Verde cheese." Jerry slapped Ross on the back. "We used your recipe, and its popularity has made us double the volume three times already."

"It's the same as any around here," Ross said, in his usual humble way.

"That's not what the buyer from Dean and DeLuca thinks," Maddie said excitedly. "The woman happened to try some and they want to talk to you."

Cain's phone buzzed as everyone started talking about Ross's good luck. Emma glanced at her, but she smiled and shook her head to let her know it was nothing to worry about. The caller was Remi, and she wasn't expecting any bad news.

"Hey, thanks for the ride up here. Emma and the kids are getting spoiled with that kind of service."

"Glad to do it," Remi said. Judging from the background noise, she was at the Pescador Club, her father's favorite business. "I don't want you to worry on your vacation, but Nicolette was here earlier. She came in with two guys to offer us the deal you walked away from. Her tone was almost desperate, but she did take her time telling me what a shit you are. I guess she forgot we *were* part of the original deal."

"Then half my message got through."

"How's that?"

"She came to the house and wasn't too nice to Emma. Before she got to be a pest like she had been the night before at Emma's, I paid her and Luce a visit, with a message to leave. She's moving on, apparently, but finding new takers wasn't what I had in mind." She looked about into the darkness, at ease with the number of guards Katlin had roaming close to the house.

"According to her, she's not going anywhere."

"Do me a favor and call her back and set up a meeting next week. If you want to make it sound better, tell her you want your dad there and he's not available until then." The lights from the porch had attracted a swarm of bugs, which gave her the idea to take the kids fishing, since she'd had the lake stocked.

"No problem. I'm not interested in anything this woman has in mind, from the way she approached me. She should've stuck with Maximo to finish our contract. He was reasonable, and what he'd agreed to would've been good for everyone. Nicolette comes across as half-hinged."

"Keep in touch, and let me know if you need any help." She ended the call.

"Problems?" Katlin asked.

"Nicolette's trying to find new wine lovers, and Remi was tops on her list." She'd moved into the office, which had been Emma's idea, and she'd designed and decorated it. Like in New Orleans, it had some mementos of her family's history, as well as Emma's touches that were, as always, tasteful. "Before we head back I'll give Michel Blanc a call and ask him to come for a visit. That'll be the easiest way to put a leash on Nicolette and her girlfriend."

"I know we just arrived, but Muriel called during dinner with some interesting information."

"She's okay, right?"

"Don't worry. I put a fence around her. What happened to Merrick and Emma isn't going to be repeated, if I have anything to do with it." Katlin came close and stood next to her. "I think about it all the time too, so I go over all the potential holes in our security constantly. These people who'd hurt the women we love, they won't get close again."

"Do you remember that hole we filled not that long ago?" Cain turned and put her hands on the sides of Katlin's neck. "When I have Juan in that same place, then I'll stop thinking about it."

"Muriel might've gotten us one step closer to that."

"Is she doing okay?" She waved Katlin to one of the faux-cowhide chairs Emma thought would be perfect.

The decanter and glasses were her father's and had been in the office for years. Emma had asked her to consider moving them because of the crystal stag head on the bottle that matched the etchings on the glasses. Unlike the other glasses at home, this set had been a gift from Cain's mother, so they weren't that old, but she did love them as much as her dad had.

She poured Katlin a small amount of whiskey and some for herself. "After what happened with Shelby, I think she covers up her feelings so I won't find any weakness in her. The way that all went down, I don't know, it changed her."

"Do you mind me being honest?"

"That's why I'm talking about this."

Katlin sipped her drink as if to fortify herself. "What Shelby did cut deep into who Muriel thought she was, and it gutted her. Muriel felt, hell, feels like an idiot for allowing someone so dangerous that close to the family. Right afterward, Brent the asshole put you in the hospital, and Emma and I wouldn't let her in to see you. She told me later it was like losing everyone who loved her right after Uncle Jarvis died."

"I didn't blame Emma for what she did, considering the circumstances. Maybe it'll take time, though I want her to know we may disagree at times, but we're her family."

"Talk to her then, cousin. Think about what her relationship was with Uncle Jarvis right before he passed. You're the rock in her life now. She needs your reassurance and faith. I'm convinced that's what's sped up Merrick's recovery, so don't take for granted that everyone always knows what's in your head."

Cain laughed, forever grateful that she'd lucked out with the family she'd been blessed with. "Thanks for the advice, and just so you know, I love you. When Emma came back to me, I asked you to step up, and you have. I'm proud to have you with me."

"I wasn't fishing for compliments, but I'll take that one. Your Da and Uncle Jarvis helped me get here, and Mum and I'll never forget that. She wants to have us over for dinner when we get back." Katlin's mother was Dalton's cousin who'd married young, but to a bastard who'd given her only one good thing in her life—Katlin.

Katlin was a baby when her mother Laura received her last black eye from her husband's fists, and she'd finally turned to Cain's Da for help. Neither Katlin, when she was old enough, nor Laura ever asked what happened to him, and most probably never would. Cain's Da hadn't killed him, but he'd disappeared like fog on a sunny day after their talk. In Katlin's life, Dalton and Jarvis were the fathers she knew and loved, and she'd never ventured beyond that.

"How is she? It's been a while since she's been to the house."

"You know Mum and her daily masses. I swear the day we both go, a troop of angels will fall from the heavens to carry us away, she prays so much."

Cain laughed at that too, since her mother was exactly the same way. "Tell her we'd love to, though she might be sorry when I drag my rowdy bunch along. Now tell me what Muriel found."

"Something you and Ramon did once. Do you remember the name Jerome Rhodes?"

"He was the one who'd rented rooms for Gracelia and company, supposedly. Is he back?"

"Arrived the day after the first bout of bad luck, only this time he's staying in Metairie at that place by the lake. Muriel put the word out after that last time, on the off chance he came back, and one of the girls at the front desk called this morning. He's got four rooms this time under J. Rhodes."

"Get Sabana on the phone and ask how hard she's willing to work to get back in my good graces. If she goes off on these people and I lose Juan, let her know there's no hole big enough for her to hide in. Send her over there and watch to see if Gracelia has finally poked her head out from whatever rock she's been hiding under."

"You sure? Sabana's good and doesn't hesitate, but she's still too high-strung for me to trust completely."

"She wants off that wall more than she wants to pull the trigger, so let's see what happens. If my judgment's off that bad I might have to consider retirement."

"Retirement? And leave me with all this crap? Forget about it," Katlin said as she left.

The need to get back on the plane and see if Gracelia really was with this guy Jerome was something Cain had to beat down and put back in its cage. She'd promised the kids and Emma the week, and that's what she was going to give them.

"We'll see soon enough, Gracelia, what kind of devotion you

have for your child. Will you give him up at the first sign of pain, or will you die with his secrets intact, like I would if our positions were reversed?"

❖

"Judice, this is Victoria."

The call was unexpected; she'd caught up on everything before she left and informed all her clients when she'd be home from her brief vacation. Victoria worked for Salvatore Maggio, a man you never wanted to disappoint.

"Hello, is everything all right? I'm surprised to hear from you."

"Everything's ready for your return, and I'll get into a world of trouble if Sal knows I'm making this call."

"If anything's wrong he won't hear it from me."

"Colin Mead called Sal and told him someone was asking about your kid, but the interest shifted to you quick enough. You know how much Sal likes questions, so what are you doing down there?"

Victoria might've been Sal's assistant, but she was also his mistress, and he loved pillow talk. No subject about his business was off-limits. If someone like Fiona ever flipped someone like Victoria or her, the head of the mob on the West Coast would go away for life. Then the streets would run red with blood for the betrayal. Sal had been good to her, as had Colin Mead, but a lifetime of lying to Fiona about who her mother really was had been burdensome. There was no way out, though, except a pretty casket for a job well done.

"Someone called Colin about me?" Colin's operation wasn't as large as Sal's, but he was as deadly. The Chicago transplant was a big Irishman who loved to laugh and drink, and his crew ran part of the docks. He'd been one of her first clients and still tried to get her in bed whenever he came to the house for his ledgers. "Who?"

"You know someone named Casey?" Victoria's voice dropped, and Judice pictured the pretty brunette hunched over her phone somewhere in Sal's office.

"Cain Casey?" Dread spread through her like fire through dry brush.

"No, it was Muriel Casey. Colin talked to her because Sal said they were somehow related. Maybe this Muriel was asking because they want to use your services, but I'd suggest coming by when you get back and talking Sal off the ledge. He's not paranoid about much, but he's rethinking outsourcing his books. You could hurt him if you really wanted to, but I told him you weren't that stupid."

"Sal and Colin don't have anything to worry about. I took a blood oath with both eyes open, and I know the consequences of breaking that." In reality she wasn't worried about herself. Fiona was her priority. If Cain felt threatened by her daughter, she knew from experience how she'd react. "Do you think I should talk to him now?"

"No." Victoria's voice rose suddenly. "You promised you wouldn't say anything," she said through what sounded like clenched teeth. "That goes for Colin too."

"Did Sal say what Colin told Muriel Casey?"

"All I know is what I just told you, so relax and enjoy your visit. If anything else comes up I'll call you."

"Thanks." She hung up and grabbed her stomach. Such sudden fear always made her nauseous, as did not having a good answer to avoiding a bad situation.

Her phone rang again, and she lunged for it as if whoever the caller was held the key. "Hello."

"How are you, pretty lady?" Colin's voice boomed through the receiver, and she had to pull it away from her ear.

"Enjoying my visit with Fiona, but I'm looking forward to coming home."

"Good," Colin said, in a more normal tone. "Good," he repeated. "Judice, you know I trust you, and I've stuck by you even when that kid of yours picked the road she did. Having the woman I trust with my money living with a detective of the LAPD was a gut check for me. You promised, though, that this wouldn't ever be a problem, and so far you've been right. Fiona's gone about her business, which was to stay the hell away from ours."

She glanced at the clock, grateful Fiona wasn't due for another hour. "Colin, nothing's changed from our end."

"Don't stress yourself. As far as I'm concerned, your place with me is the same, but Sal ain't as quick to calm as I am. From what we hear, little Fiona's gotten herself a gig with the FBI that's concentrating on organized crime."

"That's true, but in Louisiana," she said as the room closed in on her. Eventually there'd be no place to hide, and Fiona's badge couldn't protect either of them. "She moved here and has no interest in you or Sal."

"If she was working the same as she was here, I'd agree and start flirting with you, but the 'F' stands for Federal. NOPD might not have heard of us, but I can promise you the FBI has, and they'll keep coming until they know all about us."

"I've tried talking to her, but she's hardheaded when she feels strongly she's doing the right thing."

"I got a call about Fiona from Muriel Casey," Colin said to cut her off. "Muriel's a sharp one, but nothing like my distant kin Cain. That's who Muriel was calling for, so your Fiona's been noticed."

"What did you tell her?"

"I told her not to worry about Fiona because I personally vouched for you. Don't make a liar out of me. Muriel doesn't know exactly what you do, and for now that's how we'll keep it."

"I won't betray you, please believe that. How are you related?"

"Cain's a cousin a couple of times removed on our daddy's side, and we've done some business with her that's been nothing but legit. I care for you, Judice, but if I'm pressed I'll side with Cain on this one. If I pull my patronage and my business, I'll give you fair warning so you can try and run. The only way that'll happen is if Fiona turns on us. I don't like talking about such harsh subjects, but I thought you deserved the truth from me."

She'd realized this side of things going in, but had gambled with their lives anyway. "Thank you, and please think about my years of loyalty before you make any decisions. Fiona blames Cain for something, and it motivated her to work with the FBI. She'll never get any help from me, I swear it."

"The problem is though, darling, if she gets too close something will be done, and if that comes to be, that loyalty you've shown Sal and me will dry up and die. I can't protect you from anything if I'm having to protect my livelihood at all costs."

"I know." She took a while to lower the phone after he'd hung up. She jumped when it rang again. "Hey, how's your day going?" she asked Fiona, trying to sound upbeat.

"It's a short day. You want to eat early and go to a movie or something?"

"I'd love to." She hung up again and she tried not to cry while she slowly got ready.

"Damn the Caseys. Damn them to hell," she said as she stared at her reflection.

❖

"But, Papa," Nicolette screamed into her phone to try to talk over her father, Michel.

"Do not interrupt me again," he said in a stern voice. She hoped he was alone in his office so she wouldn't have to deal with the embarrassment when they returned home. He'd lectured from the moment he'd answered. "You and that imbecile begged me to let you go close a deal that needed nothing else but to shake hands with those involved. That was it."

"You can't blame Luce for trying to sweeten the deal."

"Then Luce didn't tell you the truth of what happened. She tried to piss on Cain Casey to mark her territory, and she got slapped down for it at our expense." Michel took a breath, which signaled her he was starting to calm. "I gave Luce the job she has with us at your urging, my love, but I'm leaving it up to you to clean this mess up. You have to start realizing I won't live forever, and you need to use your head in business instead of your heart. You built Cain up to mythical status, then sent Luce to do business with her."

The hospital waiting room wasn't crowded, but the few people waiting to hear how their loved ones fared through surgery stared at her, she assumed, for her volume and the French she spoke. Luce was finally in surgery to repair the damage to her nose, since the doctor had waited for the swelling to go down. The time and pain had worked Luce into a lather, and she'd concocted a different plan to kill Cain every hour, it seemed.

"This is my fault and I'll fix it. Have some faith. I've already tried to get Remi back to the table, but she laughed and told me to get the hell out of her club."

"Faith in you has never and will never be a problem for me, but you knew the stakes before you left. We need to expand to survive, and it makes me angry that Luce knew that as well and still chose to screw this up." He'd softened his tone earlier, but now he was starting to get loud again. "And of course Remi Jatibon brushed you off. That's what your girlfriend did to her and her family. Insults are hardly forgiven in our business, Nic. It's time you learned that lesson even at the expense of some of the others."

"Tell me what you want me to do, Papa, and I'll do it." The young couple in the corner who'd been praying the rosary the entire time she'd sat there jumped to their feet when a man in scrubs came to the door. What would it be like to love someone like that? "I promise not to disappoint you again."

"We need capital, Nic, so write this number down," Michel said, and rattled off some numbers. "This isn't what I had planned, but we must do what we have to in order to survive."

"Who is this?" The only clue she had was that it was a local number.

"His name is Jerome Rhodes. He's currently the second for Gracelia Luis, but he's interested in branching out. Meet with him and see if this is a good fit for us."

"You want to move us into drugs?"

"I want to sell wine at inflated prices. Leave the judgment to God, and concentrate on the survival of our family."

She got up and the guards followed her out. Luce could wait, but her father's wishes couldn't. "This will be better than the original deal, you'll see." She tried to sound confident, but unknowns were, in her opinion, the first step toward ruin.

❖

"It's a shame we can't keep the shades open so we can wake up to that view," Emma said as she took off her earrings and bracelet.

"You can if you want to. Believe me, you can see out, but no one's peeking back at you." Cain sat on the bed in her sleep pants and watched Emma's nightly ritual. The jewelry went into a small pile; then she brushed her hair, removed her makeup, and applied some kind of cream to her face. When they'd been apart and she'd snapped the bathroom light off, she'd lie there alone and miss the sight.

Emma wore a silk robe and smiled at her in the mirror. "What are you thinking so hard about over there, mobster?"

"Hard is the operative word, so hurry it up in there."

When Emma turned she pulled the tie on the robe so Cain could see she was naked underneath. Emma was incredibly beautiful, and she'd thought so from the beginning, but this surpassed all that. She'd forgotten how extraordinary she was pregnant, but it all came back. The swell of her belly and the larger breasts made her even more gorgeous in her eyes, and it made her want her.

"You're a gift to me, lass," she said, but didn't get up. Right now she didn't want to so as not to miss this very personal view. She didn't give a damn what was outside the window.

"From the day I met you, I've wanted to always see this look on your face," Emma said as she started for her, the robe billowing out as she moved. "Take your pants off."

Cain stripped and sat back down. Emma straddled her leg when she did and reached down to open her sex so it pressed against her thigh. Cain could feel how wet she was, but she wanted Emma to set their pace.

"You always appear so hungry whenever my clothes are off." She opened her mouth to Emma's finger and her heart to her words. Emma never spoke like this to anyone but her, and never outside their bedroom. "Do you know how flattering that is? You could have anyone, but you want me."

"Therese Casey raised no fools," Cain said after she'd sucked on Emma's fingertips. "What I should do, though…" She placed her hands on Emma's hips and helped her slide forward a little. The friction was enough to make Emma moan and Cain clam up.

"You should do what?" Emma placed her hand under her breast and pressed the nipple to her lips.

"I ought to put you over my knee and spank you for the torturous night you put me through."

"Tonight I'm yours to do with anything you please," Emma said with a smile as she stood and lay across her lap before she could protest.

"Are you comfortable?" Her concern was for the baby with Emma in this position.

"Incredibly so," Emma said, her voice peaking at the end when she grabbed her ass.

"Good." She squeezed both sides before she slid her finger down Emma's sex to the hard clit, then back up to ease it in to the knuckle. Emma lifted her bottom the fourth time she repeated the move, and from how she was dripping, she was ready. One small taste and she'd give her what she wanted.

She put two fingers in, then put them in her mouth. Emma was unique and she savored her until she got a slap to her foot. "A faster tempo would be good," Emma said.

Another slap came when she laughed, but she gave Emma what she wanted and filled her up, letting her move however she wanted. The first orgasm of the night was fast and hard, and made Emma press her legs together when she came. She was so limp, Cain was able to pick her up and carry her to lay her down. Once her head was on the pillow, Emma kissed her and fell asleep. Another side effect of pregnancy she'd forgotten and had to get used to.

"I love you, lass, even if you've left me in a sorry state," she said as she wrapped her arms around her and tried to ignore the pounding between her legs. As much as she tried concentrating on what Muriel had found, she couldn't hold the thought with Emma this close to her.

She closed her eyes and found sleep instantly, with her parents waiting in her dreams. They both had the same wide smiles and the same message. "Be sure of who you are, love, and what your position is," her father said first, like he had so many times in his life. "Nothing can change that."

"Listen to your father," her mum said. "There's a little boy on his way who's counting on you like his brother and sister are."

"I'll do right by what you taught me, and by my name," Cain said, and became peaceful when her parents turned and walked away toward a beautiful sunset. "Keep watch over us."

CHAPTER SEVENTEEN

Y ou were talking in your sleep last night," Emma said as she came up from between her legs. Having an intense orgasm right after you woke up was both wonderful and aggravating. Wonderful since any orgasm was great unless you disliked sex, and aggravating because you somehow slept through the buildup.

"I'm surprised you heard anything over all your snoring," Cain said jokingly, grabbing Emma's hands as she started to tickle her and then gently pulling Emma's body over hers. "I'd puff my chest out over the coma I put you in, but all this fresh air might kill me."

"Get up and take your children for a swim, and if that tires you out, I might take a nap with you later. Maybe I can stay conscious this time until the festivities are over. Oh, and while *you* were snoring, Muriel phoned. She said to call when you got a minute."

"How about we pay someone to take the kids swimming and we stay naked." Cain ran her hands up the curve of Emma's butt. "Maybe it's not too late for twins. I think we can do it."

"I'm not exactly immune to your persuasion, so don't make this harder than it has to be, mobster. You keep me in here all day and I'll probably go into labor from the full-body blush that'll cause." Emma seemed so happy that any trace of the horror Juan had put her through was gone.

"Put your bathing suit on, Mama, after you take a shower with me."

Cain called Muriel and found out about Jerome and her call to Colin. Before Muriel finished, she'd asked her to fly up and join them so they could get through all their business from the new study in the cabin. Muriel didn't hesitate to accept her offer, and she promised herself to try to help Muriel find what she'd lost when Jarvis died.

They swam and had lunch on the back patio, where it was hard to keep the kids quiet as they played with the baby. For some reason the dream she'd remembered from the night before came to mind, and she took it to mean she had to enjoy moments like this, to savor the light so the dark times weren't so bad to bear.

"I had a dream last night about my parents," she whispered to Emma.

"About what?"

"Mum said we have a little boy on the way, so you were right." The news wasn't exactly scientific proof, but it made Emma smile and tear up as she kissed her.

After lunch she walked the field they'd herded the cows out of with Ross and Hayden, all of them cradling shotguns. Lou had set up the skeet machine and checked the field the day before to make sure it was clear of anyone who'd be in the line of fire, especially any brave federal agents.

"Let the cheese and casino king go first," Cain said to Hayden as Lou loaded the clay pigeons into the machine.

Ross kidded back, "I might want to put money on this, so watch it."

It was on Ross's second shot that she noticed the small satellite dish halfway up a tree. Someone had put it up and pointed it toward the house. She cocked her head in that direction so Lou would hopefully notice what she was staring at.

"It wasn't there yesterday, boss."

"You want to go next, Mom?" Hayden asked when she stepped in front of him.

"Give me a second." She loaded two shells into the chambers of the crack barrel she owned. "Anyone out there?" she yelled, and walked closer to the tree line. "This is private property, so show yourself and any warrant you've got on you, or I call my pal the sheriff." She snapped the gun closed so it was ready to fire.

"Last chance." She repeated her warning before she put the gun to her shoulder and seated it. The dish splintered when the buckshot hit it, and she hoped they were listening like rats in a wall when it did. Lou jogged to catch up as she entered the woods because her gut told her the dish was a decoy. The Feds had to have more sophisticated equipment than that.

A hundred feet in she saw the short wand-like mic about the same height as the dish, so she let loose the other shell. "I can do this all day, and Lou here is calling to close off all the access roads to the property. Why not save yourself some embarrassment, Agent Chapman?"

"For future reference, it's Special Agent Chapman," Ronald said from somewhere deeper in, but still not in view.

"There's not a fucking thing special about you, Ronald." She removed the two empty shells and replaced them. "I'm not usually one for cursing, but you and your little minion are out of place here. Do you have a warrant or not?"

"I already told you, you live the way you do, Ms. Casey, and you have to accept certain things."

"What's that? Being spied on while I'm enjoying a vacation with my family? Were you after my father-in-law's secret cheese recipe, or are you curious about what my wife and I are up to in the master bedroom?" She snapped the gun closed again and kept walking. "Lou, call some guys and let's flush these people out of here."

"Ms. Casey, I'm warning you that you're coming precariously close to threatening the lives of a number of federal agents."

"My attorney will go through the finer points of people on my property claiming they're agents but not showing themselves." She saw another distance mic and blew it out of its tree. Lou fired from fifty feet away, and that got Ronald to step out from behind the tree that hid him.

"Let's take a breath before this gets out of hand," he said, his palms showing. "What the hell's the matter with you? I could have you shot and I'd be justified."

She laughed at Ronald's dress shirt and slacks. This guy really was an odd duck who must always have trouble fitting in. "I find you a threat, not because of why you're here but because of my recent experience at the hands of your people. You're right. You can have me shot and get away with it and get a medal for your troubles. It's happened before, but you can't have it both ways either, Ronald." She removed the shells from her gun and left it open; she didn't want someone like Brent to take a free shot.

"What do you mean?"

"A guy with a badge with the discretion to do anything he wants makes me *have* to defend myself. If you think I'm letting Cehan beat me while I'm cuffed again, you don't know me at all. *You* were the one who forgave him, so I'm done with this and your tough-guy act." She looked at him and came close to laughing at his glare. "Get out of here now, and I don't call George Talbot."

"George is the U.S. Attorney, not your personal crusader, and the reputation of someone like Agent Cehan will trump you in court every time."

"We'll see about that. You're right, George is so very far away right now, but eventually we'll find out in court who wins that argument. Will it be you in your frilly shoes or me with the family and pregnant wife who had to sit by my bedside while I recovered from the head injury that asshole gave me?" The taunts were hitting their mark, and she never looked away from his face as it twisted in anger.

"This isn't the last of this." He turned his back on her and walked away.

"He's going to double down now," Lou said as he pumped his weapon.

"What a better alibi then," she said low, but didn't really care if she'd missed any microphones. "I've come to the end of my patience with this," she said, this time louder.

Lou nodded as if he understood this sudden break in composure. She seldom called the watchers out, especially the way she'd done with Ronald. It'd been a knee-jerk reaction, but she realized she could work it in her favor if she could convince Emma of a few things once they got back to the house.

"Let's finish up with Hayden. Tell everyone not to make like a clay disk while we're out here."

They were out for another hour and were laughing by the time they walked home. She never glanced back, secure that Ronald hadn't ordered his people to leave. When the prey was hostile and coming apart because you had them backed to a wall, they seemed easier to catch. Right now she needed Ronald to relax because she'd be cakewalk prey, in his opinion.

When Ronald turned around he shoved his hands into his pockets and tried to calm his gut. He was so close to throwing everything he'd planned into the toilet for the chance to strangle the life out of the bitch who'd dared treat him like a punk with no balls.

"Agent Chapman," Lionel said, but shut up when he shot him a look.

"Leave, and I'll transfer you somewhere you're guaranteed to be miserable."

"She's not kidding about the sheriff." Shelby moved Lionel behind her. "It's happened before, and he'll rush over here given the chance because he loves her."

"We still have ten mics pointed at the house, with double that in cameras," Joe said, obviously much more comfortable than him in his jeans and hiking boots. "We can monitor from the hotel room."

"If you have a hearing problem, then you're worthless to me as a field agent." Ronald kept going until he reached the car and came close to hitting Brent as he tried to get in the passenger side.

The game was harder than he imagined, but nothing in Casey's file mentioned a reaction like today's. Maybe confronting her from the beginning had thrown her and he was getting to her. If that was true, any humiliation she wanted to give him would be worth it. His priority would have to be keeping the respect of the team and prohibiting them from reporting back to Annabel.

"Fuck," he screamed, and slammed his hand on the seat next to him. Of all the places in the world for this to happen. He needed something to get himself together, but it'd have to wait.

The car fishtailed down the dirt road and Shelby stared at the receding taillights. "What exactly happened?" she asked the others. "And who's volunteering to walk to town and pick up the other car?"

"I vote for Brent," Claire said. "You're team leader. Lionel and I have to stay with what's left of our equipment, and Joe's the best shot of all of us."

"Kiss my ass," Brent said, but did start the walk toward the highway where they'd left their car.

"In all our years together, have you ever seen Cain do something like that?" Joe asked, and Shelby nodded. "This feels like the first time we were here. She totally did a one eighty of how she did things, and she played us."

"This time, though, she's not planning anything out of the ordinary that we know of. You all had to notice the split second she saw that dish. The short-fuse reaction felt real to me," she said, because she understood that point where you snapped.

"How do we play this?" Joe asked.

"Not like we did last time." She thought about all she could get out of Cain with a little leverage. That's what she'd been missing before. Something on Cain was better than her great idea of giving her their complete playbook in exchange for help in finding the men she was searching for. "We need to be ready for anything."

"It's good to have you back," Joe said as they sat back on their camping folding chairs. "Anything you need to help you get past the rest of what you're going through, just ask."

"Thank you, but this is better than moping around my house. Like

I told Annabel, Cain might not be responsible for ordering the hit on my parents, but it'll tie back to her somehow." Again she went with a little of the truth. "Someone wanted us to zero in on Cain, and when that happens, you take your eyes off something else."

"Or you use the cops to get rid of your competition," Joe said.

"Her competition's a possibility, but they're nowhere around here, so let's hope ape man brings coffee. It's going to be a long week."

❖

Muriel studied the notes she'd made on her conversation with Colin and the research she did afterward. There was a lot that didn't make sense and even more she couldn't find, which to her was as troubling as finding too much on someone. She took off the reading glasses she'd recently had to get and pinched her nose.

Alone in the cabin of Remi's plane, she stared out the window and wondered if her parents had been reunited again and if she'd ever find someone she'd cherish as much as her father had her mother. Even after she'd encouraged him to search for someone to share his life, he'd smiled and declined.

"We're a hundred miles out. It shouldn't be long now." One of the attendants had come out and was clearing away the remnants of the sandwich and soda she'd served.

"Thank you." Muriel went back to staring at clouds.

The plane stopped, and when the door opened only one person was waiting by a big SUV. She laughed at the shorts and plain T-shirt. Cain never looked this undone, but it was a good thing. "Are those your cow-milking clothes?"

"It's my fishing outfit, smart-ass, and I bought you some, so don't make too much fun of me." Cain accepted her bags and tossed them in the backseat. "Come on. Let's go have lunch in town. I'm sure the waitress needs new shoes by now."

"I guess I don't have to ask if you're having fun. We should've talked you into a vacation home years ago." The last time Muriel was here she'd seen only this small part of the airport. It felt like a million years ago, when her life had been as uncomplicated as a ten-year-old's.

"I'm already planning to add on." Cain put her hand on the back of Muriel's neck. "Something occurred to me as I was in a rowboat baiting Hannah's hook. I want them to grow up the way we did. When we were kids I had Billy and Marie, and you and Katlin were always there. Think about how much harder this would be without that foundation we had from the beginning."

"You sure about that?"

Cain had come alone with a plan to spend a day trying to get Muriel to open up. It might turn out to be easier than she'd thought. "Why don't you want to believe me?"

"About what? I haven't accused you of lying, that I know of."

She parked a block from the café, glanced in the rearview mirror, and saw the blue sedan about fifty feet behind them. "Will you promise me something?"

"Sure. If you need something I'll be happy to help out. All you have to do is ask."

"You see that?" She pointed at the mirror. "We can't talk now, but tonight, once everyone's asleep, I want you to have a drink with me." She shook her head to keep Muriel quiet. "Only accept if you're ready to talk to me."

It took a long pause for Muriel to get out and join her on the sidewalk, but she did after peering back at the sedan. She recognized Joe Simmons and Claire, but that was all. Shelby would come back eventually, and Cain needed to have Muriel in a better place to deal with seeing her as an adversary every day.

"Did Emma like the house?"

Their conversation at lunch started there and ended with what had happened with Ronald the day before. Muriel smiled as Cain whined about the pressure of not ever being out of the Feds' spotlight. *I think they got it*, Muriel wrote on a napkin she pushed toward her.

"You'd think so." Cain winked.

At the house she pushed Muriel into the pool fully clothed, and Katlin went in right after, an easy target because she was laughing so hard. The roughhousing was a good reminder of what they were like as children, back when they didn't have to worry about anything and their only real responsibility was school.

"Give us a bit, then I'll call y'all in," she said to Katlin and Lou once dinner and fun were over.

Muriel had changed and watched her as she moved around the room. "You don't have to do this, you know. If you're worried I'm cracking up on you, I'm not."

"Stop bullshitting me," Cain said sharply. The approach was harsh, but her father had used it plenty of times when he wanted something stubborn to shake loose, as he'd put it. "I'm not going to judge you, and it's time you hear some truths from me."

"I've heard everything I need to hear from you, and I know how you feel, so let's get back to work."

"Sure, once you answer my question from today. Why don't you believe me?" She grabbed Muriel by the jaw and made her look her in the eye. "What did I do to make you lose faith in me? Better yet, what do I do to change that?"

"Goddamn it, this is something I have to work out for myself, so don't let it eat at you. If one of us fucked up here it was me, not you. Hell, if it wasn't for you, we'd be in real trouble because of what I did."

"The problem is, it does eat at me because I promised your father I'd let you know word for word what was in his heart before he had to go. I've repeated them to you over and over, but you haven't heard a single thing I've said."

"The words that play in my head in a loop are the last ones Da and I exchanged, and that we fought over that bitch I allowed in my bed makes me want to crawl into a ball and stay that way. Jesus, what an idiot he must've thought I was." Muriel's voice rose to a scream and she slammed her hands into the arms of the chair.

"We all make mistakes, Muriel, but if we don't learn from them, life loses every bit of happiness. You made a mistake in trusting that Shelby cared more for you than her job, but it wasn't fatal."

"No, not fatal, but don't lie and say it wasn't damaging."

"A few years ago I trusted a man because technically we shared blood, and he took something precious from me. That mistake was fatal for my sister, and if I hadn't been able to get past it, Emma would still be up the road and Hannah would still be under the same roof as that witch who's her grandmother. For a long time it felt so good to let the anger build—it was all I had. It made it easy to dump all that pain on Emma's head. My love for her won out, and it's caused that gash Danny made to heal." She moved up so their knees were touching. "Danny was never Emma's fault, but it was so convenient to blame her, to hate her even, but losing her made me bleed more than losing Marie."

"You're not suggesting I take Shelby back?"

"I'm suggesting you let it go and move on. If you don't, the right woman will fall on you and you'll be too bitter to allow her in." Cain tapped over Muriel's heart. "You're my family, and I love you. Nothing in this life or the next will ever change that. If what happened had made me lose faith in what you mean to me, you wouldn't be here, you'd know nothing of my business, and I would've been honest about letting you know that."

"That I believe hands down." Muriel laughed. "You left out that you would've kicked my ass."

"I did kick your ass in the pool today to soften you up for this." She framed Muriel's face with her hands and smiled. "You forget I know you, cousin, and I know the pain you're in." She choked up when Muriel's eyes watered and a few tears dropped down her cheeks. "Uncle Jarvis is gone and I know you miss him, but don't forget you're a part of me. You're my family, and I'll be here for you however you need me."

"Thanks." Muriel wiped her face and blinked furiously, as if to dry up her emotions. "If I'd lost your trust and Katlin's, I'd be a goner, so I appreciate that you didn't turn your back on me. And I'm sorry I've been such a weakling lately. I'm sure you're ready for me to drop the maudlin act."

"You move at your own pace, and if anyone gives you shit about it, punch them in the face. That always makes me feel better."

"That might land me in jail. Assaulting a federal agent isn't a wise move."

"Haven't you heard?" Cain laughed. "We're criminals, cousin, but we're damned good ones. We've got a lot of ill-gotten gains to bail you out of anything."

Muriel laughed and stood so Cain could put her arms around her. She hugged her as hard as Jerry had at their arrival and didn't let go right away. Muriel had coasted since Jarvis's death, but Cain felt they'd finally made headway in knocking the boulder of guilt she carried off her shoulders.

❖

"What do you think they're talking about?" Claire asked as she watched Cain and Muriel with their heads together. Cain had finally relented from playing the theme from *Bonanza* after months, only to replace it with Disney's "It's a Small World" again. "She should become a contract worker at Guantanamo. You'd tell her whatever she wanted to know after a day of listening to this on a loop. How do you think she does it without going crazy herself?"

"The same way she's convincing Muriel what an evil bitch I am," Shelby said with a pain in her chest as she watched Muriel cry.

"Do you mind if I ask you something? Believe me, I won't be insulted if you don't answer."

"Sure." She glanced away from the monitor and rubbed her eyes from fatigue.

"If you could do it over again, would you change anything? That night when we all had dinner at your place and Cain showed up, I was convinced you really cared for Muriel. I never thought it was all about the assignment."

"I still care. You don't suddenly stop what you feel because they toss you to the curb." She went back to the monitor and remembered what it was like to be in Muriel's arms. "My mistake was thinking I could crack through that." She tapped her nail against the image of Cain and Muriel. "They take family commitment to heart, and I wasn't ever going to be enough to break that engrained sense of Caseyness. I might change my tactics if I got another shot, but I would take another shot, if that's what you're really asking."

"We thought we'd lost you, so that's good to hear."

"Grief makes you do crazy shit." She stared at Muriel's profile as she laughed at something Cain had said. "Look at what she almost sacrificed because of it."

❖

"Get Colin on the phone tomorrow and ask him if he's up for a visit," Cain said to Muriel as a wrap-up on their business for the night.

After Muriel's call to Colin, she'd researched Fiona and Judice O'Brannigan and found something disturbing to Cain—nothing. Judice had no past, no history except for giving birth to a daughter, Fiona. If not for that, there'd be no trace of the woman at all, and as with Dallas Montgomery, there had to be a reason. People hid from all sorts of situations and enemies, and finding them sometimes proved to be a dangerous proposition, even with the assurance of someone like Colin Mead.

"You want him to come to us, or do you want to go there?"

"Whichever's convenient for him. I want him happy and at ease so he'll be willing to tell his tales."

"You obviously haven't spoken to him recently." Muriel closed her files. "Give him a chance and he'll talk your ears off."

"Go to bed, and we'll hear it soon enough."

Cain went up and gently eased in next to Emma, to not wake her. Muriel's information had perked her up, but even though she wasn't sleepy, she didn't want Emma to wake up alone. Finding that Fiona and her only known family were ghosts was enough to almost make her forget about Juan—almost.

She'd seen enough movies to know that eventually someone would be smart enough to infiltrate the one arena that could tip the scales one way or the other. A family with someone loyal to them in the police department would be huge. Big Gino had almost pulled it off with Barney, but Barney wasn't really loyal to him. He'd only played a part for Gino to get what he wanted. Masquerading as a federal agent had been Barney's true acting job, not what he'd been willing to do for Gino to break the law. Only he'd done it for personal gain, not for the betterment of the Bracato family.

Her mind wandered from subject to subject, and the man in her parents' house that she'd seen later on watching them from his car finally pinged her memory. It was that brief glimpse of him at the shooting range with Hayden that afternoon. It was the same guy, and she remembered how she'd felt compelled to stop and look. The guy with the big shiny gun, the blond hair that clashed with those jet eyebrows, and how he stood almost arrogantly at the top of the steps in her old house.

There was something she realized now that she didn't then—when he'd descended the steps to leave and glanced back, his eyes weren't on her. They were on Emma. The way he stood at the top of the steps should've tipped her off. His hands were behind his back, and he rocked on his feet as if he were blessing you with the gift of his company. Only two other people she'd ever met made a habit of doing that, and one of them was dead.

Juan Luis, though, was not.

That habit had driven her nuts when she'd had to deal with his uncle Rodolfo, and after watching him as a boy, Juan must've picked it up. The fucker had been smart enough to change his face, but not those little things that identified him as completely as a goddamn fingerprint would.

"Shit," she said softly, and Emma stirred in her arms but didn't wake. When Cain went to leave the bed, she did.

"Where are you going?" Emma asked, without opening her eyes.

"I'll be right back, I promise." She put a robe on and went down the hall to where Merrick and Katlin were staying and knocked.

"You'd be in trouble if we'd been busy," Katlin said, blinking at the light in the hallway. "What's wrong?"

"Who'd you put on the guy outside the Columns Hotel?"

"What guy?"

"Wake the hell up and tell me you put somebody on him," she said, grabbing Katlin by the collar of her robe.

"I wasn't with you that day, remember? You and Merrick went alone and met Sept and that chick Fiona. What guy are you talking about?"

She heard the tap of Merrick's cane and the door opened wider. "I put Shaun Quinn on him, since he was the closest to us that day. He's young, but I'm sure he knows not to drop the ball on this, especially when I told him to find someone to relieve him when he was off. You want me to call him?"

"Wait, what guy are y'all talking about?" Katlin repeated.

"That's a good question that I'm sure Cain would love to answer over a cup of coffee since I'm up now," Emma said from behind her.

"It's too early for coffee. Let's go downstairs and make a few calls."

Cain got Muriel up as they headed down, and she waited for Merrick to make the call. "Whoever he is, he's at the Piquant, so I'd rule out FBI, and Shaun said he's in for the night. Actually he hasn't been out much since we left, but he does have another guy with him when he goes out to eat and such. If it makes you feel better I told him to put someone at all the entrances to make sure we don't lose him." Merrick sat next to Katlin when she was done and yawned. "Now, will you tell us why we're up in the middle of the night?"

"It's Juan."

Despite them all having been asleep five minutes earlier, they stared at her with the silence that could only come from shock. But saying it out loud made her believe it more. He was right in front of her with his hand on Hannah, and she'd never realized it until now.

"What do you mean it's Juan?" Emma grabbed Cain's forearm.

"There was only one way for him to come back, and he did it. The man at the top of the steps the day we went to Remi and Dallas's new place was Juan."

"I hate to argue with you, honey, but that guy wasn't Mexican and looked nothing like Juan," Emma said, but she stared at her as if something was starting to come back.

"He changed his face through surgery. It was his only escape, and hell if I didn't fall for it. Do you realize how close he was to you, Hannah, and Hayden? If he'd been his usual stupid self I would've lost every single one of you before I could stop him." She'd been right all along—Juan couldn't help himself. He'd come back to finish what she'd denied him. "He was there the last time Hayden and I went to the gun range and at the house that day."

"How can you be so sure?" Katlin asked. "Not that I'm trying to disagree with you."

"Think about Juan when we first met him, but not how he talked or acted. Think about his mannerisms."

"Oh, my God," Emma said, as if the truth had been dumped in her lap. "That day in Jackson Square when he confronted me and Lou was with me. We'd had our mock fight and you'd stormed away toward the church. He came out from the coffee shop and stood there with his hands behind his back. He rocked as he spoke, only showing his fists when Lou talked back to him. If Shelby hadn't shown up right then I believe he would've been arrogant enough to have Lou shot in broad daylight."

"There's no way in the world that stupid bastard did that on his own," Muriel said.

"He didn't." Cain put her arm around Emma, not wanting to worry her any more than she had to. "Anthony Curtis helped him get out of town, and he ran all the way home to his mother. Gracelia, from my understanding, is at times hasty, but she's a lot smarter than Juan. Think about it. She stole Rodolfo's business from him and killed him without much trouble. If Anthony is still part of that equation, then he's gone all in, because he certainly can't come back to his old life after what happened with Emma and Merrick."

"So we go back and kill the little shit?" Katlin asked.

"We'll get to that, but if we kill Juan right away it scares away his accomplice. I want Juan so bad I'm willing to sell my soul to the devil, but if I'm going to do that, I want both of them."

"How do we find Anthony?" Merrick asked. "Especially if he went through the same drastic overhaul of his face as Juan."

"We start with Vincent and see what that shakes loose."

"What's that supposed to mean?" Emma asked.

"Sometimes to catch a snake, you need a rat to bait the trap."

CHAPTER EIGHTEEN

Jerome walked the levee again and puffed on his cigarette as he casually glanced behind him. He hadn't chanced any other calls, but the young woman in the lobby was there again this morning. It was the third day he'd come down to get out of the room where Gracelia was cursing him for making her go through the hell she was in stuck with only him to count on.

Pablo followed him out and looked over his shoulder as well when Jerome did. He waved him over to make him walk faster. The more time passed when he wasn't getting anything done, the antsier he got, and not even the coke he was consuming was helping.

"Señor, I hear from Miguel Gonzalez. If you say yes, we can go soon, but Señor Delarosa no is here," Pablo whispered excitedly, even though they were alone. It was one of the reasons Jerome liked this guy more and more. Pablo was a nervous little ninny, but that kept him alive and out of trouble.

"When, then?"

"He say to come at the end of week. We got problem before we start."

"Pablo, call me Jerome, okay, and try and ease up a little bit. I'm not going to throw you to the wolves for telling me the truth. Try to remember that I'm not Gracelia and I'm not going to shoot you in the head on a whim." Sometimes he doubted Pablo understood half of what he was saying, but he was reasonable when he compared him to the others Gracelia had surrounded herself with.

"Delarosa, he want to know why Señora Gracelia no come to talk to him. He no know you and he no trust no man he no know."

"So does he want to talk to me or not?"

"He say you gamble to come, but he want to see if you have *cojones* or no."

The young woman stepped outside to the small coffee stand right by the door and seemed to be ordering something. She never really paid attention to them, and the guy serving her was engaged in a conversation with her. From everything Jerome saw, whatever the bitch was there for, it seemed it wasn't to spy on him. Even though she was young, the woman was good.

"Tell him we'll be there, but you're not responsible for me."

"What you mean?"

"If he doesn't want to work with me, or trust me, I'll take that alone. You can tell him you work for Gracelia Luis and I made you call. Whatever happens, I want you to be able to walk out of there because of your loyalty."

"*Gracias*, Jerome," Pablo said, and took his hand. "You go and I go, but I tell Señor Delarosa I with you, and trust you."

"Let's go, then." Jerome tossed the car keys to Pablo. It was still early, but he wanted to find out if they'd hit someone's radar. "I need to do some other things."

They headed back toward the hotel since the parking garage was located through the back of the lobby. As they walked past the coffee shop the young woman barely gave them a look, seeming to concentrate on her magazine and drink. Jerome stopped in the lobby and waited, putting his hand on Pablo's arm to make him stop. When five minutes went by and the woman didn't come in after them, he relaxed.

Jerome asked Pablo to stop at one of the larger gas stations down the large boulevard the hotel was on. He went in with a baseball cap low on his head, not wanting to take any chances of anyone remembering him. The throwaway phones were close to the register, and he picked up two, along with a card, and paid cash. The girl who rang him up smiled as she chewed her gum and pointed to where the restrooms were when he asked.

He checked under each stall and ripped one of the phones out of its plastic container. The number he needed was hidden in his shoe under the liner, another technique he'd learned in his time with the Bureau. It rang six times before someone answered, and he waited for them to say something.

"Do you want to talk now or should I enjoy the beach?"

"Have you told Mom that I'm okay?" He sat on the toilet, not caring how dirty it was. The roller coaster he'd been on was exhausting, and his father's voice made him want to lie down and sleep.

"Where are you now? Wait. Don't tell me specifically. Are you in the States?"

"Yeah, and I'm making my way to you. Are you willing to help me or should I go it alone?" One of the greatest disappointments of his life was the day he'd taken his oath to enter the Bureau and his father wasn't there. He'd worked his ass off to follow in his father's footsteps, but by that time his dad lived under a cloud of suspicion that got heavier and darker by the day.

The academy director had told him it would be better if his dad skipped the ceremony, but his mother was welcome. By the time he'd gotten his post at the New Orleans office where his dad had last served, Matt Curtis, decorated agent, had taken a voluntary-retirement offer. He'd explained it saved him and his mother from a lengthy investigation and the embarrassment of shredding his reputation.

He'd grown to hate Annabel, who he blamed for what had happened to his father, even if she hadn't come to New Orleans permanently until after Barney was taken in. It was Annabel who had come down to lead the witch hunt against his dad. Her success had been why she'd gotten the job once Barney had been caught with his hand up Big Gino's ass.

"What are you into?" Matt asked.

"I don't have time for that, but know that if you decide to help him, I'm way ahead of where you were. It's enough of a lead that we can set things straight. Money is the only thing you need to get even, that's what you always said."

"Don't use your own trouble and compare it to mine to try to drag me into whatever this is," his dad said, and sounded old and scared to him. "I'm not saying no, but your mother, she's been through enough, and I'm not sure she can stand one more thing. On most days I think that, as hard as it is for her to accept that you're gone, it's best that you stay dead."

"So that's your answer?" He couldn't fucking believe it. Whatever came next, all he had were Gracelia and Pablo. He was screwed.

"For now leave your mother out of it, and we'll see where this takes us. Don't get crazy on me and think I'm going to leave you to hang. You're my son and I'm going to do whatever I can to help you. When can you get close enough?"

"I've got something important later, so give me time. I'll call you the same way, and if nothing's wrong, answer the same way. If you've been made or you think someone's on your ass, answer by asking if I can talk because it's raining. You understand?"

"Perfectly, and take care of yourself. Don't do anything that's going to get you hurt or worse before I can get to you. One wrong move because you mistake someone's kindness, and you're sunk. Don't forget that."

"I've made it so far, but I'll be happy to have you watching my ass. Take care yourself."

❖

"No." Emma crossed her arms over her chest, which Cain interpreted as defiance. The longer they were together, the stronger and more assured Emma became, and she wasn't sorry about that. Having a partner in every aspect of her life was something Cain appreciated and should've figured out sooner. "Think of something else because I'm not staying here like a damsel in distress while you go home where there's a list as long as my arm of people who want to hurt you."

"Lass, think about it. If we leave together, the kids are going to complain about coming back with us. Remember the last time. The best thing is for you to stay here, and I'll be back as soon as I'm done. You give me the opportunity, and I can finish this without having to worry about that bastard coming anywhere near you or our kids."

"Don't ask me to do that. Please don't, because I don't think I can handle it, not anymore." Emma looked deflated and fell against her. "I can't let you go alone and stay here going out of my mind."

Cain put her arms around Emma and looked out at the lake, trying to spot any of Ronald's men. It would be best for her to go alone, without the FBI detail tailing her, and come back before they realized she was gone. That probably would never happen, but she had simple dreams about stuff like this. They stood together, and she imagined Emma was working on her argument when the door opened behind them. Hayden came in and put a hand on each of their shoulders.

"Mama's right about this, Mom." He made eye contact with Cain, and his smile mirrored hers. "Right now it's not a good idea to make her worry too much."

"Did you raise his allowance or something?" she asked Emma as she gave her a mock glare.

"He's your son and was tops in his class, so don't try to beat him in this debate." Emma pinched her on the butt.

"We have to discuss this seriously. I don't like talking about what happened, but you know what this guy wants, and if we give Juan the chance he won't hesitate to try again. If I'm right, and I know in here that I am," she patted the side of her stomach, "think about what he's done to try again. How crazy do you have to be to go through reconstructive surgery to press the restart button?"

Emma and Hayden appeared at a loss for words after she'd explained her side of the argument. She didn't want to hurt them with the truth, but it was easy to forget when you were somewhere safe and no one could touch you. "If I say yes—" She stopped when Emma's smile widened. "I said *if*, so pay attention. You have to stay home and not make yourself a target. Are you going to have a problem with that?"

"I just want to be there for you, because even if you've figured out Juan's secret, this still won't be a cakewalk. I don't want to be a target, but I do want to be a comfort as you go through this ordeal."

Hayden grinned. "And I'll take care of Hannah here and wait for you to return. If you go back to work, then we can finish our vacation and wrap up the wedding plans. When I start high school I can finally say my parents are married."

They went into town as a family and had lunch while Ronald and Brent stood across the street within view, as if they wanted her to see them. It was humorous in a way, since Ronald's face was still tight and his movements vicious, as if he was still angry. She and Emma got up to go to the bathroom, and though she didn't think it would work, they walked out the back door and got a ride to the airport from her favorite waitress. This time Remi's plane wasn't there waiting, but they took a small hopper plane to Chicago and a commercial plane from there. When they boarded that one, she called the café and told Ross to go ahead and head back to the house. He'd move into the cabin until they returned.

The night before, she'd had a great talk with Hayden, and she came away thinking that after her lecture about anger, he finally understood. Granted, they had a few years before his education started in earnest, but stuff like this was important for him to learn now. Ronald had fallen for everything she'd thrown at him, and his anger had blinded him and his team to a couple of things or people. The night before, Katlin, Lou, and about six guards had left, with the help of Jerry and a few of the small carts they used on the farm. When she and Emma landed, the people she trusted most with both their lives would be waiting.

"Have you thought of how best to do this?" Emma asked in a whisper.

"This is an interesting dilemma, if you think about it. Before, with problems like this, you take care of them and they go away."

"But this time one of the problems used to be an FBI agent," Emma said, close enough to kiss her on the nose.

"You can never know, considering what Shelby and Brent did, how much leeway these guys have in an undercover assignment to bend the rules. Anthony might've been turned by Juan, or he could be the greatest undercover agent in the history of the world. If I take care of a problem that's a problem for the FBI too, then maybe there won't be much fallout, but," she waggled her hand, "if he's the greatest at his job, then we'll have a problem for a while."

"What's your best guess?" Emma turned her head and kissed her, which made the woman across from them stare. Cain was about to tell the bitch something when Emma grabbed her by the collar and kissed her again. "Not worth it. Save your anger for later."

"You're good for me, lass. The last thing I need is for air marshals to take me in. To answer your question, I don't think he's getting any awards for his fantastic job performance and his dedication. Even after what that guy Brent did and got away with, I can't believe they'd give him that much rope to close a case. Especially since Juan and his mother aren't the Bureau's business. Not really."

"Remember not to do anything that'll make you have to change your face." Emma rested her head on Cain's shoulder. "The only thing that scares me about all of this is that I should've known or felt something when he was that close to us. When I remember his hand on Hannah's I'm tempted to ask you to let me come along. It's so strange that he became so fixated on us."

"Not really." Cain moved a little so the attendant could put their drinks down. "What Carlos told me was that Rodolfo, for some reason, never acknowledged him as his son until the very end, but spoiled Juan from birth and never gave him many responsibilities. When Juan wanted anything, he got it." She took a drink from her soda and pushed Emma's water closer to her. "Anyone who's raised that way never becomes a reasonable person. *No* has to be part of any child's vocabulary. If not, Juan is the result."

They finished their talk on the plane and were able to walk through the airport to the outside in no time, since they didn't have luggage. Lou was parked close to where they exited, and she signaled for him to stay behind the wheel. She wanted to get out of there as soon as she could so Emma wasn't outside and exposed.

"Talk to me, Lou."

"Sabana's not answering her phone," He started down the ramp and waited until they were at a traffic light to glance back at her. "Shaun is at the Piquant but hasn't spotted the guy you had him following. Now that we know it's Juan, he's covered every exit, but still nothing."

"Stop by Vincent's first. I'm interested in old rumors, but only if Vincent's willing to either confirm or deny them."

Vincent's office was in the building next to the restaurant, and like her place, had a large garage door so he and any visitors could drive in without having to deal with anyone outside. In Vincent's case a mix of agencies loved to spend taxpayer dollars following him around. Vinny's business had attracted the DEA, Vincent's women and rackets had fans in the NOPD, and the FBI wouldn't mind wrapping it all up, including his money-laundering operation.

"I know you love me, but don't tell me you cut your trip short to come see me." Vincent helped Emma out and hugged her. "Come inside and let me get you something to eat."

Patrick, Mook's brother, shook her hand but stopped with Lou outside Vincent's private office. "Let me know if you need anything, boss," he said to Vincent before he closed the door.

"What do you need, Cain?" He put together a plate of snack items for Emma.

"What can you tell me about Matt Curtis?"

"There aren't too many secrets out there that you and your father didn't know about." He laughed.

"Actually I'm asking because I don't know. Rumor isn't something I often engage in, and that's not what I'm here for."

"Matty, that's what he wanted us to call him," Vincent said as he gave her a plate of salami and cheese. She looked at Emma, knowing how queasy her stomach was during pregnancy, but he'd given her only bread, fruit, and cheese, which she was eating. "He came to us, not the other way around, because no one's that crazy."

"What did Matty want? And Big Gino would definitely agree with you now if he had it to do over again. Happy-to-help-you agents aren't good additions to your payroll."

"Mostly this jerk wanted money, and to relieve my wallet of a lot of it. If I agreed, though, he promised me the moon."

"Stuff like federal secrets, or was he willing to run errands for you like Barney did for Gino? I don't know much about Matty, but he wasn't much to worry about since Da never brought him up except for the snippets he'd heard on the streets." She took the glass of wine Vincent offered her.

"According to him, he'd do whatever I wanted. The problem was, Matty wasn't tied real tight. I told him to fuck off and warned him not to make me say it again," Vincent said, then slapped the side of his head. "Sorry, Emma."

"Pretend I'm not here."

"So he wasn't working for you. If that's the case, why did Barney and the rest of those guys drum him out?" She wasn't confused often, but this didn't make sense. She was planning to use Matt to lure his son out of hiding and thought she could use Vincent to do it.

"If it hadn't been for Barney, then Matty would most probably be fat and rich by now. I didn't hire the fool, but someone did. Gino started shelling out cash, and his business got better because the heat all but disappeared. That's how we figured out who he was working for."

"How in the hell did I miss that?" she asked, more for her own benefit.

"You aren't and never will be a dumbass as big as Big Gino," Vincent said.

"Amen to that," Emma said.

"Thanks, I guess."

"Let me put it this way. Things were going good for Matty once he found his sugar daddy, but he didn't count on one thing."

"Could it be that Barney Kyle was a greedier bastard than he was? He got Annabel down here to investigate for him, that part I know. She was ultimately responsible for drumming him out."

"That's right, and once all Gino had was Barney, he made him rich as long as the favors kept coming in. When Barney wanted to retire, Gino was willing to bankroll that too, as long as his last act was killing you."

"That part of the story we know," Emma said. "If anyone deserved the end he got, it was Barney. Can I ask you something?"

"Pretty ladies can ask me whatever they want."

"How did you find all this out? Cain figured out only a little, but you've got it all."

"Emma." Vincent took her hand and smiled at Cain before kissing her knuckles briefly in a friendly way. "I'm a bad man. Well, if you ask all those time wasters outside, that's what they'll tell you. Bad men go to confession when asked by their bishop, and they donate to good things when asked. A new computer lab for a children's program might not buy me a ticket to heaven, but it helped me get enlightenment."

"Thanks for sharing all that with me," Cain said. "Most times religious experiences aren't things I like to share with anyone."

"I'm glad too because the first part was something God's servants wanted you to know, and the second part is between me and our Savior. When I can't get divine intervention, I count on my friends to help me out."

"I hope I'm at the top of that list."

"You know it, but what's your take on this?"

"It's a fascinating story, and now that I know Matty's interest in money, I'm going to offer him the opportunity to supplement his retirement fund. If I can get him to bite, I'll toss him out there and hopefully lure his son out of hiding."

"You got plans for him? The son, I mean," Vincent asked when she glanced at her watch.

"It's time for him to retire like his father. Maybe they can do all those father-son things they missed out on." She got up and held her hand out to Emma. "Thanks, old friend. You really helped me out."

"You've done wonders for Vinny and his future, so I'm glad to. All this new business has a new set of people sniffing around, but let them fight for space out there. Do they honestly think I've got drugs on my shelves in here alongside the olives?"

"That was interesting," Emma said when they were in the car.

"It was a learning opportunity, and I love those. I understand now the possibilities of how Juan was able to flip Anthony, and why he was so cooperative. It's a genetic flaw." She moved her neck from side to side and cracked the bones. "In his pea brain he blames the world for what happened to his father, and I'm a part of that. Because of me, Barney stole his dad's job, reputation, and chance at the big money."

"It's strange, but Shelby never mentioned anything to Muriel about Anthony. He was on Shelby's team, and because he was, he knows all about us. Think about it. Everything about you and our children, where to find you, what schools we picked, and who's closest to us every day. He shared that with Juan, knowing why he wanted to know."

Cain nodded as Emma spoke but cut her off when she got a call from Muriel. "Are you all okay?"

"We're back in the pool and have fishing plans for later, so concentrate on what you have to do. The kids are fine, and Mook, Merrick, and I'll keep it that way. I wanted to let you know Ronald went in and searched the café after you left. We still have company, but not the group you'd think would be here if you were still on property. Mook followed the primary team to the airport and watched them board a private jet. I'd expect them by tonight at the latest. The wayward Shelby is back on duty. The team left with her and Ronald in the lead."

"Thanks, and don't forget what we talked about. You okay about everything?"

"I'll wait for your call. After hearing that from Mook, I'm looking forward to what comes next."

"They're coming?" Emma asked when Cain ended the call.

"Yeah. Should be here tonight, so let's make one more stop, if you're up to it."

Lou got on the interstate and headed for the Ninth Ward and Jasper's. She wanted her plan in place before Shelby got back. Ronald, though, she was looking forward to seeing again. If the FBI kept making this so easy for her, she'd have to start sending Christmas presents to everyone in the New Orleans office.

"Muriel said Shelby was back at work."

"That's a good thing. She needs to see Shelby for who she is. Once her heart closes that part of her life, the quicker she'll find what we have."

"Shelby's going to find something, all right, because I'm going to throw it at her feet. There'll be no walking around it or over it, so she'll have to deal with it."

❖

"Are they still there?" Gustavo said when Andre came back with a pizza and beer. He hadn't been out the room at the Piquant in days and had found relief only when he snorted coke and masturbated to the porn on pay-per-view.

Andre had first told him about the man parked across from the back door of the hotel two days before. The man, whoever he was, didn't attempt to hide himself, and the car was always there, even when a different guy was sitting in it at night. Andre had taken it upon himself to check out the garage and front, since they were the only other ways out. In the garage another car was parked close to the street but still inside, and when he'd stared the guy had gotten out and smiled at him. The woman on the street was obviously part of the group, and if Andre had any questions as to who they were there for, they vanished when the woman followed him to the pizza parlor and back.

"Yeah, the woman I told you about walked behind me the whole time again, but stayed outside when I got back." Andre pushed the paper plate away as if he'd lost his appetite from the new developments. "Who do you think it is?"

"It has to be the police. They must've recognized you and they're waiting to see who you're with." He folded a slice in half and took a huge bite. "We got to go by Casey's and see if they're back." He spoke with his mouth full and wiped his fingers on his shirt. This life of hiding bored him, and he wanted to get out and start his hunt again. He was also still mad at his mother, but he missed her. Once he was on the streets that night, he was going to chance a call. "Tonight we'll go check some stuff out, but I want you to go down first. If those people take off after you, I'll go alone."

"Where are you going? Do you realize this is my first time in the States?"

"If you can come with me you'll see, but if not you'll have to wait until you learn not to be so obvious. They spotted you because you act like a virgin in a whorehouse."

"I can go back to Gracelia, if you think you can do better." Andre dropped onto his bed. "Why do you even want me here? From what Gracelia says, Jerome's in charge and I could lose my job for cutting out."

"You mention that guy's name again and the only way you make it back to Gracelia is if you can get there with a bullet in your head." Gustavo slammed the door to the bathroom and started the shower. He hadn't been bothered with bathing, but it was time to pull himself together and get back to work.

When he finished and went out for fresh clothes, Andre was gone, so he took his time getting dressed. Certain that the people outside, whoever they were, were busy following the idiot with him, Gustavo slicked his hair back and picked up the wad of cash he'd hidden in the room safe. Along with his money, he took the valet ticket and called down for the car Andre didn't know about. He tucked the pistol into the waistband at his back and prayed the Caseys were back so he could get on with things.

He drove slowly, but not so much that he'd attract attention, and passed by the studio offices to see if Remi was there. Once he'd finished with Cain, this would be his next target for the assistance she'd offered his enemies to defeat him. The parking lot was almost empty except for some small cheap cars that wouldn't be Remi's.

"Where are you, Cain?" he said as he headed uptown. He'd followed the convoy of cars to a smaller airport near the lake and seen Cain take her family away. The thrill of getting so close to her had faded when he saw that, since he couldn't follow her. His only choice had been to wait.

The house was lit and there was more activity at the gate as a car came up the street from the opposite direction. It entered the yard and, even from his limited view, he saw Cain get out first, then turn and help Emma. They'd returned, and suddenly he was curious if the kids were with them. The Casey children had never been in his plan, but all that time alone had changed his mind about that. If Cain lost Emma it'd drive her mad, but add her fake kids and the pain would be nirvana for him.

Cain stopped on the way to the door and answered her phone. Her head dropped and she shook it when Emma said something to her. Whoever had called had made Cain angry, and she took it out on Emma when she yelled something at her. He wished he could hear, but it was too big a risk to get out of the car. Cain jabbed a finger in Emma's face, and he was shocked when the small spitfire hauled back and slapped Cain.

This was the second time he'd seen this go down, and again he laughed at how weak Cain was for not hitting back. Any woman who'd dare do that to him wouldn't live to see the morning, but Cain stood there like a moron and took it. She stared Emma down but turned and walked into the house and left Emma alone.

Emma got back in the car, and the big buffoon that'd been out there with them got back in to drive her. When they pulled away he saw Emma with her head down and her face covered with her hands. It was as if the heavens had opened and God had given him everything he'd begged for.

The car moved at a good clip by the boutiques and antique stores of Magazine Street toward the warehouse district and stopped in front of a building that had a sign with Emma's name in neon. It was early, yet there was already a line to get in, but no one stopped Emma as she went up the steps and entered. Her driver tried to follow her, but he put his hands up when she obviously told him something from the other side of the door.

Gustavo parked down the street and got in line, ready to start handing out money to work his way in faster. The bouncer made his way through the crowd and tapped random women on the shoulder, which was their pass in. When he got close, Gustavo held up five one-hundred-dollar bills, and he was able to go with the women.

The nightclub was fairly full when he entered, and he strode to the bar before he decided to scan the room. If only he'd brought a taste of coke with him or waited for Andre. If Emma fought him, he wouldn't be able to make it out with her without getting killed. This was Casey's

place, her turf, her woman. Angry or not, it'd take skill to force her to
come with him.

"Need anything?" the bartender asked, waking him from his
stupor. "Do you need a drink?" the guy said slowly.

"Tequila." He faced the man and the mirrored wall behind him
with the name *Emma* etched in the glass. "Another," he said, after he
downed the first drink and put money under the empty shot glass. The
guy poured a second and moved on.

He took it and held it, only wetting his lips with it as he turned and
roamed the large space with his eyes. They had to have a connection
since he found her right away at a table in the corner, and she was
alone.

He started toward her seat as if searching for a place to sit. Emma
didn't seem to notice him as she sipped what looked like a club soda,
so he sat two tables from her and went back to his people-watching.
When he glanced back she appeared to be crying, and then she made
eye contact and smiled briefly. That was validation for all the work he'd
put into this.

When he stood so did she, only it had nothing to do with him. The
large man had entered and pointed to a door, but not the front one, then
to his phone. Emma nodded and started walking, but she had to pass
Gustavo to get to the guard.

"Excuse me," Emma said, because he'd gotten up and blocked
her path.

"Are you fine?" he asked, since this close he could see her red
eyes.

"I'm sorry, what?"

"You don't look okay. I can help you?" He reminded himself not
to touch her. It was too early for that, and the guard that drove her there
was too close. He decided to take the opportunity to just break the ice.

"Thanks, but no. Do you mind?" Emma made a motion for him
to move over.

He could tell she was really pregnant, and the thought of who
she was sharing this experience with made him sick. "I wish you a
good night. It's not a good time for you to cry," he said, and lapsed
on his promise when he reached out and started to touch her belly. He
immediately closed his hand into a loose fist and dropped it to his side.
"Please," he said, and moved.

"Thanks," Emma said, and seemed comfortable as she passed.

He hadn't blown it, and this break in her routine proved that perhaps Cain's relationship with this beautiful woman wasn't as good as everyone thought.

"Soon, Emma," he said, and downed his second shot. Emma disappeared through the door with the man, and just like that she was away from him again. "I never thought you'd make it this easy for me, Cain."

CHAPTER NINETEEN

Emma looped her arm though the bend of Lou's elbow because she needed something familiar to hang on to until she reached Cain in Muriel's office. If she was this off-kilter, she could imagine how Cain was doing after their ruse. Not that she doubted what Cain had figured out about how Juan had changed himself, but after the brief encounter she was sure. His mannerisms, his subdued aggression, the accent, and his voice were all the same. When he'd moved closer, she'd remembered his habit of studying her like a bug on a slide.

"Are you all right?" Cain asked as soon as the elevator door opened. The time it would've taken Emma and Lou to get up there had obviously been too long for her to wait.

"With Lou and the other people you had around me, I never worried about anything." When Cain wrapped her arms around her she did feel more centered. "It's him. You were right, and brilliant for figuring that out."

"If I'd been brilliant, I would've figured it out the day we first saw him."

"Think about what position we could eventually be in if you hadn't. He went through all that trouble to get his fresh start, but he never accounted for who he was up against." When they reached Muriel's office, Emma held Lou back and closed the door to the conference room. "I was as close to him as you were that day, and I've had more contact with him, but I never knew. There's no way anyone would've surmised that right then, honey. I mean, who in the hell goes to this much trouble?"

"Are you sure you're okay with what we have planned?"

When Shaun had called and told them Juan was on the move and headed toward them, Cain had formulated a plan instantly. If this new man who appeared more American with a slimmer nose and sandy-blond hair really was Juan, the satisfaction of killing him would have to wait. By using him and guiding him in a certain direction, they could perhaps lure Anthony out, along with Gracelia.

The first step toward that was the very public view of their deteriorating relationship for Juan's benefit. They'd had a physical fight before, for the FBI's sake, so Cain had sacrificed her cheek again. Then came the illusion of Emma out in public alone, or barely alone, to lick her wounds away from her supposed tormentor. Cain had been right again when Juan saw her at the table. He'd been so fixated on her, he'd missed the four guards around her, aside from Lou.

"It's not often I get to help you, so please don't ask me to stop now." Emma kissed Cain and placed her hand on her chest. "I can do this, and I'll feel good about it. Juan didn't want me because he secretly loved me. He wanted me to get to you *and* because I wasn't interested. You might be a great motivator, but I think when I said no he became obsessed. I want to be part of getting rid of him because of what he did to both of us."

"I'm not comfortable or crazy about putting you out there, though."

"You know I'm forgiving to a fault sometimes." Emma caressed the cheek she'd slapped and smiled, which made her appear sadder. "It's cost us so much…you so much when I mistakenly put my faith in someone else. Not this time, and when he reached out to touch our baby, it confirmed it for me. That's something sacred to you and me, a child that's ours and will be such an important part of who we are together, but I know he doesn't see it that way. I'm sure Juan wants nothing but to destroy this baby to complete his conquest."

"Okay, but we stick to the whole plan. No ad-libbing and no trying to ditch the people I put with you." Cain tapped the tip of Emma's nose with her finger.

"Trust me. I don't want a repeat of what happened any more than you do. You want to go by Remi's place before we head home?"

"Yeah." Cain helped Emma to her feet and kissed her again. "We still have too many unknown variables in this, and with any luck, Remi's found the answer to some of them."

"We'll need to fill them in on what's going on, so I'll meet you there. If we get home early enough, we can call the kids. I'm surprised Hayden hasn't phoned already. He seemed okay being left behind, but I'm sure he's learned to hide disappointment well," Emma said.

Lou pressed the elevator call button for them and kept his eyes pointed at the door.

"He called on my way over here, and he sounded okay with us reporting in later. He was really sweet about it."

"Of course he's sweet. He gets that from me."

Lou's shoulders shook from laughter after he heard her squawk from Emma's pinch to her side. They rode down and she waited ten minutes before going out the back. Emma and Lou had gone through the front, where she hadn't spotted Juan in any monitor. Patience might be a virtue, but it was damn hard when she had this guy in her sights.

"Where is he?" she asked Shaun.

"Fell in line with Lou and Miss Emma. He's doing his best to hang back, but he's as subtle as chickenpox."

"Any luck with a name?"

"Unfortunately the staff at the Piquant is immune to bribes for stuff like that, so I don't have it yet. The guy he was with took off and headed into the Quarter. I've got someone following him, and he said he looked pissed and is drinking it off at Pat O's."

"Stay with Juan and have whoever's watching his friend call me. There might be a way to speed up this process without showing my hand."

"You got it, boss."

"Well, it's within sight now, anyway."

❖

Remi took her jacket off in the elevator and rolled her head from side to side to crack the bones in her neck. The studio was getting busier here and in LA, which meant more travel in her future, as well as for Dallas. They'd signed a few projects that her people said Dallas would be perfect for, only they weren't going to be filmed in New Orleans. Now that Dallas didn't have to fear the past and she'd decided to take them, it'd mean star billing and the paycheck to go with it.

The condo was quiet and she headed for the bedroom and changed for a night in, then fixed herself a drink. After Dallas and Kristen moved in she'd promised not to smoke inside, so she took her cigar and aged rum to the balcony. Dallas didn't particularly care for the habit but had gotten her a comfortable chair to enjoy the view and the Cuban Cohibas she was fond of.

As she watched the huge freighters go by she thought about the house they'd bought and the history of the place. She remembered visiting often as a child and playing with Cain and Marie while Mano ran off with Billy. Their fathers were starting to do business together, and her family had been fortunate that Dalton had instantly liked her father when they met. It wasn't often that her dad humbled himself to anyone like that, but he'd lowered his head and forgotten his pride when he begged Dalton to give him a chance.

She'd committed her family to the amount of business they were doing with Cain because of how Dalton had received him that day. Dalton had listened to his story, his requests, and the manner in which he'd asked for them. An hour later he had the keys to the Pescador Club, the loan that launched the place, and Dalton's protection. Dalton had also told her father to bow to no other man again, especially him, and if someone wanted him to, he gave him his personal number. It took a day for their friendship to take root, and Dalton had kept his word about everything he'd promised. His final gift had been the deed to the club.

When it was her turn, she found the same kind of friendship and loyalty in Cain. Even her father was impressed with the profits they'd made with the purchase of the studio and using it to launder money for both families. Cain had shown selflessness there as well because she'd only wanted 49 percent to keep the authorities away from them as much as possible.

The sliding-glass door opened behind her and she held her hand up, assuming it was Dallas. Someone's hand slowly slid down hers and she immediately knew it wasn't Dallas, and when she lowered it and pulled the person closer, she found Kristen smiling at her. Maybe Simon had a point, because the caress wasn't what you'd expect from an in-law. She let Kristen go and decided to set things straight between them when she leaned against the railing in a pose that made her breasts jut out.

"How was school?"

"It was good. A summer semester is always fun since you get it out of the way faster. Did you have a hard day?" Kristen asked, and she nodded. "Want a neck rub?"

"Your sister will take care of that when she gets here." The statement made Kristen's smile vanish and her shoulders slump slightly. "So no more cute stuff, okay? Dallas sacrificed plenty to keep you safe, and I'm not interested. She doesn't deserve the disrespect from you, and I'll never hurt her like that. Do we understand each other, or do I need to make it plainer?"

"I was just being nice so you'd like me. I didn't mean anything by it. Besides, I'm lonely."

"I'm not mad, but I also don't want any misunderstandings. We've got a new house to enjoy, and I want you to think of it as home. Hell, it's big enough that you can stay for however long you want, even if it's forever. But try to find someone who'll give you everything your sister and I have. Until then, get a cat if you're lonely."

Kristen's focus went to the elevator doors and Remi stood and turned. She'd been expecting Cain and Emma, and they were a great diversion to end this conversation. Before she moved to open the door she hugged Kristen and kissed the top of her head. "It's been a hard life, I know that, but you'll get there."

"Thanks, Remi."

"I love you, and we'll be fine."

"I ordered dinner." Cain winked at her when she rolled her eyes from behind Kristen. "When's Dallas finished for the night?"

"She should be scrubbing makeup off now, so give her a few minutes. Drink?"

"I'll have whatever you've got." Cain helped Emma into one of the leather chairs in the den. "And my partner will take juice, if you have it."

Remi came back with two glasses and found Kristen sitting close to Emma, Cain near the door to the balcony. "Cigar?" she asked when she handed her the drink.

"Only one," Emma called out from the other room.

They went out and she listened to what Cain had discovered, amazed that Juan had gone to such lengths to get close to them again. But the really bizarre part of what had happened was Anthony actually going along willingly with these people.

"You're probably his first target, but I can't imagine we'll be too far behind. What do you need from us?"

"If I'm right, Juan has walked through your new house so he's familiar with the layout. He's got to eliminate me before you have to worry about anything, and in reality he might not have any plans for you or your family at all. To play it safe, though, tell Emile to keep Dallas close. Someone like Juan is set on what he wants to do, but if an easy target jumps out at him, he'd probably risk it." Cain took a long drag from her cigar and seemed to follow the smoke as the wind blew it south. "Don't repeat my mistakes."

"Have you spotted Anthony at all?"

"Not yet, but we might have a lead on Gracelia. Even if I find her I believe it's smart to wait until I have them all. Mother and son might be easy targets, but I don't want to give Anthony the opportunity to run back to his former employer and cut a deal."

"Whatever you need, it's yours."

Cain smiled and held up a finger when the phone rang. "Where is he now?" She listened and pointed inside. Dallas had just come in and was already making over Emma. "Wait until he's closer to Canal Street, where it's less crowded, then offer him a ride. Once you have him, call Katlin."

She dialed Katlin next. "Go by the electric company and find out what you can."

"What are you curious about?"

"The good. We've got the bad and the ugly covered."

❖

Fiona drove with more confidence now that she was becoming more familiar with the streets and their sometimes stranger names. She'd done her best to get assigned with Sept whenever possible, but so far Special Agent Ronald Chapman's request had come to nothing. After Cain pulled Sept aside at the Columns, Sept had never mentioned her again.

The call from Ronald that Cain was back, but with only a skeleton crew, had surprised her. A coward like Casey seemed to always need a crowd around her. It was the only way for such people to stay in power. She'd waited at the lakefront airport but never saw the Caseys get off any aircraft. The place was basically closed for the night, the manager had said, so she was headed back downtown to pick up her mother.

They only had two more days together, and her opportunity to talk her mother into staying was getting slim. Her mom seemed driven not only to return to California, but to take her back as well. She'd hinted and prodded, but so far her mom hadn't given her anything as to why that was so important to her.

As she got closer she saw her mother outside on her cell, having what looked like an intense conversation. Something was up and she wanted to know what it was. Her mom had always been secretive, but if she was in trouble she needed to say what the problem was so she could help.

"Call me if there's anything else, and I mean right away. I don't care what time it is," Judice said, loud enough for her to hear her through the open window of the car. Judice hung up when she spotted her and immediately plastered a smile on her face. "Hey, you're early. That's great." Judice hugged her and did an amazing transformation from frustrated to happy.

"Is there a problem?" Fiona asked.

"No, well, a problem with an extension for one of my clients. Nothing a call to the IRS in the morning won't fix, even if it'll be a pain in my ass." Judice laughed, but Fiona couldn't help thinking that it was all an act. "Let me treat you to whatever you want tonight. I've been looking forward to this all day."

It wasn't the time to start an argument, so she put the car in Drive without another word. The place she wanted to try was crowded, but everyone seemed content to wait at the bar while waiters performed a dangerous ballet with loaded trays of food between crowded-too-close tables. The atmosphere was really too loud to have a good conversation with her mother, but that wasn't why she'd wanted to venture in.

The Irish pub and restaurant wasn't all that far from the one Cain owned, and from what some of the beat cops had told her, Cain liked to stop by often for the potato stew made from her mother's recipe. She needed more contact with Casey so she could figure out the crack in her defenses. Once she was in she'd rip her to the ground.

"Are you sure you don't want to try somewhere nicer?" her mother asked. "New Orleans isn't exactly known for their Irish cuisine."

"Let's just stay for a beer. Then we can go."

"This has to do with this case of yours?" The veneer of happiness dropped off her mother's face, and she appeared more angry than hurt.

"You don't talk to me anyway, so why shouldn't I get something done while I can?"

"Then play with fire on your own time." Her mother turned to leave. Fiona grabbed her by the biceps to keep her from going. "Fiona." Judice stared at her hand. "You want to work, then work, but it's best you leave me out of it."

Fiona stood and looked at her mother's finger as if it were a gun, since she pointed at her. A few of the rowdier patrons bumped into her, but she stayed in place as her mother left. The smart move would've been to go after her, but she was tired of playing twenty questions and getting no answers. It didn't matter right then that their time was limited; she needed to do something constructive.

"Get you something, my darlin'?" The bartender's Irish accent sounded authentic.

"A Guinness and a few minutes, if you've got them."

The man poured and set her glass on the counter to let it settle. "There you go." He wiped his hands on a bar towel. "I get off at two, if you're interested in my time."

"Not like that. I only want to ask if you know Cain Casey."

"Who's asking?"

She showed him her badge and put a ten on the bar for her drink. "Detective Fiona O'Brannigan."

The man glanced at the badge then at her money before taking the glass back and throwing it in the sink. "Keep your money and take your questions out the door with you."

"Loyalty can sometimes buy you more trouble than favors, so you want to try again?"

"Get out of my place before you get hurt, little lady." He crossed his arms over his chest and glared down his somewhat crooked nose at her.

"Threatening the NOPD isn't a wise move. Is Casey worth jail time to you?"

He picked up the old yellow phone on the wall and dialed a number he obviously knew from memory. She felt her phone vibrate against her hip when he hung up, and she read the number from her precinct on the display.

"Get the fuck out of there, and get back here now."

"Yes, sir." She didn't have to ask who it was; her superior officer had a recognizable voice.

The smug expression on the bartender's face made her realize how far Cain's reach went in the city, but also how deeply she'd corrupted the police. "The answer to caging you for life might not be found in whatever the Feds think you're doing, Casey. It might lie on a more local level," Fiona said as she drove the couple of blocks to work. "That'd be hilarious since you think you're so smart."

She dialed Ronald's number, but this time there was no answer. "Call me. I might have something."

❖

Ronald had gone by the office when they'd landed and ordered a team out to find wherever Casey was in the city. The sarcasm in everything Annabel had said, along with her sweet, sickening smile, had irritated him from the second she'd greeted him. "You lost Casey in a small backwoods café in dairy-town Wisconsin? Really, Ronald. I thought your being here was the answer to all our prayers."

It hadn't gotten any better throughout the day, and in a way he'd lost the upper hand because she'd been right. Casey had waved every single time she'd seen him, insulted him in front of the others, and pretended she knew something about him. She was nothing but a lying punk, like every other asshole he'd ever confronted. No way in hell Casey or anyone else knew anything about him, at least not anything he didn't want them to.

He'd gone to his hotel room and changed into jeans, T-shirt, and biker boots, but that wasn't all he'd done to hide the rigid personality he prided himself on. The wig made him appear younger, since the hair was longer and braided in a Jamaican style. So far, his theory that people concentrated on shit like hair and tattoos instead of facial structure had held true. He laughed about it as he glanced at the large snake tattoo that ran down his forearm. It'd come off later in the shower, but for now it was yet another clue someone would eventually give police if they were brave enough.

From the reports the Bureau had on file, Airline Drive—a few miles out from downtown—was where he'd find what he was looking for. It was maddening that he had to do this, since he found it disgusting that he actually needed it, but it was like the steam release on a pressure cooker. If he blocked it too long then the whole pot exploded, and he'd do anything to avoid that.

The first guy was too fat and actually appeared grotesque in the tight pink leopard-skin Lycra pants he wore. When he smiled at him he was also missing teeth, so he kept going. He was cursing as he reached the end of the strip, but the last guy who stood by a few women was the one. He was a slight, light-skinned teenager—perfect. Ronald was about to give him the night of his life.

"Get in." He pointed to the guy with a hundred between his fingers.

"Big man like you needs more than skinny Minnie here," one of the women said.

"You coming or what?"

The guy got in and didn't immediately start spouting the usual phrases or try any of the tired moves that the more seasoned prostitutes felt were expected of them. "I'm Frankie."

"I didn't pick you up for conversation, so shut the fuck up." Frankie cringed and pressed closer to his door as he screamed. The fear made Ronald hard. On nights like this he could do whatever he wanted, and in turn he'd get what he sometimes couldn't as an agent—respect and satisfaction.

He stopped behind the large grocery, which he'd already checked out and found free of security cameras, and unzipped his jeans. The pink condom Frankie put on him was almost comical, but the way Frankie sucked dick wasn't. He slowed him down, not wanting to come too quick, and Frankie complied. As his head bobbed like a fishing cork, Ronald put on the golf gloves he used in situations like this. They protected his hands and left none of his DNA, but were thin enough to enjoy the sensation he was about to experience.

Frankie stopped when he prompted him to, and a little of his edge dulled. "Take that pretty outfit off," he ordered.

He watched as it all dropped to the floor of the car and enjoyed how shy Frankie acted. When he was naked and the expanse of skin was within reach, all Ronald could think again was *perfect*. Frankie's skin was flawless, with no scars, bruises, or blemishes. Unfortunately for Frankie, that was about to change.

"I bet you're popular," he said, and wished he had a quicker recovery period. He knew himself, though, so what came next was necessary if he wanted to get off a second time. "Pretty thing like you." His comment made Frankie look at him. "Work it until it's hard."

He didn't touch as Frankie masturbated for him, and he was impressed that, for such a smallish man, Frankie's dick resembled his physique in that it was long and skinny. Once his hand started to move faster he gazed for another moment, then couldn't stand it. "Stop," he screamed.

Frankie's eyes opened, and he put his hands up like a well-trained pet used to following commands. "Tell me what you want," he said, thrusting his hips toward him.

"Get out so we'll be more comfortable." Frankie did as he asked and stood in the shadow of the Dumpster, not appearing alarmed when Ronald took his belt off.

That didn't last past the first lash from the wide leather and buckle. When Ronald dropped that and used his fists, all Frankie could do was whimper from the fetal position he'd rolled himself into, as if to make a smaller target. Every red line and blotch on the once-beautiful skin would be a bruise soon, and the thought of them made Ronald hard again.

He stood over Frankie's motionless body and jerked off with only one thought on his mind. Soon this would be Cain Casey, and the exercise would the sweetest of his life. Bringing her down and humiliating her like this would be epic. When he squirted over Frankie's back the familiar tableau was done, so he opened his trunk and got the bleach wipes he always carried with him.

Frankie whimpered as he wiped him down and put each wipe in a bag that he'd take with him. All that was left was to get Frankie's clothes out of his car and pay him. He threw the rumpled outfit on his head and pressed two hundred bucks in his hand. He'd given him a little extra for being such a good sport.

"Thanks, kid. That was great."

He drove away. The more distance he put between them, the mellower he got. Tomorrow he'd start over and make the necessary changes to get back to why he was here. It'd be easier now that he was under control again.

"When I find you, Casey, you're going to pay for the humiliation I just endured."

CHAPTER TWENTY

Two weeks passed and Juan seemed to follow the same routine, which was to drive close to the house and follow Emma wherever she went. Lou and Emma reported that he hadn't touched her again, but he was starting to build confidence by getting closer to them when he could.

Sabana still sat on the hotel where Gracelia was staying, but still hadn't seen her. Cain told them all to hold on. They weren't going to lose anyone by casting a net too early.

"What did that guy you picked up tell you?" Emma asked as they lay together in the quiet of the early morning.

Andre Reyes—that was the one thing the man Katlin had picked up knew for sure. His name and who he worked for. He'd started, according to him, with Gracelia, but after a phone call went with Gustavo Katsura. That's who he worked for now, but all they did was sit around the room Gustavo had rented and watch television. Gustavo had alluded to a plan, but nothing had come of it. Even with Simon there for translation purposes, Katlin had discovered nothing else. If he'd had something to give up, he would've when the first shock went through his balls. Hell, she might've been tempted to make something up if she'd been in his position, but that's all he'd said.

"He was never really close to Gracelia, and Gustavo never gave specifics. I'm willing to wait them out." Cain moved behind her so Emma could use her as a body pillow. "What I don't, I take that back, can't wait for anymore is getting the kids and everyone back. I thought my wakeup call would've prompted Gracelia to try to punch back, but she went silent. It doesn't make any sense."

"Maybe you should try something to entice her out in the open." Emma rubbed her foot up and down her leg as she spoke. "Something you might want to do, but don't want to be blamed for."

"What's going on in that beautiful head of yours?" She kissed a spot above Emma's ear and enjoyed when she pressed closer.

"There's nothing you can do to that ass from the FBI who beat you while you were cuffed? That still bothers me. He did it and got away with it to the point of gloating that day at Hayden's game. Maybe you should get rid of the idiot and blame it on the other idiots messing up our days."

"If Brent shows up dead I don't think the FBI will look at the Luis family first, lass. I haven't forgotten about him." She ran her hand down Emma's back, then up again. "Annabel's been good at cultivating short fuses in her people, and if left to fester, Brent will eventually decide the law is too slow. Once he does, he'll hurry things along like he did before."

"Maybe Annabel needs to go. That day I went to see George Talbot when they'd taken you in, she was so condescending. When there's a problem and you get rid of it, but it keeps happening, there has to be a common denominator. My guess is Annabel."

"I don't know for sure, but I think that's why Ronald Chapman is here. He agrees with you about Annabel, but he wants something badly." Emma's eyes started to droop as Cain spoke, but she didn't stop, wanting her to go back to sleep. She kept up her gentle stroking as well to encourage drowsiness. "When someone wants something there has to be a good explanation. I'd rather have someone I know fairly well, since I know what Annabel's about, over the unknown with an agenda."

"What are you going to do?" Emma's voice was soft as satin and as slow as molasses. Sleep was close.

"We'll talk about that tomorrow, but I've got something in mind." She kissed Emma's forehead and stayed quiet after that because Emma needed her rest.

After a talk with Sabana the night before, she'd found that whoever Jerome Rhodes was, he was a creature of habit. Every day, a couple of times a day, he walked the levee and smoked. After those initial calls he hadn't phoned anyone else. His only company was two men who trailed him but seldom talked to him.

Cain knew something would come of it because the two guys who kept Jerome company appeared Mexican. She'd studied the pictures Sabana had gotten of Jerome, and he too had the same coloring, but his facial features were much more refined. He didn't stand out as a part of Rodolfo's crew, so she assumed he'd started with Gracelia.

Today she was going for a walk, not to threaten or talk to Jerome, but to put him on the radar of her watchers. Whatever his role was with Gracelia, she was interested in how he'd react not only to her, but to who else would be looking on. If he was one to panic, then he'd run somewhere, and maybe once he did, they'd get somewhere.

After that she planned to meet with Carlos, who had finally made it in to town and was staying at the Piquant as well. He'd come for his business, she guessed, but was also there because Gracelia was possibly close. As much as she wanted to kill Juan, Carlos wanted to kill Gracelia, maybe even more.

The other thing they needed to decide was whether to bring the kids and the rest of their family home. She wanted Muriel back by her side to make sure she continued to put the hurt behind her. Family was the most important thing to Cain, and Emma was right—it was time to stop running. The fear the different scenarios she'd thought of when it came to Juan had given him more power in her mind than he deserved. She was ashamed to admit that to herself, but a repeat of what had happened to Marie would've driven her mad.

"It's time to go back to the basics," she whispered, and kissed Emma's forehead when she whimpered in her sleep. "So put your running shoes on, Juan. I'm coming."

❖

"Señor," Pablo said early that morning when Jerome came out of the bedroom for coffee and the paper. He'd become obsessed with all forms of news since he figured that's how they'd find the dumb bastard Gustavo. "Miguel Gonzales call and he want us at the house today at five. Señor Delarosa no is in the city, but he want to hear what you say."

Jerome stared at Pablo and wanted to kiss him. Finally there might be a way out of this hellhole with the witch he was sharing his bed with. The more days that passed with no word from Gustavo, the more worried and frantic she became, and she had forgotten all her grand statements and promises about taking her son out of the picture. If Gustavo called, she swore to God she'd give him whatever he wanted if only he'd come back to her.

"Good." He motioned Pablo closer to him so he could hear him whisper. "Get the car and park a block away. When I go out for my walk, I'll make it down the levee and meet you. For now I don't want anyone else to know."

"I understand."

He skimmed the paper and ate a large breakfast now that his

appetite had returned. No matter what, he had to go, but if he could get in with Hector and get him to trust him enough to give him a job, he wouldn't have to start over on his own with only the skeleton crew he could steal from Gracelia. The longer he stayed here, the quicker he'd be found by accident because of the Luis family. Guilt by association in this case would only get him killed.

That was especially true of Cain Casey. The first time he wanted Cain to see him with this face was when he was in close proximity to Hector. That's where he wanted her to form her history with him going forward, thus eliminating any chance she'd put him together with Gracelia and then hear from someone that Juan had brought him to his mother. He'd watched her for years, and no one escaped justice that long without a quick mind and high intelligence.

"If Gracelia gets up early let her know I'm out for a walk. Wait here and tell everyone not to follow me. I want to be alone." Pablo nodded and sat in front of the muted television with some Spanish show he liked to watch.

Jerome ignored the girl who sat in the same place every day and headed for the walking path on the levee. The last of the disposable phones he'd purchased was charged, in his pocket, and ready for a call. He headed down the path and never glanced back in case one of the men ignored Pablo. He'd get enough distance between them not to be overheard.

The number he dialed rang twice, and his father answered. "I'm sorry. I've got the wrong number." He hung up and waited. It'd take his dad about fifteen minutes to make it to the pay phone they'd agreed on, so he kept walking at a good clip.

He glanced at his watch and dialed the number and waited for the phrase that meant everything was okay from Matt's end. "What's new?" his dad asked.

"I got the meeting I've been waiting for, so hopefully by the end of the day today I'll get my promotion. Once I do I'm moving from my current location and getting a bigger place so you can join me."

"Is your assistant still with you?"

"Yeah, and as loyal as ever. I figure if he comes with me it'll be easier to get the rest of the crew to come along. The house where I was before might be a good place for us to work from," he said, meaning Gracelia's house in Cabo. If she and Gustavo were eliminated, he planned to move in and eventually get the paperwork done to transfer the deed.

"Be careful and don't plan too far ahead. Things get missed like that, and this isn't the time for big mistakes. There's too much at stake."

"Don't worry. I think my qualifications will be what they're looking for. I'm not going to brag and tell them about all my experience so as not to give them the wrong impression." Despite his father's warning he couldn't help but spin some fantasies in his head about what was in store for them. Finally he'd have people around him that respected him as well as money and power. It was all within reach.

"Be careful and don't do anything to piss off this guy. You want to walk out of there…" His dad paused as if to give him a warning about Hector and his tendency to kill anyone he deemed not to his liking. "Walk out with more than you came in with, or at least with what you have now."

"I got us this far, so—" He'd started his statement by wanting his father to give him some credit when he turned around. Cain Casey was perhaps fifteen feet behind him and had never made a sound. From the way she was dressed, she wasn't here for a morning run. "Fuck," he said, and cursed his weakness for showing any kind of reaction.

"What?" his father screamed.

"It was good talking to you, and I'll have to get back to you on all the other stuff we talked about. I don't have the information in front of me right now." He hung up and slipped the phone into his pocket as if he'd finished his call and was on the way back to the head of the trail. She didn't move and stood in the middle of the trail as he started walking, so he smiled and started to go around her.

"What's your hurry? It's beautiful out here this time of morning. Not so hot, like when you're out here in the afternoon." Cain stared him down, and it'd be a mistake to pass without saying something.

"I'm late for a meeting, so have fun." He got about three feet on the other side of her when she spoke, and he had to stop again.

"I'm sure Gracelia is still sleeping off the high, so I wouldn't rush on her behalf," Cain said, since she'd changed her mind not to actually talk to this guy. It'd been his initial reaction to her that'd made her decide to go a step further than she'd planned. He'd been flying high with whoever was on the other line, but he'd crashed hard when he'd glanced behind him and found her there.

"I'm sorry. I really have to get going." Jerome lifted his hand in a poor excuse for a wave and started running down the path, slowing only when he noticed Katlin at the end where she'd left her.

She waved at Katlin to let him by, and after the very short encounter she was angry with herself for not coming sooner. Jerome not only knew her, but recognized Katlin as well, so her family wasn't a foreign thing to him. And he knew enough about them to be afraid. Why would he be? She was after Juan and would gladly hand Gracelia over to Carlos to do whatever Carlos had planned, but Jerome was an unknown to her.

"If he ran any faster he'd have fallen in the lake," Katlin said as she met her halfway. "What'd you tell him?"

"He said he was in a rush to not miss a meeting, so I told him his boss was probably sleeping off her high. Interesting reaction, though, don't you think?"

"Sometimes you have that little something extra in your smile that sends people running. They don't know you like we do, so don't ask me to explain."

"Did you pull Sabana from the lobby?"

"Yeah, she's waiting at the car and ready to polish your shoes if you ask her to. Your lesson must've sunk in because she didn't give her usual lip."

"Good. Call her and tell her to drive around. I promised Carlos I'd stop by for coffee."

"Do you think Gracelia will run after this?"

"The smartest move—if she wants to live longer than the time it'll take Carlos to drive out here and stuff her in a pillowcase and drag her off—would be to run back to Mexico. If she still has people loyal to her, then she might have a chance to fight him off, but from what I hear, Carlos is the new popular guy and fast-rising star. His father would be proud of him if Juan and his sister hadn't tied him to a tree and fed him to the ants."

"Will he eventually be a problem?" Katlin pointed to where Sabana had stopped.

"I understand the allure of drugs, but I want no part of them. If I explain that plain enough, then we can both do business in close proximity and not have a problem. Maybe he'll understand that better than Hector, because no matter how I put it, it never sinks in."

"Maybe he's got a crush on you?"

"If that's true I'll send Emma over there to explain the facts to him, after I tell her he said she looked fat. By the time she'd finish with him, they might have a little left to bury." Cain laughed.

"Head to the Piquant, Sabana," Katlin said.

"We'll meet with Carlos and then I want you to follow Lou and Emma to their appointment. Make sure no one sees you. We need them to appear vulnerable and easy pickings."

"Do you promise you'll stay home?"

"Believe me. We're too close to them to want to take any chances."

❖

"What happened?" Matt asked.

"Cain Casey was out there this morning," Jerome said, panting from his sprint inside.

"Did she make you?"

"She knows I'm with Gracelia, but that's it. I'm still going with what we talked about, only I'm going to try to move it up some. I'll call when I'm done, so be ready to move and make sure you don't pick up any viruses along the way." He stripped off his clothes and started the shower. "If Hector doesn't work out, we still have the other option I told you about."

"Don't worry about me, and concentrate on what you're doing," his dad said, and paused. "Make sure you're all right when you finish. Keep your head on your shoulders and you'll do fine."

"Even if I don't do fine, I'm planning to keep my head on my shoulders."

❖

Cain met with Carlos and got his promise not to move on Gracelia until the other pieces of her wish list were in sight. He thanked her and told her that once they were finished with what had to be eliminated from both their lives, he'd never bother her again unless she needed something from him. For the favors she'd done him so far, he owed her a few in return.

"Make sure that nothing happens to her," Cain told Lou when they got home.

"Don't worry, boss. I'd take a clip full of bullets for Emma, and I told the restaurant-reservations people it was important to keep the next table open."

Emma was having lunch with Dallas to discuss house plans and volunteered to go out to a restaurant where they'd be in full sight of

Juan. Emil and Lou would be at the next table, and the table to the other side of Emma and Dallas could be taken by Juan, if he showed up. If Emma complained loudly enough about her and how everything was wrong between them after this pregnancy, it'd open the door for Juan to provide a shoulder to cry on when Dallas was called away.

Cain wasn't thrilled with what Emma was willing to do, but to positively lure Juan away from any guards they hadn't spotted yet, she needed him to grab for a carrot that was too big to pass up. If Emma was within reach he'd forget about everything else, including his personal safety, and he'd probably call for backup. If luck was on her side, his helper would be Anthony again, and if it was, she'd hand Gracelia over and take care of the other two together.

"Call me if he comes with more force than you anticipated. Katlin will be there, but if he's got ten guys with him we might have a problem."

"Honey, you need to calm down," Emma said as she smoothed her light-blue linen dress. "I wouldn't be doing this if I thought the baby or I would be in danger. Think of it this way. If everything goes well, maybe he'll ask me out, and if you hear anything else, I can give him an answer and bring him home with me."

Jerome had run to the Delarosa house and had been in there for a couple of hours with another man he'd brought with him. She was waiting to see where he headed next, and if he actually survived to leave, he might be another avenue to Anthony.

"It's my job to worry about you, lass, and it's a lifetime commitment on my part. I know it has to be done, but I don't have to like it."

"Remember that." Emma kissed her hard, able to reach because she'd stopped on the second step. "I need you to repeat it word for word when I get you to an altar." She smiled as if trying to lighten Cain's mood. "If not, I have Lou as a witness. No running out on me."

"I've been running *to* you all my life."

"I love it when you talk to me like that," Emma said as she wiped Cain's mouth free of lipstick with her index finger. "But then, I just love you."

"I love you too, so stay safe and come home. When you get here I'll have a surprise waiting for you."

Emma nodded and kissed her again. "We'll call no matter what, so try to eat something while we're gone."

"She'll be in a knot by the time we get back," Lou said as they walked to the car. "But you can't change that about her because she loves you." He opened the door for her and held her hand as she sat. "When it comes to her family, that worry keeps her vigilant like it did her father."

"I know, but it takes its toll. Changing that about Cain is like asking her to change the color of her eyes. It'd be impossible." Lou nodded and started out toward Commander's Palace restaurant. "What about you, Lou? You need a family to cluck around and worry about. You'd be a wonderful father."

"I'd love that, but finding a girl isn't that easy. Don't think I'm complaining about my job. I love what I do and I'd never willingly leave the family, but finding someone who'd understand it will be hard." He was a good driver but constantly looked in every direction as well as what was in front of them. "I can't change who I am either, so she'll have to live with what I do."

"Sometimes what we wish for is right in front of us. We have to simply pay attention."

"What are you talking about?" He seemed momentarily distracted and met her eyes in the rearview mirror.

"I believe your special attention to Sabana after Rick's death was something she appreciated then, but now she wants something more from you. I've seen how she looks at you."

"She's just a kid who needed me to show her the ropes."

"Once upon a time she did, but those aren't the signals she seems to send out now. Every woman has the right to change her mind, but in this case she didn't change. She just wants so much more from you."

"You can tell that from a look?"

"Cain values you, but that doesn't mean you're not a caring, gentle man."

"Thanks, but I'm going to put my teddy-bear persona in my back pocket for now." Lou winked before he got out. He opened her door and offered his hand again. "Two cars back," he said softly, but didn't glance in that direction. "Stay on my right side, and don't make eye contact."

She went in as if Lou was her date and took the steps slowly to the garden room where Dallas already waited. The hostess followed Lou's instructions, and the man Cain figured was Juan arrived a few minutes later and took the table next to them.

"You look prettier every time I see you," Dallas said when she stood and hugged her. "How are you feeling?"

Their visit started like it usually would, and they laughed together while they were waiting for their lunch. She started her complaints after they went through the paint choices and other decorating ideas Dallas brought with her. She tried to be convincing about why they were there, and she wasn't loud enough to garner anyone's attention but Juan's.

"It's like she doesn't even love me anymore," she said, and dabbed at the corners of her eyes with her napkin. "Last night she said I might as well leave." The words weren't true but made her tear up anyway.

"Don't give up," Dallas said as she picked up her phone with a disgusted expression and listened for a few minutes. "I'm sorry, but I can't fix this over the phone," Dallas said apologetically when she finished the call. She got up and bent to hug Emma good-bye. "Please be careful," she said.

Emma could see why Dallas was such a good actress since she did appear to be off to handle some problem. "I will, but I don't know how much more of this I can take." She wiped her tears again and glanced at Juan and smiled when he stared at her. It took him a few beats to return the gesture, since he seemed to be in a trance.

She waited for him to move, but he didn't. He couldn't take his eyes off her, but he didn't do anything. When she thought about a younger version of herself and what she would've done in this situation, she figured this was where the kernels of doubt would begin. What if Cain was wrong and she killed an innocent? She looked at him, unwavering in her eye contact, and she was sure.

"I'm sorry for staring, but you look so familiar to me," she said, and ignored Lou clearing his throat. "Have we met?"

"I see you at the club Emma's."

"You're right." She smiled at him even though she was getting nauseous. She stopped, not wanting to overdo it and make him bolt. "Nice seeing you again," she said, and stood. There was no reason to stay since Cain hadn't called to ask her to stretch this out.

"Would you like coffee?"

She gazed at Lou and hesitated. "Sure. I don't have anywhere to be."

They sat quietly while the waiter went for their order. Juan had clammed up after his brief show of bravery, but he'd gone back to that trancelike stare. It reminded her of the few times they'd been around him.

He'd always looked at her in a way that made her feel naked and exposed, his thoughts plainly written on his face. The silence unleashed the memory of all those things he'd said when he was tying her to that table. The words and their intent made her wake in a sweat some nights.

"Do you see someone?" Juan asked when she glanced away from him.

She took a sip of her tea and carefully put her cup down. It'd taken being this close to him again to know she didn't want to for any reason. Every second with him somehow tainted her, her unborn child, the life she had with Cain, and everything in her life. His viciousness had come so close to killing what was good in her.

Escape was all she thought about when she got up and headed for the bathroom. Lou stayed, but Katlin was right behind her. "Cain," she said, when Cain answered her call. "It's him, and I can't—I don't want to be here. I'm sorry I'm letting you down, but I can't sit and pretend." She hated that she was crying.

"Are you okay? You're not alone, are you?"

"I'm fine. Katlin's with me."

"Lass, listen to me." Cain sounded upset. "Come home."

"I'm sorry."

"No, don't say that. You didn't do anything wrong."

When she hung up and opened the door, Lou stood outside. She walked with him, never glancing toward the table. She was suddenly desperate to get back to Cain, so Lou got her into the car and drove home without another word.

Cain waited outside and opened the door and her arms as soon as they stopped. After everything she'd accomplished since her return, she'd let Cain down. Cain had given her so much more trust and responsibility so they'd be true partners and equals, and she hadn't come close to repaying her when it counted. Her weakness had cost them, and her failure physically made her hurt. She'd wanted to be the one who brought Juan in. Cain picked her up and carried her inside when she started to sob.

"Lass," Cain said, and put her fingers under her chin so she'd see her face. "This is my fault, and I should've said something sooner. What happened to you isn't something you let go of easily. I was an idiot to put you in front of this guy again. He might have a new face, but he's still the same in here." Cain put her hand over her chest.

"I wanted to make it easier for you to get him."

"You did, and I'll prove it to you." Cain kissed her and helped her to her feet. "Tonight this is all over."

❖

Gustavo watched Emma leave and noticed how upset she was as she hung on to the gorilla usually with Cain. The woman Emma had with her that day had to be dead, from the gunshot he'd fired into her head, so the big man didn't surprise him. Whatever was going on was what confused him, but now was the time to get Emma away from Cain.

From the car he dialed Andre again, and the same message that he wasn't taking calls came through. He cursed the bastard for leaving him. He had no choice but to do something he'd wanted to avoid.

He took a deep breath and dialed another number. "Hello," his mother said, and her voice made his throat constrict. He missed her, and that he'd lost her to a man like Anthony made him hurt. His stupidity had cost him the most important relationship in his life.

"Mama," he said, and quickly wiped away his tears.

"Juan." His name from her lips made him cry harder. "Tell me where you are."

"Why, so you can tell Jerome? I gave you everything. I killed Uncle Rodolfo for you, and you betrayed me for someone who doesn't respect you."

"I made a mistake, but give me a chance to make it right. I love you and I've been sick since you left."

He rested his head on the wheel and decided whether to believe her. When the passenger door opened and the guy who got in put a gun to his neck, he froze from surprise and sudden fright. No way would he be unlucky enough to get mugged, but that had to be it. No one could know who he was.

The back door opened and someone else got in. "Give me the phone," the man behind him demanded. "Gracelia Luis, please," he said when he had the phone and put it on speaker.

"This is Gracelia Luis Ortega."

"We have your son, but we're willing to give him back for a price."

"My son is dead."

"Your son is alive and pissing his pants in front of me. You could buy him a new face and pretty hair, but spines aren't for sale. Do you want Gustavo back or not?"

"Tell me when and where, and I'll pay you whatever you want."

Shaun gave her an address and instructions to be there at ten that night with fifty grand. If Emma had been able to lure Juan away, Cain would've gone with that part of the plan so Emma would feel good about bringing him to justice, and so Juan and Gracelia would know they'd die on the same night. But, as he was fast learning, Cain always had a contingency for everything.

"What do you want?" Juan sounded unsure of his mother's commitment.

"I want a lot of things, but my boss wants you to die a slow and horrible death."

"I double whatever he pay. Who you work for?"

"I'd hand you over for free just to see Cain Casey smile," Shaun said as he hit the back of Juan's neck with the butt of his gun. When Juan slumped over, Dino bound his hands and got out to drive.

"You want to call?" Dino asked.

"Not until we get there and we're sure we have no tails. If we can fucking do this, Dino, we're on our way."

"Yeah. I've waited for this break my whole life." Dino laughed. "Good thing we're not this poor bastard."

"He's about to learn the consequences of touching what doesn't belong to him. Play with fire and the devil burns you."

❖

Jerome sat with his seat reclined and his eyes closed as Pablo drove them toward the Gulf Coast. The meeting with Miguel Gonzales had been long, with no results, but he really couldn't blame the guy. He'd come with nothing to trade except the ragtag group that was left of the once-strong Luis family. Miguel didn't completely turn him away, but he didn't bite either, or promise a meeting with Hector.

"What we do now?" Pablo asked, and at least he'd stopped crying.

While they were in the meeting Chico had called and had a frantic conversation with Pablo, but Pablo had wisely waited to tell him about it once they were in the car. They couldn't go back to the hotel, and he'd thought about what he was becoming when he grieved the loss of his coke stash more than Gracelia. According to Chico, the men who'd practically ripped the door from its hinges had killed everyone around Gracelia, but carried her out alive.

"Did Chico recognize anyone?" It slowly sank in that he was free of Gracelia and Juan, but damn if he didn't miss her a little. She'd been a pain in his ass, but she'd gone out of her way to do more for him than anyone in his life.

"One man he say is for Carlos." Pablo started to wipe at his face again and his voice quivered. "If he work for Carlos, la señora is dead."

"Don't think about that right now," he said, and tried to sound sincere. That Gracelia had little time left was a given, so he had to get his parents and leave. They'd regroup, but in Mexico from the house he'd claim as Gracelia's lover. Once he was behind the fortress-like walls he'd set up the business the way Gracelia should've, and when he did, people like Hector and Cain would have no choice but to respect him and give him a wide berth. "If we could help Gracelia we would, but we have to accept she's gone."

"You call Carlos?"

"Gracelia killed his father. Nothing I say is going to make him let her go. She should've considered that this might happen." He turned away from Pablo and his sniveling, and immediately spotted the car not far behind them. It made him sit up and become instantly alert. "Pull over."

"Here?"

"Pull over now."

The car passed them, but slowed. "What I do?" Pablo asked.

"Get off at the next exit." It wasn't the authorities, since they wouldn't be this blatant; whoever it was, he couldn't lead them to his parents' front door. "Pull into that gas station." He got out and went to the bathroom to make a call alone.

"How's the weather?"

"Not great. It's hot, too hot for you to visit. You'd be miserable with all your old friends hanging all over you." His dad tried to sound like there wasn't a problem, but the FBI was obviously outside the house watching, listening, and waiting for him to show up.

He probably could visit since they'd never recognize him, but Casey had seen him. If her people were driving the car that was now across the street, all it would take was a quick search to see who the house belonged to. And if she did that, it wouldn't take much to make him. He gave her that much credit.

"Come for a visit instead. I'll make the arrangements when I can."

He rested his head against the cinderblock wall and couldn't believe he was having to run from this bitch again. There was no way to know for sure it was Cain, but the visit had thrown him and he just knew it was her. He also didn't have any choice but to run if he wanted to live. They'd have to drive until they reached a decent-size airport where they could board a direct flight to Mexico. This time, though, no one would be on the other end to help out or protect him.

"God have pity on you, Gracelia, because Carlos won't," he said as he dropped the phone into the trash. He'd come back eventually, but not until he was either in a position of power or became someone else with no past that'd haunt him.

"It's time to save myself."

CHAPTER TWENTY-ONE

The kids, Roth, and Muriel arrived later that afternoon, and the kids' rundown of what they'd done cheered Emma up. She was about to turn down Cain's offer to go out, but changed her mind when Cain said it was important.

She took her time dressing and found it both comforting and sexy to have Cain sit and watch her. It made her feel wanted as well as loved.

When she finished, Cain opened the safe and removed the diamond choker that had been her mother's, a gift from Dalton because she'd said yes. "I promised you a surprise today and I think I did good in delivering."

"I needed them back here with us, so thank you."

"Tonight isn't about trying to get away from them. I simply want to give you something else." Cain put her hands on the necklace and kissed the side of her head. "My father gave this to my mother the day they married. It was his way of presenting her something precious for the promise of the life he'd have with her. That's what I want to do as well."

"I have everything I need already."

"Let's see about that."

They arrived at Vincent's restaurant and stopped briefly at the door so the folks in the van would see them before they entered. Vincent escorted them to the private room and locked the door so he could access the room they held their meetings in.

"I've always been curious about this place," Emma said as they descended slowly. She didn't seem prepared for what waited in the basement and leaned on Cain as if to regain her composure.

Cain had destroyed the house where Marie died—had stood outside the day the company she'd hired crushed it and trucked it away, but she kept one single piece with this night in mind. It sat in the middle of the room, sturdy and ready for one more act of violence. Dino and Shaun had done a good job of following her directions before they took off. Juan was spread on the table where Marie had lost her life the same way he'd tied Emma down. They'd stripped him bare and only covered his groin with a towel.

"My gift tonight is peace of mind," Cain said as she left Emma's side and moved to the table and grabbed Juan by the hair and lifted his head. "I wanted you to see him like this so you'd know he can't hurt us anymore."

Juan pulled against his bindings and she briefly mourned the loss of the opportunity to beat him to death, but it was important for Emma to remember this sight. She wanted Emma to know what would happen to anyone who tried to harm her or their family, and how she'd deal with it. On her watch, rabid animals would always be put down.

"You were planning this again, weren't you?" Emma asked Juan as she stepped next to her. "What did I ever do to you that made you this crazy?"

She motioned for Katlin to remove his gag, but gave her a serious look. If he was going to be the same ass he usually was, he'd die without another word. "You belong to me," Juan said, after he'd taken a few deep breaths. "I show you that. I take you to make you happy."

"He missed his chance to deny who he was," Emma said as she looked at him with an expression Cain had never seen on her face. When she took another step toward him, Katlin replaced his gag. "Do you remember the day we met?" Juan had gone back to straining and glaring. "I told you then my name is Emma *Casey.* I belong to her." Emma pointed at Cain and moved closer to him. "You should've walked away that night because she's relentless, and I love that I belong to her. There wasn't a chance in hell you would beat her."

Cain held up her hand for Katlin to back off when Emma raised her fist over his head and held it there. When she brought it down, the echo of the slap rang clearly in the room. Five more came in quick succession before Emma stopped and gripped the table.

"Go upstairs, lass, and I'll be up in a minute." Cain put her arms around Emma from behind and held her.

"Are you going to kill him?"

"I've thought about it."

Emma swung around and looked at her, as if not believing her answer. "I'm not asking because I'm upset about it. I want to know for sure. He's taken too much from us for you to show mercy now." Emma placed her palm against her cheek. "I can't watch you lose another minute of sleep over trash like that. He deserves everything you have in mind."

"Juan hurt you," she said, and kissed Emma, which made Juan groan. "So no, he's not leaving here alive." Katlin handed her something and she released Emma to take it. The bottle usually held ketchup, but not tonight. "I've thought about it for a long time—how to kill him, I mean. His family has a tradition of sorts." She squeezed the bottle and aimed it at his crotch, after she'd removed the towel.

"They tie a man to a tree and coat his genitals in honey so *fire* ants finish the job." She squeezed another stream until it puddled under his ass. "It's slow and painful, and it's a Luis signature." She squirted his hands next, and the liquid dripped from his fingers to the cement floor.

"That's how Juan's father died," she said, and he flared his lips, trying to get the curses around the gag. "But from what Hector told me about him, it wasn't a big loss."

She emptied the bottle on his penis. "This is how Juan killed his uncle Rodolfo too, so I wanted to give him a part of his family's heritage but put my own twist on it. When I light him up he can start the journey to hell the way his daddy and uncle did, but someone deserves to punch his final ticket more than me." She waved to the corner, and Merrick stepped forward with one of her pistols in hand. Her gait was still slow but she made it without a cane.

"So go upstairs, lass, and we'll finish this. When we do, Juan will never be a problem to you again." Emma nodded but took the time to kiss Merrick's cheek and Cain's lips before Lou helped her up and relocked the door behind them.

She waited until she heard the door close before Katlin took the gag off again. "You stupid bitch," Juan said when his mouth was clear. He clicked his jaw shut when she pressed the tip of her switchblade under his eye hard enough to pierce the skin.

"It amazes me that people like you issue threats at times like this," she said, and Simon translated from the corner. She'd volunteered to come since Cain wanted him to understand completely why he was here and what would happen to him. "If you give me Anthony Curtis, I'll allow Merrick to kill you fast and without prolonged pain."

He spoke in fast Spanish, so she waited for Simon. "Anthony and my mother will hunt you until they slaughter you and your family. So kill me, and your family and these bitches are dead," he said, and lifted his head to stare at Merrick and Katlin.

"Your mother is somewhere with Carlos and some of his best men," she said as she pressed the knife to his forehead and brought his head down with it. "I'd say they're threatening her with rape before they kill her, but I hear Gracelia loves to fuck anything that moves."

"You lie."

"He asked me for Gracelia because she's got to pay for what happened to Rodolfo, and I agreed." When he opened his mouth she made another cut. "I just want to know she's dead. I only care about you and Anthony, so take my offer. If not, you'll die like your father, only I won't bother with ants."

"I hate Anthony, but you won't get anything from me," Simon translated.

"Katlin," she said, and the gag was back in place.

Juan's eyes grew comically huge when she slowly dragged a match across the side of the box and lit it. "This is for putting your hands on my wife after she asked you not to." His body arched off the table when his hands started to burn. "And this is for why you touched her at all." She dropped another match onto his dick.

Large, fat tears spilled from his eyes as his skin blistered, and she let him suffer before Merrick shot him in the head. Katlin put out the last of the small fire on the table, and they all stared at his lifeless body.

"Have Lou go with Dino and Shaun to meet Tina C at the cemetery. She'll be there around three at the entrance to the mausoleum. I want no trace of this one."

"You paid to bury this asshole?" Merrick laughed. "Tina didn't have an available hole to throw him in?"

"I insisted this time because if Emma's nightmares come back, I want a place for her to be able to see. A small plaque was worth the reminder of what a nobody this man is to us, so we'll put him in a space under the name Juan Nadie," she said, and tried to repeat it the way Remi had. "*Nadie* means *no one* in Spanish, so he's effectively a John Doe."

"What about Gracelia?" Merrick asked.

"Gracelia has a date with Carlos tonight. In a few hours he'll be the last Luis left alive." She looked at Juan's pained expression, frozen by death, and the weight she'd carried from the afternoon he'd taken Emma dropped from her shoulders. "I asked him for only one thing before she died, and he gave me his word."

"What?" Katlin asked.

"A gift for someone frozen in time."

❖

"I'll understand if you don't want to eat and want to head home," Cain said when she came back in the room where Emma sat with Lou. Emma didn't appear shocked or sick, but she moved slowly toward her, nonetheless, since this was the first time she'd shown her partner the dark side she'd never denied having. She couldn't blame her for her fear.

"I'd like to go home, but not for the reason you think." Emma stood with her hand out. "I want you to hold me while I tell you how much it means to me that you'd do something like this for me. To not have to look over my shoulder for the rest of my life is a blessing. Juan kept trying until you either killed him or he succeeded."

"It's my honor to protect you and take care of you, and you'd do no less for me. I'm positive of that." She held Emma's hand and led her out to the dining room. The place had gotten crowded in the time they'd spent downstairs, so Lou walked ahead to make sure they didn't run into problems before they made it outside.

She noticed Fiona O'Brannigan at a table with an older attractive woman who was drinking from a wineglass. Their hair was the same color, only it seemed time had dulled the color of the older woman's somewhat, and since they shared the same cheekbones Cain guessed it was her mother.

The woman turned slightly after Fiona said something, and Cain also noticed the low-cut neckline of the woman's dress. This was the ghost Muriel had found, and even with the distance between them she could see the piece of jewelry the woman wore around her neck. "Wait a second, lass."

She stepped closer to Fiona's table and stared at the ring hanging around the woman's throat from a thick gold chain. The woman looked at her with panic clearly etched into her face and subtly placed her hand over her chest. If it was what Cain thought it was from her brief glance, Fiona's companion had tried her best to hide it from her. Even after what she'd just done, this was bizarre. It was like finding a needle in a haystack as big as the universe.

"What the hell do you want?" Fiona stood up, but the woman put her hand on her wrist. "What?" Fiona repeated, when the woman didn't move or say anything.

"Cain Casey," she said, and offered the woman her hand.

"Judice O'Brannigan," the woman said softly as she shook it, but her other hand stayed on the jewelry.

"Nothing that's lost ever stays buried." Cain moved her finger close to the woman's chest.

"Touch or bother her and I'm taking you in," Fiona warned her as her hand got close.

"If you want to play it that way we will, but I've put off my call to Colin Mead long enough. Have a nice meal and we'll see what he says."

"What do you know about Colin Mead?" Fiona asked as she glanced between her mother and Cain.

"Fiona, how about you go back to the pretend world you live in, and I'll return to my life," Cain said. "Ronald isn't going to help your career, you aren't going to save Shelby, and the list of your friends in this town keeps getting shorter. What you should ask yourself instead is if you have a place to go back to if this doesn't work out."

"My daughter isn't a threat to you," Judice said, now pale. "Believe me, she's not. You have my word on it."

"Learn that lesson from your mother. Family should be the most important thing in your life, and at the end of it it's the only thing real. I love mine with a devotion that people seldom have anymore, and I'd give anything to keep them safe."

"I've done the same for mine, even if it's only Fiona." Since Cain's eyes had never left Judice's chest, she took her hand away and let her look. "Mementos only mean you're trying to remember something special."

"Something like the brutal death of someone who was a wonderful husband, father, and friend? A man whose life ended in betrayal, and because it did he died without ever meeting his grandchildren? If that's what you're trying to remember, then believe me. I'm not the forgiving kind."

"That's it," Fiona said, and reached for her. "Turn around, I'm taking you in."

"Fiona," Judice said loudly. "Leave it be."

Cain walked away before she had to endure any more of Fiona's delusions of grandeur and took Emma's hand. The sight of Judice O'Brannigan meant that even though Juan was dead, something else was brewing, and it had nothing to do with Fiona. She needed to be sure the past didn't rear up and present a bad surprise.

"What was that about?" Emma asked when they were in the car on the way home.

"I need to call a distant cousin to listen to a story about the woman we just saw. Colin Mead runs a branch of our family in California, and he's got such an eye for the ladies that sometimes he's not the brightest bulb in the box."

"You think he's involved with that woman?" Emma rubbed her hand between Cain's.

"It's more than that, but I'm not going to worry until I talk to Colin."

"Are you concerned that this Colin guy told Fiona's mother something about your business? If he did, she wouldn't be stupid enough to share it with Fiona, would she?"

"I'm not really interested in what she does with Colin, or how stupid she is, but I do want to know why she has my father's ring around her neck. He lost the original that'd been in our family for generations before he and my mother got married. How'd she end up with it?"

"Are you serious? Come on, honey. He made a copy of the original, so maybe it was popular back in the day."

"I'd almost believe that, but did you see her face when I got there? She had a definite reaction, and when I walked over there, she looked almost afraid. Something's up, and then there's what Muriel found, or didn't find, on her. Think of Dallas when we first met her. When someone doesn't have anything in their past, there has to be a reason for it."

"Her daughter isn't exactly an unknown to you. She's been nothing but pushy since she got here with the idea of who killed Shelby's parents."

"Fiona's harmless, and if people like Sept aren't willing to play along with her theories about certain crimes, she's not going to last long in that job. Her last option will be Ronald Chapman, if he puts her on his task force permanently, but that won't happen either."

"You're not giving her a recommendation?" Emma said, and smiled at her.

The joke made her laugh, but she was sure about Ronald. His day was coming, and all that starch he loved in his shirts was going to strangle him when she pounced. "Let's see what Colin has to say."

Muriel met them at the door and followed them to the office. She handed over Colin's number and sat next to Emma while she dialed. "Colin, please. Tell him Cain Casey wants to talk to him."

"Shit, I haven't heard from you in ages. From what Muriel tells me you're married with kids. Who in the hell would've believed that with all the women you bedded in the old days." Colin was, as always, loud and brash. Her father had found him annoying, but she and Billy loved him for his honesty even if he was crass.

Emma laughed and shook her head, having heard his comments on speakerphone.

"Thank God I've already told her about the old days, since she's sitting here with me, so put that beer down and pay attention."

"Is this about Judice and that kid of hers?"

She glanced at Muriel, then Emma before she tapped the side of her head. "Her kid, as you put it, wants my head on a wall, and her mother doesn't exist. Believe me, if she did, Muriel would've found her, so tell me what she does for you."

"Judice is a magician with the books. She works for me and Sal."

"Sal as in Salvatore Maggio? Sal trusted someone outside his family anywhere near his money? Did this woman lie and tell him she's secretly Mother Teresa?"

Colin laughed, and she could hear him beating on something. "I would've thrown her out on her ass, but she came with a recommendation I couldn't ignore."

"Al Capone was her grandfather?"

"No…your Da was her boyfriend." He spit the last part out fast.

"Judice was with Da?" She found it hard to believe that, since her father, no matter how many his relationships, had told her about all of them. A life with no secrets, he'd said, was one with very few surprises from the past. She'd been so much like him in so many aspects of his life, but the one thing she was the most proud of was how she'd changed when she'd met Emma and committed. There'd been no one else after that. Period.

"Are you saying he was with this woman after he met Mum?"

"Hear what I'm saying, Cain," he said, and he lowered his voice. "Once Dalton met Therese, no woman had a chance with him. Judice came before and disappeared a little before your Da fell in love. There was nothing between them again, and she ran out of New Orleans like she'd never find another man again and the devil was chasing her. She came here, and I found her working behind a bar a few months after she left there and gave her a job when she asked. She's been a nun ever since. All she does is work and fuss over Fiona."

"Who was she back then?"

"What?" Colin asked, stringing out the word.

"Colin, don't make me pull your spleen out through your nose. Who was she back then?"

"When your Da knew her she was Bridget Cleary. She was a looker, and she's aged well. I've tried to show her she could have another chance at love, but she never budged after Fiona was born."

Cain had to stop and think, and it was getting to her that she had to ask so many questions about a woman she should've known all about. "Did she ever get in touch with Da after she got there, that you know of?"

"He never asked, and I didn't ask when she changed her name. Considering what she does for me, I don't give a shit what name she goes by. All I know is that she stays home, makes the IRS think I'm an altar boy, and hides the rest so good that only I know where it is. All Judice really cares about is Fiona, and when I asked about using the kid's new position to help us out, she came down on me so hard my balls are still blue. Fiona's got a great head on her shoulders, but she decided on the police thing when she was about twelve, and nothing could change her mind."

"Thanks, Colin. Don't forget to send in your response to the wedding invitation you got."

"You should've asked the girl a long time ago, like before she decided to give you three kids."

Emma laughed again as she hung up. "He sounds interesting, and after that talk I think I need to order more alcohol. Go on and don't be late." She pointed to the door. "Take Muriel with you so she can pay attention if you get mad and lose track."

"I think we've gotten to that point in our relationship where we share a brain." Muriel left them alone for a moment, and Cain took advantage by kissing Emma softly at first, but then with more intensity. "I won't be long."

"Where's she staying?" Emma asked.

"We'll find out before we get there."

"Who'd you leave behind?"

"No one. Judice will call before the night is done. She gives me the vibe that she'd offer me anything to keep me away from Fiona. Once I talk to her she'll give me even more than that."

In the middle of their next kiss the phone on the desk rang, and she let it until she was done with Emma. "Cain, Judice O'Brannigan is on one for you," Muriel said.

"I could work on the psycho hotline, couldn't I?"

"I think you mean psychic hotline, honey." Emma handed her the receiver.

"Ask our friends outside and see which one they agree with." She smiled and pressed the extension button. "Take a cab to my address," she said, and provided it. "If you want it to go well, leave Fiona not only behind but in the dark. I'll give you fifteen minutes."

"Do you want me to go upstairs?" Emma asked.

This wasn't going to be anything like Juan's death, but Cain wanted to shield Emma anyway. She didn't know what Judice was going to say, but her gut said she wasn't going to like it. "You can stay if you want, but if you're tired, head on up."

"I want to stay."

"I don't know why, but I want you to."

CHAPTER TWENTY-TWO

Emma and Cain sat together and waited. Strangely, the dream Cain had when they'd been at the cabin came back to her, and she put her hand over the son her parents had promised. She wanted to take the time to enjoy this baby since she didn't know if Emma wanted any more kids.

"After the summer's over, I'd like for Merrick to go back to work if she wants to," she said, and Emma nodded. "I think she's ready to team up with maybe Dino or Shaun to go out with you."

"She'll kiss the ground you walk on if you give her back her job, but she deserves it. I can't believe the progress she's made, but then she's always been strong."

"That's why I want her with you and the baby. She loves you too much to let anything happen to either of you."

They talked about nothing important after that, just to fill the time until Judice arrived. Muriel showed her in a few minutes later, and Judice stood by the door with her hand on her chest again. She'd wisely worn the necklace, so Cain stood and stepped closer to her. Judice didn't say anything when she raised her hand and worked her fingers under the gold chain.

With one quick tug the necklace came apart and she held up the ring that dangled from the bottom up for Judice to see. "What do you want me to call you?" she asked as she turned and rejoined Emma. "Is it Judice or Bridget?"

"I haven't heard that name in years, so please, it's Judice. That was my grandmother's name and I picked it to remind me of her."

"Sweet, but this isn't a friendly visit where we'll get to know each other. First, I want to know why you stole this." She held up her father's ring again. It was definitely his, since the saying and the name marked it as the Casey heirloom. "Then I want to know what kind of game you and Fiona have going. What's the mother of a police detective doing keeping the books for Colin Mead and Sal Maggio?"

"I didn't steal anything, and my life is none of your business." Judice changed from weak to sounding defiant. "I told you at the restaurant that neither of us is a threat to you."

"You're telling me that my father gave you this? This was something he loved so much he wore a replica until he was killed. You're going to come into my home and tell me he waited his whole life for his turn to wear it, and he gave to you?" Her voice rose with each word, and she'd never wanted to slap someone so much in her life.

"He betrayed me, so he owed it to me."

"I'm going to give you one more chance. Tell me why you have this. Why was it so important to you that you had a copy made for Fiona? I've looked all my life, and the only one I've ever found that resembles it is the one on my son's finger."

"You're just like him, a bull in a china shop that smashes everything good in their lives. I loved him and he threw me away when that bitch came into his life and acted like pure snow."

Emma's hold was easy to break, and Cain moved too fast for Judice to get away from her. She raised her hand and Judice dropped to her knees. "My parents are dead. I don't know who raised you, but in my family you don't speak about the dead that way to their last surviving child, since I take it the bitch you're referring to is my mother. Disrespect her again and you won't leave the same way you walked in, and Fiona won't be able to help you."

"I wanted him to love me that way, and I gave up plenty to be with him and do everything he wanted. When he was done he threw me away, so I took something he treasured as well as all the money I could find in the house." Judice didn't get up and Cain made no move to help her. "I ran where he couldn't find me and stayed there."

Cain removed the ring from the chain, put it in her pocket, and dropped the broken jewelry in front of Judice. "Get out of my house."

Judice appeared relieved, as if she'd passed some test and there'd never be another one. "I have your word that you'll leave Fiona alone." She stood and smoothed her dress down.

"I'm an animal." Cain sat behind her desk. "I'm going to act like animals act. The one thing that's not in a beast's nature is to give their word, but I'm going to tell you what I *am* going to do. Before you get back in the cab outside, I'm going to call Colin and tell him Fiona is not only after me, but she's going to use him and Sal to get to me. She's going to receive every medal the police can pin on her for getting her mother to give them both up, and with that information it's only a matter of time before I'm next to them in a cell with no windows."

"You can't do that," Judice said as she put her hands on the edge of her desk as if she couldn't hold up her weight.

"I can and I'm going to, gladly. I'm not usually so cruel, but when people come in here and feed me some story that's nothing but bull, it's like daring me to try my best to destroy them. There's that and the fact Fiona's been nothing but an annoyance since her arrival."

"Fiona's dedicated and she's trying to impress her bosses. Once she's settled you'll never see her again, so I'm begging you to leave her be."

"I doubt that, now that I've talked to you. Her hatred of me might not be all about me, but simply because my name is Casey. Perhaps that's something she learned growing up, so she's so dedicated to make mama proud of her. Whatever it is, my advice is to run and think about whatever you're hiding when you find a rock to live under. Colin might cut you some slack, but Sal will hack you into little pieces when he finds you. And he will find you, even if you hide in a hut in the middle of the Amazon jungle."

"You didn't know I existed until tonight. Leave me alone and I'll go back to California and you can pretend you never met me."

"You do exist, Bridget Cleary, and I won't forget you now. I gave you a chance to explain yourself, but not explaining yourself was your choice." She opened her book and searched for Colin's number. "If you really knew my father well, then you've got a clue as to how Caseys handle threats. I'm the heir the bull sired, and he raised me in the same china shop you described."

"I took the ring from him as a reminder. Dalton was good to me, and to my family, but your mother did turn his head from the first day he saw her." When Judice started talking, Cain put the phone down and listened. "He was working for his father already and had gotten my father some stuff to do around the warehouse. My father was a drinker and not a very nice man when he hit the bottle, but Dalton was the deterrent that kept his hands off my mother and me. It took him only one time to see the bruise on my mother's cheek to explain some things to my father in terms only Dalton could deliver. That he cared that much made me love him more."

Emma got up and came to sit on the arm of her chair, so Cain waved Judice into a visitor's chair. "He never mentioned you. All the others he did, but not you."

"The last time we were together, he took that damn ring off and touched me like he couldn't wait to love me. He hadn't been that passionate in a long while, but then I figured out that he was thinking about someone else. The pretty girl with the light-green dress with lace around the collar we'd seen walking from St. Louis Cathedral that afternoon. At least that's what I accused him of."

"That part of the story he did tell me." The first time he'd seen her mum was one of her father's favorite memories.

"I'd been late that day, so I only noticed her because his eyes were glued to her, and he was hooked. It wasn't long after that he was a fixture at the Baxter Sunday dinners, and from what I hear he took it slow until he'd swept Therese off her feet. He'd never taken that kind of time with me."

"So the ring was a trophy to appease your jealousy?" she asked, and Judice nodded. Something was missing, though. It was like something she was trying to remember and it was right at the tip of her recollection, but she couldn't get to it.

"I wanted to be what Therese was in his life, but he didn't see me that way. My father started hitting us again when Dalton left, and he told me over and over all that I was to Dalton Casey was a whore. He used me and then tossed me aside when more suitable wife material came along." Judice wiped her tears and gazed at Cain as if to read every emotion that crossed her face.

"I'm sorry my father-in-law treated you that way, but I'm curious about something," Emma said. "Why would you have to move across the country and change your name only because your boyfriend broke up with you and married someone else?"

"We'll get to that, lass, but I have a better question. If you hated him for picking my mum over you, why make Fiona a copy of the ring?" Judice's eyes widened and she moved to the edge of her seat. "The motto on the outside is something the Caseys have believed for generations. 'Mine but for a moment.' It makes sense for you and how your relationship with Da ended. But it doesn't explain why Fiona wears it." Saying it out loud made the pieces fall into place so easily she imagined hearing them click tightly together. The realization must've shown on her face because Judice paled, and her own stomach felt like it had dropped to her knees.

"Oh, God," she said as she slowly stood up.

"Wait," Judice said, and jumped her feet. "Let me explain."

"It's too late for explanations."

"What?" Emma held her by her belt, and it was the only familiar and comforting thing that was real. The truth Judice had hidden for so long had untethered her from the foundation of who she was.

"Why would a woman move across the country, change her name, and live a solitary life with a child that she had a ring made for? A ring that summed up a man's whole family in a circle of gold and one short phrase."

Judice started to cry and shake her head. "I wanted more for Fiona than she'd have here. If he found out he'd have taken her from me, and that wasn't his right. You didn't know him back then. Dalton was strong, but he was something to fear too. And your mother, she'd never give Fiona the life I could because she would've never accepted her. She was mine."

Cain pounded on the desk and took a deep breath to keep from throwing up. "Shut up," she said loudly. "My father was nothing like that, and if what you're saying is true, you stole more than a goddamn ring from him."

"Your father slept with me and then told me to not come around anymore. After he got dressed he offered me money to make sure I'd be okay. I liked to drink, smoke, and have fun back then, but I wasn't anyone's whore. All the things he loved about me one minute were what he hated the second he saw someone he could walk down the aisle." Judice was still crying, but she was spitting the story at her like bullets from a machine gun. "When I found out about Fiona, I ran as fast and as far as I could, and once I set up in California I started working the bar at the first pub I could find. Colin was the only one I told my real name, and he could give a shit why I wanted to change it."

"He knew?"

"Colin was like your father. He wanted to bed me and show me a good time. Fiona was a baby and he had his own family to worry about, so he never asked questions and I never told him that part. Dalton's name was good enough for him to trust me with the job he gave me, and I worked my ass off to give Fiona a decent and good life."

"So you're telling me that Fiona is my father's child?"

"Yes." Judice said it, and Cain hit the desk again. "But give me this secret, I'm begging you. Fiona wears the ring because she's admired mine all her life, and I don't wear it for the reasons you think. It has nothing to do with Dalton, Therese, or the Casey family as a whole. I wear it as a reminder that Fiona is mine, but if she ever knows the truth, it'll only be for a moment." Judice held up the broken gold chain. "The life I've built, the things I've given her, and the love I have for her can snap in a second, and I'll never be able to repair any of it. I ran as far as I could, but Agent Shelby dragged Fiona here after her parents were murdered, and she hates you. I tried to shield her from your family and she's found you anyway."

"Why not tell her?"

"Because she's mine, and she's no Casey. Your father was only a sliver of why she exists, but I'm her mother and the one who's fought for her from the day she was born. I was blessed that she doesn't look like him, and her spirit is pure. She'll never be a part of this life. She's better than that. You can wax over your Da's true nature, but I know the truth of who he was. He was a butcher who played the part of a nice guy when he was at home, but he's burning in hell for all those people he killed on a whim." The slap sounded hard and loud, and Emma appeared ready to deliver another one. It was the only reason Cain didn't get up and do it herself. This woman had to have become suicidal after such a solitary life.

"O'Brannigan is something you made up. What kind of heritage is that?"

"Fiona O'Brannigan was my grandmother who lived out her days on a farm in Ireland. She was strong, honest, and had plenty of history, only none of it had to do with booze or killing. That's what I wanted for Fiona, and she's made me proud."

"Get out of my house," Emma said when Cain dropped back in her chair, exhausted physically and mentally. "And remember this before you do. If you ever talk about my family again I'll be the one to kill you. There was no honor in what you did. Believe me, I tried running with a child for what I thought were the right reasons, and it turned out to be disastrous. Nothing built on a lie survives the light of day."

"You're like Therese, a good Casey wife with a good set of blinders."

"I can see why Dalton tossed you aside," Emma said.

"He wanted a virgin who didn't ask a lot of questions."

"The ice is thinning under your feet," Cain warned Judice. She'd had her fill of disrespect for one night.

"He wanted a partner who'd help him through life. That's what Cain and I have, and we're teaching our children to look for that when their time comes. You, though, were raised by drunks who obviously knew nothing about love, so that's the legacy you passed to your child. You hid away and stole from her the family that would've given her not only love, but a sense of who she really is." Emma pointed at Judice when she started to say something. "I know, we're killers with no morals. Look at Fiona for who she really is, and be honest with yourself. You've raised a petty loner who has no regard for anyone but her own self-importance."

"You don't pull any punches."

"Not when it comes to the safety and happiness of my family. Now get out." Emma buzzed for Katlin or Lou.

"What about Fiona?" Judice asked from the door.

"I don't know," Cain said. "She's no more welcome here than you are, but knowing what I do now won't save her if she tries to harm my family." Cain turned her chair around. "Go back to wherever you came from and stay out of my sight, and be careful not to talk about my parents the way you did tonight to anyone else. You do, and Fiona will know my true nature after she finds herself alone in this world." As much as she prided herself on the load she could carry, she couldn't listen to another word out of this woman's mouth.

When the door closed she rested her head in her hands and felt like she was underwater with no way up.

"Oh, Da, what now?"

❖

Judice pulled the hair on the sides of her head as one of Cain's men drove her back to her hotel. The pain at the base of her skull and at the center of her gut built to the point she knew she'd be sick. The fear that had tickled her spine when she packed for this visit bloomed until she was frantic as to what to do next.

She'd gladly given up her past and her family for the opportunity to raise Fiona, and after so many years, she'd stupidly thought it safe to return to New Orleans since the city held nothing but ghosts of her past. The reality that Therese had given Dalton something she hadn't had never occurred to her, but Cain was his twin not only in appearance but intelligence. One short introduction and Cain had peeled away every one of the lies she'd hidden behind for more than half her life.

"You want to get out here?" the man asked. "Your kid's waiting out front for you."

She bumbled with the door, not ready to face Fiona, but she couldn't avoid it when Fiona quickly walked toward her and put her fingers on her cheek.

"What happened to you? Where'd you go?" Fiona asked, her fingers on the spot where Emma had hit her.

"I was walking and I tripped."

"And you fell on someone's hand? Come on." Fiona led her inside and didn't say anything until she'd placed a towel with ice against her face.

"Did this have anything to do with Casey?" Fiona asked after the silence between them had become deafening.

"You don't want to tell me every aspect of your life, so don't ask me about mine." Pulling away even as drastically as she'd moved away from her parents and family might be the only way to save Fiona.

"I've allowed you your secrets all my life, so if you want to keep quiet now, go ahead. But have you ever asked yourself why I became a cop? One of the main reasons, anyway."

She stared at Fiona's face, trying to find a trace of Dalton aside from the blue eyes. When she was this serious, Fiona's intense expression was Dalton's down to the scowl. "It gave you the power and opportunity to search for the answers I denied you." She sighed and felt like a spool of yarn that Cain had cut enough to unravel. "What did you find?"

"Not you." Fiona's delivery was soft.

"What else?"

"Casey was right about Colin Mead, but I couldn't verify the rumors about Sal Maggio."

"You didn't go through my stuff to make sure? I locked my office, but curiosity is a great motivator if you really wanted to know." Maybe if she'd been honest she would've seen that this ending was inevitable.

"I know who you work for, what they do, but not why you did it."

"If you decide to pursue it, you'll sign my death warrant. I'm not saying that to stop you. I knew who I was dealing with, and the consequences, but know the reality before you do anything."

"I would've already, if that was my plan. All I've ever wanted is the truth, not to hurt you," Fiona said, and walked out.

❖

The drive to Cain's didn't take long, and Fiona stood at the gate, not wanting to be there. To ask permission to enter was begging for Cain to laugh at how in the dark she was about her own mother. Cain knew more than she did, judging from their exchange at dinner.

The wrought iron felt cool despite the heat, but she let go as if it'd burned her when Cain stepped out of the darkness.

"Are you lost?" Cain asked.

"What'd you do to my mother?"

"I asked you a question."

"Fuck you and your questions."

Cain laughed and she forced herself not to curl her hands into fists. "My partner is right about you," Cain said, as if she'd known what she meant. "If you're smart, Fiona, you'll turn around and forget about me and my family. You have no place here."

"Just spit it out."

"I'll leave you and your mother alone if you return the favor. Don't make me repeat that. You and Judice deserve each other, and I want you both gone from my sight."

"Wait," she screamed when Cain turned to leave.

"You won't find any answers here, so run back to Judice. Me and mine are off-limits to you."

Fiona wanted to fling a curse at her but thought it important not to alienate Cain. From the moment Shelby had mentioned Cain's name, she'd felt their futures would intertwine until one of them was dead. That, she still predicted, was true, but she didn't wish that on either of them as Cain disappeared from view.

CHAPTER TWENTY-THREE

Emma gave Cain the time she needed to process the news and didn't press her to talk about it. Not that she could. Judice and Fiona had arrived in town and put a crack in the truth of who Cain thought she was, and who her Da had been. She'd taken a break from the business and everything else until she could regain the confidence she needed to do what she did.

The only meeting she'd accepted in the three and a half weeks she'd taken to sort things out was with Carlos, and he'd come through for her and gotten the information she asked of him. He was going back home and appeared so much lighter now that he'd avenged his father. With his personality he'd be successful in a short time. After what they'd been through together and how their problems had overlapped, she was sure that unless he changed dramatically, they wouldn't be enemies. Never business partners or great friends, but not enemies either.

"We need to think about whether we want to evacuate for this thing," Emma said as she opened her eyes. There'd been a few small storms that had come to nothing, but Katrina appeared to be gathering strength as it rolled off the Florida coast.

"I've already talked to the airport and they have a plane available for charter. The guys are packing and we'll be ready by tomorrow morning. I called, and Maddie and Jerry are ready for us. We'll pack everything and wait it out up north." Cain scrubbed her face with her hands, tired of the disconnect she felt from the life she'd had before her conversation with Judice.

"You think it'll pass before the wedding?"

"I hope it blows itself out before it gets here, but I don't want to take any chances. Don't worry. No matter what, I'm planning to meet you at the end of an aisle somewhere and smile as you put a ring on my finger."

"Is there something I can do to make you feel better?" Emma sounded sad. "I hate to see you suffer."

"It's time to move on, but I'm not sure how. This thing, it's not like finding an old letter that spills a family secret. Fiona shares half my blood, and I can't accept it. As much as I love my family, I consider only Billy and Marie my siblings. I really don't see myself opening my arms and welcoming this woman into my life." She meant it and smiled when Emma moved slowly and sat across her hips. The baby was much more active now, and she wondered what this one would be like. Would he be shy or rambunctious like Hayden and Hannah?

"I love you, and I'll stand by your side no matter what you decide. What I need right now, though, is for you to touch me. I want to remind you of a few things." Emma pulled her nightgown over her head. She was gorgeous.

"What do I need to remember?" The sight of Emma's swollen belly made her smile. She put her hands on Emma's hips and loved that her nipples hardened, telegraphing her need.

"No matter what life throws at you, you are Derby Cain Casey." Emma leaned back, reached between her legs, and touched herself to get her fingers wet. "You're the true heir of Dalton Hayden Casey." Emma painted her lips and the taste made her wet in return. Cain groaned when Emma did it again and carefully rolled her onto her back. But when she began to move down to put her mouth on her, Emma held her in place and shook her head.

"Tell me, love," she said as she put her hand between Emma's legs and kissed her. "What do you want?"

"Put your fingers inside and make me come, but I want you to hold me while you do. I miss you." Emma ran her finger along the outside of her ear and gasped when she put her fingers in. As she stroked, Emma hung on to her and planted her feet into the mattress so she could move her hips. She raked her nails up her back with one hand and pinched her own nipple with the other. "Faster and harder. You aren't going to hurt me and I need you," Emma said breathlessly.

"I'll give you whatever you need." Her hand was so wet and Emma's clit was so hard she craved putting her mouth on her, but she stayed and watched Emma shut her eyes as she came. Right then Cain forgot everything that had been bothering her. What Emma had said made sense.

There was only one Casey heir, and even if Judice could prove Fiona was his child, nothing in their life would change. Clans were built and had survived for generations through a strict code of honor and trust. Fiona had no clue what that was about.

"Thank you," Emma said, and the words made her feel shame. Her partner shouldn't have to be thanking her for this.

"I'm sorry, lass, for not handling all this better."

"Don't do that. I was thanking you because you make me feel good and wanted. Not because I think you took pity on me and made love to me."

"You can't believe that. Even when I'm in a gloomy mood I still find you beautiful, and I love you."

"Then come love me in the shower and help me pack, if we have to get out of here. I'm sure it's only going to be a few days up at the lake house, but the kids are looking forward to it. Do you need to get anything done before we go?"

"I've got a few stops, so take as many guys as you need to get things done."

"Do you think we can reschedule our ceremony if this goes on longer than necessary?" She'd lost count as to how many times Emma had asked the question.

"You put a lot of work into that, so it's done, lass. If any of the places gives you a hassle when we get home I'll take care of it." She walked the line of not trying to sound too casual about a storm coming ashore during their commitment ceremony and not giving away the other plans she'd made on the chance that happened and their return was delayed.

"I don't want to miss the chance to put a ring on your finger," Emma said as a joke, and she winked over her shoulder. She put up a good front, but Cain could see the slight slump of her shoulders.

They showered and tried to get the kids to calm down from the hysteria that'd taken over the city about the possible evacuation. Cain had been through this before and knew there was no reason to panic, but she had to put aside everything she had no control over and concentrate on getting her people ready for whatever the weather might throw at them.

She took Katlin and Lou with her as they went by every store that did business with them and made sure they had the money and resources to survive the storm. As they headed through the French Quarter she told Lou to stop at the side of Jackson Square, and she got out to head in to the cathedral. The ten o'clock mass was ending so she sat in the back and watched her old friend Father Andrew Goodman go through the religious rituals.

"Lost your way?" he asked when he came back in after he'd spent time with the parishioners outside.

"You were at my house last month drinking my whiskey so keep your guilt to yourself, you old fraud." She stopped at the donation box and dropped in a few hundred dollars. "I came to ask you something, and if you don't have the answer I'll settle for some advice."

"Call in your flock from outside." He made a shooing motion and waited in the main aisle. "Put in a good word for yourselves while I deal with your boss," he told Lou and Katlin.

She told him about her conversation with Judice and her possible relation to Fiona. Andrew listened and tapped his fingers together as he did. "Your Da came to see me before he was killed, you know we've talked about this before, and he mentioned Bridget Cleary."

"I thought confessions were something you'd never share with me."

"There are confessions and talks between friends, Derby, so don't make me take a ruler to your butt. You know better than that." He poured her a little bit of whiskey from the bottle she gifted him on a regular basis. "He talked about Bridget and the relationship he'd had with her. Whatever this woman told you, your Da didn't throw her out like a bag of trash. He didn't feel the same about her as he did about your mum, but he did break it off before he met Therese formally."

"You don't have to protect him. I've heard about Da and his women, actually from Da. It was a lesson for me when I was enjoying my youth and the barrel of oats I'd been given." She laughed. "He told me that once I committed, the rest would have to go because the woman who gifted your life with children didn't deserve the disrespect. Once he married Mum, I believed him when he said he'd never strayed. Judice had his ring, though, and even made a copy for her daughter."

"I'm not saying her story's not true as far as her daughter, but I believe in my heart that what your father described to me was the end of the relationship." As his priest he knew the consequences to his soul if he lied, and as his friend he had no reason to. Andrew put his hands over hers. "What this woman told you I can tell has shaken your belief in your Da, but he's still the man you remembered the minute before she told you, so don't do that to yourself. He can't defend himself, and if you start doubting what kind of man he was, it will only rob you of something special."

"I'd never betray his memory, but I don't know how to accept this."

"Even God took more than a day to create the world, Derby. Give yourself some time and let that decide for you. If you want to pursue it, fine, and if you don't, then that's going to be fine too." He moved his hand to her shoulder. "Judice did all this for a reason, and until she tells you what that reason is, I suggest you withhold any judgment against Fiona."

"Even if Fiona's made it her life's mission to arrest me or, better yet, shoot me with cause?"

"I keep telling you that the Lord loves even his wayward sheep. Your mum isn't going to just sit playing a harp while someone tries to do you harm. Go home to your family and know she won't be the only one praying for you."

"So wait and see what God has planned for me?"

"You'd be surprised, and don't play the tough guy with me. You're like your father in that way."

"Don't forget about everything else I asked for."

"That's the last thing I'm going to do."

"Take care and thanks for listening."

"That's my job," he said, and put his hand over her hand and whispered a prayer, "but I'm also your friend. Right now worry about what's right in front you, not what's coming up from the sides. Emma, Hayden, Hannah, and a new baby are what should be on your mind."

"For always."

❖

The airport was busier than usual when they landed, and a few of the townspeople were in the lot with their vehicles. Emma got off the plane and held Hannah's hand as if she'd fly off if she let go. "What's going on?" she asked as Cain came down behind her.

By the time they'd boarded, Katrina was in the Gulf, strengthening by the hour, and had started drifting west. The spaghetti models resembled a child's scribbles, but the state governments had started their warnings and told people to get out of the low-lying coastal areas. Nothing lay in Katrina's way that'd bring down the intensity, and they estimated that wherever she hit would be devastated for months.

Emma had worried about all those less fortunate, but Cain also knew she wasn't thrilled that the one casualty so far had been their ceremony. "They're making money by running a taxi service this weekend."

"Is there a convention in town or something?" Emma asked, and laughed.

"Since we're evacuating up here, I guess they thought there might be an influx of people running from bad weather."

Jerry had come with some of his hands and brought the vehicles, as well as some of the farm trucks, to handle the luggage and crowd with them. As they left the tarmac Cain saw another private jet landing and didn't recognize it, so she figured it was Shelby and company, ready to set up for the duration of their stay. This time she hoped they'd booked ahead, because they were going to have to sleep in the plane unless some nice farmer took them in.

The road to the lake house came into view. The crew that'd arrived a day before them had done a good job with the decorations. Emma started to cry when she spotted the yards of white ribbon and lamps that now lined the way along with the pines.

Maddie was in the yard, along with Vincent and his catering staff, as they both directed people where to put tables, chairs, and a dance floor. The Jatibons, Dallas, and Kristen were enjoying the pool and deck to the back.

Cain opened Emma's door and walked to their tree before she dropped to a knee. "You worked hard getting all this together, and I don't want to wait until whatever's going to happen to stand before all these people and declare to the world how I feel about you. If you want we'll wait, but tomorrow is a great day for a wedding, and since we can't have it at home right now, I had it flown up here."

"You're too good to be true."

"There are a lot of people in the world who wish I weren't," she said, and smiled as she held Emma's hand. "Say yes."

"Yes."

"Don't forget that's supposed to be your answer tomorrow."

❖

Cain left the party their friends had put together as a night-before event to walk the field where they'd shot skeet earlier that summer and waited. The land was beautiful here with the fields of green and the cows lazily ripping it out in clumps. She stared at the woods and lifted her hand and motioned whoever was out there forward.

Shelby, she knew, was back on the job, but it was Ronald she was interested in seeing now. "Ronald, a moment of your time, please."

He stepped out after she didn't add anything to that and stood at the edge of the woods. He'd obviously packed smarter this time around and seemed more comfortable in his jeans and golf shirt. "What do you want? Or is this another attempt to go around our procedures?"

"Meet me halfway and I'll tell you."

She started walking with Lou the same distance behind her as Brent was behind Ronald. Emma hadn't liked the idea of her going out in an open field with so many people hidden right in front of her, but in life you had to at times take chances.

"What do you want?" Ronald said, that smug expression he'd mastered firmly planted on his face.

Lou stepped forward with a large, thick, yellow envelope, and Brent drew his weapon. She wasn't worried about him at the moment, but she had Katlin with a rifle behind her on the off chance she was wrong. She was a gambler but she wasn't crazy.

"I know usually the guests bring gifts to a wedding, but I made an exception, so this is for you." She handed him the package and smiled. "Please go ahead and open it. I'm dying to know if you like it."

He folded the metal piece that kept it closed but didn't take his gaze off her. "What the hell is this?"

"When you introduced yourself I took an interest in you, Ronald, since you made your intentions so clear, and I told you then that everyone has secrets. *Everyone* has them, and you never know how the world will react when they're exposed. Sometimes you recover, and sometimes you can't find a hole deep enough to hide in, but it takes walking that gauntlet of shame to find out. These are some of my secrets, Ronald, and I thought you'd enjoy them."

He glanced down and widened the top without taking anything out. It was almost comical to her when his eyes closed momentarily, as if he couldn't believe what he was seeing, and his mouth went slack. If she had to guess, his asshole had tightened to a pinhole.

"How did you...what are these for?"

"I haven't made up my mind about that, but you should go back to Washington while I think about it." Behind them Joe and Shelby were now in view, as if they couldn't wait to join the little party, but Annabel stood alone to the side. She'd invited Annabel before leaving the city and told her she might have a solution to the problems she was experiencing.

Annabel had been reluctant until she'd explained sometimes she enjoyed the landscape she was accustomed to. She didn't want to peer out at a world of Ronald's making any more than Annabel did. The only payment she wanted in return was Fiona's expulsion from any task force she was on or would ever be interested in. "Remember, though, Ronald, the thing about secrets is that once they're found, people tend to copy them many times over." She pointed to the other envelope under Lou's arm. "If I'm shot or something like it by someone like this guy you've got behind you, then they won't be secrets anymore."

"Someone like you, though, I can't trust you. I could do whatever you ask, and you'd probably do your worst for kicks."

"What the hell is this about?" Brent asked, and Ronald cut him off with a glare.

"Like I said, I haven't made up my mind yet, but I'd feel less crowded making up my mind without you and your friend standing out here scaring my cows. Leave tonight. That's my deal."

He started walking without a word, with Brent asking a ton of questions as he followed. Her investment in night-vision camera had proved to be smart, and when Ronald read through everything she'd given him he'd figure out she had the wig, wipes, his favorite belt, and the gloves he was fond of in a safety-deposit box outside New Orleans. She'd never seen Annabel appear so relieved as when Ronald practically ran from the field.

"Shelby, a moment of your time now if you can spare it."

Shelby moved faster than Ronald and held Joe back. "What was that about?"

"Ronald has a need to return to Washington for a while, but that's got nothing to do with you." She took out a small piece of paper from her pocket gingerly between her knuckles. She'd had it typed, and the only fingerprints on it would be Shelby's, if she accepted it. "Have you given any thought to our talk about orchards and sin?"

Shelby had to lean in to hear her, but she nodded. "I've planted mine, but I can't harvest until I know where to find what I'm looking for."

She handed over the names Carlos had gotten from Gracelia before she died. He didn't give details as to how he'd done it, but it had taken hours, and she'd given him every bit of information he'd asked for. It had been Anthony's idea to kill Shelby's parents, but it'd been Gracelia who hired the gangbangers from LA to do the job. She'd demanded names to make sure they could be trusted to not leave clues.

"They should all be in the system, but make sure you can live with the consequences of your actions."

"Thank you, but why would you do this?"

"For saving Emma for me. But now we're even. If you want me to owe you one, take Fiona with you and talk her into staying in California."

"Don't tell me someone's finally getting to you."

"She doesn't belong in my world, and I doubt she ever will."

Chapter Twenty-four

"Let us rejoice, for this is the day the Lord has made," Andrew said as he stood before them under the arbor Ross had made close to the shore of their lake. Ross had walked Emma down the aisle between the chairs set out, appearing both incredibly nervous and equally proud.

"A long time ago as a boy, I was befriended by a someone who came to change my life for the good because he was not only generous of spirit, but he was also generous with his family when he shared them with me. My friend Dalton and I chose different paths in life, but seeing the love he had for his wife and his children made me believe even deeper in God." He smiled at Cain when she nodded. "So, Derby, face this beautiful woman and tell her your intentions."

"My Da taught me some things as well, and one of his most important lessons was how to welcome a Casey into our family. It's a long tradition, and it applies for everyone except on their wedding day." Emma's smile didn't change, but she narrowed her eyes a little. "I met you a lifetime ago, and you demanded to be seen, respected, and loved. You are my partner, the mother of my children, and the love that lights my way."

Hayden moved closer and handed her a ring. "You're mine, not for just this lifetime, but forever. You own my heart, my soul, and I'll only know peace with you at my side." She slipped the ring in place and kissed Emma's hand.

Hayden handed Emma her ring as well, but it made a slight clink when it landed in her hand. "I met you a lifetime ago, and you blinded me to anyone else. It was easy to love you, to respect you, and to help you through anything in this life because my love for you is the basis of my happiness." Emma held up the wedding band she'd picked and slipped it on her finger. "You're mine, but not for just this lifetime. I love you with all that I am, and I want this ring to be a sign of everything you mean to me." Emma held her finger in place and positioned another ring to follow hers. It was the original Casey ring that Judice had stolen.

"I know what it's like to come home where I belong after being lost, so I think it's time to put this where it belongs." Emma placed it on her finger below the wedding band and kissed her knuckles. "I'm a Casey and, for always, I'll be your Casey."

Andrew finished the ceremony, and the kiss Emma gave her made Cain optimistic for the future. Only time would tell what shape their home would be in when they returned to New Orleans, and how Fiona and her mother would fit into their lives, but today was for celebration, not questions about the unknown. So as they raised the first glass for a toast, Katlin and Muriel shouted simply one word.

"Clan."

The Casey Clan was hers, and no one would take it from her.

About the Author

Originally from Cuba, Ali Vali has retained much of her family's traditions and language and uses them frequently in her stories. Having her father read her stories and poetry before bed every night as a child infused her with a love of reading, which carries till today. In 2000, Ali decided to embark on a new path and started writing.

Ali now lives in the suburbs of New Orleans with her partner of twenty-eight years, and finds that living in such a history-rich area provides plenty of material to draw from in creating her novels and short stories. Mixing imagination with different life experiences makes is it easier to create a slew of different characters that are engaging to the reader on many levels. Ali states that, "The feedback from readers encourages me to continue to hone my skills as a writer."

Books Available From Bold Strokes Books

Date with Destiny by Mason Dixon. When sophisticated bank executive Rashida Ivey meets unemployed blue-collar worker Destiny Jackson, will her life ever be the same? (978-1-60282-878-0)

The Devil's Orchard by Ali Vali. Cain and Emma plan a wedding before the birth of their third child while Juan Luis is still lurking, and as Cain plans for his death, an unexpected visitor arrives and challenges her belief in her father, Dalton Casey. (978-1-60282-879-7)

Secrets and Shadows by L.T. Marie. A bodyguard and the woman she protects run from a madman and into each other's arms. (978-1-60282-880-3)

Change Horizon: Three Novellas by Gun Brooke. Three stories of courageous women who dare to love as they fight to claim a future in a hostile universe. (978-1-60282-881-0)

Scarlett Thirst by Crin Claxton. When hot, feisty Rani meets cool vampire Rob, one lifetime isn't enough, and the road from human to vampire is shorter than you think... (978-1-60282-856-8)

Battle Axe by Carsen Taite. How close is too close? Bounty hunter Luca Bennett will soon find out. (978-1-60282-871-1)

Improvisation by Karis Walsh. High school geometry teacher Jan Carroll thinks she's figured out the shape of her life and her future, until graphic artist and fiddle player Tina Nelson comes along and teaches her to improvise. (978-1-60282-872-8)

For Want of a Fiend by Barbara Ann Wright. Without her Fiendish power, can Princess Katya and her consort Starbride stop a magic-wielding madman from sparking an uprising in the kingdom of Farraday? (978-1-60282-873-5)

Swans & Clons by Nora Olsen. In a future world where there are no males, sixteen-year-old Rubric and her girlfriend Salmon Jo must fight to survive when everything they believed in turns out to be a lie. (978-1-60282-874-2)

Broken in Soft Places by Fiona Zedde. The instant Sara Chambers meets the seductive and sinful Merille Thompson, she falls hard, but knowing the difference between love and a dangerous, all-consuming desire is just one of the lessons Sara must learn before it's too late. (978-1-60282-876-6)

Healing Hearts by Donna K. Ford. Running from tragedy, the women of Willow Springs find that with friendship, there is hope, and with love, there is everything. (978-1-60282-877-3)

Desolation Point by Cari Hunter. When a storm strands Sarah Kent in the North Cascades, Alex Pascal is determined to find her. Neither imagines the dangers they will face when a ruthless criminal begins to hunt them down. (978-1-60282-865-0)

I Remember by Julie Cannon. What happens when you can never forget the first kiss, the first touch, the first taste of lips on skin? What happens when you know you will remember every single detail of a mysterious woman? (978-1-60282-866-7)

The Gemini Deception by Kim Baldwin and Xenia Alexiou. The truth, the whole truth, and nothing but lies. Book six in the Elite Operatives series. (978-1-60282-867-4)

Scarlet Revenge by Sheri Lewis Wohl. When faith alone isn't enough, will the love of one woman be strong enough to save a vampire from damnation? (978-1-60282-868-1)

Ghost Trio by Lillian Q. Irwin. When Lee Howe hears the voice of her dead lover singing to her, is it a hallucination, a ghost, or something more sinister? (978-1-60282-869-8)

The Princess Affair by Nell Stark. Rhodes Scholar Kerry Donovan arrives at Oxford ready to focus on her studies, but her life and her priorities are thrown into chaos when she catches the eye of Her Royal Highness Princess Sasha. (978-1-60282-858-2)

The Chase by Jesse J. Thoma. When Isabelle Rochat's life is threatened, she receives the unwelcome protection and attention of bounty hunter Holt Lasher who vows to keep Isabelle safe at all costs. (978-1-60282-859-9)

The Lone Hunt by L.L. Raand. In a world where humans and Praeterns conspire for the ultimate power, violence is a way of life…and death. A Midnight Hunters novel. (978-1-60282-860-5)

The Supernatural Detective by Crin Claxton. Tony Carson sees dead people. With a drag queen for a spirit guide and a devastatingly attractive herbalist for a client, she's about to discover the spirit world can be a very dangerous world indeed. (978-1-60282-861-2)

Beloved Gomorrah by Justine Saracen. Undersea artists creating their own City on the Plain uncover the truth about Sodom and Gomorrah, whose "one righteous man" is a murderer, rapist, and conspirator in genocide. (978-1-60282-862-9)

The Left Hand of Justice by Jess Faraday. A kidnapped heiress, a heretical cult, a corrupt police chief, and an accused witch. Paris is burning, and the only one who can put out the fire is Detective Inspector Elise Corbeau…whose boss wants her dead. (978-1-60282-863-6)

Cut to the Chase by Lisa Girolami. Careful and methodical author Paige Cornish falls for brash and wild Hollywood actress Avalon Randolph, but can these opposites find a happy middle ground in a town that never lives in the middle? (978-1-60282-783-7)

Every Second Counts by D. Jackson Leigh. Every second counts in Bridgette LeRoy's desperate mission to protect her heart and stop Marc Ryder's suicidal return to riding rodeo bulls. (978-1-60282-785-1)

More Than Friends by Erin Dutton. Evelyn Fisher thinks she has the perfect role model for a long-term relationship, until her best friends, Kendall and Melanie, split up and all three women must reevaluate their lives and their relationships. (978-1-60282-784-4)

Dirty Money by Ashley Bartlett. Vivian Cooper and Reese DiGiovanni just found out that falling in love is hard. It's even harder when you're running for your life. (978-1-60282-786-8)

Sea Glass Inn by Karis Walsh. When Melinda Andrews commissions a series of mosaics by Pamela Whitford for her new inn, she doesn't expect to be more captivated by the artist than by the paintings. (978-1-60282-771-4)

The Awakening: A Sisterhood of Spirits novel by Yvonne Heidt. Sunny Skye has interacted with spirits her entire life, but when she runs into Officer Jordan Lawson during a ghost investigation, she discovers more than just facts in a missing girl's cold case file. (978-1-60282-772-1)

Blacker Than Blue by Rebekah Weatherspoon. Threatened with losing her first love to a powerful demon, vampire Cleo Jones is willing to break the ultimate law of the undead to rebuild the family she has lost. (978-1-60282-774-5)

Murphy's Law by Yolanda Wallace. No matter how high you climb, you can't escape your past. (978-1-60282-773-8)

Silver Collar by Gill McKnight. Werewolf Luc Garoul is outlawed and out of control, but can her family track her down before a sinister predator gets there first? Fourth in the Garoul series. (978-1-60282-764-6)

The Dragon Tree Legacy by Ali Vali. For Aubrey Tarver time hasn't dulled the pain of losing her first love Wiley Gremillion, but she has to set that aside when her choices put her life and her family's lives in real danger. (978-1-60282-765-3)